THE FISHING EXCURSION,—"PIERRE AND JEAN"

THE WORKS OF
GUY DE MAUPASSANT

PIERRE AND JEAN
FATHER AND SON
BOITELLE

AND OTHER STORIES

Translated by
ALBERT M. C. McMASTER, B. A.
A. E. HENDERSON, B. A.
MME. QUESADA AND OTHERS

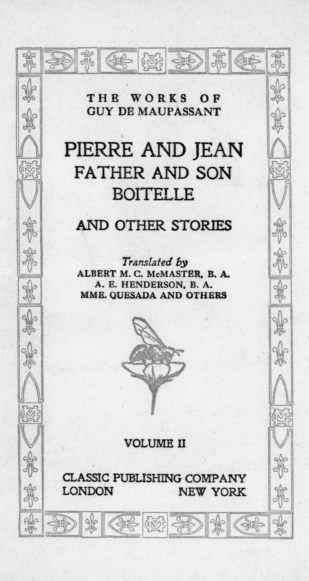

VOLUME II

CLASSIC PUBLISHING COMPANY
LONDON   NEW YORK

CONTENTS

Guy de Maupassant

"THE NOVEL"

INTRODUCTION TO PIERRE AND JEAN

I HAVE no intention of pleading here the cause of the following little novel. On the contrary, the ideas which I shall attempt to elucidate would involve rather a criticism of the style of psychological study which I have undertaken in "Pierre and Jean."

I wish to discuss the novel in general.

I am not the only one to whom the same reproach is addressed by the same critics every time that a new book appears.

In the midst of eulogistic phrases I regularly find the following, by the same pens:

"The greatest defect of this work is that it is not a novel, properly speaking."

One could reply by the same argument:

"The greatest defect of the writer who does me the honor to sit in judgment on my work is that he is not a critic."

What, in fact, are the essential characteristics of a critic?

He must, without partisanship, without preconceived opinions, without the ideas of any school, without any connection with any clique of artists—he must comprehend, distinguish, and explain the most opposite tendencies and the most contrary temperaments, and appreciate artistic essays of the most diverse forms.

The critic who, after "Manon Lescaut," "Paul and Virginia," "Don Quixote," "Les Liaisons Dangereuses," "Werther," "Elective Affinities," "Clarissa Harlowe," "Emile," "Candide," "Cinq-Mars," "René," "The Three Musketeers," "Mauprat," "Le Père Goriot," "Cousine Bette," "Colombe," "Le Rouge et le Noir," "Mademoiselle de Maupin," "Notre Dame de Paris," "Salammbo," "Madame Bovary," "Adolphe," "M. de Camors," "L'Assommoir," "Sapho," etc., still dares to write, "This is a novel and this is not," seems to me to be endowed with a perspicacity which is very much like incompetence.

Such a critic usually understands by a novel an adventure more or less probable, arranged like a drama in three acts, the first containing the exposition, the second the action, and the last the dénoûment.

This manner of composing a novel is certainly admissible on condition that we deal with all in the same manner.

Do there exist rules for writing a novel, outside of which a written narrative ought to bear another name?

If "Don Quixote" is a novel, is "Le Rouge et le Noir" another? If "Monte Cristo" is one, is "L'Assommoir" another? Can any comparison be established between the "Elective Affinities" of Goethe, the "Three Musketeers" of Dumas, "Madame Bovary" by Flaubert, "M. de Camors" by Octave Feuillet, and "Germinal" by Zola? Which of these works is a novel? Where âre the famous rules? Where did they come from? Who established them? In virtue of what principle, what authority, what course of reasoning, do they exist?

It seems, however, that these critics know, in some certain, indubitable manner, what constitutes a novel, and what distinguishes it from another which is not one. This simply means that, without being producers, they are enlisted in a certain school, and reject, just as the novelists themselves do, all works conceived and executed outside of their code of æsthetics.

An intelligent critic, on the contrary, ought to seek for everything that is as different as possible from the novels already written, and to urge young authors, as earnestly as they can, to strike out new paths.

All writers, Victor Hugo as well as Zola, have persistently claimed the absolute, indisputable right of composing—that is, of imagining or observing—according to their personal conception of art. Talent comes from originality, which is a special manner of thinking, seeing, understanding and judging. Now, the critic who assumes to define the "novel" according to the ideas he has formed from the novels he likes, and to lay down certain invariable rules of composition, will always be hostile to the genius of the artist who introduces a new style. A critic, to really deserve the name, should be nothing but an analyst, without bias, without preferences, without passions; and, like an art critic, take into account only the artistic value of the object of art submitted to him. His comprehension ought to be all-embracing, and ought so completely to absorb his personality that he can praise and commend the very books which, as a man, he does not like, and which he must estimate in the character of a judge.

Most critics, however, are merely readers; and the result is that they nearly always lash us unmercifully, unreservedly, and without stint, or else compliment us.

The reader who seeks in a book merely to satisfy the natural bent of his mind demands that the writer shall minister to his predominating taste; and he invariably describes as remarkable or "well written" the work or the passage which pleases his imagination, be it idealistic, gay, loose, sad, dreamy, or realistic.

In brief, the public is composed of numerous groups that cry out to us:

"Comfort me."

"Amuse me."

"Touch my sympathies."

"Make me sad."

"Make me dream."

"Make me laugh."

"Make me shiver."

"Make me weep."

"Make me think."

Some chosen spirits alone ask of the artist:

"Make something beautiful, in the form which suits you best, according to your temperament."

The artist essays, succeeds, or fails. The critic ought to judge of the result only by the nature of the effort: he has no right to take account of tendencies.

This has been written a thousand times already, but it will be always necessary to repeat it.

Thus after the literary schools which have sought

IV

to give us a deformed, superhuman, poetic, tender, charming, or superb vision of life, there has come a realistic, or naturalistic, school, which professes to show us the truth, the whole truth, and nothing but the truth.

These different schools of art must be accepted with equal interest, and the works that they produce must be judged solely from the point of view of their artistic value, admitting *a priori* the general ideas which give birth to them.

To deny the right of an author to compose a poetic work, or a realistic work, is to seek to force him to modify his temperament, to reject his originality, and not to allow him the eye and the intelligence which Nature has bestowed on him.

To reproach him for seeing beautiful or hideous things, small things or epics, gracious or displeasing things, is to reproach him with being made in such or such a manner, and with not having a power of vision that agrees with our own.

Let us leave him free to understand, to observe, to convince as he pleases, provided he be an artist. Let us rise to the heights of poetry when we criticise an idealist, and show him that his dream is commonplace, vulgar, not mad enough or magnificent enough. But if we criticise a naturalist, let us show him wherein the truth in life differs from the truth in his book.

It is evident that schools that differ so widely must employ absolutely opposite methods of composition.

The novelist who transforms the brutal, unpleasant, unvarying truth, in order to draw from it some charming and exceptional incident, ought, without any exaggerated regard for probability, to manipulate events at his pleasure, and prepare and arrange them so as to arouse the reader's pleasure, emotion, or sympathy. The plan of his novel is a mere series of ingenious combinations, skillfully leading to the dénoûment. The incidents are disposed and graduated to the climax and the termination, which is the crowning decisive event, satisfying all the curiosity awakened at the beginning, barring any further interest, and terminating so completely the story told that we no longer desire to know what will happen to-morrow to the personages who had enchained our interest.

The novelist, on the other hand, who professes to give us an exact image of life ought carefully to avoid every concatenation of events that seems exceptional. His object is not to tell a story, to amuse us, to touch our pity, but to compel us to think, and to understand the deep, hidden meaning of events. Through having seen and meditated, he looks at the universe, things, facts and men, in a manner peculiar to himself, the result of the combined effect of observation and reflection. He seeks to impart to us this personal vision of the world by reproducing it in his book. In order to move us as he himself has been moved by the spectacle of life, he must reproduce it before our eyes with scrupulous accuracy. He will have, then, to compose his work so skillfully, with such apparent simplicity, as to conceal his plot and render it impossible to discover his intentions.

Instead of taking an incident and developing it in a manner to render it interesting down to the dénoûment, he will introduce his character or char-

acters at a certain period of their lives, and conduct
them, by natural transitions, down to the following
period. In this way he will show, at times, how
minds are modified under the influence of surrounding circumstances; and, again, how sentiments and
passions are developed, how we love, hate, combat
each other, in all social conditions; how business interests, money interests, family interests, and political interests, all vie with one another.

The skillful execution of his plan, then, will not
consist in emotion or charm, in a fascinating beginning or an affecting catastrophe, but in the adroit
grouping of everyday facts from which the
definitive meaning of the work may be gathered.
If, in three hundred pages, he can portray ten years
of a life for the purpose of showing its peculiar and
characteristic significance in relation to all the beings that surrounded it, he ought to know how to
eliminate, among the innumerable little daily events,
all those which are useless to him, and to place in a
strong and distinct light all those which would have
remained unperceived by less clear-sighted observ-
ers, and which give his book its power and its value
as a whole.

One can understand how such a manner of composition, so different from the old method, apparent
to all eyes, often bewilders the critics, and that they
do not discover the fine, secret, almost invisible
threads employed by certain modern artists in place
of the single thread which was called "the plot."

In brief, if the novelist of yesterday selected and
related the crises of life, the poignant emotions of
soul and heart, the novelist of to-day writes the his-
tory of the heart, the soul, and the intellect, in their

normal condition. To produce the effect he aims at, that is, the feeling of simple reality, and to bring out the artistic lesson which he desires to draw from it, that is, the revelation of the real contemporary man before his eyes, he must employ only actual and incontestable facts. But if we place ourselves at the very point of view of those realistic artists, we must discuss and contest their theory, which seems to be summed up in these words, "The whole truth, and nothing but the truth."

Their intention being to bring out the philosophy of certain current everyday facts, they are often obliged to change events in the interest of probability and to the detriment of truth, for

"Le vrai peut quelquefois n'être pas vraisemblable."

"Truth may sometimes be improbable."

The realist, if he is an artist, will seek, not to show us a vulgar photograph of life, but to give us a more complete, striking and convincing vision of life than the reality itself.

It would be impossible to narrate everything, for it would require at least a volume a day to enumerate the multitude of insignificant incidents that fill up our existence.

Some selection is therefore imposed on the writer, and this is the first blow at the theory of the "whole truth."

Life, besides, is composed of the most different, most unforeseen, most contrary, and most incongruous things; it is brutal, without sequence or connection, full of inexplicable, illogical and contradictory catastrophes which ought to be classed under the heading, "Various Events."

That is why the artist, having chosen his theme, selects in this life, incumbered as it is with accidents and trivialities, only those characteristic details necessary to his subject, and will cast all the rest aside.

One example out of a thousand. The number of people in the world who die every day by accident is considerable. But we cannot make a tile fall on the head of a principal character, or throw him under the wheels of a carriage in the middle of a story, under pretext that it is necessary to introduce an accident.

Life, again, leaves everything just as it finds it, precipitates action, or drags it out indefinitely. Art, on the contrary, consists in using forethought and care in elaboration, bringing into prominence, through sheer skill in composition, the essential incidents, and in giving to all the rest the degree of prominence proportioned to their importance, in order to produce a convincing impression of the special truth it seeks to portray.

To make things real consists, therefore, in giving a complete similitude of truth according to the ordinary logical sequence of facts, and not in transcribing them, servilely, one after another, in the order of their successive occurrence.

Hence, I conclude that the realists of art ought rather to call themselves the illusionists.

How puerile it is, besides, to believe in reality, when we each carry our own idea of truth in our mind and our senses. Our eyes, our ears, our sense of smell, our taste, are all different, and create as many ideas of truth as there are men on the earth. And our minds, receiving their information from these senses, are diversely impressed, and understand, analyze and judge as if each of us belonged to a different race.

Each of us, then, simply creates a world according to his own imagination, a poetical, sentimental, joyful, melancholy, obscene, or lugubrious illusion, according to his nature. And the writer's only mission is to faithfully reproduce this illusion by means of all the devices of art of which he is master and that he knows best how to employ.

Illusion of the beautiful, a mere human convention! Illusion of the disagreeable, a varying opinion! Illusion of the true, never immutable! Illusion of the ignoble, attractive to so many! Great artists are those who impose on mankind their particular illusions!

Let us not, then, lose our tempers over any theory, since each one of them is simply the generalized expression of an individual temperament.

Two theories, in particular, have frequently aroused discussion through being opposed to each other, instead of both one and the other being accepted on an equal footing; these are the theory of the analytical novel, and the theory of the objective novel. The partisans of analysis demand that the writer shall devote his attention to describing the slightest evolution of a soul, and all the most secret motives that determine action, giving to the action itself a place of very secondary importance. It is merely a peg on which to hang the story. According to them, these analytical, dreamy novels in which imagination is confounded with observation should be composed after the manner of a philosopher writing a book on psychology, revealing causes by tracing them back to their most distant origin, telling all the whys of all resolves, and discerning all the struggles of a soul acting under the impulse of interest, passion, or instinct.

The partisans of objectivity (what an odious word!) profess, on the contrary, to give us an exact representation of what takes place in life; they carefully avoid all complicated explanations and all dissertations on motives, and limit themselves to placing before our eyes personages and events.

In their view psychology ought to be concealed in a book, as it is concealed, in reality, beneath the facts of existence.

Novels conceived on this plan gain thereby in interest, in action, in color, and in stirring life.

In place, then, of describing at length the condition of mind of a character, authors who deal with the objective seek for the special action or gesture to which this state of mind would inevitably lead under certain definite conditions. And they make him conduct himself in such a manner, from one end of the volume to the other, that all his acts, all his movements, shall be the reflection of his inmost nature, of all his thoughts, all his resolves, all his doubts. They hide their psychology instead of displaying it; they make it the framework of the book, as the invisible bony system is the frame of the human body. The painter who paints our portrait does not show our skeleton.

It seems to me that a novel thus executed gains likewise in sincerity. In the first place, it is nearer the truth, for the people we see in action around us do not confide to us their motives of action.

We must next take into account that if, by dint

of observation, we can ascertain the nature of men so exactly as to foresee their course of conduct under almost all circumstances; if we can say with precision: "Such a man, of such a temperament, in such a case will do thus or so"—it does not follow that we can ascertain, one by one, all the secret evolutions of his mind, which is not our mind; all the mysterious temptations of his instincts, which are not similar to ours, nor all the confused proclivities of his nature, with its senses, nerves, blood, and flesh differing from our own.

Whatever be the genius of a weak, passionless man, loving solely science and work, he can never enter so completely into the body and soul of a robust, sensual, violent nature, stirred by every desire and even by every vice, as to comprehend and describe the secret impulses and sensations of such a different being, even though he may clearly foresee and narrate all the acts of his life.

In brief, the author who deals with psychology alone can only describe himself in describing his characters in the various situations in which he places them; for it is impossible for him to change his senses, which are the sole intermediaries between ourselves and external life, and impress us with their perceptions, determining our sensibilities and creating in us a soul essentially different from those that surround us. Our point of view and our knowledge of the world, acquired by the aid of our senses, and our ideas of life, can be only partially transferred to all the characters whose inmost, unknown being we pretend to be unveiling. It is always ourselves whom we exhibit in the form of a king, a murderer, a thief, or an honest man; of a courtesan, a nun, a young girl, or a market woman; for we are obliged to state the problem to ourselves in these terms: "If *I* were king, murderer, thief, courtesan, nun, young girl, or market woman, what would I do? What would I think? How would I act?" We can, then, only diversify our personages by changing the age, sex, social position, and all the circumstances of the life of our *I,* which nature has surrounded with an impregnable barrier of organs.

Skill consists in not letting the reader recognize this *I* under all the different masks which serve to hide it.

But if, from the sole point of view of complete accuracy, purely psychological analysis is open to question, it may, nevertheless, give us as noble works of art as all the other methods of work.

To-day we have the symbolists. Why not? Their dream as artists is one to be respected; and they are particularly interesting, inasmuch as they know and proclaim the extreme difficulty of art.

In fact, one must be very mad, very daring, very presumptuous, or very stupid to write anything nowadays! After so many masters of such varied dispositions, of such manifold genius, what remains to be done that has not been done, what can be said that has not been said? Who among us can boast of having written a page or a phrase which cannot be found, almost verbatim, somewhere? When we, who are so saturated with French writings that our whole body gives us the impression of being kneaded up with phrases, take up a book, do we ever find a line or thought which is not familiar, or of which we have not had at least a confused presentiment?

The man who seeks only to amuse the public by already known methods writes with confidence, in the candor of his mediocrity, for the ignorant, the idle. But those on whom all the ages of past literature weigh heavily; those whom nothing satisfies, whom everything disgusts because it does not come up to their dreams; those to whom every flower seems to have been plucked, to whom their work always gives the impression of a useless and common labor—arrive at the opinion that literary art is an intangible, mysterious thing, only partially revealed to us in some of the pages of the greatest masters.

Twenty verses, twenty phrases, may suddenly thrill us to the heart as a surprising revelation; but the following verses resemble all verses, and the prose that follows resembles all other prose.

Men of genius, doubtless, do not experience this anguish and torture, because they have in themselves a resistless creative power. They do not sit in judgment on themselves. The rest of us, who are simply conscientious and persistent workers, can only by continued effort fight against overwhelming discouragement.

Two men by their simple and lucid teachings gave me this power of persistent effort—Louis Bouilhet and Gustave Flaubert.

If I speak of them and of myself in this place it is because their advice, summed up in a few lines, may be useful, perhaps, to some young writers with less self-esteem than is usually found in literary débutants.

Bouilhet, with whom I formed a rather intimate acquaintance about two years before I gained the friendship of Flaubert, by dint of repeating to me that a hundred verses, or even less, insured the reputation of an artist, provided they were faultless and embodied the essence of the talent and originality of a man, even of second-rate talent, made me understand that.

I also learned that the best-known writers have seldom left more than one volume; and that the first essential is to have the luck to find and discern, amid the multiplicity of subjects that present themselves, that subject that will absorb all our faculties, all our ability, all our artistic power.

Later on Flaubert, whom I sometimes saw, conceived a liking for me. I ventured to submit to him some of my attempts. He kindly read them, and replied: "I do not know if you have talent; what you have shown me proves that you possess a certain degree of intelligence. But do not forget this, young man, that talent—to quote the saying of Buffon—is merely 'long patience.' Keep on working."

I did so, and often revisited him, as I perceived that he liked me, for he laughingly called me his disciple.

For seven years I wrote verses, I wrote stories, I wrote novels, I even wrote a detestable play. Of these nothing survives. The master read them all, and on the following Sunday at luncheon he would give me his criticism, and inculcate little by little two or three principles that sum up his long and patient lessons. "If one has any originality, the first thing requisite is to bring it out; if one has none, the first thing to be done is to acquire it."

Talent is long patience. Everything which one desires to express must be considered with sufficient attention, and during a sufficiently long time, to discover in it some aspect which no one has as yet seen or described. In everything there is still some spot unexplored, because we are accustomed to look at things only with the recollection of what others before us have thought of the subject we are contemplating. The smallest object contains something unknown. Let us find it. In order to describe a fire that flames, and a tree on the plain, we must keep looking at that flame and that tree, until to our eyes they no longer resemble any other tree, any other fire.

This is the way to become original.

Having, besides, laid down this truth that there are not in the whole world two grains of sand, two specks, two hands, or two noses exactly alike, he compelled me to describe, in a few phrases, a being or an object in such a manner as to clearly particularize it and distinguish it from all the other beings, or all the other objects of the same race or the same species.

"When you pass," he would say, "a grocer seated at his shop door, a janitor smoking his pipe, a stand of hackney coaches, show me that grocer and that janitor, their attitude, their whole physical appearance, including also by a skillful description their whole moral nature, so that I cannot confound them with any other grocer or any other janitor; make me see, in one word, that a certain cab horse does not resemble the fifty others that follow or precede it."

I have stated elsewhere his ideas on style. They are closely related to the theory of observation which I have just explained.

Whatever be the thing one wishes to say, there

is only one noun to express it, only one verb to give it life, only one adjective to qualify it. We must search, then, till that noun, that verb, that adjective, are discovered; never be content with an approximation, never resort to tricks, however happy, or to buffooneries of language, to avoid a difficulty.

We can interpret and describe the most subtle things if we bear in mind the verse of Boileau:

"D'un mot mis en sa place enseigna le pouvoir."

"He taught the force of a word in the right place."

There is no need of the eccentric, complicated, multifarious sort of Chinese vocabulary, which is inflicted on us at the present day under the name of artistic writing, to enable us to describe every shade of thought; but it is necessary to discern, with the utmost lucidity, all the modifications of the value of a word according to the position it occupies. Let us have fewer nouns, verbs and adjectives with almost incomprehensible meanings, and more varied phrases, differently constructed, ingeniously turned, sonorous and full of skillful rhythms. Let us endeavor to be excellent stylists, rather than collectors of rare terms.

It is, in fact, more difficult to turn a phrase to suit one's self, to make it say everything (even that which it does not express), to fill it with hidden meanings, and with secret suggestions which are not formulated, than to invent new expressions, or to seek in the depths of old forgotten books all those that are obsolete and have lost their significance, and for us are only dead words.

The French language, moreover, is a limpid stream which mannerists have never been able, and never will be able, to trouble. Every century has thrown into this limpid current its fashions, its pretentious archaisms, and its affectations, without any of these useless attempts and impotent efforts rising to its surface. The nature of the language is to be clear, logical and nervous. It refuses to be enfeebled, obscured, or corrupted.

Those who to-day write descriptions without careful attention to abstract terms, those who make the rain or hail fall on the *cleanness* of the window panes, may also fling stones at the simplicity of their fellow workers. They may hit, perhaps, the fellow workers that possess a body, but will never reach the simplicity which has none.

GUY DE MAUPASSANT.

La Guillette, Étretat, Sept., 1887.

PIERRE AND JEAN

CHAPTER I

SURPRISING NEWS

"AH!" exclaimed Monsieur Roland abruptly after a quarter of an hour's silence, during which he had remained motionless, his eyes fixed on the water, occasionally raising his line very gently to see if he had a bite by a slight movement, feeling the line he had dropped down into the sea.

Madame Roland had been dozing at the stern by the side of Madame Rosémilly, who had been invited to join the party, but roused herself at her husband's exclamation, and, turning her head toward him, asked:

"Well, what is it, Gérôme?"

He replied in a tone of vexation:

"Can't get another bite. Since noon I've caught nothing. One ought never to go fishing with women; they delay one in starting."

His two sons, Pierre and Jean, who were sitting, one on the starboard, the other on the port side, each with a line over his forefinger, began to laugh at the same instant, and Jean replied:

"You are not very gallant to our guest, papa!"

Monsieur Roland was confused, and made his excuses.

"I beg pardon, Madame Rosémilly, but I cannot help it. I invite ladies because I like their company, but as soon as I find myself on the water, I think of nothing but fish."

Madame Roland was now wide awake, and was gazing with a softened air at the wide stretch of cliffs and sea. She murmured:

"Still, you have had good sport."

Her husband shook his head in negation, while he cast a satisfied glance at the basket where the fish, caught by the three men, were still gasping weakly with a low sound of sticky scales and quivering fins, of weak, ineffectual struggles, as they opened their mouths in the deadly air.

Monsieur Roland took the hamper between his knees and tipped it till the silver flood of creatures reached the edge, in order to see those at the bottom. They gasped more perceptibly in their death agony, and their pungent odor, the wholesome smell of the sea, arose from the full basket.

The old fisherman inhaled it greedily, as if it were the scent of roses, and declared:

"By George! They are fresh, these fellows," and then continued:

"How many have you caught, doctor?"

The elder son, Pierre, a man of thirty, with black whiskers closely trimmed, but without mustache, replied:

"Not many. Three or four."

The father turned to the younger son.

"And you, Jean?"

Jean, a tall, light-haired youth, with a full beard, and considerably younger than his brother, smiled as he answered:

2

"About the same as Pierre. Four or five."

They always told him the same lies, and delighted the old fellow beyond measure.

He rolled his line round a rowlock, and, crossing his arms, announced:

"I'll never again try to fish in the afternoon. After ten o'clock, it is all over. The rascals will not bite; they take a siesta in the sun."

The good man looked at the surrounding sea with the satisfied air of a proprietor.

He had been a jeweler in Paris, but an irresistible love of sailing and fishing dragged him from his counter as soon as he had acquired a modest competence. He left Paris and betook himself to Havre, where he bought a boat and became an amateur sailor. His two sons, Pierre and Jean, remained in Paris to continue their studies, and came occasionally, during vacation, to share their father's amusements.

The elder son, Pierre, five years older than Jean, on leaving college had felt a vocation for various professions in succession. He tried half a dozen, one after another, and, quickly disgusted with each, plunged at once into new attempts.

Finally, medicine tempted him, and he set to work with such ardor that he received his degree as doctor after a brief course of study, further shortened by exemptions granted by the authorities. He was intelligent, changeable and tenacious, full of utopian and philosophical ideas.

Jean, as fair as Pierre was dark, as calm as his brother was excitable, as sweet tempered as his brother was spiteful, had quietly studied law, and obtained his diploma at the same time that Pierre graduated in medicine.

Both were now taking a holiday with their family, and both had formed the project of establishing themselves at Havre, if they could succeed in doing so satisfactorily.

But a vague jealousy—one of those dormant jealousies which grow up almost invisibly between brothers or sisters, till they mature and burst forth on the occasion of a marriage or of a piece of good luck happening to one—kept them on the alert in a state of fraternal and inoffensive hostility. They certainly loved each other, but they spied on each other. Pierre, who was five years old when Jean was born, regarded, with the dislike of a spoiled little animal, this other little animal, which suddenly appeared in the arms of his father and mother, and was so caressed and beloved by them.

Jean had been from childhood a model of gentleness, goodness, and even temper; and Pierre gradually became wearied of hearing the continual praise of his big brother, for to him his gentleness seemed effeminacy, his goodness, foolishness and his kindness, blindness. His parents, good, easy people, who dreamed of their sons occupying honorable commonplace positions, reproached him with his fickleness, his enthusiasms, his abortive attempts, all his ineffective impulses toward larger ideas and the ornamental arts.

After he attained manhood, they no longer said to him, "Look at Jean, and follow his example," but whenever he heard, "Jean did this, Jean did that," he understood clearly this hidden allusion, and the meaning of the words.

4

Their mother, a good housewife, rather sensi-
mental, was continually appeasing the little rivalries
that sprang up every day between her two big
sons, over little matters of everyday life. At this
moment her peace of mind was disturbed by a
trifling event which she feared might lead to a
complication. During the winter, while her sons
were completing their special studies, she made the
acquaintance of a neighbor, Madame Rosémilly,
widow of a ship captain who had died at sea two
years before. She was quite young, only twenty-
three, a capable woman, who knew life by instinct
like a wild animal, as if she had seen, experienced,
comprehended and weighed all possible events, of
which she formed an estimate in a sound, narrow
and benevolent spirit. She had fallen into the habit
of coming over in the evening with her embroidery
to chat with her neighbors, who always offered her
a cup of tea.

Monsieur Roland, whose craze for a sailor's life
was taking a greater hold of him, inquired about
the deceased captain from their new friend, and she
spoke of him, of his voyages, his old yarns, without
embarrassment, like a sensible woman resigned to
her loss, who loves life and respects death.

The sons, on their return home, finding this pretty
widow installed in the house, at once began to pay
her attention, less through a desire to please her
than from a longing to supplant each other.

Their mother, with her practical common sense,
hoped that one of them would be successful, for the
young widow was rich, but she did not wish the
other brother to feel hurt.

Madame Rosémilly was a blonde, with blue eyes,

a crown of fluffy hair that fluttered in the slightest breeze, and a little bold, defiant air which was not in keeping with her sensible disposition.

She seemed already to prefer Jean, attracted to him by a similarity of character. This preference, however, was only shown by an almost imperceptible difference in voice and look, and by the fact that she sometimes took his advice.

She seemed to divine that Jean's opinion would agree with hers, while that of Pierre would as surely be different. When she spoke about the doctor's ideas in politics, art, philosophy or morals, she would occasionally say "Your nonsense." Then he would look at her with the cold stare of a magistrate who is preparing an indictment against all women, poor creatures.

Before the return of his sons, Monsieur Roland had never invited her to go out fishing; nor, indeed, did he ever take his wife with him, for he liked to set out at daybreak with Captain Beausire, an old skipper whom he had met on the quay at high tide, and who had become an intimate friend, and the old sailor, Papagris, commonly called Jean Bart, who was the boatkeeper.

One evening in the preceding week, Madame Rosémilly, who had dined with them, observed, "Fishing must be amusing, is it not?" and the retired jeweler, flattered in his ruling passion, and possessed with a desire to make converts, exclaimed:

"Will you come with us?"

"Oh, yes."

"Next Tuesday?"

"Yes, next Tuesday."

6

"Have you the courage to start at five in the morning?"

"Oh, no, certainly not!" she cried in astonishment.

He was disappointed and chilled and began to doubt her earnestness. Nevertheless, he asked:

"At what hour can you start?"

"Well—at nine!"

"Not before?"

"No, not before. Even that is too early!"

Monsieur Roland hesitated. They would certainly not catch anything, for when the sun is bright the fish do not bite; but the two brothers were zealous in making all the arrangements and settling everything at once.

On the following Tuesday the *Pearl* cast anchor beneath the white rocks of the cape of La Hêve; they fished with success till noon, then rested, and fished again without catching anything, and Roland, discovering somewhat late in the day that Madame Rosémilly really cared for nothing but the sail, and, seeing that there was no sign of a nibble at his lines, uttered, in an access of unreasoning impatience, an energetic "Bah!" which was addressed as much to the uninterested widow as to the fish that would not be caught.

He was at present engaged in gazing on the captured fish, with the trembling joy of a miser; then he looked at the sky and remarked that the sun was sinking.

"Well, boys," he said, "shall we go back toward shore?"

The sons both drew in their lines, reeled them,

7

cleaned their hooks, and stuck them into their corks, and then waited.

Monsieur Roland stood up to look at the horizon in seafaring style.

"No more wind," he said; "we must row, my lads."

Then, with his arm pointing to the north, he addded:

"Look, there's the Southampton packet."

The smooth sea lay stretched out like a piece of blue cloth, boundless, gleaming with reflections of gold and fire, and away in the direction indicated a blackish cloud ascended against the rosy sky. Below it was seen the ship, which at such a distance seemed quite small. Southward were numerous other clouds of smoke, all approaching the pier of Havre, the white line of which, with its tall, erect lighthouse at the end, was scarcely visible.

Roland asked:

"Isn't the *Normandie* due to-day?"

Jean replied:

"Yes, papa."

"Give me my glass. I believe she is down there."

He pulled out the brass tube, adjusted the instrument to his eye, and then, delighted at seeing her, exclaimed:

"Yes, yes, it is the *Normandie;* I recognize her two smokestacks! Will you have a look, Madame Rosémilly?"

She took the glass and turned it toward the distant American steamer, doubtless without bringing it into the field, for she could distinguish nothing but some blue with a circle of color, a round rainbow, and then strange objects, like a kind of eclipses, which made her feel quite sick.

She returned the glass with the words:

"I never could use that instrument, and it always provoked my husband, for he would remain for hours at the window watching the ships pass."

Monsieur Roland was vexed as he replied:

"It must be the fault of your eyes, for my glass is a very good one."

Then he offered it to his wife.

"Will you take a look?"

"No, thank you; I know beforehand that I could not see."

Madame Roland, a woman of forty-eight, who did not show her age, seemed to enjoy, more than the rest, the sail and the close of the day.

Her chestnut hair had just commenced to whiten. She had a calm, thoughtful air—a happy, kindly air pleasant to see. According to a remark of her son Pierre, she knew the price of money, which did not prevent her from enjoying the charm of revery. She loved to read romances and poetry, not for their value as works of art, but for the tender and melancholy dreaminess they awoke in her. A verse, often commonplace, often bad, set the little chord in vibration, as she would say, and gave her the feeling of a mysterious desire almost realized. She felt a pleasure in these light emotions that somewhat troubled her soul, which was as well kept as an account book.

Since her arrival at Havre she had become visibly stouter and this made her once slender and supple figure rather heavy.

This excursion on the water had charmed her.

Her husband, without being ill-natured, bullied her just as despots in an office bully underlings, without anger or dislike, and with whom a command is like an oath. In the presence of strangers he restrained himself, but in his family he was not so careful, and assumed terrible airs, although he was afraid of everybody. She, in her dislike of noise, scenes and useless explanations, always yielded and never asked for anything; she had not dared even ask, for a long time back, to join in a sail. It was with joy, then, that she seized this occasion, and tasted this rare and novel pleasure.

From the time they left the shore, she gave herself up utterly, body and soul, to the enjoyment of gently gliding over the water. She did not think, she did not dwell on memories or hopes; it seemed to her that her heart, like her body, was floating over something soft, fluid, delicious, which lulled her into apathy.

When the father gave the order, "Come, get to your oars," she smiled as she saw her two big sons take off their jackets and roll up their shirtsleeves.

Pierre, who was nearest the two ladies, took the starboard oar, Jean that on the larboard side, and they waited till the master cried, "Oars all!" for he stickled about having these manœuvres executed according to rule.

Then, at one dash, they dipped their oars, and swung back with all their force, and tried to rival each other in the vigor of their strokes. They had set out quietly, with sails set, but the breeze had fallen, and the masculine pride of the two brothers was at once aroused at the prospect of measuring their strength against each other.

Whenever they went fishing with their father alone, they rowed without the rudder, for Roland prepared the lines while watching the course of the boat, which he guided by a word or gesture. "Easy, Jean." "Now, Pierre, pull," or perhaps he would say, "Come, *one,* now *two,* more elbow grease." Then the lazy one pulled stronger, and the other took it more easily, till the boat resumed a straight course.

To-day they wanted to show their muscle. Pierre's arms were hairy, rather thin but nervous; those of Jean, plump and white, rather pink, with a mass of muscles that played beneath the skin.

Pierre had the advantage at first. With teeth set, brow wrinkled, legs stretched, hands clenching the oar, he made it bend at every stroke, and the *Pearl* would swerve aside. Monsieur Roland, sitting in the bow to leave the stern to the ladies, roared out, "Easy, number *one;* pull, number *two.*" Then number *one* pulled harder, and *two* could not reply to his disorderly stroke.

At length the captain gave the word "Stop." The two oars rose together, and Jean, by his father's orders, pulled a few strokes alone. But from that moment he had the advantage; he grew animated and heated, while Pierre, out of breath and exhausted by his rash efforts, grew weak. Four times Monsieur Roland made them stop in order to give the elder time to recover his wind, and to get the boat on her course. The doctor, his forehead covered with perspiration, his cheeks pale and vexed and humiliated, stammered out:

"I do not know what ails me. I have a spasm

at the heart. I started in very well, but that has strained my arm."

Jean asked, "Would you like me to take both oars?"

"No, thanks. It will soon pass."

Madame Roland, in a tone of annoyance, said: "Now, Pierre, what is the sense of putting yourself into such a condition? You are not a baby now."

He shrugged his shoulders and resumed his rowing.

Madame Rosémilly pretended not to see, notice, or hear anything. Her little blonde head, at every movement of the boat, gave a pretty little toss backward, which shook the soft hair on her temples.

But Monsieur Roland cried, "Hallo, there's the *Prince Albert* overtaking us!" They all looked. Long, low, with its two smokestacks sloping astern, and its two yellow paddle boxes like round cheeks, the Southampton packet came on at full speed, her deck covered with passengers and open parasols; her swift, noisy paddlewheels struck the water, making it foam, and giving her an air of haste, as of a special courier; while her upright bows cut the sea into two swelling waves, which glided, thin and transparent, along her sides.

When she was quite near the *Pearl,* Monsieur Roland lifted his hat, the two ladies waved their handkerchiefs, and the greeting was answered by half a dozen parasols waved from the steamer as she passed on, leaving a few slow waves behind her, on the tranquil and gleaming surface of the sea.

Other steamers came into view, hastening from all points of the compass to the short white dock, which swallowed them up, one after the other. Fishing boats and large sailing vessels, with their slender masts gliding against the sky, in tow of almost invisible tugs, all approached, slowly or swiftly, that devouring ogre, which at intervals seemed gorged to satiety, and would vomit forth to sea another fleet of steamers, brigs, schooners, and three-masters, with their network of masts and spars. The steamers sped on, right or left, over the smooth bosom of the ocean, while the sailing ships, cast off by the tugs that had hauled them out, remained motionless, spreading from topmast to foremast their white or brown canvas, which seemed red in the setting sun.

Madame Roland, her eyes half closed, murmured: "How beautiful the sea is!"

Madame Rosémilly replied, with a prolonged sigh, which, however, had no sadness in it:

"Yes, but it does plenty of mischief sometimes."

Roland exclaimed:

"There's the *Normandie* going into port. Is she not huge?"

Then he told all about the opposite coast yonder on the other side of the mouth of the Seine—which was twenty kilometres wide, that mouth, he said. He pointed out Villerville, Trouville, Houlgate, Luc, Arromanches, the river of Caen, and the rocks of Calvados, which render navigation dangerous as far as Cherbourg. Then he discussed the sandbanks of the Seine, which shift at every tide, and mislead even the pilots of Quillebœuf if they do not examine the channel every day. He bade them remark that Havre separated Upper and Lower Normandy. In Lower Normandy the flat coast, consisting of pasture lands, meadows and fields, slopes down to the water's edge. The coast of Upper Normandy, on the other hand, descends by steep, precipitous cliffs full of clefts and indentations to the sea, forming an immense white wall as far as Dunkirk, every cleft containing a village or a port—Étretat, Fécamp, Saint Valery, Tréport, Dieppe and so on.

The two ladies, who were in a state of apathetic comfort, were not listening; they did not speak, for they were somewhat overpowered by the vast expanse of air and water, and by the calm magnificence of the sunset. Roland, alone, never stopped talking; he was one of those whom nothing affects. Women, more nervous, sometimes feel that the sound of a useless voice is as irritating as an impertinence.

Pierre and Jean, now pacified, rowed on slowly, and the *Pearl* advanced to the harbor, looking diminutive by the side of the large ships.

When she touched the quay, the sailor, Papagris, who was waiting for them, assisted the ladies to land, and the party entered the town. A numerous, quiet crowd, the crowd that goes to the pier every day at high water, was also returning townward.

Mesdames Roland and Rosémilly led the way, followed by the three men. As they went up the Rue de Paris, they paused occasionally before a milliner's or goldsmith's shop to look at a hat or a trinket, and, after an exchange of ideas, resumed their walk.

Before the Place de la Bourse, Roland, as he did every day, looked at the merchants' dock, which was filled with ships and led into other docks, where the large hulls, with their sides touching, lay four or five deep. The countless masts along the many miles extent of quays, the masts with their yards, their vanes, and their ropes, gave to this opening in the middle of the town the aspect of a great dead forest. Above this leafless wood the gulls were circling, watching for all the refuse cast in the water, and dropping on it like a falling stone. A ship boy, who was fixing a pulley at one end of the yards, looked as if he had climbed up to get a bird's nest.

"Will you take dinner with us, to finish the day together?" said Madame Roland to Madame Rosémilly.

"Yes, with pleasure. I accept informally. It would be melancholy to go home alone this evening."

Pierre, who had heard the remark, and whom the indifference of the young widow began to annoy, muttered, "Humph! the widow is putting on airs now." For some days he had called her the "widow." The word meant nothing, but the tone in which it was uttered seemed to him ill-natured and slighting.

The three men did not say another word until they reached their home. It was a narrow, two-story house, in the Rue Belle-Normande. The servant, Josephine, a country girl of about nineteen, at low wages, in whom the startled, animal look of the peasantry was exaggerated, opened the door, closed it after them, and followed her master to the reception room on the first floor. Then she said:

"A gentleman has been here three times."

Monsieur Roland, who never spoke to her without shouting and cursing, cried:

"Who is it that's been here? confound it!"

She was not disturbed at any time by these outbursts of her master, and continued:

"A gentleman from the notary."

"What notary?"

"Well, Monsieur Canu."

"And what did the gentleman say?"

"That Monsieur Canu would come himself this evening."

Monsieur Lecanu was the notary, and, to some extent, the friend of Roland, whose business he transacted. For him to announce a visit in the evening argued some urgent and important affair. The Rolands all looked at each other, as worried at this news, as people of small means always are at the intervention of a lawyer, who awakens in their minds a host of ideas about contracts, legacies, lawsuits and other things agreeable or disagreeable. After some seconds, Roland murmured:

"What can this mean?"

Madame Rosémilly began to laugh.

"Why, it is a legacy, I'm sure. I bring good luck."

They were not however, expecting the death of any one who was likely to leave them anything.

Madame Roland, blessed with an excellent memory for pedigrees, at once began to recall to mind all the marriages on her own and her husband's side, and to trace out the connections and the various branches of cousins.

She asked, before even taking off her hat:

"Tell me, father" (she called her husband "father" at home, and sometimes "Monsieur Roland" before strangers), "tell me, father, do you remember whom Joseph Lebru married when he took a second wife?"

"Yes, a little Dumenil, daughter of a paper man-ufacturer."

"Has he any children?"

"Four or five, at the least, I believe."

"No; there is nothing from that quarter."

She was becoming eager in this inquiry, and clung to this prospect of a little competence falling to them from the sky. But Pierre, who loved his mother dearly, who knew her to be somewhat of a dreamer, and feared if her illusions were shattered, and the news, instead of being good, should turn out bad, that she would be annoyed and saddened, checked her by saying:

"Do not indulge in romance, mamma; there are no more rich American uncles. For my part, I should sooner believe that it is about a marriage for Jean."

All were surprised at the idea, and Jean was somewhat annoyed that his brother should have spoken of such a thing before Madame Rosémilly.

"Why for me rather than for you? Your sup-position is open to question. You are the oldest; you would be the first to be thought of. And then, as for me, I do not want to marry."

Pierre giggled.

"You must be in love, then?"

The other, annoyed, replied:

"Must one be in love to say that one does not want to marry yet?"

"Good. The 'yet' explains all. You are wait-ing."

"Let us grant that I am waiting, if you like."

M. Roland, who had listened and reflected, all at once found the most probable solution.

"By Jove! we are all stupid to rack our brains thus. Monsieur Lecanu is a friend of ours. He knows that Pierre is looking for a doctor's office, and Jean for a lawyer's office: he has found how to place one of you."

This was so simple and probable that everybody agreed.

"Dinner is ready," said the maid. All went to their rooms to wash their hands before sitting down to table.

Ten minutes later they were seated in the little dining-room on the ground floor.

They did not talk much at first, but after a few minutes Roland once more expressed his surprise at the visit of the notary.

"In brief, why did he not write? Why did he send his clerk three times? Why is he coming himself?"

Pierre thought this quite natural.

"He wants an immediate answer, and perhaps he has to communicate some confidential matter, which one does not care to put in writing."

They remained, however, preoccupied, and somewhat out of sorts at having invited Madame Rosémilly to dinner, for it would prevent them from freely discussing the matter and forming their plans.

They had just ascended to the drawing-room when the notary was announced.

Roland rushed to meet him.

"Good-day, my dear maître."

He used the word *maître*, which is a title given to lawyers in France.

Madame Rosémilly rose.

18

"I am going home. I am very tired."

They feebly attempted to detain her, but she did not consent, and went off alone, without any of the three gentlemen escorting her as usual.

Madame Roland was very attentive to the new-comer.

"A cup of coffee, Monsieur Lecanu?"

"No, thanks. I have just risen from table."

"A cup of tea, then?"

"I will not say no, but a little later. We must first talk business."

In the profound silence which followed these words nothing but the rhythmical ticking of the clock was heard, and the noise from the lower story of the dishes being washed by the girl, who was too stupid to even listen at keyholes.

The lawyer began.

"Did you know at Paris a certain Monsieur Maréchal—Léon Maréchal?"

M. and Madame Roland uttered the same exclamation, "Of course I did."

"He was one of your friends?"

Roland declared:

"Our best, sir; but a rabid Parisian. He never was away from the boulevard. He was head clerk in the treasurer's office. I never saw him after I left the capital. Then we ceased to write to each other. You know when one lives far apart——"

The lawyer continued gravely:

"Monsieur Maréchal is dead."

Husband and wife made the same little gesture of sorrowful surprise, real or feigned, with which such news is received.

M. Lecanu continued:

"My colleague in Paris has just communicated to me the chief clause in his will, making your son, Monsieur Jean Roland, his sole legatee."

So great was their astonishment that no one had a word to say.

Madame Roland was the first to master her emotion, and stammered out:

"*Mon Dieu!* Poor Léon—our friend. *Mon Dieu, mon Dieu!* Dead!"

Tears glistened in her eyes, those silent tears of women that spring from the soul and overflow the cheek, and seem so mournful because they are so limpid.

Roland, however, thought less of the sadness of the loss than of the hope it held out. Still he dared not immediately ask about the clauses of the will, or the amount of the fortune; but in order to approach to the interesting question indirectly, he asked:

"What was the cause of poor Maréchal's death?"

M. Lecanu was completely ignorant.

"I only know," he said, "that, dying without direct heirs, he leaves all his fortune, twenty thousand francs per annum placed out at three per cent. interest, to your second son, whom he saw born and grow up, and whom he deemed deserving of this legacy. Should Monsieur Jean refuse to accept the legacy, the property will go to the orphan asylum."

"That's a noble idea. If I had had no children I certainly would not have forgotten him, either— my dear friend."

The lawyer smiled.

"I was very much gratified," he said, "at being

able to announce the matter personally. It is always a pleasure to bring people good news."

He did not give a thought to the fact that this good news was the death of a friend, of the best friend of M. Roland, who himself had suddenly forgotten the intimacy which he had just proclaimed with such conviction.

Madame Roland and her sons alone preserved a sorrowful countenance. She continued to weep quietly, and to wipe her eyes with her handkerchief, which she then placed to her lips to check her heavy sighs.

The doctor, in low tones, observed:

"He was a good fellow, very kindly disposed. He often asked us to dinner, my brother and me."

Jean, his large eyes open and sparkling, with a gesture habitual to him, clasped his beautiful beard in his right hand, and slid it through his fingers.

He opened his lips twice to utter some suitable phrase, but could think of nothing, and finally said:

"He was very fond of me indeed, and always kissed me when I went to see him."

But the father's thoughts were galloping, galloping round about the legacy, just announced, and already acquired, round this money hidden behind the door, which would come in at once, to-morrow, as soon as the words "I accept" were uttered.

He asked:

"There is no possible difficulty? no suit? no contest?"

M. Lecanu was quite at his ease.

"My colleague in Paris describes the situation as absolutely uncomplicated. We only want Monsieur Jean to accept."

"Good, then; and the fortune is quite clear?"

"Quite clear."

"All formalities have been gone through?"

"All."

Suddenly the old jeweler felt a touch of shame —a vague, instinctive, transitory shame—at his haste in reassuring himself, and continued:

"You understand, of course, that if I ask you all these things at once, it is to spare my son annoyances which he might not foresee. Sometimes there are debts, embarrassments, how can I tell? And one finds one's self entangled in a labyrinth of complications. In fact, although I am not the legatee, I think of the little one before all."

In the home circle Jean was always called "the little one," although he was much taller than Pierre.

Madame Roland suddenly seemed to come out of a dream, to recall something far away, almost forgotten, which she had heard at some time and was not sure of, and she stammered out:

"Did you not say that our poor friend Maréchal had left his fortune to my little Jean?"

"Yes, madame."

She replied simply:

"It gives me great pleasure, for it proves that he loved us."

Roland rose.

"Do you wish, dear sir, that my son should sign at once the deed of acceptation?"

"No—no, Monsieur Roland. To-morrow—to-morrow, at my office at two o'clock, if that suits you."

"Yes—yes; certainly."

Then Madame Roland, who had also risen, and

was smiling after her tears, took two steps toward
the lawyer, laid her hand on the back of his armchair, and, gazing on him with the tender look of
a grateful mother, asked:

"That cup of tea, Monsieur Lecanu?"

"I will take it now, gladly, madame, with pleasure."

The servant was called, and brought in first
those dry crackers in tin boxes—those tasteless,
hard English biscuits that seemed made for parrots' beaks, then went for some colored napkins,
folded in little squares—those tea napkins which are
never washed in thrifty families. She came in a
third time with the sugar bowl and the cups; then
she went out to boil the water.

The company waited.

No one could speak; they all had too much to
think of and nothing to say. Madame Roland alone
made some commonplace remarks. She told about
the fishing party, and praised the *Pearl* and Madame Rosémilly.

"Charming, charming woman!" repeated the
lawyer.

Roland, leaning his back against the marble
chimneypiece as in winter when the fire is burning,
his hands in his pockets, his lips puckered up as if
to whistle, could not keep still, as he was tortured
with an imperious desire to give vent to his joy.

The two brothers, in similar armchairs, their
legs crossed in the same fashion, sat at right and
left of the central round table, looking straight before them in similar attitudes, but with different
expressions.

The tea appeared at last. The lawyer took,

sugared and drank his tea, after crumbling into it a little cracker too hard to bite. Then he rose, shook hands, and left.

"The arrangement is, then," repeated Roland, "to-morrow at your office, two o'clock."

"That is right; to-morrow, two o'clock."

Jean had not said a word.

After the departure of the lawyer there was again silence, till Roland, Senior, clapped his two hands on the two shoulders of his younger son, exclaiming:

"Well, you deuced lucky dog, why don't you embrace me?"

Jean smiled and kissed his father, saying:

"That did not seem indispensable."

But the father could not restrain himself for joy. He walked about, thrummed on the furniture with his clumsy fingers, pirouetted on his heels, and repeated:

"What luck! what luck! Here's luck indeed!"

Pierre asked:

"You knew Maréchal well, then, at one time?"

His father replied:

"By Jove! he passed all his evenings at our house. Don't you remember that he went to the college to fetch you on holidays and often took you back again after dinner? Why, the very day Jean was born, it was he who went to get the doctor! He had break-fasted with us when your mother felt ill. We knew at once what was the matter, and off he went at a run. In his hurry he took my hat instead of his own. I remember that, because we laughed a good deal about it afterward. It is even likely he remembered this circumstance when he was dying,

24

and, as he had no heir, said to himself: 'I contributed my assistance when the little fellow was born, and now I'll leave him my fortune.'"

Madame Roland, buried in a deep easy-chair, seemed lost in memories. She murmured as if she were thinking aloud:

"Ah! he was a noble friend, devoted, faithful; a rare man, as times are now."

Jean rose. "I am going to take a little walk," he said.

His father was surprised and wished to detain him, for they had to talk, to make plans, to form resolutions. But the young man was obstinate, alleging an appointment. Besides, there would be plenty of time to come to an understanding before the legacy came into his possession.

But Jean was obstinate, pretending he had an appointment. He went away, for he longed to be alone, in order to reflect. Pierre, in his turn, said he was going out, and some minutes later followed his brother.

When Roland was alone with his wife he took her in his arms, kissed her half a score of times on each cheek, and, in reply to a reproach she often had made to him, said:

"You see, my darling, that it would have been no good for me to stay longer in Paris, and work myself to death for the children, in place of coming here to recover my health, since a fortune has dropped to us out of the clouds."

She became very serious.

"It falls from the clouds for Jean," she said; "but Pierre?"

"Pierre! why, he's a doctor, he will make—money —and then his brother will do something for him."

"No. He would not take anything. Besides, the legacy is for Jean, nobody but Jean. Pierre, you see, finds himself at great disadvantage."

Poor Roland seemed perplexed.

"Then, we will leave him the most in our will."

"No. That would not be just, either," she cried out.

"Ah, pshaw! What then? What do you want me to do? You are always looking out for something unpleasant. You spoil all my enjoyment. I'm off to bed. Good-night. All the same, it is a stroke of good luck, right down good luck!"

He went his way, enchanted in spite of everything, and without a word of regret for the friend who died so generously.

Madame Roland returned again to dream beside the lamp which was now smoking.

CHAPTER II

PIERRE IS PUZZLED

As soon as he was out of doors, Pierre turned his steps toward the Rue de Paris, Havre's principal thoroughfare—well-lighted, animated and noisy. The rather fresh breeze coming from the sea played about his face, while he walked slowly, his cane under his arm, and his hands behind his back.

Somehow he felt ill at ease—dull, disappointed, like one who has heard bad news. This unpleasant impression had not been formulated into thought, and had he been suddenly called upon he would have been puzzled to have told the cause of this heaviness of spirit, this torpor of body. He was out of sorts —suffering from an uneasy feeling he could not explain. He had within him somewhere a sensitive spot, a scarcely perceptible moral wound that he could not place his finger upon, but which, nevertheless, annoyed, fatigued, saddened and irritated him; an unnamed and trifling trouble, a mere foreboding of sorrow.

Arrived at the Place du Théâtre, he felt attracted by the lights of the Café Tortoni, and slowly sauntered up to the illuminated façade; but just as he was about entering, he reflected that he might encounter friends and acquaintances—people with whom he would be compelled to converse—and a sudden repugnance for this commonplace goodfellowship of *demi-tasses* and *petits verres* took possession of him. Then, retracing his steps, he again followed the main thoroughfare in the direction of the harbor.

He asked himself, "Where shall I go?" seeking some new place that would be agreeable to him in his present frame of mind. He did not find any, for he felt annoyed at being alone, and still did not wish to meet any one.

On reaching the principal quay he hesitated a moment and then turned toward the pier: he had decided in favor of solitude.

As he passed near a bench on the breakwater, he stopped and sat down, tired of walking and disgusted with his proposed promenade.

Again he asked himself, "What is the matter

with me this evening?" and set to work to recollect
what disappointment he had met with, much as one
interrogates a patient to determine the cause of his
fever.

He was at once excitable and thoughtful—at one
moment in a quandary, the next in full possession
of his logical powers, approving or blaming his impulsive actions; but, in the end, his original nature
always gained the upper hand—the man of feeling
dominating the man of intellect.

He now sought to discover the reason of his temporary weakness; of the necessity he felt to keep
moving without any object in view; of the desire
to meet some one who would disagree with him at
the same time that he had a disinclination for the
society of those he might see, and a distaste for
what they might say to him.

At last he put this question to himself:

"Could it be Jean's inheritance?"

Yes, that might, after all, have been the cause
of his discomfort. When the lawyer had brought
the news, he had felt his heart beat a little faster
than usual. We are certainly not always masters
of ourselves, but are subject to spontaneous and
persistent emotions against which we struggle in
vain.

He reflected deeply on this physiological problem
—the impression produced by an event on the
psychic individuality, and creating within one a current of ideas and sensations, joyful or painful, the
opposite of what the Thinking Being desires, demands or considers good and wholesome—the
Thinking Being, which is its superior through the
cultivation of the intellect.

He tried to picture to himself the state of mind of a son who inherits a large fortune, and who is about to test many longed-for pleasures, hitherto forbidden by a father's avarice—a father whom he nevertheless loved and pitied.

He rose and walked toward the end of the pier. He already felt better, glad to have understood— to have surprised himself, as it were, and unveiled the other personality that is within us.

"So I was jealous of Jean," he thought; "certainly a rather unworthy sentiment. I am sure of it now, for the first thought that came into my head related to his marriage with Madame Rosémilly. I don't fancy that sensible little goose, who seems made to disgust one with sound sense and goodness. Thus it is uncalled-for envy—its very essence—that which is because it is! I must beware of it."

He had reached the signal-mast that indicates the depth of water in the harbor, and lit a match in order to read the list of ships that had been signaled outside and were waiting to come in with the next tide. Steamers were expected from Brazil, La Plata, Chili and Japan, besides two Danish brigs, a Norwegian schooner, and a Trukish steamer. This latter announcement surprised Pierre as much as if he had read of a Swiss steamer, and caused him to conjure up the vision of a large vessel swarming with men in turbans, who sprang up the rigging in wide trousers.

"But how stupid of me," he thought; "the Turks are a seafaring people."

A few steps farther on he stopped to look at the bay. On his right, above Sainte Adresse, the two electric lighthouses of Cape de la Hêve, like a monstrous twin Cyclops, darting across the water their continued powerful glances. The two parallel rays of light resembling the giant tails of two comets reached in a straight line of limitless length from the summit of the hill to the edge of the horizon. On the two piers, two other lights—the children of these Colossi—marked the entrance to the harbor; while yonder, across the Seine, could be seen still others, some steady and others intermittent, with brilliant flashes and dark eclipses, opening and closing like eyes—the eyes of harbors, yellow, red, green, watching over the dark sea covered with ships; living eyes of the hospitable shore, saying by the simple mechanical movement of their lids:

"It is I; I am Trouville; I am Honfleur; I am the river of Pont Audemer."

And overlooking all the others, so high up and so far off that it could easily be mistaken for a planet, the aerial lighthouse of Étouville, lighting the way to Rouen across the sandbanks at the mouth of the great river.

Then on the deep, boundless sea, darker than the heavens, here and there stars seemed visible. They trembled in the nocturnal mist—small, near, and distant, and also white, red, or green; generally they were motionless, but some seemed to move. They were the lights on vessels at anchor that were waiting for the rising tide, or on those still in motion that were seeking an anchorage.

Just then the moon rose behind the town. It, too, looked like some huge, celestial beacon, placed in the heavens to guide the immeasurable flotilla of stars.

Pierre said, half aloud:

"And yet we allow ourselves to be annoyed by trifles."

Suddenly, quite close to him, a shadow—a great, fantastic shadow glided into the wide, black opening between the two piers. Leaning over the granite parapet, he saw a fishing boat coming in without hum of voices, sounds of waves, or splashing of oars, gently gliding along, its tall brown sail filled with the breeze from the ocean.

"If one could live on that boat," he thought, "perhaps one's mind might be calm."

Then, advancing a few steps farther, he saw a man seated at the end of the mole.

Was he a dreamer, a lover, a sage, a happy man, or an unhappy one? Which was he? He came nearer, curious to see the face of this solitary watcher. In a second he recognized his brother.

"What! Is it you, Jean?"

"What! Pierre? What are you doing here?"

"Getting a breath of fresh air. And you?"

Jean began to laugh.

"I am following your example."

And Pierre sat down by the side of his brother.

"Is it not beautiful?"

"Yes."

From the tone of his voice Pierre understood that Jean had not been looking at what was around him. He continued:

"When I come here I have a wild longing to go away with these ships—to the north, or to the south. Only to think that those lights yonder come from every quarter of the globe—from the lands with gigantic flowers and beautiful pale, or copper-colored girls; the lands of humming birds, elephants, roaring lions, negro kings; from all the lands that furnish fairy tales for those of us who no longer believe in 'Sindbad the Sailor' or the 'Sleeping Beauty'! Wouldn't it be splendid to be able to treat one's self to a journey there? But that would take money, and a good deal of it——"

He stopped suddenly, all at once remembering that his brother now had the necessary means, and that, liberated from every care—from daily toil—free, without trammels of any kind, happy, joyous, he could go where fancy might dictate, toward the home of Swedish blondes or of Havanese brunettes.

Then one of those involuntary thoughts, common with him, so sudden, so rapid, that they could neither be foreseen, checked, nor modified, came to him as from the mind of a second, independent and powerful personality.

"Bah! he is too stupid; he will marry the little Rosémilly."

He had risen to his feet.

"I leave you to dream of your future; I feel the need of exercise."

He pressed his brother's hand, and continued in cordial tones:

"Well, little Jean, you are now wealthy. I am glad that I met you alone to-night, to tell you how pleased I am, how heartily I congratulate you, and how much I love you."

"Thanks, thanks, my good Pierre, thanks!" stammered Jean, his gentle, sympathetic nature greatly moved.

And Pierre turned back, sauntering slowly, his cane under his arm, and his hands behind his back. When he had reached the town he again asked himself what he should do, annoyed at having his walk cut short, at having been turned from the direction of the sea by the presence of his brother.

Suddenly an idea came to him.

"I'll go drink a glass of liqueur at Père Marowsko's," and he turned back toward the Ingouville quarter.

He had known Père Marowsko in the hospitals at Paris. He was an old Pole—some said a political refugee, who had had tragic experiences in Poland, and who had come to France to carry on his business of a druggist after passing some fresh examinations. Nothing was known of his past career, although various legends had found currency among the internes and externes at the hospitals, and later among his neighbors. His reputation as a formidable conspirator, a Nihilist, a regicide, a patriot ready for any enterprise, had proved attractive to the vivid imagination of Pierre Roland, and he had become the friend of the old Pole, without, however, having obtained from him any details regarding his life. It was owing to the young physician that the old man had come to Havre to establish himself in business, relying upon the patronage that the former had promised to bring him.

In the meantime he lived economically in his little shop, selling medicines to the small dealers and working people of the neighborhood.

Pierre often dropped in to see him after dinner and have an hour's chat, for he had taken a fancy to Marowsko's calm face and occasional lapses into conversation, believing that his long silences were an indication of much profound reflection.

A single gas jet burned over a counter filled with

phials. Those in the window had not yet been lighted, from motives of economy. Behind the counter, seated on one chair with his feet resting on another, a bald-headed old man, with a large, beaklike nose that, continuing the line of his forehead, gave him the solemn look of a parrot, was fast asleep with his chin resting on his breast.

At the sound of the bell he awoke, rose, and on recognizing the doctor, came forward to greet him with outstretched hands.

His black coat, spotted with stains of acids and sirups, and much too large for his small, lean frame, somewhat resembled an ancient cassock. Marowsko spoke with a strong Polish accent, that gave his weak voice a lisping, childish character, and intonations like those of a child just beginning to talk.

Pierre sat down.

"What's the news, my dear doctor?" asked the Pole.

"Nothing; the same old story!"

"You don't seem lively this evening."

"No, I'm not often so."

"Come, come! You must rouse yourself. What do you say to a glass of liqueur?"

"Thanks; I should be glad to have one."

"Well, then, I will astonish you with a new preparation. For two months I've been trying to make something out of currants, from which thus far we have made nothing but sirup. I—well, I've found it—I've found it—a good liqueur, very good!"

And beaming all over he went to a closet, which he opened, and took out a phial. He moved about in an undecided way, with short, incomplete gestures—never fully extending his arms or his legs, or making an entire motion. His ideas were of the same order as his movements. He suggested, indicated, sketched them, but never went the length of stating them.

His principal business in life seemed to be the preparation of liqueurs and sirups. "With a good sirup or a good liqueur, one can make a fortune," was a frequent remark of his; and he had invented hundreds of sweet concoctions, without being able to place a single one of them on the market. Pierre declared that Marowsko made him think of Marat.

Two small glasses were brought from the back room and placed on the preparation counter. Then the two men examined the color of the new liquid by holding it up to the light.

"Beautiful ruby!" was Pierre's verdict.

"Isn't it?"

And the old parrot-like face was wreathed in smiles.

The doctor tasted the precious cordial, held it in his mouth, pondered, tasted again, again reflected, and at last spoke:

"Good, very good, and with a decidedly original flavor. A genuine find, my dear sir."

"Yes, I am quite satisfied."

Then the old man consulted his visitor as to how the new liqueur should be named. He thought of calling it "Essence de Groseille," or, rather, "Fine Groseille," or "Grosélia," or "Groséline."

Pierre was not satisfied with either of these. Marowsko then had an idea.

"What you said just now is good, very good—'Beautiful ruby.'"

35

The doctor argued against the appropriateness of the title, although it was his own invention, and advised strongly in favor of "Groseillette," which Marowsko thought admirable.

Then he lapsed into silence, and remained for several minutes seated under the single gas jet without saying a word.

"Something strange happened to us this evening," said Pierre at last, almost in spite of himself. "One of my father's friends has died, and left his fortune to my brother."

The druggist did not at first seem to understand, but after reflection, hoped that the doctor would get half. When the affair had been fully explained, he seemed surprised and vexed, and as an expression of his dissatisfaction at seeing his young friend sacrificed, he kept repeating:

"That will not look well."

Pierre, whose lassitude was again getting the upper hand of him, wanted to know what the old man meant. What evil could result from his brother's having inherited a fortune from a friend of the family? But the worthy man, circumspect in his day and generation, would not explain.

"In such a case, it is customary to divide the fortune equally between the two brothers. I tell you it will not look well."

And the doctor, out of patience, went away, returned to the paternal roof, and retired for the night.

For some time he could hear Jean softly walking up and down the adjoining room; then he fell asleep.

CHAPTER III

THE DEMON OF JEALOUSY

The doctor awoke next day with a settled determination to make his fortune.

He had already come to this decision several times before, but without acting upon it. At the outset of all his attempts to enter upon a new career, the hope of becoming suddenly wealthy had buoyed him up and given him courage until he encountered the first obstacle, the first repulse, which would at once turn him in some new direction.

Cozily ensconced in his warm bed he meditated. How many physicians had become millionaires in less than no time! All that was needed was a little skill and ability, for, in the course of his studies, he had gauged the most celebrated professors of the healing art and set them down as jackasses. Surely he was as clever as they, if not more so! If he could manage in some way to capture the patronage of the wealthy and fashionable in Havre, he would be able to make 100,000 frs. a year easily. And he ran over items of this imposing income. In the morning he would call on his patients. Taking the very lowest average, he would make ten visits a day, which, at 20 frs. each, would give him 72,000 frs. a year, or more probably 75,000 frs., since he would be certain to be called to see more than ten patients. In the afternoon he would devote himself to office practice; and, if he only received ten visits at ten francs, he would have 36,000 frs. at the end of the year. Thus he would have an income of 120,000

37

frs., in round numbers. Former patrons and friends whom he would call on for ten francs a visit, and for whom he would prescribe at his office for five francs, might slightly diminish this total; but this again would be made up by consultations with other physicians and the numerous petty perquisites of the profession.

Nothing easier than to reach this point by dint of skillful if indirect advertising—the insertion of paragraphs in the *Figaro* calling attention to the fact that the whole body of Paris savants had their eyes fixed on him, and were deeply interested in the surprising cures performed by the young and modest physician of Havre. He would be richer than his brother—richer and celebrated—and satisfied with himself, for he would be the architect of his own fortune, and he would be generous to his aged parents, who would be justly proud of his renown. He would not marry, not caring to embarrass himself with one exacting woman; but he would have intimate friends among the prettiest of his women patrons.

By this time he felt so sure of success that he sprang out of bed as if intent on at once grasping it, and dressed himself in order to look through the town for a suite of rooms that would suit him.

Then, rambling about the streets, he thought how insignificant are the trifles that sometimes affect our most important actions. For three weeks he had been hesitating about taking some decided step, when this course suddenly occurs to him—doubtless as a consequence of his brother's having received a legacy.

He stopped before doors beside which were cards

advertising "beautiful" or "luxurious" apartments
or "apartments" pure and simple, the latter only in
spiring his contempt. Then he inspected several
with a haughty air, measured the height of ceilings,
sketched on his memorandum book the plan of the
apartment, showing the communicating doors and
those opening into the hall, informing them that he
was a physician and received many visits. The
staircase must be large and well kept; he could not
go higher up than one flight.

After taking seven or eight addresses and scrib-
bling down a mass of information, he returned to
breakfast a quarter of an hour late.

In the vestibule he heard the rattling of dishes.
Could they have begun without him? Why? Meals
were never very punctual in that household. He
felt hurt and dissatisfied, as he was a little sensitive.
As soon as he entered the room his father said to
him:

"Come, Pierre, make haste! You know we are
going to the lawyer's at two. This is no day for
loitering."

The doctor sat down without replying, after having kissed his mother and pressed the hands of his
father and brother. He then took from the dish in
the centre of the table the cutlet that had been left
for him. It was cold and dry. It was also probably
the poorest. He thought that it might have been
left in the oven until his arrival, and that they
should not have so completely forgotten their other
son—the eldest. The conversation that had been
interrupted by his entrance was continued.

"As for me," said Madame Roland to Jean,
"this is what I should do, and at once. I should

take showy apartments—something striking; I would go into society, buy a horse, and select one or two interesting cases to plead, thus securing a foothold in the higher court. I would seek to be a kind of very special amateur advocate. Thank Heaven! you are beyond the reach of want, and if you follow a profession, it will be in order not to lose the fruits of your studies, and because no man should remain idle."

Père Roland, who was peeling a pear, said:

"*Cristi!* In your place I should buy a fine craft—a cutter, built on the model of our pilot boats —and should sail as far as Senegal."

Pierre, in his turn, gave an opinion. It was to the effect that a man's intellectual or moral worth did not depend on his fortune. To those of only moderate intelligence money was too often the cause of their degradation, while in the hands of the strong it was a powerful lever. The latter, how-ever, were rare. If Jean was really a man above the average, he would now be able to give proof of it, since he found himself beyond the reach of want. But he would have to work a hundred times harder than he would have been called upon to do under ordinary circumstances. It was not a question of pleading for, or against, the widow and orphan, and of pocketing a certain number of crowns for a case won, or lost; but of becoming an eminent jurist —a great legal light!

And he added in conclusion:

"If I had money, I should dissect bodies!"

Père Roland shrugged his shoulders:

"Tra, la, la! The wisest thing to do is to take life easy. We are not beasts of burden, but men.

When one is born to poverty, one must work—and, so much the worse, one works; but when one has an income, one would be a fool to kill themselves with work."

"Our inclinations are not the same," replied Pierre with dignity. "As for me, all that I respect in the world is knowledge and intellect—everything else is contemptible."

As Madame Roland always endeavored to avert the collisions that were constantly occurring between father and son, on the present occasion she turned the drift of the conversation by referring to a murder that had been committed the week previous at Bolbec-Nointot. The attention of the family was soon occupied by the details of the tragedy, their atrocity, and the attractive mystery inseparable from even vulgar, scandalous and loathsome crimes—a mystery that exercises a strange and fascinating power over the imagination.

Père Roland, however, frequently consulted his watch.

"Come," he said, "it is time to be going."

"It is not one yet," was Pierre's sarcastic comment. "As there is abundance of time, it was scarcely worth while to give me a cold cutlet to eat."

"Are you coming to the lawyer's with us?" asked his mother.

"What should I do there? My presence is entirely unnecessary."

Jean remained as silent as if he were in no way interested in the matter. When the Bolbec murder was being discussed, he had laid down certain legal principles, and made certain points regarding crimes and criminals. Now he had relapsed into silence; but the brilliancy of his eyes, his red cheeks, and even his glossy beard seemed to proclaim his happiness.

After the family had set out, Pierre, finding himself again alone, continued his morning's search for furnished apartments. After two or three hours of ascending and descending stairs, he finally discovered, on the Boulevard François I, something really desirable—a large mezzanine apartment with doors opening on two different streets, two reception rooms, a corridor inclosed in glass where patients, while waiting, might stroll about among the flowers, and a charming circular dining-room with windows looking out on the sea.

Just as he was about to take it, the rent—three thousand francs—proved a stumbling block, as the first quarter must be paid in advance, and he had not even a sou of his own.

The small fortune that his father had been able to put aside did not yield quite eight thousand francs a year, and Pierre had often reproached himself for having caused his parents difficulties through his indecision in the choice of a profession, his invariably abandoned experiments, and his continual taking up of new studies. He therefore let the matter stand, promising a decision in two days. Meanwhile it occurred to him that he might ask his brother to advance the money for the first three or even six months—fifteen hundred francs—as soon as the latter should come into possession of his legacy.

"That would only be a few months' loan at the longest," he thought. "I should probably repay it even before the end of the year. Nothing would be more natural, and he would be glad to be able to accommodate me."

As it was not yet four o'clock, and he had nothing, absolutely nothing to do, he sauntered into the Public Gardens and sat down. There he remained on his bench, not even giving himself the trouble to think, his eyes fixed on the ground, a prey to a sense of lassitude that was fast developing into real discomfort.

Still, he had passed all the preceding days in this way since his return to the paternal roof, without suffering as he was now doing from the void in his life and from inaction. How had he been able to pass the hours from the time he rose until bedtime?

He had lounged on the pier when the tide came in, lounged on the streets, lounged in the cafés, lounged at Marowsko's, lounged everywhere. And now this kind of life, that had seemed tolerable enough up to the present time, had become hateful to him. If he had had money he would have taken a carriage and gone for a long drive in the country along roads shaded by beeches and oaks; but he was forced to count the price of a glass of beer or a postage stamp, and such extravagance was not within his means. It suddenly occurred to him how hard it was, when a man is past thirty, to be obliged from time to time to blushingly ask his mother for a louis, and he muttered to himself as he scratched the gravel with his cane:

"*Cristi!* if I only had money."

And the thought of his brother's legacy again came to him like the sting of a wasp; but he dismissed it impatiently, not wishing to surrender himself to envy.

Fair, light-haired children were playing around him in the dust of the paths, and carefully constructing imposing mountains of sand, only to tumble them down with a kick as soon as built.

This was for Pierre one of those depressing days when one looks into all the corners of one's mind and shakes out all its creases.

"Our own tasks," he reflected, "resemble the work of these youngsters." Then he asked himself whether it were not the wisest course in life to beget two or three of these little, useless beings, and watch them grow up with a pleased curiosity. And the desire to marry came to him. One would at least hear some one moving about in the hours of trouble and uncertainty; it is something to have woman's sympathy when one is suffering.

He began to think about women. He knew them but slightly, his flirtations in the Latin Quarter having seldom lasted more than a fortnight, being exhausted, and continued or replaced by a new one when the next remittance arrived. There must, however, be kind creatures. Was not his mother the good sense and the attraction of his father's fireside? How he would like to meet a woman—a real woman!

He rose suddenly with a resolution to call on Madame Rosémilly. Then he sat down again as suddenly. She was displeasing to him. Why? She was too vulgarly practical; besides, did she not appear to prefer Jean? Without admitting it in so many words, this preference counted for much in his low estimate of the widow's intelligence; for, although he loved his brother, he could not help considering him rather commonplace intellectually, and as inferior to himself.

He did not intend, however, to remain where he was until nightfall, and, as on the previous evening, he anxiously asked himself, "What shall I do?"

He now felt within him the necessity of being petted, embraced and consoled. But consoled for what? He could not have told; but he was passing through one of those periods of weakness and lassitude in which the presence of a woman, the caresses of a woman, the touch of a hand, a glance from eyes blue or black, seem suddenly indispensable to our hearts.

And the recollection came to him of a waitress in a wine shop whom he had one evening taken home, and whom he had seen again from time to time.

He again rose to go and drink a "bock" with this girl. What should he say to her? What would she say to him? Nothing, no doubt; but what did it matter? He would hold her hand a moment. She seemed to have taken a fancy to him. Why, then, did he not see her oftener?

He found her taking a nap on a chair in the almost deserted wine shop. Three customers were smoking their pipes, with their elbows on the oak tables; the cashier was reading a novel; while the proprietor, in his shirt sleeves, was asleep on the bench.

As soon as she saw him the girl rose quickly and came forward, saying:

"Good-day; how are you?"

"All right; and you?"

"Oh! very well. What a stranger you are!"

"Yes, I have but little time to myself; you know I'm a physician."

"Well, why didn't you tell me so before? If I had only known it, I would have consulted you when I was ailing last week. What will you take?"

"A beer; and you?"

"I'll have one, too, as you pay for it."

She brought the glasses, and, seated opposite each other, they chatted. Every now and then she would take his hand with the easy familiarity of her class, and looking at him with tender glances, she said:

"Why don't you come oftener? I like you ever so much, you know."

But he had already had enough of her, and she appeared in his eyes what she really was—stupid, common and vulgar.

"Women," he said to himself, "should come to us only in dreams, or surrounded by the aureole of luxury, that idealizes what is commonplace."

"You passed here the other morning with a handsome light-haired gentleman with a long beard," she remarked; "was it your brother?"

"Yes, it was my brother."

"He is awfully good-looking."

"You think so?"

"Certainly; and he looks as if he lived well."

What uncontrollable impulse suddenly urged Pierre to tell this wine-shop waitress of Jean's legacy? Why did the story, that he would have forced back had he been alone, come to his lips at that instant, and why did he allow it to make its way out from between his lips as if he felt compelled to relieve his heart, swollen with bitterness, before some one?

"He's a lucky fellow, my brother," he said as he crossed his legs; "he's just fallen heir to an income of twenty thousand francs."

She opened wide her blue, covetous eyes.

"And who left it to him? His grandmother, or his aunt?"

"No, an old friend of my parents."

"Only a friend? Impossible. And you didn't get anything?"

"No; I scarcely knew him."

She thought a moment, and then, with a peculiar smile, said:

"Well, your brother is fortunate in having friends like that. No wonder he doesn't look at all like you."

His first impulse was to slap her face, without exactly knowing why; but he only asked, in a constrained way:

"What do you mean?"

"Me?—oh, nothing," she replied, with affected ingenuousness; "only he's luckier than you."

He threw twenty sous on the table, and went out.

Then he kept repeating the phrase: "No wonder he doesn't look at all like you." What was she thinking of? What hidden meaning lay concealed in these words? They were certainly inspired by malice and spitefulness. They were insulting. Yes, the girl must have thought that Jean was Maréchal's son.

The emotion that this slur on his mother's good name aroused in him was so violent that he stopped and looked about for some place to sit down.

He saw another café opposite, went in, took a chair, and ordered another "bock."

He felt his heart beat; cold chills ran over him. Suddenly he remembered what Marowsko had said the day before: "It will not look well." Had the same thought—the same suspicion—occurred to him and to this waitress?

Leaning over his beer glass, he watched the white foam rise and melt, while he asked himself: "Can people really believe a thing like that?"

The reasons that gave rise to this odious hypothesis in the minds of others now appeared to him, in their order, clear, evident, exasperating. That an old bachelor without heirs should leave his fortune to the two children of a friend—nothing seemed simpler or more natural; but when he gave the whole of it to one only, no doubt the world would at first be surprised, then gossip, and finally smile. Why had he not foreseen it? Why had his father not had an inkling of it? Why had his mother not suspected it? No, they were too happy over this unexpected windfall; such a thought would not occur to them. Besides, how could these worthy people entertain such an ignoble suspicion?

But the public, the neighbors, the tradesmen, all who knew them—would they not repeat this odious slander, laugh and jest over it, ridiculing his father, and despising his mother?

And the remark made by the wine-shop girl, that Jean was light and he dark, that they did not resemble each other either in face, gait, figure, or mind, would likewise occur to every one. When they referred in future to Roland's son, people would ask: "Which, the real or the false one?"

He got up, having decided that his brother must be warned—put on his guard against the terrible danger that threatened their mother's honor. But what would Jean do? The simplest way out of the difficulty would be to refuse the legacy, which would then go to the poor, and to say to friends and acquaintances who had heard of the will that the latter contained objectionable clauses and conditions, that would have made Jean not an heir, but a trustee.

As he entered the house he decided that he ought to see his brother alone, so as not to have to speak on such a subject before his parents.

As he opened the door he heard the sound of voices and laughter in the salon, and on entering that apartment he discovered that his father had brought back with them Madame Rosémilly and Captain Beausire to dinner in honor of the joyful occasion.

Vermouth and absinthe were handed round to excite an appetite, and the party were already in the best of spirits. Captain Beausire was a little roly-poly man, whose angles had been rounded off by much rolling about on the sea, and whose ideas were as smooth as his person—like pebbles on the beach —who laughed heartily and seemed to consider that there was good in everything in life.

He clinked glasses with Père Roland, while Jean filled those of the ladies a second time.

Madame Rosémilly refused, when Captain Beausire, who had known her husband, exclaimed:

"Come, come, madame, *bis repetita placent,* as we say in *patois,* which signifies: 'Two Vermouths can't do one any harm.' Now as for me, since I no longer follow the sea, I give myself, every day be-

fore dinner, two or three of those artificial 'rolls.'
I supplement them with a little 'pitching' after
the coffee, which makes the sea rise during the rest
of the evening. However, I never go the length of
raising a 'tempest,' never, never never, for I fear
'shipwreck.' "

Roland, whose passion for the sea was encouraged by the old sailor, laughed heartily, his face
already glowing, and his eye unsteady from the absinthe. He had a paunch—a capacious abdomen in
which all the rest of his body appeared to have been
absorbed—one of those soft, yielding corporations
with which men who sit a great deal are afflicted,
and who seem to have neither thighs, chest, arms,
nor neck—all being apparently heaped up together
on the seat of their chair.

Beausire, on the contrary, although short and
stout, was as well filled out as an egg and as hard
as a ball.

Madame Roland had not yet finished her first
glass; and, rosy with happiness, her eyes shining,
she was lost in the contemplation of her son Jean.

His cup of enjoyment seemed at length to be
full. The affair was concluded, the papers had been
signed, and now he had an income of twenty thousand francs. By the way in which he laughed, from
his speaking with fuller, more sonorous tones than
was his wont, from his more decided manner and
his greater degree of assurance, it was evident that
he already had acquired the self-poise that money
brings.

Dinner was announced, and as old Roland was
about to offer his arm to Madame Rosémilly, his
wife interposed:

"No, no, father, to-day everything is for Jean."
The table groaned under unaccustomed plenty.
Jean took his father's seat, and before his plate
stood a huge bouquet with silk favors—such as only
grace very ceremonious occasions—which rose like
a flag-decorated dome. At its sides were four glass
dishes, one containing a pyramid of superb peaches;
the second, an immense cake filled with whipped
cream, and covered with bells made of frosting—
a regular cathedral; the third, slices of pineapples
in a white sirup; and the fourth—unheard-of extravagance—black grapes brought from the tropics.

"Bigre!" said Pierre, seating himself. "We seem
to be celebrating the occasion of Jean le Riche!"

After the soup they drank Madeira, and everybody began to talk at once. Beausire told of a dinner that he had eaten in Santo Domingo, at the
table of a negro general. Père Roland listened to
him, but endeavored to get in edgeways a story of
his own about a certain repast given by one of his
friends at Meudon, as a consequence of having par-
taken of which every guest had to pay the penalty
of a fortnight's illness. Madame Rosémilly, Jean,
and his mother talked over a proposed excursion to
Saint Jouin, and a breakfast there, from which they
promised themselves much unalloyed pleasure;
while Pierre bitterly regretted not having dined
alone, at a cheap seaside restaurant, where he would
have escaped all the noise, laughter and joyful
manifestations that were unnerving him.

He reflected as to how he should manage to communicate his fears to his brother, and to induce him
to give up the fortune that he had already accepted,
that he was even now enjoying, and that was exer-

cising its intoxicating influence upon him. It would no doubt be hard for him, but the necessity was there; he could not hesitate since their mother's good name was at stake.

The appearance of an enormous trout started Roland off into a series of tales about fishing. Beausire matched them with wonderful adventures at Gaboon, at Sainte Marie, in Madagascar, and, particularly, on the coasts of China and Japan, where, he declared, the fish had faces as comical as those of the inhabitants. And he described them, their great, golden eyes, their blue or red bellies, their queer fins, like fans, their crescent-shaped tails—so vividly and with so much humor that his hearers laughed until tears stood in their eyes.

Pierre alone seemed incredulous, and muttered to himself:

"No wonder that the Normans are called the Gascons of the North!"

After the fish came a "vol-au-vent," then a roast chicken, a salad, kidney beans, and a pâté of Pithiviers larks. Madame de Rosémilly's maid assisted in waiting on the table, and the general good humor sensibly increased with each successive glass of wine. When the cork of the first bottle of champagne popped, Père Roland, greatly excited, and imitating the sound with his lips, exclaimed:

"I like that better than the sound of a pistol."

Pierre, more and more annoyed, replied with a sneer:

"Still, it may be more dangerous for you."

Roland, who was about to drink, replaced his full glass on the table, and asked:

"How so?"

For some time past he had been complaining of his health—of torpor, giddiness and certain constant and inexplicable unpleasant sensations. The doctor replied:

"Because the pistol ball might miss you; but the wine goes straight into your stomach."

"And then?"

"And then it burns in the stomach, disorganizes the nervous system, renders the circulation sluggish, and paves the way for apoplexy, with which all men of your temperament are threatened."

The fumes of increasing intoxication that had gradually been overpowering the ex-jeweler were suddenly dispersed as by a gust of wind, and he looked at his son with anxious, restless eyes, endeavoring to make out whether he was not jesting.

"Oh, these plaguy doctors!" exclaimed Beausire; "they're all just alike. You mustn't eat, you mustn't drink, or make love, or dance round dances! It is all detrimental to your precious health. Well, I've done everything they forbid in all parts of the world, wherever I could, and as often as I could, and I don't see that I'm any the worse for it."

"In the first place, captain," replied Pierre, with a touch of sarcasm in his voice, "you're stronger than my father; and, besides, all good livers talk just as you do until the day when—and they never return to say to the prudent medical adviser: 'You were right, doctor.' When I see my father do precisely what he ought not to do, what is most dangerous for him to do, it is only natural that I should warn him. A pretty son I should be if I did not."

"Come, Pierre," interrupted Madame Roland, greatly annoyed, "what is the matter with you? It can't do him any harm for once. Think what an occasion it is for him—for us all! You will spoil his pleasure and ours, too. You are very ill-natured."

"Let him do as he likes," Pierre muttered to himself, shrugging his shoulders; "I have warned him."

But Père Roland did not drink. He looked at his glass full of clear, sparkling wine, whose intoxicating essence was coming to the surface in minute bubbles that were pressing eagerly, rapidly upward, and bursting as they reached the air. He looked at it with the distrust of the fox that has found a dead fowl, but suspects a trap.

"You think that would do me much harm?" he asked hesitatingly.

Pierre was touched with a feeling of compunction, and upbraided himself for having caused others to suffer through his ill humor.

"No, go ahead," he said, "you may drink this time; but don't abuse the privilege, and don't make a practice of it."

Then Père Roland raised his glass, but without having quite decided whether he would drink or not. He again looked at it in a woe-begone fashion, at once desirous and fearful; then he smelt it, tasted it, sipped it, keeping the wine in his mouth, but all the time the prey of many an anxious thought, distracted by weakness and the desire to gratify his palate, and filled with regret as soon as he had drained the last drop.

All at once Pierre met the eye of Madame Rosémilly. It was fixed on him—clear, blue, penetrating and stern. He at once divined the meaning of the look—the irritation that had possessed the simple-minded, straightforward little woman, for her glance said to him:

"You are envious; that is disgraceful."

He bent down his head, and went on eating. But he was not hungry, and nothing pleased him. He was tormented by a desire to go away from these people, so that he would no longer hear them talking, jesting and laughing.

Meantime Père Roland, the fumes of the wine having again gone to his head, had already forgotten his son's advice, and was looking askance at a bottle of champagne, still nearly full, that had been left by the side of his plate. He dared not touch it, for fear of receiving another admonition, and he was therefore meditating by what means he could gain possession of it without attracting Pierre's attention. Finally he decided in favor of the most natural course possible. He took the bottle carelessly, and, holding it at the bottom, reached across the table, and first filled the doctor's glass, which happened to be empty; then he filled up the other glasses round the table, and when he came back to his own, he began talking very loud, so that if any one noticed him filling his glass they would have declared that it had been done inadvertently. However, no one seemed to notice him.

Pierre, without thinking of what he was doing, drank a good deal. Nervous and annoyed, he frequently, but unconsciously, raised his glass with its clear, efferverscing liquid to his lips.

Gradually a pleasant warmth spread over his body and diffused itself throughout his entire being, like a tepid, gracious wave bringing with it joy and comfort. He already felt better, less impatient, less discontented; even his resolution to speak to his brother that very evening was weakened—not that he had gone so far as to think of abandoning his intention, but he was not anxious to disturb his newly-found serenity.

At last Beausire rose to propose a toast. Having bowed all around, he said:

"Very gracious ladies and gentlemen: We have met to celebrate a happy event in the life of one of our friends. It was formerly said that Fortune was blind. I believe that she was only short-sighted, or malicious, and that she has just purchased an excellent pair of marine glasses, which have enabled her to make out in the port of Havre the son of our gallant comrade Roland, captain of the *Pearl*."

"Bravos" were uttered by all lips, reënforced by much clapping of hands, and Père Roland was happy.

After coughing, for he felt husky, and his tongue was somewhat unwieldy, he stammered out these words:

"Thank you, captain; thanks for myself and for my son. I shall never forget your conduct on the present occasion. May you always be happy."

His eyes being filled with tears that ran down his nose, he sat down, not thinking of anything more to say.

Jean, who was laughing, took the floor:

"It is I who should thank the devoted, the dear" (here he looked at Madame Rosémilly) "friends who have to-day given me this touching proof of their affection. But it is not by words that I can testify my gratitude. I shall prove it to-morrow, every instant of my life—always; for our friendship is not of the kind that passes away."

"Well said, my child!" murmured his mother, much affected; but Beausire exclaimed:

"Come, Madame Rosémilly, say something in behalf of the ladies."

She raised her glass, and in a gentle voice, a little tinged with sadness, she said:

"I drink to the blessed memory of Monsieur Maréchal."

There was a pause for a few seconds—a calm, as for contemplation after a prayer. Then Beausire, who was handy at compliments, remarked:

"It takes the women to think of those little refinements of sentiment."

Then, turning to Père Roland, he said:

"But, after all, who was this Maréchal? You were very intimate with him, were you not?"

The old man, somewhat maudlin in his cups, began to shed tears, and in disjointed sentences explained:

"A brother—you know—one of those we never meet any more—we were never separated—he dined with us every evening—and he paid for our seats at the theatre—I can't say any more than that—than that—than that. A friend—a true—true—wasn't he, Louise?"

"Yes, a faithful friend," replied his wife simply.

Pierre looked at his father and mother, but, as the conversation turned on other subjects, he began to drink again.

He had little recollection of what occurred after that, except that they drank coffee and liqueur and laughed and joked. He retired toward midnight, his mind confused and his head heavy, and slept like a log until nine the next morning.

———

CHAPTER IV

A SUDDEN QUESTION

Slumber, steeped in champagne and chartreuse, no doubt soothed and calmed him, for he awoke in a very kindly disposition of mind. As he dressed himself, he examined, weighed and summed up the emotions of the preceding evening, and sought to disentangle from them, clearly and completely, the real secret motives, the personal as well as the external motives.

It was, in fact, quite possible that the girl in the wine shop had conceived a vile idea, on learning that only one of the sons of Roland had received a legacy from an unknown person. Have not such creatures always such suspicions, without the shadow of a motive, about every honest woman? Do they not, whenever they talk, insult, calumniate, defame, every woman whom they imagine to be beyond reproach? Whenever an unimpeachable character is mentioned in their presence, they become annoyed as if they were being slandered, and cry, "Ah, yes, indeed, I know your married women— models of propriety. They have more intrigues than we, only they conceal them because they are hypocrites. Oh, yes; models of propriety!"

Under any other circumstances, he certainly

would not have listened to, nor even supposed possible, such insinuations against his poor mother, so good, so simple, so worthy. But his soul was troubled by the leaven of jealousy fermenting in him. And in his over-excited state, on the watch, in spite of himself, for anything which might be of detriment to his brother, he had perhaps attributed to this waitress odious meanings of which she was innocent. It was possible that his imagination alone, the imagination which he did not control, and which incessantly outstripped his will, was straying and roaming untrammeled in the infinite universe of ideas, and bringing thence shameful, unavowable thoughts, which he hid away in the depths of his soul, as in some unsounded abyss, like something stolen. It might be that his imagination alone created and invented this horrible doubt. His heart assuredly, his own heart, had its own secrets; and this wonderful heart perhaps had found in this abominable doubt a means of depriving his brother of the inheritance that he envied. He suspected himself, at present; and, as devotees interrogate their conscience, he questioned all the mysteries of his thoughts.

Certainly Madame Rosémilly, limited as was her intelligence, had the tact, the keen scent, the subtle perception of women. But this idea had never occurred to her, for she drank, in perfect good faith, to the blessed memory of Monsieur Maréchal. She would not have done so if the slightest suspicion had touched her. Now he no longer had any doubts; his involuntary displeasure at the fortune that had fallen to his brother, and also, assuredly, his religious love for his mother, had intensified his scruples—pious and honorable scruples indeed, but exaggerated.

On arriving at this conclusion, he had a feeling of satisfaction as at the accomplishment of a good action, and he resolved to be amiable to all the world, beginning with his father, whose whims, stupid assertions, vulgar notions, and too apparent mediocrity incessantly irritated him.

He did not come in late to breakfast, and he amused all the family with his wit and good humor.

His mother, delighted, said to him:

"Dear Pierre, you do not know how witty and amusing you can be when you please."

And he talked on, making epigrams, and exciting their mirth by ingenious caricatures of their friends. Beausire was his butt, and at times Madame Rosémilly; but he treated her in a discreet fashion, not too ill-naturedly. And he thought as he looked at his brother: "Why don't you stand up for her, stupid? It is all very well, your being rich, but I can cut you out whenever I choose."

Over the coffee he said to his father:

"Are you going to use the *Pearl* to-day?"

"No, my boy."

"Can I take her and Jean Bart?"

"Oh, yes; whenever you like."

He bought a good cigar at the first tobacconist's he came to, and, with a joyous air, went down to the harbor.

He looked at the clear, luminous sky of delicate blue, freshened by the sea breeze.

Papagris, the sailor, called commonly Jean Bart, was asleep at the bottom of the boat, which it was his duty to have ready for sailing every day at noon, when there was no fishing party in the morning.

"Only ourselves, skipper," cried Pierre, as he descended the iron ladder from the quay and leaped into the boat.

"How is the wind?" he asked.

"Still from the north, Master Pierre. We'll have a good breeze in the offing."

He hoisted the foresail, and raised the anchor, and the boat, unmoored, began to glide gently toward the pier on the calm water of the harbor. The slight land breeze struck the top of the sail so gently as to be imperceptible, and the *Pearl* seemed endowed with a life of its own—the life of vessels—urged on by a mysterious and hidden force in itself. Pierre took the tiller, and, cigar in mouth, his legs stretched out on the seat, his eyes half closed in the blinding rays of the sun, watched, as they passed them, the huge tarred timbers of the breakwater.

When they reached the open sea, at the extreme end of the north pier, the freshening breeze, as it passed across the doctor's face and hands, seemed like a chilly kiss. He drew a long breath and inflated his lungs, as if drinking it in. It filled the brown sail that bellied out, gave the *Pearl* a list to leeward, and enlivened her speed.

Jean Bart quickly hoisted the jib, and its triangle, filled with the wind, looked like a wing. Then, taking two strides aft, he threw loose the driver which was lashed to its mast.

The boat abruptly keeled over, and, as she flew on at full speed, there was a gentle swishing, bubbling sound as she cut through the water.

The stem cut the sea like the share of a plough

run wild, and the waves it raised, in white curves of foam, curled up, and fell back just as the heavy brown earth falls back from the furrow.

Every wave they encountered—and they were short and close together—gave the *Pearl* a shock from the jibboom to the rudder, which quivered in Pierre's hands; and when the wind blew stronger for some seconds the water skimmed the gunwale as if it would overflow the boat. A steam collier from Liverpool was at anchor, waiting for the tide; they passed under her stern, and then visited the ships in the roadstead, one after the other, and then stood a little farther out to admire the coast.

For three hours Pierre, in calm and motionless content, went hither and thither on the rippling water, steering as though it were some winged creature, swift and obedient, this thing of wood and canvas that came and went at his caprice, at a pressure of his hand.

He was plunged in revery—such revery as comes to one on horseback or on a ship's deck. He thought of his future, which was to be prosperous, and of the pleasure of a life of intelligence. To-morrow he would ask his brother to lend him, for three months, fifteen hundred francs, so that he could move at once into the pretty suite of rooms in the Boulevard François I.

The sailor said, all at once:

"Here's the fog, Master Pierre. Better put about."

He raised his eyes, and saw in the north an extensive gray light shadow that obscured the sky, and covered the sea, and was advancing toward them like a cloud fallen from the sky.

He veered round, and, with the wind astern, directed his course to the jetty, followed by the driving fog, which gained on them. As it reached the *Pearl*, and enveloped it in its intangible density, a cold chill ran through Pierre's limbs; and a smoky, musty odor, the strange odor of sea fog, made him close his mouth that he might not swallow this damp and icy mist. When the boat reached its anchorage in the dock, the whole town was already buried in the fine vapor, which, without falling, wetted one like rain, and spread over the houses and streets like a river overflowing.

Pierre, with his hands and feet chilled, hurried home, and flung himself on his bed to sleep till dinner time. When he entered the dining-room, his mother was saying to Jean:

"The corridor will be charming. We will put some flowers there. You'll see. I will take on myself to attend to them and renew them. When you give a party, it will be a fairy scene."

"What are you talking about?" the doctor asked.

"A delightful suite of rooms I have just rented for your brother—a real treasure on the mezzanine floor overlooking two streets. It contains two reception rooms, a glass corridor, and a little round dining-room, perfectly lovely for a rich bachelor."

Pierre grew pale. His heart was filled with anger.

"Where is it?" he said.

"Boulevard François I."

He doubted no longer, and took his seat, so exasperated that he longed to cry out, "This is too much! Is he to have everything?"

His mother, radiant with pleasure, continued:

"And, fancy, I got it for two thousand eight hundred francs. They asked three thousand, but I obtained a reduction of two hundred francs by taking a lease for three, six, or nine years. Your brother will be admirably settled there. An elegant apartment is all that is necessary to make a lawyer's fortune. It attracts clients, charms and retains them; it inspires them with respect, and lets them understand that a man living in such style must be well paid for his words."

She was silent a few seconds, and resumed:

"We must find something like it for you, but more modest, as you have nothing—still very nice, all the same."

Pierre replied in an indignant tone: "For me! It will be by work and science that I shall succeed!"

His mother persisted:

"Yes, but I assure you a pretty apartment will be a great help, all the same."

About the middle of the meal, he asked abruptly,

"How did you make the acquaintance of this Maréchal?"

Monsieur Roland raised his head, and tried to refresh his memory:

"Wait, I do not remember very well. It is so long ago. Oh, yes, I know! Your mother made his acquaintance in the shop—was not that the way, Louise? He came to order something, and often returned. We knew him as a customer before knowing him as a friend."

Pierre, who was eating French beans, and sticking the point of his fork into them one after the other, as if he were spitting them, rejoined:

64

"At what time did you make his acquaintance?"

Roland again tried to recollect, but, recalling nothing, appealed to his wife's memory:

"What year was it, Louise? You cannot have forgotten, as you have so good a memory. Let's see. Was it in—in—in '55 or '56? Just think; you must know better than I do."

She reflected for some time; then, with a steady and tranquil voice, replied:

"It was in '58. Pierre was then three years old. I am certain I make no mistake, for it was the year when the child had the scarlatina, and Maréchal, whom we then knew but little, was of great assistance to us."

Roland exclaimed:

"True, true, he was wonderfully kind. When your mother was worn out with fatigue, and I was busy in the shop, he went to the druggist's to bring the medicines. He had, indeed, a noble heart. And when you were well again, you cannot imagine how happy he was, and how he kissed you. It was from that time that we became great friends."

Then this thought entered Pierre's mind, like a bullet that tears and wounds: "Since he knew me first, was so devoted to me, loved and kissed me so fondly; since I was the cause of the great intimacy with my parents—why did he leave all his fortune to my brother, and nothing to me?"

He asked no more questions, and remained moody rather than thoughtful, nursing a new, as yet undefined disquiet, the secret germ of a new calamity.

He left the house early, and began again to roam the streets. They were buried in the fog, which rendered the night oppressive, opaque and sickening. It might have been called a pestilential vapor bearing down on the earth. It could be seen streaming past the gas lights, which it seemed momentarily to extinguish. The street pavements became slippery, as from an icy coating, and all evil odors seemed to come out of the houses—putrid odors from cellars, from gutters, from spouts, from filthy kitchens—and blend with the odor of the flying mist.

Pierre, with his shoulders to his ears and his hands in his pockets, not wishing to remain longer out in the cold, went to call on Marowsko.

The old druggist was still sleeping under the gaslight of his store. When he recognized Pierre, whom he loved with the attachment of a faithful dog, he shook off his torpor, went to look for his glasses, and brought out his new liqueur.

"Well," asked the doctor, "how are you coming on with your liqueur?"

The Pole explained that four of the principal cafés of the town had consented to give it a trial, and how the *Phare de la Côte* and the *Sémaphore Havrais* would write it up in exchange for some pharmaceutical products presented to the editors.

After a long silence, Marowsko asked if Jean was really in possession of his fortune and put two or three further vague questions on the same subject. His sullen devotion to Pierre revolted against this preference. Pierre believed he could follow his thoughts; he divined, understood, read them in his averted eyes, in the hesitating tone of his voice, in the phrases which rose to his lips, but which he did not utter, and which he would not utter—he so discreet, so timid, so cautious.

He no longer doubted that the old man was thinking: "You ought not to have let him accept this legacy, which will cause evil reports about your mother." Perhaps he even believed that Jean was Maréchal's son. Certainly he believed it. How could he help believing it, as it must appear so probable, so natural, so evident? Had not he himself, Pierre, her son, been struggling for three days with all his force, all the subtle arguments of his heart, to deceive his reason? Was he not still struggling against this terrible suspicion?

And once again the necessity of being alone in order to think, to discuss with himself, to face boldly, without scruples or feebleness, this theory so possible, and yet so monstrous, dominated him so forcibly that he rose without even tasting the liqueur, shook the astonished druggist by the hand, and plunged into the fog of the streets.

He said to himself: "Why did this man Maréchal leave all his fortune to Jean?"

It was now no longer jealousy that made him ask this; it was no longer that rather mean and natural envy which he knew was hid in his bosom, and which he had fought against for the last three days; it was the dread of something horrible—the dread of believing, himself, that Jean, his brother, was the son of that man!

No, he did not believe it, he could not even put to himself so criminal a question. This suspicion, however slight, however improbable, must be rejected by him, utterly and forever. He must have light and certainty, he must have complete assurance in his heart, for his mother was all he loved in the world.

And as he wandered alone in the night, he would submit his memory and his reason to a minute examination, through which the startling truth would be evolved. That done, he would think of it no more, never again. He would go to sleep.

He thought: "Let me see. Let me, first of all, examine the facts; then I will recall all I know of him, his treatment of my brother and me; I will seek for all the motives that could possibly have occasioned this preference. He was there when Jean was born? Yes, but he knew me before that. If he had entertained a mute, secret love for my mother, he would have preferred me; for it was through me, thanks to my scarlatina, that he became the intimate friend of my parents. Logically, therefore, he ought to have chosen me, to have had a more vivid affection for me, unless he felt for my brother, as he saw him growing up, an instinctive attraction and predilection."

Then, with a desperate effort of thought, of all his intellectual power, he retraced his recollections, in order to reconstruct, bring before his mind, recognize, understand this man—the man whom he had constantly seen, without caring for him, during all the years he had passed in Paris.

He felt, however, that walking, the slight motion of his steps, somewhat troubled his ideas, disarranged their order, weakened their reach, and obscured his memory.

In order to throw on the past and its unknown events a keen look from which nothing could escape, he must remain motionless, in some large, empty place. He decided to go and sit on the pier, as he had done the other night.

As he drew near the harbor, he heard, in the direction of the open sea, a melancholy, sinister moan, like the bellowing of a bull, but longer and more powerful. It was a fog horn, the cry of ships lost in the fog.

A shudder shook his flesh and wrung his heart, such an echo was there in his soul and nerves of that cry of distress, which he fancied he had uttered himself. Another similar voice moaned in its turn, but farther away, then close by, the fog horn of the harbor replied to them, rending the night with its clamorous tone.

Pierre walked quickly to the pier without further thought, satisfied to plunge into the lugubrious and moaning darkness.

He sat down at the end of the pier, and closed his eyes to avoid the sight of the electric lights, veiled in mist, which made the port accessible at night, and of the red light of the lighthouse on the south jetty, which, however, could scarcely be distinguished. Then, turning sideways, he leaned his elbows on the granite, and covered his face with his hands.

His mind, without his speaking the word, kept repeating, as if to summon, evoke and challenge his ghost, "Maréchal—Maréchal." And in the darkness of his closed eyelids he suddenly saw him as he had known him—a man of sixty, with a pointed, white beard, and heavy eyebrows that were likewise white. He was neither tall nor short, had an affable air, soft gray eyes, a modest bearing, the look of an honest, tender and simple soul. He called Pierre

and Jean "my dear children"; he never appeared
to prefer one to the other, and asked them together
to dinner.

Pierre, with the persistence of a hound following
a lost trail, began to recall the words, the gestures,
the tones, the looks of this man who had disappeared from earth. He recalled him, gradually, just
as he was, in his rooms in the Rue Tronchet, when
he received his brother and himself at table.

Two maids waited on him, both old, who, for a
long time past, doubtless, had acquired the habit
of saying "Monsieur Pierre" and "Monsieur
Jean."

Maréchal stretched out both hands to the young
people, the right to one, the left to the other, as
they entered.

"Good-day, my children," he would say. "What
news have you of your father and mother? As for
me, they never write me a line."

The conversation went on pleasantly and familiarly on common topics. There was nothing ex-
traordinary about the man's intellect, but he was
gentle, charming and gracious. He was certainly
a good friend to them—one of those good friends of
which one seldom thinks, because one is so sure of
their friendship.

Memories now began to pour in upon Pierre.
Maréchal, seeing him sometimes melancholy, and
guessing at his poverty as a student, had offered
and lent him money, spontaneously—some hundreds
of francs, perhaps forgotten by both, and never
repaid. The man, then, always loved him, always
took an interest in him, since he was troubled about
his needs. Then—then—why leave all his fortune

to Jean? No; he had never apparently shown more affection for the younger than for the elder brother, been more thoughtful for one than the other, less tender apparently to this one than to that one. Then—then—he must have had a powerful and secret reason for giving all to Jean—all—and nothing to Pierre.

The more he thought of it, the more he revived the past of later years, the more the doctor considered the distinction made between them improbable and incredible.

An acute pang, an inexpressible anguish, entered his breast, and made his heart flutter like a shaken rag. Its springs seemed broken, and the blood, gushing through it, made it tremble violently in streams, tumultuously shaking and tossing it.

Then, half aloud as one speaks in a nightmare, he muttered: "I must know! My God, I must know!"

He went back now still further, to the earliest days when his parents lived in Paris. But faces escaped him, and this muddled his recollections. He was, above all, anxious to recall Maréchal with blond, chestnut, or black hair. He could not do so; the later appearance of the man, when he was old, had effaced the others. He remembered, however, that he was slender, that he had a soft hand, and often brought flowers, very often, indeed; for his father constantly repeated:

"More bouquets. Why, it is madness, my dear fellow; you will ruin yourself on roses."

Maréchal would reply:

"Let me alone; it gives me great pleasure."

And suddenly the remembrance of his mother's

71

tones, as she smiled and said, "Thanks, my friend," crossed his mind, so distinctly that he fancied he could hear her. She must have pronounced these three words very often, as they were so engraven on the memory of her son!

Maréchal, then, used to bring flowers—he, the rich man, the gentleman, the customer—to this little shopwoman, the wife of a small jeweler. Did he love her? How could he have become the friend of these shopkeepers if he had not loved the wife? He was a man of education and refinement. How many times he talked to Pierre of poetry and poets! His appreciation of writers was not that of an artist, but of a bourgeois who can feel emotion. The doctor had often smiled at his sentimental ideas, which seemed to him rather silly. To-day he understood that this sentimental man could never, never have been the friend of his father, who was so matter-of-fact, so earthy, so heavy, for whom the word poetry had no meaning.

Maréchal, then, young, free, rich, open to all tender emotions, one day, by chance, entered a shop, having probably noticed the pretty woman behind the counter. He bought something, came back, and talked day by day more familiarly, through his frequent purchases, acquiring an entrée to the house, the privilege of smiling at the young wife, and of shaking hands with the husband.

And afterward—afterward—O God!—afterward.

He had loved and caressed the first child, the jeweler's child, till the birth of the second; then down to his death he had remained a stranger; then, his tomb closed, his body decomposed, his name effaced from the names of the living, having disappeared wholly and forever, having no longer to take any precautions, nothing to dread or to hide, he left all his fortune to the second child! Why? The man had intelligence; he must have understood and foreseen that he might, that he would almost infallibly, arouse a suspicion that this child was his. He would thus dishonor a woman! How could he have acted as he did if Jean had not been his son?

And suddenly a precise, terrible recollection crossed Pierre's mind. Maréchal was fair-haired, fair as Jean. He remembered now a little miniature which he had seen in Paris on the parlor chimneypiece, once upon a time, but which had disappeared. Where was it? Lost, or hidden? Oh, if he could only have possession of it for a second! His mother, perhaps, had it in the secret drawer where relics are hidden.

His agony at this thought became so poignant that he groaned aloud—one of those brief moans wrung from the heart by keen anguish. And suddenly, as if it heard him, as if it understood his condition and replied to him, the fog horn on the pier bellowed close to him. Its voice—the voice of a supernatural monster, more sonorous than thunder, a wild, formidable roar, made to overpower the voice of the winds and waves—spread through the darkness across the invisible sea buried in the fog.

Then, through the mist, near and far, similar cries arose in the night; terrible were these appealing screams from the huge blind steamers.

Again all was still.

Pierre opened his eyes, and stared in surprise at being there, aroused from his nightmare.

"I am mad," he thought; "I suspect my mother." And a flood of love and tenderness, of repentance, prayer and desolation, inundated his heart. His mother! Knowing her as he knew her, how could he suspect her? Was not the soul, the life, of this simple, chaste, loyal woman more transparent than water? Any one who saw and knew her could not but judge her beyond suspicion. And it was he, her son, who doubted her! Oh, if he could have taken her in his arms at that moment, how he would have embraced and caressed her! How he would have knelt to her to ask pardon!

Could she have deceived his father? His father! Certainly he was an honest man, honorable and upright in his dealings, but his soul had never crossed the horizon of his shop. How could this woman, formerly very pretty, as he knew, and as could be still seen, endowed with a delicate, affectionate, tender nature, have accepted as her betrothed, and as her husband, a man so different from herself?

Why ask? She had married him as a girl marries the lad with money whom her parents present to her. They installed themselves at once in their store in the Rue Montmartre; and the young woman presiding at the counter, animated by the spirit of her new home, and by that subtle, sacred sense of community interest which replaces love and even affection in most of the homes of the business people in Paris, had begun to work with all her active and refined intelligence for the fortunes of the house. And her life had passed, in quiet, honorable uniformity without tenderness.

Without tenderness! Could a woman live with-

out love? A young, pretty woman living in Paris,
reading books, applauding actresses who die of
passion on the stage, could not pass from youth to
age without her heart being touched, if only once?
He would not believe it of any other woman—why
should he believe it of his mother?

Certainly she might have loved as others did!
Why should she be different from others, even if she
was his mother?

She had been young, with all the poetic weak-
nesses that trouble the heart of the young. Con-
fined and imprisoned in the shop by the side of a
vulgar husband who always talked business, she
had dreamed of moonlight, of travels, of kisses in-
terchanged in the evening shadows. And then one
day a man had entered, as lovers enter in books,
and he had spoken as lovers do.

She had loved him. Why not? She was his
mother. Well, was he to be blind and stupid to the
extent of rejecting evidence because his mother was
involved?

Had she listened to him? Yes, since the man had
had no other friend; yes, since he had remained
faithful to her when she was old and at a distance;
yes, since he had left all his fortune to her son, to
their son!

Pierre rose, quivering in such wrath that he
would have liked to kill some one. His outstretched
arms, his open hand longed to smite, to slay, to
bruise, to choke! Whom? All the world—father,
brother, the dead man, his mother!

He started to return home. What should he do?

As he passed before a little tower near the sig-
nal pole, the strident scream of the fog horn

sounded right in his ear. His surprise was so great that he almost fell, and recoiled to the stone parapet. There he sat down, with no strength left, so great was the shock.

The steamer which was the first to answer seemed quite near, and appeared at the entrance, the tide being high.

Pierre turned and saw its red eye dimmed by the mist. Then, under the diffused gleam of the electric light, a huge black shadow outlined itself between the two piers. Behind him the voice of the watchman, the hoarse voice of a retired captain, cried:

"Ship ahoy!"

And, in the mist, the voice of the pilot standing on the bridge, with equal hoarseness, replied:

"*Santa Lucia.*"

"Where from?"

"Italy."

"What port?"

"Naples."

Before his troubled eyes, Pierre fancied he could see the crest of flame of Vesuvius, while at the foot of the volcano the fireflies were dancing in the orange groves of Sorrento or Castellamare. How often had he dreamed of those familiar names, as if he had known the districts! If he could but go away, at once, no matter where, and never come back, never write, never let it be known what had become of him! But, no; he must return, return to his paternal home, and sleep in his bed.

So much the worse. He would not return, he would wait till day. The sound of the fog horns pleased him. He rose and began to march like an officer keeping his watch on deck.

Another enormous and mysterious ship followed the first one. It was an English ship returning from India.

He saw many more come in, emerging one after the other out of the impenetrable darkness. When the dampness of the fog became intolerable, Pierre set off toward the town. He was so cold that he entered a sailor's drinking place to get some grog, and when the hot brandy and pepper burned his palate and throat, he felt hope revive in him.

He had deceived himself, perhaps? He knew right well his own vacillating unreason. He had deceived himself beyond doubt. He had accumulated facts as one draws an indictment against an innocent person, whom it is always easy to condemn when one wishes to believe him guilty. After a night's rest, he would think quite differently. Then he went home to bed, and by force of will ended by falling asleep.

CHAPTER V

THE TELLTALE PORTRAIT

But the doctor had not lost himself for more than an hour or two in a troubled sleep before he awoke in the darkness of his warm, closed room. He felt, even before he was able to think, that painful oppression, that unrest of soul, which the sorrow on which we have slept leaves in us. It would seem as if the unhappiness, the shock of which had only struck us the evening before, during repose insinuated itself into our very flesh, and tortured and wearied like a fever. Recollection came to him abruptly, and he sat up in bed.

Then he went over again, slowly, one by one, all the arguments that had agonized his heart on the pier, while the fog horns were screaming. The more he thought, the less he doubted. He felt himself borne along by his logic to the intolerable certainty as by a hand that drags you along and strangles you.

He was thirsty, he was hot, his heart throbbed. He rose to open the window and breathe fresh air, and when he was up a slight noise reached him through the wall.

Jean was sleeping quietly, and snoring gently. He could sleep! He had no forebodings, he had suspected nothing! Their friend, Maréchal, had left him all his fortune. He accepted the money, as it seemed to him right and natural.

He slept, rich and satisfied, not knowing that his brother was worried and suffering. And there arose in Pierre a rage against this care-free and contented sleeper.

The day before he would have knocked at his door and, going in, would have sat beside the bed and said to him, before he was fairly awake, after being startled suddenly:

"Jean, you ought not to keep this legacy, which to-morrow might bring on your mother suspicion and dishonor."

But to-day he could not speak; he could not say to Jean that he did not believe him to be their father's son. At present he must guard in secret, keep buried in his heart, the shame he had discovered; he must hide from all the blot he had detected, and which no one must discover, not even his brother—above all, not his brother.

Little did he think now of empty respect for public opinion. He would have liked all the world to accuse his mother, provided that he—he alone—he knew her to be innocent. How could he bear to live near her every day, and believe, as he saw her, that his brother's father was a stranger?

How calm and serene she was, nevertheless! How sure of herself she seemed! Was it possible for a woman like her, with pure soul and upright heart, to fall without exhibiting later any signs of remorse, or any stings of conscience?

Remorse, remorse! It must formerly, in the early days, have tortured her; then it was blotted out, as everything is blotted out. Certainly she had wept for her fault, and by degrees had almost forgotten it. Have not all women, all, this prodigious faculty of forgetfulness, which makes them scarce recognize, after a few years, the man whose lips have kissed them again and again? The kiss strikes like lightning, love passes like a tempest; then life once more becomes calm as the sky, and begins again as before. Do we remember a passing cloud?

Pierre could not remain in his room. He felt the roof press on his head, and the walls stifled him. And, as he was very thirsty, he lighted his candle to go and drink a glass of water, fresh from the kitchen faucet.

He descended two flights; then, as he ascended with the carafe full, he sat down, in his nightshirt, on one of the steps of the stairs where a current of air was blowing, and drank out of the bottle in long gulps, like a runner out of breath. When he was quiet again, the silence of the dwelling affected him; then, one by one, he distinguished the slightest noises. At first it was the clock in the dining-room, and its ticking seemed to him to grow louder second by second. Then again he heard some one snoring, the short, labored snoring of an old man; his father, no doubt; and he shuddered at the idea, as if it had only just come to him, that these two men, sleeping in the same house, father and son, were nothing to each other! No tie, not even the frailest, united them, and they did not know it! They talked affectionately to each other, they embraced each other, they were glad or sorry together over the same things, as if the same blood ran in their veins. Yet two persons born at the two extremities of the world could not be more alien to each other than this father and this son. They believed they loved each other, because a lie had grown up between them. It was a lie that produced this paternal love and this filial love—a lie impossible to expose, and which no one should ever know but himself, the true son.

Still, still, if he were mistaken? How could he find out? Ah, if there were only a likeness, even a slight one, between his father and Jean, one of those mysterious likenesses that pass from great-grandfather to great-grandson, and show that the whole race descends directly from one source. It would be an easy thing for a medical man like him to recognize it—the form of the jaw, the curve of the nose, the distance between the eyes, the nature of the hair or teeth; even less than these, a gesture, a habit, a trick of manner, a transmitted taste, some sign or other quite characteristic for a trained eye.

He could recall nothing—no, nothing. But he had not looked carefully, he had not observed carefully, as he had had no reason for tracing out these imperceptible indications.

He rose to reënter his room, and began to mount the stairs with slow steps, pondering all the time. As he passed before his brother's door, he stopped short, his hand extended to open it. He was seized with an imperious desire to see Jean at once, to take a long look at him, to surprise him in his sleep, while the peaceful face and the relaxed features were in repose, and when all the artificiality of life had disappeared. In this way he would seize the sleeping secret of his physiognomy, and if any appreciable resemblance existed, it would not escape him.

But if Jean awoke, what should he say? How explain his visit?

He remained standing, his fingers grasping the door handle, and seeking a reason or pretext.

He remembered, all at once, that, eight days before, he had lent his brother a phial of laudanum to allay the pain of toothache. He might have toothache himself this night and come to get the bottle. Then he entered, but with a furtive step, like a thief.

Jean, with his mouth half open, was sleeping a profound animal sleep. His beard and fair hair made a splash of gold in the white linen. He did not awake, but he stopped snoring.

Pierre bent over him and gazed on him with eager eye. No; this young man did not resemble

Roland; and, for the second time, his mind returned to the miniature of Maréchal that had disappeared. He must find it. If he saw it, perhaps he would doubt no longer.

His brother stirred, disturbed doubtless by his presence, or by the light of the candle in his face. Then the doctor retreated on tiptoe toward the door, which he closed noiselessly. He returned to his room, but did not go to bed.

The day was slow in coming. The hours struck, one after another, by the drawing-room clock, which had a deep, serious tone, as though this little specimen of the clockmaker's art had swallowed the bell of a cathedral. The sounds rose up through the empty staircase, traversed walls and doors, and died away in the rooms, in the unhearing ear of the sleepers. Pierre walked to and fro from his bed to the window. What should he do? He was too much upset to pass the day at home. He wished still to be alone, at least till the next day, in order to reflect, to become calm, to fortify himself for the everyday life which he had to resume.

Well, he would go to Trouville, and watch the crowd swarming on the beach! It would divert him, change the current of his thoughts, and give him time to prepare himself for the horrible thing that he had found out.

At earliest dawn he rose and dressed himself. The fog had lifted; it was a beautiful day. As the Trouville boat did not sail till nine o'clock, the doctor thought that he ought to kiss his mother before leaving.

He waited for the hour when she usually rose, and then went down. His heart was throbbing so fast as he touched the door, that he paused to take breath. His hand, as it lay on the door handle, was weak and quivering, almost incapable of the slight exertion of turning the knob to enter. He knocked. His mother's voice asked:

"Who is there?"

"Pierre."

"What do you want?"

"To say good-morning, because I am going to pass the day at Trouville with some friends."

"But I am still in bed."

"Do not disturb yourself, then; I can kiss you on my return, this evening."

He hoped that he could get away without seeing her, without pressing on her cheeks the hypocritical kiss which nauseated him beforehand.

But she replied:

"Wait a moment; I'll open the door. You must wait till I get back into bed."

He heard her bare feet on the floor, and then the sound of the bolt sliding. She cried:

"Come in!"

He went in. She was sitting up in bed, while beside her Roland, with a silk handkerchief round his head and his face to the wall, continued to sleep. Nothing but a shake of the arm could have awakened him. On the days he went fishing, the maid, who was rung up at the appointed hour by the sailor Papagris, would come and drag her master out of this invincible sleep.

Pierre, as he approached, looked at his mother, and it seemed to him all at once that he had never seen her.

She held up her face; he kissed her on both cheeks, and then seated himself on a low chair.

"You arranged this party yesterday evening?" she said.

"Yes, yesterday evening."

"You will be back for dinner?"

"I do not know yet. In any case, do not wait for me."

He examined her with astonished curiosity. It was his mother, this woman! Her entire countenance, seen from childhood, since his eye could distinguish, her smile, her voice, so well known, so familiar, all at once appeared to him quite new, quite different from what they had been hitherto to him. He understood now that, loving her, he had never looked at her critically. Yet it was she, and her knew every smallest detail of her countenance; but he perceived these little details clearly for the first time. His anxious attention, as he scrutinized this beloved face, revealed to him a difference in it, a physiognomy which he had never before discovered.

He rose to go, and then, suddenly yielding to an unconquerable desire to know what had been gnawing his heart since the evening before, he said:

"I say, mother, I thought I remembered a miniature of Maréchal that we had in our parlor in Paris."

She hesitated a second or two, or at least he imagined that she hesitated; then she said:

"Why, yes!"

"What has become of this portrait?"

Her answer, again, might have come quicker:

"That portrait—wait—I do not quite know—perhaps I have it in my desk."

84

"I would be very pleased if you would find it for me."

"Yes, I'll look. Why do you want it?"

"Oh, not for myself! I thought it would be quite natural to give it to Jean, and it would please my brother."

"You are right. It is a happy thought. I will look for it as soon as I get up."

He left the room.

It was a cloudless day, without a breath of air. The people in the streets seemed lighthearted; merchants were going to their business, clerks to their office, girls to their shops. Some of them were singing, happy in the brightness of the day.

The passengers were already going on board the Trouville boat. Pierre took his seat on a wooden bench at the very end of the boat.

He asked himself:

"Was she disturbed by my question about the portrait, or only surprised? Has she mislaid it, or hidden it? Does she know, or does she not know, where it is? If she has hidden it, why did she do so?"

Advancing steadily from deduction to deduction, he reached this conclusion:

The portrait, the portrait of a friend, the portrait of a dear friend, had remained in the parlor in full view till the day when the wife or the mother had been the first to perceive, before any one else, that it resembled her son. Doubtless, for a long time she had been looking for this resemblance; and when she detected it, and recognized the fact that every one might, some day or other, detect it also, she had one evening removed the dangerous little

85

miniature, and, not daring to destroy it, had concealed it.

Pierre now remembered very well that the miniature had disappeared long before their departure from Paris. It had disappeared, he believed, when the growth of Jean's beard brought out the likeness between him and the fair-haired young man who was smiling in the picture.

The motion of the boat as she put off disturbed the course of his thoughts. He rose and looked at the sea.

The little steamer passed the piers, turned to the left, and puffing, panting and quivering, took her course to the distant coast, which was visible through the morning mist. Here and there the red sail of some heavy fishing smack, lying motionless on the smooth sea, had the appearance of a big rock rising from the water. The Seine, as it flowed from Rouen, looked like a large inlet of the sea, dividing two neighboring countries.

In less than an hour Trouville was reached, and, as it was the time for bathing, Pierre betook himself to the beach.

From a distance, it had the look of a long garden full of blooming flowers. On the great stretch of yellow sand, reaching from the pier to the Roches Noires, parasols of every color, hats of every shape, dresses of every shade, were seen in groups before the bathing houses, in lines along the beach, or scattered here and there, looking actually like enormous bouquets on a boundless prairie. The confused sounds, near or far, of voices sharpened by the thin air, the calls, the cries of children wading in the surf, the clear laughter of women, all mingled in a gentle, unceasing murmur, which blended with the imperceptible sea air, and was absorbed with it.

Pierre walked in the middle of these people, more lost, more separated from them, more isolated, more immersed in torturing thought, than if he had been flung from a ship's deck into the sea, a hundred leagues from shore. He brushed against them; he heard, without listening, a few phrases; and he saw, without looking, the men talk to the women, and the women smile on the men.

Then, all at once, as if awaking from sleep, he perceived them distinctly; and a feeling of hatred seized him, for they seemed happy and content.

He went on, brushing against the groups and walking round them, a prey to new thoughts. All these many-colored toilets that covered the sands like so many flowers, these pretty materials, these showy sunshades, all the ingenious inventions of fashion, from the tiny shoe to the extravagant hat, the seduction of gesture, voice and smile—the whole coquetry displayed on the beach—suddenly seemed to him an immense unfolding of feminine perversity. All these dressed-up women wanted to please, to captivate, to tempt, some one. They had made themselves beautiful for men, for all men except the husband whom they no longer needed to conquer. They had made themselves beautiful for the lover of to-day and the lover of to-morrow; for the stranger they met, noticed, perhaps expected.

And these men seated by them, gazing into their eyes, speaking to them with faces close together, attracted them, desired them, hunted them like game, like elusive and fleeing game, although it seemed so near and so easy. The beach was, then, only a marketplace, where some sold themselves and others gave themselves, where some bargained for their caresses and others only held out promises. All these women had only one thought—to make them desire that which was already given, sold, or promised to other men. And he reflected that it was always the same thing, the whole world over.

His mother had done like the rest; that was all! Like the rest? No! There were exceptions—many, many exceptions. The women he saw around him, rich, silly seekers for love, were, on the whole, coquettes of the elegant world of fashion, or even coquettes of a more brazen kind; for respectable women did not mingle with this beach crowd, this legion of idlers.

The tide rose gradually, driving before it the first line of bathers. Groups were seen to rise with a start, and run from the yellow wave fringed with foam, taking their chairs with them.

The bathing boxes on wheels, drawn by a horse, were also taken in shore; and on the board walk, which ran along the beach from one end to the other, there was now an unbroken, dense, slow stream of elegant toilets, which formed two contrary currents, that jostled and mingled. Pierre, in a state of nervous exasperation, fled and plunged into the town, where he took breakfast at an ordinary wine shop near the outskirts.

When he had taken his coffee, he stretched himself out on two chairs before the door, and, as he had scarcely slept the night before, dozed in the shadow of a lime tree.

After some hours of repose, he roused himself,

and, seeing that it was time to return to catch the
boat, he set out, feeling overcome by a sudden weakness that had fallen on him during his slumber. He
was determined to return, and learn if his mother
had found the portrait of Maréchal. Would she
mention it first, or would he have to ask her again?
Beyond question, if she waited till he interrogated
her once more, she had a secret reason for not showing the portrait.

But when he had entered his room he hesitated
to go down to dinner. He was suffering too much.
His throbbing heart had not yet calmed itself. However, he made up his mind, and appeared in the
dining-room as they were sitting down to table.

They all appeared to be very happy.

"Well," said Roland, "how are you getting on
with your shopping? I do not want to see anything
before it's all in place."

His wife replied:

"Oh, very well. Only it requires a good deal of
thought to avoid making a mismatch. The question
of furniture is taking up our attention."

She had spent the day visiting with Jean the
carpet stores and furniture stores. She wanted rich
materials, rather gaudy, to strike the eye. Her son,
on the other hand, wanted something simple, but
elegant. So, over every sample shown them, they
both of them reiterated their opinions. She main-
tained that the client required to be impressed, that
he ought to feel, when he entered the reception
room, that it gave the effect of wealth.

Jean, on the contrary, wishing to attract only
an opulent and fashionable clientèle, desired to con-

quer the refined class by his modest and impeccable taste.

The discussion, which had lasted all day, began again with the soup.

Roland had no opinion. He repeated:

"I do not want to hear about anything. I'll go and see it when it is finished."

Madame Roland appealed to the judgment of her elder son.

"Come, Pierre, what do you think?"

His nerves were so excited that he longed to reply with an oath. He said, however, in a dry tone, vibrating with indignation:

"Oh, I quite agree with Jean, for my part! I like simplicity, which, as regards taste, is comparable to uprightness as regards character."

His mother resumed:

"Remember, we live in a town of business people, where good taste is not met everywhere."

Pierre replied:

"What matter? Is that a reason to imitate fools? If my townsfolk are stupid or dishonest, am I bound to follow their example? A good woman will not commit a fault because her neighbors set her a bad example."

Jean burst into laughter.

"Your comparisons sound as if they were taken from the maxims of a moralist."

Pierre made no rejoinder, and his mother and brother recommenced their talk of draperies and easy-chairs.

He looked at them as he had looked at his mother, in the morning, before he left for Trouville. He looked at them like an observant stranger; and, in fact, he felt as if he had, all at once, entered a stranger's family.

His father, in particular, astonished him as he looked at him and thought about him. This fat, flabby man, this contented simpleton, was his father —his! No, no, Jean was not a bit like him.

His family! Two days ago an unknown, maleficent hand, the hand of a dead man, had rent and shattered, one by one, all the bonds that held together these four souls. It was all over; they were broken forever. No mother now for him, for he could not love her when he could not venerate her with that absolute, tender and pious respect which is necessary to the filial heart. No brother now for him, for this brother was the child of a stranger. There remained for him only a father—this fat man, whom he could not love in spite of himself.

He said abruptly:

"Oh, mamma, did you find that portrait?"

She opened her eyes in surprise.

"What portrait?"

"Maréchal's."

"No—that is, yes; I have not found it, but I think I know where it is."

"What are you talking about?" Roland inquired.

Pierre answered:

"A miniature of Maréchal, that used to be in our little parlor in Paris. I thought that Jean might like to have it."

Roland exclaimed:

"Yes, certainly, I remember it perfectly. I saw it as lately as the end of last week. Your mother pulled it out of her desk when she was arranging her papers. It was Thursday or Friday. You remember, Louise, don't you? I was just going to shave when you took it from a drawer and placed it on a chair beside you, with a heap of letters, half of which you burned. Why, is it not strange that you should have handled that portrait scarcely two or three days before Jean's legacy came? If I believed in presentiments, I should call that one."

Madame Roland quietly replied:

"Yes, I know where it is. I will go and get it at once."

Then she had been lying! She had lied that very morning, when she replied to her son's question as to what had become of the miniature: "I do not know exactly—perhaps I have it in my desk."

She had seen it, touched it, handled it, looked at it, a few days before, and then she had put it back in the secret drawer with some letters—his letters.

Pierre looked at his mother who had lied to him. He looked at her with the exasperated wrath of a deceived son whose sacred affection had been betrayed, and with the jealousy of a man who, after being blinded for a long time, at length detects a shameful treason. If he had been that woman's husband, he, her son, he would have seized her by the wrists, by the shoulders, or by the hair, and have hurled her to the ground, and have struck, wounded and crushed her! Yet he could say nothing, do nothing, state nothing, reveal nothing. He was her son, he had nothing to avenge, he had not been betrayed.

But yes, she had betrayed his affection, his filial respect. She owed it to him to be irreproachable, as all mothers owe it to their children. If his anger amounted almost to hatred, it was because he felt her to be more criminal toward him than toward his father himself.

The love of man and wife is a voluntary pact, where the frail one is guilty of perfidy only; but when a wife becomes a mother, she is more responsible, for Nature has confided to her a race. If she succumbs then, she is cowardly, unworthy, infamous!

"Well, well," said Roland suddenly, extending his legs under the table, as he did every evening, to sip his glass of ratafia. "It is not unpleasant to be idle when one has a little competence. I hope Jean will invite us to some special dinners now, even if I should sometimes get a pain in my stomach."

Then, turning to his wife:

"Go bring the portrait, dear, as you have done eating. I should like to see it again."

She rose, took a candle, and left the room. After an absence which seemed long to Pierre, although it only lasted three minutes, Madame Roland returned, smiling, and holding by its ring an old-fashioned gilt frame.

"Here it is," she said. "I found it almost at once."

The doctor was the first to extend his hand. He took the portrait and examined it, holding it at arm's length. Then, feeling that his mother was looking at him, he slowly raised his eyes to his brother's face to compare it with the picture. He almost said in the impulse of his violence: "Why, this is like Jean." If he did not dare to utter these terrible words, he displayed his thoughts by the

Vol. 1—8

way in which he compared the living face and the painted face.

They had, certainly, some traits in common, the same beard and the same brow, but nothing definite enough to warrant the declaration, "There is the father, and here is the son." It was rather a family resemblance, a similarity of physiognomy as of those in whose veins flows the same blood. But what was more decisive to Pierre's mind than this look in the two faces was the fact that his mother rose, turned her back, and, with unnecessary delay, pretended to lock up the sugar and liqueurs in the closet.

She saw that he knew or at least suspected.

"Hand it to me," said Roland. Pierre handed over the miniature, and his father drew the candle nearer to see it better. Then in a softened tone he said:

"Poor fellow! To think that he was like that when we knew him. Heavens, how time flies! He was a handsome man, all the same, at that period, and pleasant in his manners. Was he not, Louise?"

As his wife did not reply, he continued:

"And what an even temper! I never saw him in a bad humor. Well, it's over; there's nothing remaining of him—except what he left to Jean. We can swear that he showed himself a good and loyal friend to the end. Even when dying, he did not forget us."

Jean, in his turn, extended his arm to take the portrait. He looked at it for some moments, and then said, in a tone of regret:

"I do not recognize him at all. I can only remember him with white hair." And he returned

94

the miniature to his mother. She cast on it a rapid glance which was soon withdrawn, and seemed timid; then said, in her natural voice:

"It belongs to you, now, Jean, since you are his heir. We must take it to your new rooms."

As they entered the parlor, she placed the miniature on the mantelpiece, near the clock, where it used to stand.

Roland filled his pipe, Pierre and Jean lighted cigarettes. Usually one brother would smoke walking up and down the room; the other, buried in an easy-chair, with his legs crossed. The father always sat astride a chair, and spat into the fireplace.

Madame Roland, on her low seat, near a little table on which stood the lamp, usually did embroidery, knitted, or marked the linen.

This evening she commenced a piece of wool embroidery for Jean's bedroom. It was a difficult and complicated piece of work, and required all her attention to start it. Nevertheless, from time to time, while counting the stitches, she would raise her eyes and give a furtive glance at the little portrait of the dead man which was leaning against the clock. The doctor, as he crossed the narrow room in four or five strides, his hands behind his back and his cigarette between his lips, would encounter his mother's look every time.

One might say they were playing the spy on each other, and that war would be declared between them; and a painful unrest, an insupportable unrest, wrung Pierre's heart. Tortured and satisfied at the same time, he said to himself: "How she must be suffering at this moment, if she knows that I have found her out!" And, at each return toward

the fireplace, he stopped for a few seconds to look
at the blond countenance of Maréchal, just to show
that a fixed idea haunted him. And the little portrait, smaller than an open hand, seemed a living,
malevolent, dangerous personage that had suddenly
entered this house and this family.

Suddenly the doorbell rang. Madame Roland, always so calm, was startled, and the start revealed
to the doctor her condition of nervousness.

She said, however: "It must be Madame Rosémilly," and her anxious glance reverted again to the
mantelpiece.

Pierre understood, or thought he understood, her
terror and her anguish. Women's eyes are sharp,
their wits nimble, their minds suspicious. When the
incoming visitor should perceive this unknown
miniature, she might, perhaps, at the first glance, discover the resemblance between that face and Jean's
face. Then she would know and understand it all!
He was seized with dread, a sudden, horrible dread,
that the disgrace would be unveiled; and, turning
back as the door opened, he took the portrait and
slid it under the clock without his father or brother
seeing the action.

As he again encountered his mother's eyes, they
seemed to him changed, troubled and haggard.

"Good-day," said Madame Rosémilly; "I have
come to take a cup of tea with you."

While they gathered about her to ask how she
was, Pierre disappeared by the door that had been
left open.

They were surprised when they discovered his
departure. Jean, who feared the young woman
would deem it rude, muttered:

"What a bear!"

Madame Roland replied:

"You must not be angry with him—he is not very well to-day, and, moreover, is tired with his journey to Trouville."

"No matter," rejoined Roland. "That's no reason for going off like a savage."

Madame Rosémilly tried to smooth things down by saying:

"No, no. He took leave *à l'anglaise*. In society that is always the way when one leaves early."

"Well," replied Jean, "that may be so in society; but one does not treat one's family *à l'anglaise,* and that is what my brother has been doing the last few days."

CHAPTER VI

BITTER AND SWEET

Things went on thus in the Roland household for a week or two. The father went fishing, as usual; Jean, with his mother's assistance, moved into his new rooms; Pierre showed his gloomy countenance only at mealtimes.

His father asked him one evening:

"Why the devil do you look as if you were at a funeral? I have noticed it before to-day."

And the doctor replied:

"Because I feel the terrible burden of life."

The old fellow understood nothing of his meaning, and with an air of disappointment, continued:

"Upon my word, it is too bad! Ever since we

had the luck to receive that legacy, everybody seems miserable; just as if some accident had happened to us, or as if we were in mourning for some one."

"I am in mourning for some one," said Pierre.

"You! for whom?"

"Some one you did not know, and whom I loved too well."

Roland imagined he was talking of some love affair, and asked:

"A woman, of course?"

"Yes, a woman."

"Dead?"

"No, worse. Lost!"

"Ah!"

Although he was astonished at this unexpected confidence made to him in his wife's presence, and at his son's strange tone, he did not pursue the subject, for he thought that such matters did not concern a third party.

Madame Roland seemed not to have heard; she was very pale, and more than once looked ill.

Her husband, seeing her sink into a chair, and hearing her breathe as if respiration were difficult, had said to her:

"You really look ill, Louise; you are tiring yourself out, probably, getting Jean settled. Rest a bit, confound it all! He is in no hurry, the young swell, for he is rich."

She shook her head without speaking.

Her pallor on this day was so remarkable that Roland again noticed it.

"Come," he said, "this won't do at all, my poor old girl; we must look after you."

Then, turning to his son:

"You see, don't you, that she is ill? You have examined her, I suppose?"

Pierre replied:

"No; I did not notice that she was ailing."

"Why, a blind man could see it," said old Roland furiously. "What's the use of being a doctor, if you cannot even see that your mother is indisposed? Now, look at her! Just look at her! No, indeed; one might be dying, and this doctor here would not notice it."

Madame Roland breathed heavily, and grew so pale that her husband exclaimed:

"She's going to faint!"

"No—no—it is nothing! It will pass off—it is nothing."

Pierre had approached her, and was looking at her fixedly.

"Come, what is the matter?" he said.

"Nothing—nothing, I assure you—nothing," she repeated in a low, hurried voice.

Roland had gone for some spirits of ammonia; he returned, and, handing the bottle to his son, said:

"Here—do something for her. You have felt her pulse, of course?"

As Pierre bent forward to take her wrist, she drew back her hand with such an abrupt movement that it struck a chair near her.

"Come," he said in a cold tone, "let me attend to you, as you are ill."

She rose and held out her arm. Her skin was burning, her pulse irregular and hard. He muttered:

"It is really pretty serious. You must take a sedative. I'll go and write a prescription."

While he was bending over the paper, writing, a slight sound of suppressed sighs, of choking, of short, interrupted breathing, made him suddenly turn round.

She was weeping, with her hands over her face.

Roland, in alarm, asked:

"Louise, Louise, what is the matter? What is the matter?"

She made no response, and seemed torn by some horrible and profound sorrow.

Her husband tried to take hold of her hands and pull them from her face. She resisted, repeating:

"No, no, no."

Then he turned to his son:

"Why, what is the matter with her? I never saw her like this."

"It is nothing," said Pierre; "a slight nervous attack."

It seemed to him as if his heart was consoled by the sight of her anguish, and that this grief lightened his resentment and diminished her burden of opprobrium. He looked at her like a judge satisfied with his work.

But all at once she rose and rushed to the door, so suddenly and abruptly that it could neither be foreseen nor prevented, and ran to shut herself up in her room.

Father and son were left face to face.

"Do you understand anything of the case?" said the former.

"Yes," replied the latter. "It comes from a simple little nervous disturbance which often declares itself at mamma's age. It is likely that she will have many more attacks like this one."

Indeed, she had others, nearly every day; attacks which Pierre seemed to provoke by a single word, as if he held the secret of her strange and unknown trouble. He looked out for intermissions of repose in her face, and, with all the art of a torturer, awoke by a single word the grief which for a moment had been calmed.

And he suffered as much as she did. He suffered frightfully from the fact that he no longer loved her, no longer respected her, and that he was torturing her. When he had uncovered the wound that he had opened in the heart of this wife and mother, when he felt how wretched and how desperate she was, he would wander all alone through the town, so pierced with remorse, so racked with pity, so woebegone at seeing her thus crushed by his filial contempt, that he was tempted to fling himself into the sea and drown himself to make an end of it all.

Oh, how he wished to pardon her now! But he could not, for he was unable to forget. If he only could have avoided causing her suffering! But he could not do that, either, for he was always suffering himself. He returned home at mealtimes, full of gentler resolutions. Then, when he caught sight of her, when he saw her eyes—once so frank and direct, now timid, distracted, shrinking—he spoke in spite of himself, for he could not keep back the treacherous phrase which rose to his lips.

The shameful secret, known to them alone, spurred him on against her. It was a poison that he had at present in his veins, and that made him long to bite like a mad dog.

There was nothing now to prevent his torturing her unceasingly; for Jean lived almost altogether in his new rooms, and returned home every evening only to dine and sleep with his family.

He often noticed the bitter words and violent manner of his brother, but attributed them to jealousy. He promised himself that he would put him in his proper place and give him a lesson some day or other, for the family life was becoming very unpleasant, owing to these continual scenes. But, as he lived out of the house at this time, he suffered less from Pierre's offensive rudeness, and his love of peace induced him to be patient. Besides, his good fortune had intoxicated him, and his thoughts were occupied chiefly with matters that directly interested himself alone. He would come in full of new little cares, occupied with the cut of a jacket, the shape of a felt hat, the proper size of visiting cards. And he talked persistently about all the details of his apartment—of shelves placed in the bedroom cupboard to hold his linen, of wardrobes placed in the vestibule, and of electric burglar alarms.

It had been decided that when he formally moved into his new apartment there should be an excursion to Saint Jouin, and that, after dinner, the party should return and take tea with him. Roland wished to go by sea; but the distance and the uncertainty as to the time when they would arrive by this route, if the wind was contrary, led them to reject his proposal, and a carriage was hired for the occasion.

They started about ten o'clock, so as to arrive for breakfast. The dusty highroad traversed this Norman country district, to which the undulating plains and tree-girt farms gave the appearance of a limitless park. As the carriage rolled on at a slow trot drawn by two heavy horses, the Roland family, Madame Rosémilly and Captain Beausire, deafened by the noise of the wheels, remained silent, and closed their eyes amid a cloud of dust.

The harvest was ripe. Beside the dull green of the clover, and the bright green of the beets, the fields of yellow grain lighted up the landscape with a tawny golden gleam. They seemed to have absorbed the sunlight that fell upon them. Here and there the reapers were at work; and in the fields under the scythe the laborers were seen, swinging rhythmically as they swept the huge, wing-shaped blade over the surface of the ground.

After a drive of two hours, the carriage turned to the left, passed a windmill in motion—a gray, melancholy wreck, half rotten and condemned, the last survivor of the old mills—and then entered a pretty courtyard, and drew up before a gay little house, a celebrated inn of the district.

The landlady, who was named *La Belle Alphonsine,* came smiling to the door, and extended her hand to the two ladies, who were hesitating at the carriage step, which was awkwardly high.

On the margin of the lawn, beneath the shade of some apple trees, a party of strangers were already breakfasting in a tent; they were Parisians returning from Étretat, and the sound of voices and laughter and the rattle of dishes could be heard in the house.

All the large halls being occupied, they had to dine in a private room. Monsieur Roland suddenly saw some shrimp nets hanging on the wall.

"Ah, ha!" he cried, "do they fish for prawns here?"

"Yes," replied Beausire, "this is the very spot where they take more than on any other part of the coast."

"The devil! Let us go there after breakfast!"

It was ascertained that it was low water at three o'clock, and it was resolved that all the party should pass the afternoon on the rocks looking for shrimps.

They ate sparingly, to avoid a rush of blood to the head when they put their feet in the water. They wished, also, to reserve their appetites for dinner, which was ordered on a grand scale, to be ready at six when they returned.

Roland could not control his impatience. He wanted to buy the special apparatus for this kind of fishing, which resembles very much the nets used to catch butterflies in the fields.

Alphonsine, still smiling, lent them the nets; then she assisted the ladies in improvising a costume, so as to avoid wetting their dresses; she lent them some petticoats, thick worsted stockings, and bathing slippers. The men took off their boots, and replaced them with some wooden shoes purchased from the local cobbler.

They started out, net on shoulder and basket on back. Madame Rosémilly was charming in this costume, with an unexpected, rustic, bold style of beauty.

The petticoat borrowed from Alphonsine, coquettishly raised and held by a few stitches, so as to enable the wearer to run and leap, without fear, among the rocks, displayed the well-formed ankle of a woman at once agile and strong. She had found, to cover her head, an immense gardener's hat of yellow straw, with an enormous brim, which she turned up on one side with a sprig of tamarisk, which gave her the dauntless air of a dashing mousquetaire.

Jean, since receiving his legacy, had asked himself every day whether he should marry her or not. Each time he saw her he decided to make her his wife; but when he was alone he thought that by waiting he would have time to reflect. She was not as rich as he was now, for she had an income of only twelve thousand francs a year, but the principal was invested in real estate, in farms, and lots in Havre, on the docks, and this might, in time, be worth a large sum. Their fortunes, thus, were almost equal, and the young widow certainly pleased him very much.

As he now saw her walking before him, he thought, "Well, I must decide. Beyond question, I could not do better."

They followed the slope of a little valley, descending from the village to the cliff, and the cliff at the end of this valley was nearly three hundred feet above the sea. Framed by green banks descending to right and left of it, a spacious watery triangle, silvery blue in the sunlight, could be seen, and a scarcely perceptible sail looked like an insect on its surface. The sky, filled with radiance, blended with the water so that the eye could not distinguish a dividing line, and the two ladies, who walked in advance of the three men, cast on this clear horizon the clear-cut outline of their compact figures.

Jean, with ardent glance, saw speeding before

him the well-turned ankle, the supple waist, and the enticing hat of Madame Rosémilly. Her swift motion stimulated his eagerness and impelled him to those decisive steps which the timid and irresolute are apt to take abruptly. The warm air, in which was blended the odor of the coast, of the gorse, the clover, the grasses, and the marine odor of the rocks uncovered by the tide, intoxicated his senses still further, and he became a little more decided every second at each step, at every look he cast on the graceful outline of the young woman. He decided to hesitate no longer, but to tell her that he loved her, and wanted to marry her. The fishing party would help him; it would render a *tête-à tête* more easy, and, besides, it would furnish a pretty background, a pretty scene for words of love, with their feet in a basin of limpid water, as they watched the long feelers of the shrimps darting through the seaweed.

When they reached the end of the valley at the edge of the bluff, they perceived a little path that ran down the cliff; and beneath them, about halfway between the sea and the foot of the precipice, a wondrous chaos of enormous rocks that had fallen or been hurled down, heaped one on the other on a kind of grassy, broken plain, that disappeared toward the south, and which had been formed by ancient landslips. On this long strip of brushwood and turf, shaken down, one might say, by volcanic action, the fallen rocks resembled the ruins of a great vanished city, that, once on a time, had looked down on the ocean, itself dominated by the white and endless wall of the cliff.

"How beautiful!" said Madame Rosémilly, pausing.

Jean joined her, and with beating heart offered his hand to guide her down the narrow stairway cut in the cliff.

They went on head, while Beausire, straightening himself on his short legs, held out his bent arm to Madame Roland, who grew dizzy at sight of the abyss beneath her.

Roland and Pierre came last; and the doctor had to support his father, who was so overcome by dizziness that he sat down, and slid thus from step to step.

The young people at the head of the party went rapidly, and suddenly caught sight of a spring of clear water spurting from a little hole in the cliff, by the side of a wooden bench which formed a resting place about the middle of the slope. The water at first spread into a basin about the size of a washhand bowl, which it had excavated for itself, and then, falling in a cascade of about two feet in height, flowed across the path where a carpet of cress had grown, and then disappeared in the reeds and grass, across the upheaved plain on which were the rocks.

"Oh, how thirsty I am!" cried Madame Rosémilly.

But how could they drink? She tried to scoop up some water in her hands, but it escaped between her fingers. Jean had a bright idea; he placed a stone in the road, and she knelt on it to drink from the spring itself, which was now on a level with her mouth.

When she raised her head, covered with glittering drops sprinkled by thousands over her face, her hair, her eyelashes, Jean, bending toward her, whispered:

"How pretty you are!"

She replied in the tone one assumes in scolding a child:

"Will you hold your tongue!"

These words were their first attempt at flirtation.

"Come," said Jean, very much discomfited, "let us be off before they overtake us."

She perceived, indeed, that Captain Beausire was quite close to them. He was descending backward in order to support Madame Roland with both hands, while, higher up and farther away, M. Roland, in a sitting posture, was dragging himself down by his feet and elbows with the speed of a tortoise, and Pierre went before him to superintend his movements.

The path became less steep, and now formed a sloping road that skirted the enormous blocks that had formerly fallen from the cliff. Madame Rosémilly and Jean began to run, and were soon on the shingle. They crossed it to gain the rocks, which stretched out in a long flat surface covered with seaweed, amid which gleamed innumerable patches of water. The tide was very low beyond this slimy surface of glistening green and black wrack.

Jean rolled up his trousers to the knee, and his sleeves to the elbow, so as to go into the water without fear of getting wet, and cried "Forward," as he boldly leaped into the first pool that presented itself.

With more prudence, though with equal determination to wade into the water at once, the young woman went round the narrow basin with timid steps, for she slipped on the slimy weeds.

"Do you see anything?" she said.

"Yes, I see your face reflected in the water."

"If you see only that, you will not have any fishing to boast of."

He said in a tender voice:

"Ah, that is what I should prefer to capture above all things!"

She laughed.

"Try, then, and you'll see how it slips through your net."

"Well, if you would like——"

"I would like to see you catch some prawns—and nothing more—just at present."

"You are cruel. Let us go farther; there is nothing here."

He offered her his hand to steady her on the greasy rocks. She leaned on it rather timidly; and he, all at once, felt his being invaded by love's vibrations, filled with longing, as if the passion that had lain dormant in him had waited for that day to burst forth.

They soon reached a deeper pool where, beneath the rippling water that reached the distant sea by an invisible channel, long, fine seaweed of bright colors, like pink and green hair, floated as if it were swimming.

Madame Rosémilly exclaimed:

"Look, look, I see one—a big one, a very big one, down there!"

He perceived it in turn and went down into the pool, although the water wet him to the waist.

But the creature, moving its long feelers, quietly retreated before the net. Jean drove it toward the wrack, sure of catching it there. When it found itself blockaded, it made a sudden dash over the net, crossed the pool, and disappeared.

The young woman, who was eagerly watching his attempt, could not refrain from crying:

"Ah, clumsy!"

He was vexed, and, without thinking, dragged his net through a pool full of weeds. As he raised it to the surface, he saw in it three large transparent prawns, which had been dragged unexpectedly from their invisible hiding place.

He presented them in triumph to Madame Rosémilly, who dared not touch them for fear of the sharp, dentated point that arms their heads.

At last she decided to take them; and, seizing them between two of her fingers, she placed them, one after the other, in her basket, with some seaweed to keep them alive. Then, on finding a shallower piece of water, she stepped into it with hesitating steps, and catching her breath as the cold struck her feet, began to catch shrimps herself. She was skillful and cunning, with a supple wrist and a sportsman's instinct. Almost at every cast she brought out some victims, whom she deceived and surprised by the ingenious slowness with which she swept the pool.

Jean was catching nothing; but he followed her step by step, touched her dress, bent over her, pretended to be in despair at his awkwardness, and wished her to teach him.

"Show me how," he said, "show me!"

Then as their two faces were reflected, one beside the other, in the clear water, which the deep-growing seaweed formed into a limpid mirror, Jean smiled at the face so near his which looked up to him from below, and at times threw to it, from the tips of his fingers, a kiss which seemed to fall on it.

"Oh, how tiresome you are," the young woman said. "My dear fellow, never do two things at the same time."

He replied:

"I am only doing one. I love you."

She drew herself up and said in a serious tone:

"Come, now! What is the matter with you for the last ten minutes? Have you lost your head?"

"No, I have not lost my head. I love you, and at last dare to tell you so."

They were now standing in the pool of sea-water that rose nearly to their knees, and, with their dripping hands leaning on their nets, looked into the depth of each other's eyes.

She resumed in a playful but rather annoyed tone:

"You have taken a wrong time to speak to me. Could you not wait another day, and not spoil my fishing?"

He murmured:

"Pardon me, but I could not keep silence. I have loved you for a long time. To-day you have completely turned my head."

Then she seemed at once to take her resolution, and to resign herself to talk business and renounce amusement.

"Let us sit on this rock," she said; "we shall be able to talk quietly."

They climbed on a rock a little higher; and when they were seated, side by side, their feet hanging down in the sunlight, she rejoined:

"My friend, you are no longer a child, and I am not a young girl. Both of us know what we are about, and can weigh all the consequences of our acts. If you decide to-day to declare your love to me, I suppose naturally you wish to marry me."

He had scarcely expected such a clear statement of the situation, and answered sheepishly:

"Why, yes!"

"Have you spoken to your father and mother?"

"No. I wished to know if you would accept me."

She extended to him her hand, which was still wet, and as he placed his own in it with fervor:

"I am willing," she said. "I believe you to be good and loyal. But do not forget that I would not displease your parents."

"Do you think that my mother has foreseen nothing, and that she would love you as she does if she did not desire a marriage between us?"

"Nevertheless, I am somewhat disturbed."

They were silent. On his part, he was astonished that she was so little disturbed and so sensible. He expected some pretty airs and graces, refusals which say yes, a whole coquettish comedy of love blended with fishing and the splashing of water. And it was all over; he felt himself bound and married in a score of words. They had nothing more to say now that they understood each other; and both remained somewhat embarrassed at what had passed so rapidly between them. and were even somewhat confused, not venturing to speak or to fish, not knowing what to do.

The voice of M. Roland came to the rescue.

"This way, this way, young people! Come and see Beausire. He is emptying the sea, the old rascal."

The captain, indeed, had marvellous success. Wet

up to the loins, he went from pool to pool, detecting
at a glance the best spots, and with a slow, sure
movement of his net searching every cavity beneath
the seaweed.

And the pretty, transparent prawns, of a light
gray color, danced about on the hollow of his hand
as he took them out of the net to fling them into his
basket.

Madame Rosémilly, surprised and delighted, kept
close beside him, imitating him as well as she could,
almost forgetting her promise and Jean, who was
dreamily following her, to abandon herself to the
childish pleasure of collecting the little creatures
beneath the floating grasses.

Roland suddenly broke the silence by exclaiming:
"Here is Madame Roland coming to join us."

At first she had remained with Pierre on the
beach, for neither of them had any desire to amuse
themselves by running over the rocks and splashing
themselves in the pools, and yet they hesitated
about remaining together. She was afraid of him,
and her son was afraid of her and of himself—
afraid of his cruelty which he could not master.

They sat down then beside each other on the
shingle, and in the warm sunshine tempered by
the sea air, in presence of the limitless horizon
of blue water with silver reflections, both thought
at the same time, "How pleasant it would have been
for us here, once upon a time!"

She dared not speak to Pierre, for she knew that
his answer would be harsh; he dared not speak to
his mother, for he knew, too, that in spite of himself
he would speak rudely.

He poked among the round pebbles with his cane,

pushing and striking them. She had picked up three or four little stones, which she slowly and mechanically passed from one hand to the other. Her wandering glances presently discovered, in the middle of the field of seaweed before her, her son Jean fishing with Madame Rosémilly. She followed them with her eyes, watching their movements, and clearly comprehending with her maternal instinct that they were not talking in their usual manner. She saw them bending over side by side as they looked at each other in the water, standing up, face to face, when they questioned their hearts, and then climbing to a seat on the rock to converse with each other.

Their outlines stood out clearly defined on the horizon, looking like symbolic statues amid this wide expanse of sky, sea and cliff.

Pierre also looked at them, and a hard laugh escaped from his lips.

Without turning her head, Madame Roland said:

"What is the matter?"

Still with his sardonic smile, he replied:

"I'm taking a lesson. I am learning how men prepare themselves to be the dupes of women."

She gave a start of anger and revolt, exasperated at what she took to be his meaning.

"For whom do you mean that?"

"For Jean, by Jove. It is comical to see them."

She replied in a low voice, trembling with emotion:

"Oh, Pierre, how cruel you are! That woman is uprightness itself. Your brother could not choose better."

He laughed aloud, a forced, jesting laugh.

"Ha! ha! ha! Uprightness itself! All women are uprightness itself, and all husbands fools. Ha! ha! ha!"

She rose without replying and rapidly descended the shingly slope; and at the risk of slipping, falling into the holes concealed by the weeds, or of breaking her leg or arm, she went, without looking, almost at a run, across the pools straight toward her other son.

Jean, seeing her approach, cried to her:

"Well, mamma, have you made up your mind to join us?"

Without replying, she seized his arm, as to say, "Save me! Protect me!"

He saw her trouble, and in great surprise said:

"How pale you are! What is the matter?"

"I almost fell. I am timid on these rocks."

Jean guided her, supported her, explained the sport, and tried to interest her. But as she scarcely listened, and as he felt an intense need of confiding in some one, he drew her aside, and said, in a low voice:

"Guess what I have done."

"Why—why—I cannot!"

"Guess."

"I—I cannot."

"Well, then, I have told Madame Rosémilly that I wanted to marry her."

She made no reply; her head was in a whirl, her soul distressed so that she could hardly understand.

She repeated:

"Marry her?"

"Yes. Have I done right? She is charming, is she not?"

"Yes, charming. You have done right."

"Then you approve?"

"Yes, I approve."

"How oddly you say that! One might fancy that —that you were not pleased."

"Oh, yes. I am—pleased."

"Sure?"

"Quite sure."

To prove it, she took him in her arms and kissed him with a mother's fondest kisses.

Then, when she had wiped her eyes, which had filled with tears, she perceived down on the beach a figure lying face downward, looking like a corpse, with its face on the shingle. It was the other brother, Pierre, who was brooding in despair.

She led her "little Jean" farther away still, quite to the water's edge, and they talked long about the marriage which lay so near his heart.

The rising tide drove them toward the others, whom they rejoined, and the whole party ascended the beach to the cliff, arousing Pierre, who pretended to be asleep. They sat long at dinner, which was moistened with plenty of wine.

CHAPTER VII

THE THUNDERBOLT

As they drove home all the men except Jean were sleepy. Beausire and Roland would drop their heads every five minutes on some neighboring shoulder, which shook them off with a shrug. They then drew themselves up, stopped snoring, opened their eyes, and said, "Very fine weather," and almost immediately fell over asleep again on the other side. When they reached Havre their drowsiness was so profound that they could scarcely shake it off; and Beausire even refused to go up to Jean's rooms, where tea was awaiting them. They put him down at his own door.

The young lawyer for the first time was going to sleep in his new apartments; and he rejoiced, with a somewhat puerile joy, at the opportunity of showing, this very evening, to the woman he was engaged to, the rooms she would soon occupy.

The servant girl had gone. Madame Roland had declared that she would boil the water and serve the tea herself, as she did not like servants to sit up, for fear of fire.

No one except Madame Roland, her son, and the workmen had yet entered the rooms, so that the surprise might be complete when it was seen how pretty they were.

When they entered the vestibule Jean begged them to wait. He wished to light the candles and lamps; and he left Madame Rosémilly, his father, and brother in the dark till he exclaimed "Enter!" and threw wide the folding doors.

The glass corridor, lighted by a chandelier and glass globes of various colors concealed amid the palms, india-rubber trees, and flowers, seemed at first like a scene in a theatre. There was a pause of admiration, and Roland, astonished at this luxury, felt a desire to clap his hands as at a transformation scene.

They next entered the first reception room, a small

room with hangings of old gold to match the chairs. The large room for the reception of clients was very simple, of pale salmon color, and had an air of elegant severity.

Jean sat down in the armchair before his book-laden desk, and in a grave, rather forced voice, said:

"Yes, madame, the authorities are explicit, and, with the assent which I announced to you, give me absolute assurance that within three months the affair of which we spoke will be satisfactorily settled."

He looked at Madame Rosémilly, who smiled as she looked at Madame Roland, and the latter, taking her hand, pressed it warmly.

Jean was radiant, and, cutting a schoolboy caper, cried:

"How well the voice carries! This room would be excellent to plead a case in."

He began to declaim:

"If humanity alone, if that sentiment of natural sympathy which we feel for all suffering, was to be the ground of the acquittal which we ask from you, we should appeal, gentlemen of the jury, to your pity, to your hearts as fathers and as men; but we have on our side justice, and it is the question of justice alone that we shall bring before you."

Pierre looked at the rooms which might have been his, and was irritated at the child's play of his brother, considering him decidedly silly and witless.

Madame Roland opened a door to the right.

"This is the bedroom," she said.

In furnishing it she had lavished all her maternal affection. The hangings were of Rouen cretonne made to imitate the old Norman material. A Louis Quinze design, a shepherdess in a medallion held by the kissing bills of two doves, gave the walls, curtains, bed and chairs a coquettishly rustic air that was very attractive.

"How charming!" cried Madame Rosémilly, who became rather serious as she entered this room.

"Do you like it?" asked Jean.

"Excessively!"

"If you only knew how pleased I am!" They exchanged a momentary glance of trusting affection.

Still, she was slightly embarrassed, somewhat confused, in this sleeping room which was to be her nuptial chamber. She had noticed, on entering, that the bed was very large, a genuine family affair, chosen by Madame Roland, who had without doubt foreseen and desired the approaching marriage of her son; and this maternal foresight gave her pleasure, for it seemed to say they were expecting her to be one of the family.

When they returned to the reception room, Jean suddenly opened the door to the left, showing the round dining-room, with its three windows and its Japanese decorations. Mother and son had here indulged their fancy without restraint. This room, with its bamboo furniture, images, plaques, gold-embroidered silks, its bead curtain looking like drops of water strung together, its fans nailed to the walls to hold up tapestry, its screens, its swords, its masques, its storks with real feathers, all its little knick-knacks of porcelain, wood, ivory, paper, mother-of-pearl and bronze, had that pretentious, stiff look which awkward hands and ignorant eyes gave to things which require the highest degree of tact, taste and artistic education. Yet this room was the most admired. Pierre alone took some exception, with a rather bitter irony, which wounded his brother.

The table was decked with fruits in pyramids and cakes piled up in various forms.

No one was very hungry. They ate some fruit, and nibbled at the pastry, and, after the lapse of an hour, Madame Rosémilly demanded permission to retire.

It was decided that M. Roland should escort her to her door, and they started at once; while Madame Roland, in the absence of the servant, cast a housewife's eye over the apartment to see that nothing was lacking.

"Must I come back for you?" Roland asked.

She replied after some hesitation:

"No, my dear, go home and go to bed. Pierre will take me home."

As soon as they had left she blew out the wax candles, locked up the cakes, the sugar, and the liqueurs in a cupboard, the key of which she gave to Jean. Then she went into the bedroom, turned down the bed, and saw if the carafe was filled with fresh water and the window securely closed.

Pierre and Jean remained in the smaller reception room, the latter still sore at his brother's criticism on his taste, the former more and more irritated at seeing his brother in these apartments.

They both sat down and smoked without speaking. Suddenly Pierre exclaimed:

"By George, the widow looked pretty well tired out this evening; excursions do not suit her."

Jean felt himself being overcome by one of those

sudden and furious fits of wrath which seize good-natured men when their feelings are wounded.

His breath failed him, so strong was his emotion, as he stammered out:

"For the future do not let me hear you say 'the widow' when you are speaking of Madame Rosémilly."

Pierre turned on him haughtily:

"You are giving me orders, it seems. Are you becoming crazy?"

Jean drew himself up:

"I am not becoming crazy, but I have had enough of your manners toward me."

Pierre gave a grin.

"Toward you? Are you going to fight Madame Rosémilly's battles?"

"Madame Rosémilly is going to be my wife!"

The other laughed still louder.

"Ha! ha! Very good. Now I see why I must not call her 'the widow.' You have, however, taken a very odd way of announcing your marriage to me."

"No jesting—I won't have it. Do you hear? I won't have it!"

Jean came up to him, pale, his voice trembling, exasperated at his ironical way of talking of the woman whom he loved and had chosen.

But Pierre suddenly became just as furious; all his impotent wrath, all the bitterness that he had kept down, all the rebellious feelings he had crushed, and all his silent despair, flew to his head like a congestion of the brain.

"You dare to talk thus? You dare? Be silent, I say! Those are my orders, mine, do you hear? Those are mine!"

Jean, surprised at this violence, was silent for a few seconds, searching, in that confusion of mind into which rage throws us, for something, some sentence, some word, which would pierce his brother to the heart.

He struggled to gain the mastery over himself in order to make his words tell; and, speaking slowly to make them more cutting, he resumed:

"I have known for a long time that you were jealous of me; ever since the day when you began to say 'the widow' because you knew it annoyed me."

Pierre burst into one of his usual peals of harsh and insulting laughter.

"Ha! ha! *Mon Dieu!* Jealous of you? I jealous of you? I! I! Why? Jealous of what?— your brains or your looks?"

Jean felt that he had touched the wound to the quick.

"Yes. You are jealous of me, jealous since childhood; and you became uncontrollable when you saw this lady prefer me, while she would have nothing to say to you."

"I!—I jealous of you! On account of that silly doll—that plump little goose!"

Jean saw his blows told, and continued:

"How about the day you tried to outrow me in the *Pearl?* And all that you said in her presence, to show yourself off? Why, you are dying of jealousy! When this fortune came to me you became frantic, you detested me, and showed it in every way. You have made us all miserable. There is not an hour when you do not give vent to the anger that is choking you."

Pierre closed his fists in rage, and in an irresistible longing to rush at his brother and seize him by the throat.

"Oh, keep quiet for once! Don't speak of that fortune."

Jean cried:

"Why, jealousy is exuding from every pore of your skin. You cannot say a word to my father, my mother, or me, without letting it burst out. You pretend to despise me, because you are jealous! You pick quarrels with everybody, because you are jealous! And now when I am rich, you can contain yourself no longer; you have become venomous, you torture our mother as if it were her fault!"

Pierre had retreated to the mantelpiece, his mouth half open, his eyes dilated, a prey to one of those paroxysms of rage which lead men to crime.

He repeated in a lower, trembling tone:

"Silence, I say, silence!"

"No! For a long time I have wanted to tell you what I thought. You have given me an opportunity: so much the worse for you! I love a certain woman; you know it, and ridicule her in my presence. You drive me to extremity: so much the worse for you! But I will crush your viper fangs. I will force you to respect me."

"Respect you—you!"

"Yes, me!"

"Respect you—you! who have dishonored us all by your greed!"

"What do you say? Say it again! Say it again!"

"I say one does not accept the fortune of one man when one passes for the son of another."

Jean remained motionless, without comprehending, dazed at the insinuation of which he had a presentiment.

"What! You say—— Say it once more!"

"I say all the world is chattering, all the world is gossiping, that you are the son of the man who left you his fortune. Well, a decent man does not accept wealth which dishonors his mother."

"Pierre—Pierre—Pierre—do you know what you are saying? Is it you—you, who utter such an infamy?"

"Yes, it is I. Do not you see that I am dying of grief for more than a month; that I pass my nights without sleeping, and my days in hiding myself like a wild beast; that I do not know what I am saying or doing, nor what will become of me, so wretched am I, so crazed with shame and grief? For what was at first a surmise is knowledge now."

"Pierre, be silent! Mamma is in the next room. Remember, she may hear us—she does hear us!"

But he had to pour out his heart. He told everything, his suspicions, his arguments, his struggles, his conviction, and the story of the portrait that had again disappeared.

He spoke in short, detached sentences, almost incoherently, like a person who is crazy.

He seemed to have forgotten Jean, and his mother in the next room. He spoke as though no one heard him, because he had to speak, because he had suffered so much, and had so sternly repressed his sorrow. But now it had broken bounds.

Jean, distracted and almost convinced all at once by his brother's vehement emotion, leaned against the door, behind which he guessed that their mother had heard them.

She could not get out without passing through the parlor. As she had not done so, it was because she dared not.

Suddenly, stamping his foot, Pierre exclaimed:

"Oh, what a beast I am to have talked like this!"

And he rushed bareheaded to the staircase.

The noise of the street door, as it closed with a bang, roused Jean from the deep stupor into which he had sunk. Some seconds passed, seconds longer than some hours, and his mind was benumbed as in the dullness of idiocy. He felt that he would have to think and act before long; but he waited without even the wish to understand or know or recall anything, through fear, weakness and cowardice. He belonged to that class of temporizers who put everything off till to-morrow; and when it was necessary that he should take a resolution on the spot, he always instinctively sought to gain a few moments.

But the profound silence which now surrounded him after the loud exclamations of Pierre, this sudden silence of the walls and the furniture, with the bright gleam of the six candles and two lamps, struck him with such a shock that he longed to run away as his brother had done.

Then he roused himself and tried to think.

He had never encountered any difficulty in his life. He was one of those men who let themselves drift like running water. He had been a good scholar in the classroom to avoid punishment, and had finished his legal studies with regularity because his life was calm. Everything in the world appeared to him natural, without otherwise awakening his attention.

He had a temperamental love of order, decency and quiet, and his mind had no kinks in it; and in face of this catastrophe he was like a man who falls into the water without ever having learned to swim.

At first he attempted to doubt his brother. Had he lied from hatred or from jealousy?

And yet, how could he have been such a wretch as to speak thus of their mother, if he had not himself been frenzied by despair? And Jean still heard in his ears, still saw with his eyes, still felt in his nerves, in his inmost flesh, certain words, certain cries of suffering, some intonations and gestures of Pierre, that were so full of anguish as to be irresistible, as irrefutable as certainty.

He was too crushed to move or exert his will. His distress became intolerable; and he felt that behind the door was his mother, who had heard all and was waiting for him.

What was she doing? Not a movement, not a stir, not a breath, not a sigh, revealed the presence of a human being behind that door. Had she fled? But how? If she had fled, she must have leaped from the window into the street.

A start of terror seized him so sudden and so imperious that he burst open, rather than opened, the door, and rushed into his bedroom.

It seemed empty. A single candle on the dressing table lighted it.

Jean dashed to the window; it was fastened, and the shutters closed. He returned and scrutinized with anxious looks all the dark corners. He saw that the bed curtains were drawn; he ran and opened them. His mother was stretched on the couch, her face buried in the pillow, which she drew over her ears in order to hear no more.

At first he thought she was suffocated; then, taking her by the shoulders, he turned her round, without her ever letting go of the pillow which hid her face, and which she bit to keep from crying aloud.

But the touch of this stiffened body and of those arms clasping the pillow conveyed to him the shock of her unspeakable anguish. The energy and force with which she held, by hands and teeth, the feather pillow over her mouth, her ears, and her eyes, that he might not see her or speak to her, made him understand by sympathy to what point it is possible to suffer. His heart, his simple heart, was torn with pity. He was not a judge, not even a compassionate judge; he was a man full of weakness, and a son full of tenderness. He recalled nothing the other had said, he did not argue, he did not discuss; he simply touched with his two hands the inert body of his mother, and, as he could not pull the pillow from her face, he cried, as he kissed her dress:

"Mamma, mamma, my poor mamma! Look at me!"

She would have seemed lifeless, if an almost imperceptible shiver, a vibration as of a stretched cord, had not quivered through all her limbs. He repeated:

"Mamma, mamma, listen to me. It is not true. I am sure it is not true."

A spasm of suffocation was followed by sudden sobs in the pillow. Then all her nerves relaxed, the rigid muscles became pliant, the fingers unclasped and let go the pillow, and Jean raised it from her face.

She was very pale, very white, and tears were falling from her closed eyelids. Throwing his arms round her neck, he kissed her eyes with long, tender kisses that were moistened with her tears, and kept saying:

"Mamma, dear mamma, I am sure it is not true. Don't cry. I know it is not true."

She rose and sat up; she looked at him, and with one of those efforts of courage which are required, in certain cases, in order to kill one's self, she said to him:

"No; it is true, my child!"

They remained in silence, face to face. For some moments she still seemed suffocating, stretching her neck, and throwing back her head to breathe. At length she mastered herself and resumed:

"It is true, my child. Why tell a lie? It is true. You would not believe me if I did lie."

She looked like a madwoman. Overcome with terror, he fell on his knees beside the bed.

"Oh, be still, mamma, be still!"

She rose up with appalling resolution and energy.

"I have nothing more to tell you, my child. Farewell!"

And she walked toward the door. He seized her with both arms, crying:

"What are you doing, mamma? Where are you going?"

"I do not know. How can I know? I have nothing more to do, for I am all alone."

She struggled to escape; and he, still holding her,

could find only one word to say, over and over again:

"Mamma, mamma, mamma!"

In the midst of her efforts to break from his clasp, she said:

"No, no, I am no more your mother! I am nothing more to you, nor to any one, nothing more, nothing more! You have no longer father or mother, my poor child! Farewell!"

He understood now that if he let her go he would never see her again; so, lifting her in his arms, he carried her to an armchair, and forced her to sit there. Then, kneeling, and forming a chain around her with his arms, he said:

"You shall not leave here, mamma. I love you and will keep you with me. I will keep you always. You belong to me!"

In a low, weak voice she replied:

"No, my poor child, that is not possible. This evening you weep; to-morrow you would turn me out. You would not pardon me, either."

He answered with such an outburst of sincere love: "What, I? How little you know me!" that she gave a cry, took his head by the hair with both hands, pulled him toward her, and kissed his face wildly.

Then she remained motionless, her cheek against her son's cheek, feeling through his thick beard the warmth of his young life, and said, low in his ear:

"No, my little Jean. You would not pardon me to-morrow. You think so, and you are mistaken. You have pardoned me this evening, and that pardon has saved my life; but you must not see me again."

He repeated, clasping her tighter:

"Mamma, do not say that!"

"Yes, little one, I must go away. I do not know when, nor how I shall act, nor what I shall say. But it must be so. I would not dare to look at you or embrace you any more. Do you understand?"

Then in his turn he said, low in her ear:

"Darling mother, you will remain because I wish it, and have need of you. And you must swear to obey me, at once."

"No, my child."

"Oh, mamma, you must! Do you hear? You must!"

"No, my child, it is impossible. It would condemn us all to hell. I know, I have known for a month, what that torture is. You are softened at this moment; but when it is past, when you look at me as Pierre does, when you recall what I have told you—— Oh, my little Jean—remember—remember that I am your mother!"

"You must not leave me, mamma. I have only you."

"But think, my son, we can never see each other again without blushing, both of us; without my feeling ready to die of shame, and without my eyes falling when you look at me."

"That is not true, mamma."

"Yes, yes, yes. It is true! Oh, I understand all the struggles of your poor brother, all of them, from the first day! Now, when I hear his step in the house, my heart leaps as if it would burst my breast; when I hear his voice, I feel as if I would faint. I had you still! You! Now I have you no longer.

Oh, my little Jean, do you think I could live between you two?"

"Yes, mamma. I will love you so much that you will think of it no more."

"Oh, if that was possible!"

"It is possible!"

"How do you suppose I can forget it, with you and your brother here? Will neither of you think of it?"

"I will not, I swear!"

"You will think of it every hour of the day."

"No, I swear it. And then, listen, if you go away, I'll pick a quarrel and get myself killed."

She was distracted at the childish threat, and clasped Jean fondly, as she caressed him with passionate tenderness.

He continued:

"I love you more than you think, much more, much more. Come, be reasonable. Try to stay here only a week. Will you promise me a week? You cannot refuse me that!"

She laid her hands on Jean's shoulders, and holding him at arm's length:

"My child, let us be calm, and not be carried away by emotion. Let me speak to you, in the first place. If I should hear, once only, from your lips what I have heard for a month from your brother's mouth; if I were, once only, to read in your eyes what I read in his; if I were to surmise, by a mere word, a mere look, that I am as hateful to you as to him— one hour afterward, you understand, one hour afterward, I would leave forever."

"Mamma, I swear to you——"

"Let me speak. For a month I have suffered all

that can be suffered. From the moment when I comprehended that your brother, my other son, suspected me, and that he was, minute by minute, coming nearer to the truth, every moment of my life has been a martyrdom impossible to describe."

Her voice was so full of anguish that it brought tears to the eyes of Jean.

He attempted to kiss her, but she repulsed him.

"Let me alone. Listen—I have so much to tell you, to make you understand. But you will not understand—that is, if I should stay—I should have to—— No, I cannot!"

"Speak, mamma, speak!"

"I will, then. At least, I will not have deceived you. You want me to stay with you, do you not? For me to stay, for us to be able to see each other still, to speak to each other, to meet each other all day in the house—for I dare not now open a door for fear of finding your brother behind it—for all this, it is necessary not for you to pardon me—nothing hurts more than a pardon—but that you bear me no ill will for what I have done. You must feel yourself so strong, so different from all the world, as to say to yourself that you are not the son of Roland without blushing at the avowal and without despising me. I have suffered enough—I have suffered too much. I can bear no more. No, I can bear no more. And I have suffered, not just lately, but for a long while. You will never be able to understand. In order that we may still live together, still kiss each other, my little Jean, say to yourself, that, even though it was an unlawful union, I was even more his wife, his true wife; that I am not ashamed of it in my heart; that I regret nothing;

I still love him, dead as he is; that I shall love him always, that I loved none but him; that he was all my life, all my joy, all my hope, all my consolation, all, all, all to me, ah, for so long! Listen, little one. Before God, who hears me, I would have had nothing good in life, if I had not met him—nothing; never affection, never kindness, never one of those hours that make us so regret that we grow old—nothing! I owe to him everything. I had only him in the world, and then you two, your brother and you. Without you it would have been void, black and void as night. I would have loved nothing, known nothing, desired nothing—I would not have even wept; for I have wept, my little Jean—yes, I have wept since we came here. I gladly gave myself to him, body and soul, forever; and for ten years I was his wife, as he was my husband before God, who made us for each other. And then I perceived that he loved me less. He was always good and thoughtful, but I was no longer to him what I had been. It was over. Oh, how I wept! What a wretched deceiver is life! Nothing lasts! And we came here, and I never saw him again; he never came here. He promised in all his letters—I always expected him—and I never saw him again—and now he is dead. But he still loved us, for he thought of you. As for me, I shall love him to my last breath, and will never deny him; and I love you because you are his child, and I could not be ashamed of him before you. Do you understand? I could not! If you wish me to stay, you must accept the fact that you are his son, and me must talk of him sometimes, and you must love him a little, and we must think of him when we look at each other. If you will not, if you cannot do this, farewell, my little Jean, it is impossible for us to remain together. I will do as you decide."

Jean replied, in a gentle voice:

"Stay, mamma."

She clasped him in her arms, and began to weep afresh; then, cheek pressed to cheek, she resumed:

"Yes, but Pierre, what can we do with him?"

Jean whispered:

"We will find something. You cannot live in the same house with him any longer."

The remembrance of her eldest son shook her with anguish.

"No, I cannot, I cannot."

And, flinging herself on Jean's breast, she cried in distress of soul:

"Save me from him, save me, little Jean. Do something. I do not know—find—save me!"

"Yes, mamma; I will see about it."

"At once—you must—at once—do not leave me! I am in fear of him—such fear!"

"Yes, I will find something, I promise you."

"But quickly, quickly! You do not know how I feel when I see him."

Then she whispered low in his ear:

"Keep me here, at your rooms."

He hesitated, reflected, and with his positive good sense comprehended the danger of such an arrangement.

But he had to reason with her for a long time, and to discuss and combat with definite arguments her terror and distraction.

"Only this evening," she said. "Only to-night.

You can tell Roland to-morrow that I did not feel well."

"That is not possible, as Pierre went home. Come, take courage. I will arrange everything, after to-morrow, I promise you. I will be at the house at nine o'clock. Come, put on your bonnet; I will take you home."

"I will do as you wish," she said, with childish resignation, in timid gratitude.

She attempted to rise, but the shock had been too great—she could not yet stand up.

He gave her some water to drink and some salts to smell, and bathed her temples with vinegar.

At length she was able to walk, and took his arm. Three o'clock was striking when they passed the town hall.

At the door of their dwelling he kissed her and said, "Adieu, mamma. Courage!"

With furtive steps she mounted the silent stairs, reached her room, undressed rapidly, and, with the revived emotions of other days, crept into the bed where Roland was snoring.

Pierre alone in the house was not asleep, and heard her return.

CHAPTER VIII

PIERRE'S RESOLUTION

On returning to his room, Jean flung himself on a couch; for the grief and anxiety which inspired in his brother a longing to run away, and fly like a

hunted thing, had a different effect on his phleg-
matic nature, and crippled his every limb. He felt
himself weak beyond the power of movement, beyond the power of getting into bed; weak in body
and soul, crushed and despairing. He was not, as
Pierre was, stricken in the purity of his filial love,
in that secret dignity in which proud spirits wrap
themselves; he was overwhelmed by a stroke of
fate, that at the same time menaced his dearest interests.

When at length his mind grew calm, when his
thoughts had cleared themselves like troubled water,
he faced the situation that had just been revealed
to him. If he had learned the secret of his birth in
any other manner, he would assuredly have been indignant and experienced deep grief; but after his
quarrel with his brother, and after the violent and
brutal revelation that shook his nerves, the poignant
emotion of his mother's confession left him without
energy to revolt. The shock received by his sensitive nature had been strong enough to sweep away,
in irresistible commiseration, all the prejudices and
all the sacred susceptibilities of natural morality.

Besides, he was not a man made to resist. He
did not like to struggle against any one, still less
against himself, and therefore he became resigned;
and then, by an instinctive inclination, an innate
love of repose and of a pleasant, tranquil life, he
began to be disquieted about the annoyances which
would arise about and around him, and affect him
at the same time. He saw that they were inevitable;
and, to remove them, he resolved on superhuman
efforts of energy and activity. It was necessary
that the difficulty should be met at once, the very

next day; for he had at times that imperious need of immediate action that constitutes all the strength of the weak, who are incapable of a protracted power of will. His lawyer's turn of mind, trained, besides, to disentangle and study complicated situations and questions of domestic order in disturbed households, at once discovered all the immediate consequences of his brother's state of mind. In spite of himself, he faced the results from a professional point of view, as if he were arranging the future relations of clients after some moral catastrophe.

Beyond question constant contact with Pierre was becoming impossible. He could easily avoid him by remaining in his rooms, but it was impossible that their mother should continue to reside under the same roof as her elder son.

He meditated at length, as he lay motionless on the cushions, forming and rejecting plans, without finding anything to satisfy him.

Then suddenly this idea struck him: "Could an honorable man keep the fortune he had received?"

He was at first impelled to say, "No," and resolved to give it to some charity. It was hard, nevertheless. He would sell his furniture and work like any one else, as all have to work when beginning their career. This manly and painful determination roused his courage, and he rose and leaned his forehead against the window pane. He had been poor; he would be poor again. After all, it would not kill him. He looked at the gas lamp opposite, on the other side of the street. Then, as a belated woman passed by on the sidewalk, he suddenly thought of Madame Rosémilly, and felt a tightening at the heart. All the overwhelming consequences of his decision came to his mind. He would have to renounce his marriage with her, renounce happiness, renounce everything. Could he do this, now that he was engaged to her? She had accepted him with the knowledge that he was rich. If he were poor she would still accept him; but was he justified in asking her, in compelling her to this sacrifice? Would it not be better to keep this money as a trust, which he would later restore to the indigent?

In his soul, where egotism assumed the mask of probity, all these disguised interests struggled and fought. His first scruples gave way to ingenious arguments, then came again to the front and were once more removed.

He sat down again, seeking some deciding motive, some all-powerful pretext, to remove his uncertainty and convince his inborn integrity. A score of times already had he asked himself the question: "Since I am this man's son, since I know it and accept the situation, is it not natural to accept also his legacy?" This argument, however, could not stifle the "No" whispered by his deepest conscience.

Then he suddenly thought: "Since I am not the son of him whom I thought my father, I can accept nothing from him, neither in his life nor after his death. It would be neither noble nor just; it would be robbing my brother."

This new way of looking at it comforted him and quieted his conscience, and he went back to the window.

"Yes," he said to himself, "I must renounce the inheritance of my family. I must leave it whole and entire to Pierre, since I am not the son of his father. That is but just. Is it not just then, also, that I keep my own father's money?"

Recognizing the fact, then, that he could receive no benefit from Roland's fortune, having decided to relinquish it absolutely, he was willing and resigned himself to keep the fortune left by Maréchal; for, if he rejected both, he would find himself reduced to simple beggary.

This delicate affair being settled, he returned to the question of Pierre's presence in the family. How could he get rid of him? He was despairing of finding a practical solution, when the whistle of a steamer coming into port seemed to reply, by suggesting to him an idea.

With this thought he stretched himself upon his bed without undressing and dozed till daylight.

About nine o'clock he went out to see if he could carry out his project. After making some inquiries and a few calls, he betook himself to the house of his parents. His mother was waiting for him in her bedroom.

"If you had not come," she said, "I would never have dared to go down."

Roland was soon heard calling on the stairs:

"Nothing to eat to-day, eh? Confound it!"

There was no reply, so he roared:

"Josephine, confound it all! what are you about?"

The girl's voice came up from the depths of the basement:

"What is it, sir?"

"Where's your mistress?"

"She is upstairs with Monsieur Jean."

He raised his head toward the upper story, and shouted:

"Louise!"

Madame Roland half opened the door, and replied:

"Well?"

"Are we to have nothing to eat? Confound it!"

"We are coming, my dear."

She descended, and Jean followed.

Roland, when he saw the young man, cried:

"Ah, there you are! You are already tired of your lodgings?"

"No, father, but I wanted to chat with mamma this morning."

Jean advanced with outstretched hand, and when his fingers felt the paternal grasp of the old man, a strange, unforeseen emotion wrung his heart at the thought of a lasting separation and farewell.

Madame Roland inquired:

"Has not Pierre come?"

Her husband shrugged his shoulders.

"No, but never mind; he is always late. Let us begin without him."

She turned to Jean.

"You ought to go and look for him, my child. It hurts him when we do not wait for him."

The young man left the room. He mounted the stairs with the feverish resolution of a timid man who is going to fight a duel.

He knocked at the door. Pierre replied:

"Come in!"

He entered the room.

His brother was bending over the table and writing.

"Good-morning," said Jean.

Pierre rose.

"Good-morning."

And they shook hands as if nothing had happened.

"Are you not coming down to breakfast?"

"Well, the fact is, I have a great deal to do."

The voice of the older brother trembled, and his anxious eye asked the younger one what he was going to do.

"They are waiting for you."

"Oh, is—is our mother down there?"

"Yes. She herself sent me to look for you."

"Then I'll come down."

He hesitated at the dining-room door as to whether he should enter first. Then he opened it with a jerk, and saw his father and mother seated at table, opposite each other.

He went up to her without raising his eyes or pronouncing a word, and, bending toward her, offered her his forehead to kiss as he had done for some time past, instead of kissing her on the cheek as he did formerly. He guessed that her lips approached him, but he did not feel them on his forehead, and he straightened himself up with beating heart after this ghost of a kiss.

He asked himself: "What did they say after I left?"

Jean affectionately repeated the words "mother" and "dear mamma," and paid her great attention, handing her dishes and pouring out her wine. Pierre then understood that they had wept together, but he could not penetrate their thoughts. Did

Jean believe his mother guilty, or his brother a scoundrel?

All the reproaches which he had heaped on himself for having uttered the horrible charge assailed him afresh, choking his throat, closing his mouth, and preventing him from eating or speaking.

He was overcome, at this moment, by an intolerable desire to flee, to leave this house which was no longer his, and these people who were bound to him now only by imperceptible bonds. He would have liked to go away at once, no matter where; for he felt that it was all over—that he could no longer remain among them, that he would torture them always, in spite of himself, by his mere presence, and that they would cause him intolerable suffering.

Jean was chatting with Roland, but Pierre was not listening, did not hear what they said. He fancied, however, that there was a meaning in his brother's tones, and he began to pay attention.

Jean said:

"It will be, it seems, the finest boat in their fleet. They say six thousand five hundred tons. It will make its first voyage next month."

Roland exclaimed in surprise:

"So soon! I thought she would not be fit to go to sea this summer."

"You are mistaken. The work has been pushed so vigorously that the first trip will take place before the fall. I was at the company's office this morning, and spoke to one of the managers."

"Which of them?"

"Monsieur Marchand, a particular friend of the president of the board of directors."

"Why, do you know him?"

PIERRE AND JEAN

"Yes. And I had a slight favor to ask."

"Ah! Then you will take me over the *Lorraine* when she comes into harbor, won't you?"

"Certainly. Nothing easier."

Jean seemed to hesitate, pick his phrases, and change his subjects inexplicably. He continued:

"In brief, life on board these great Atlantic steamers is very pleasant. More than half of the month is spent ashore in two superb cities, New York and Havre, and the rest afloat with charming people. Very agreeable acquaintances can be made there, and very useful ones, too—very useful later on—among the passengers. Only imagine, the captain, if he is economical with his coal, can make twenty-five thousand francs a year, if not more."

"Phew!" exclaimed Roland, with a long whistle that bore witness to a profound respect for the sum and the captain.

Jean resumed:

"The purser may make ten thousand, and the doctor gets five thousand, fixed salary, with board, lodging, lights, heat, attendance, etc., etc. This is equal to ten thousand, at least. A good berth."

Pierre, who had raised his eyes, met those of his brother and understood him.

He asked, after a little hesitation:

"Is it difficult to obtain a place as doctor on one of these steamers?"

"Yes and no. It all depends on circumstances and influence."

There was a long silence, then the doctor spoke again:

"Is it next week that the *Lorraine* sails?"

"Yes; the seventh."

They were again silent.

Pierre was thinking. It would certainly be a solution of the difficulty if he could go as a doctor on this steamer. Later, he would see—he might leave, perhaps. Meanwhile, he would be earning his living without asking anything from his family. He had been forced, the night before, to sell his watch, for now he never asked his mother for money. This, then, was his last resort, his only means of a livelihood, except eating the bread of a home that he could no longer live in. So he said, hesitating a little:

"If I could manage it I should be very glad to sail on board of her."

"Why cannot you?" asked Jean.

"Because I know no one in the Transatlantic Company."

Roland, in astonishment, asked:

"And all your fine projects of success—what is to become of them?"

Pierre replied:

"There are times when we must learn to sacrifice everything, and renounce our dearest hopes. Besides, this is only a beginning, a means of amassing a few thousand francs to get a start with."

The father was soon convinced.

"That's true. In two years you can lay aside six or seven thousand francs, which, if well invested, will be a great help. What do you think, Louise?"

"I think Pierre is right."

Roland exclaimed:

"I'll go and speak to Monsieur Poulin, whom I know very well. He is the judge of the Tribunal of Commerce, and is acquainted with the affairs of the company. I know also Monsieur Lenient, the shipbuilder, who is a great friend of one of the vice-presidents."

Jean asked his brother:

"Would you like me to sound Monsieur Marchand to-day?"

"Yes, I would."

Then, after reflecting for some instants, Pierre resumed:

"The best way would be, perhaps, to write to my teachers and professors in the medical college, who thought very highly of me. The doctors of these steamboats are often second class. Good, strong letters from Professors Mas-Roussel, Rémusot, Flache and Borriquel would be of more service to me than any number of doubtful recommendations. It would be only necessary to present these letters through your friend M. Marchand to the board of directors."

Jean expressed his approval.

"A very good idea, very good, indeed"; and he smiled as if reassured, almost happy, and sure of success, for he was incapable of tormenting himself long about anything.

"You will write to them to-day?" he said.

"At once, immediately. I'll go and do it. I won't take any coffee this morning, I am too nervous."

He rose and left the room.

Then Jean turned to his mother:

"Mamma, what are you going to do to-day?"

"Nothing. I do not know."

"Will you come with me to Madame Rosémilly's?"

"Why, yes—yes——"

"You know it is necessary that I should go there to-day."

"Yes—that is true."

"But why necessary?" asked M. Roland, who, as a rule, never understood what was being said.

"Because I promised to call there."

"That's all. That makes a difference."

And he began to fill his pipe, while the mother and son went upstairs to get their hats.

When they were in the street, Jean said:

"Will you take my arm, mamma?"

He was not in the habit of offering it to her, for they usually walked side by side. She took it and leaned on him.

For some time they did not speak, then he said:

"You see that Pierre is quite willing to go away."

She replied:

"Poor boy!"

"Poor boy—why so? He will not be so badly off at all when he is on the *Lorraine*."

"No—I know—but I am thinking of so many things."

She kept on thinking, with her head bent, and keeping step with her son; and then, with that peculiar tone that our voice assumes sometimes when we utter the result of a long secret train of thought, she exclaimed:

"What a horrible thing life is! If by chance we find a moment of happiness in it, it is a sin to enjoy it, and one has to pay very dear for it afterward."

He said in a low tone:

"Don't talk of it, mamma."

PIERRE AND JEAN

"How can I help talking of it? I am thinking of it all the time."

"You will forget."

She was silent once more, and then, with an expression of profound regret, she continued:

"Oh, how happy I could have been if I had married another man!"

At the present moment she was exasperated against Roland, and attributed to his homeliness, his stupidity, his awkwardness, his lack of intellect, to his vulgar appearance, all the responsibility for her mistake and her unhappiness. It was this, the vulgarity of the man, that caused her to be untrue to him, that made her drive one of her sons to despair, and that obliged her to make to the other the most painful confession that could be wrung from a mother's heart.

She continued:

"It is frightful for a young girl to marry a husband like mine."

Jean made no reply. He was thinking of the man whose son he had hitherto believed he was; and, perhaps, the confused notion which he had entertained, for some time, of that man's commonplace character, the persistent irony of his brother, the disdainful indifference of others, and even the contempt of the servant girl for Roland, had prepared his mind for the terrible avowal of his mother. He did not mind so much being the son of another man; and after the terrible shock of emotion of the day before, if he did not display the revolt, the indignation, and the anger which Madame Roland dreaded, the reason was that for a long time he had been unconsciously suffering from the feeling of being the child of this good-natured fool.

They were now in front of the house of Madame Rosémilly.

She lived on the road to Saint Adresse, on the second floor of a large house that belonged to her. The windows looked out on the whole roadstead of Havre.

When she saw Madame Roland, who was the first to enter, instead of extending her hand as usual, she opened her arms and embraced her, for she guessed the object of her visit.

The furniture of the room, in stamped velvet, was always covered with chintz; and on the walls, prepared in flower designs, were four engravings bought by her first husband, the captain. They represented marine and sentimental scenes. In the first, a fisherman's wife was waving a handkerchief on the shore, while the sails of a boat bearing away her husband disappeared on the horizon. In the second, the same woman, on her knees, on the same shore, was wringing her hands as she beheld in the distance her husband's boat foundering in an ocean of impossible waves, and beneath a sky in which the lightning flashed.

The two other engravings represented analogous scenes in a higher class of society.

A young fair-haired woman, leaning in a revery over the rail of a large mail steamer, just sailing away; she looks at the already distant shore with an eye wet with tears of regret.

Then the same young woman, seated near a window looking out on the ocean, has fainted in an armchair; a letter has just fallen from her lap to the carpet.

He is dead, then! What despair!

Visitors, generally, were very much touched by the commonplace melancholy of these evidently sentimental subjects.

The chairs were placed in regular order, some against the wall, some around the centre table. The white immaculate curtains had folds so straight and so regular that one would have liked to disarrange them a little; and never a single grain of dust tarnished the gilded clock in the style of the Empire, where a globe of the world on the back of a kneeling Atlas seemed to be ripening like a hothouse melon.

The two ladies, as they took their seats, slightly disarranged the normal position of the chairs.

"Have you been out to-day?" Madame Roland inquired.

"No. I confess I am rather tired."

And then, as if to thank Jean and his mother, she told how much she had enjoyed their excursion and the fishing party.

"Why," she said, "I ate my prawns this morning and they were delicious. If you like, we will repeat that excursion some other day."

The young man interrupted:

"Before commencing a second, had we not better finish the first?"

"How do you mean? It seems to me it is finished."

"Ah, madame, for my part, I landed a fish on the rocks of Saint Jouin, which I want to take home."

She assumed a sly, knowing look.

"You? What is it? What did you catch?"

"A woman! and we have come, mamma and myself, to ask if she has not changed her mind this
morning."

She replied with a smile:

"No, monsieur; I never change my mind."

He extended to her his wide-open hand, and she
placed hers in it with a decided, resolute gesture;
then he asked:

"As soon as possible, eh?"

"Whenever you like."

"Six weeks?"

"It's all the same to me. What does my future
mother-in-law think?"

Madame Roland replied, with a somewhat melancholy smile:

"As for me, I say nothing. I only thank you
for loving Jean, for you will make him very happy."

"We will do what we can, mamma."

Somewhat touched for the first time, Madame
Rosémilly arose, and, flinging both arms around
Madame Roland, she gave her a long embrace as
though she were a child; and under the pressure of
this new caress a powerful emotion filled the aching
heart of the poor woman. She could not say what
her feelings were; they were at once sad and sweet;
she had lost a son and was gaining a daughter.

When they had taken their seats again and were
face to face, they took each other's hand and remained thus looking at each other, and smiling,
while Jean seemed to be almost forgotten by them.

Then they talked of a number of things which
had to be thought about for the approaching marriage, and when all was arranged and decided, Ma-

dame Rosémilly appeared suddenly to remember a trifling detail, and asked:

"You have consulted Monsieur Roland, I suppose?"

The same blush at once covered the cheeks of mother and son; it was the mother who answered.

"Oh, no! what is the use of it?"

Then she hesitated, for she felt that some explanation was necessary, and continued:

"We do everything without saying anything to him about it. It is enough to tell him what we have decided."

Madame Rosémilly smiled; she was by no means surprised, for it seemed quite natural as the old gentleman was of little account.

When Madame Roland and her son were again in the street, the former said:

"Let us go to your rooms. I should like to rest a while."

She felt herself without shelter, without refuge, and with a horror of her home.

They entered Jean's apartments. As soon as she saw the door shut behind her, she gave a great sigh, as if the very turning of the lock had placed her in security; then, instead of resting herself, as she had intended, she began to open the wardrobes and count the piles of linen, the number of pocket-handkerchiefs and of stockings. She changed the usual order, seeking to arrange them in a manner more pleasing to her housewifely eye; and when she had disposed the linen, she drew back to contemplate her work, and said:

"Jean, come and see how pretty this is."

He rose and expressed his admiration for the purpose of gratifying her.

When he had resumed his seat, she suddenly stepped up lightly behind his armchair, and, throwing her right arm around his neck, she kissed him, while she placed on the mantelpiece a little package wrapped in white paper which she held in her other hand.

He asked:

"What is that?"

As she made no reply, he understood, for he recognized the shape of the frame.

"Give it to me," he said.

But she pretended not to hear him, and went back to the wardrobe. He rose and, eagerly seizing this melancholy relic, he crossed the room, and double-locked it in a drawer of his desk. His mother wiped away a tear that trembled on her eyelids, and said in a rather tremulous voice:

"Now I am going to see if your new servant keeps her kitchen in good order. As she is out just now, I can inspect everything."

CHAPTER IX

THE LAST FAREWELL

Letters of recommendation from Professors Mas-Roussel, Rémusot, Flache and Borriquel, which spoke in most flattering terms of their pupil, Dr. Pierre Roland, were submitted by M. Marchand to the Transatlantic Company, and indorsed by MM.

Poulin of the Tribunal of Commerce, Lenient, shipbuilder, and Marival, assessor to the mayor of
Havre and a great friend of Captain Beausire.

It was ascertained that the surgeon of the *Lorraine* was not yet appointed, and Pierre had a chance
of being nominated in a few days.

The notification of his appointment was handed
him by the maid Josephine, one morning, as he was
finishing his toilet.

His first emotion was that of a prisoner under
sentence of death who receives a commutation of
his sentence; and he at once felt his suffering as-
suaged somewhat by the thought of his departure,
and of his calm life on board, rocked by the rolling
waves, always roaming, always wandering.

He was now living in his father's house like a
stranger, silent and reserved. Since the evening
when he had allowed the shameful secret discovered
by him to escape him in presence of his brother, he
felt that he had broken the last ties tht bound him
to his kin. He was torn with remorse at having
told it to Jean; he looked on himself as despicable,
mean and malicious, and yet he felt some comfort
in having spoken.

His eyes never met those of his mother or of his
brother. The eyes of all of them had assumed, to
avoid meeting each other, a surprising mobility, and
artifices like those of enemies who fear to cross each
other's path. He was always asking himself: "What
can she have said to Jean? Did she confess or
deny? What does my brother believe? What does
he think of her? What does he think of me?" He
could not imagine, and that exasperated him. Be-

sides, he scarcely spoke to them, except in Roland's presence, so as to avoid questions.

When he received the letter notifying him of his appointment, he showed it at once to his family. His father, who was very readily pleased at everything, clapped his hands. Jean replied in a serious tone, but with a heart full of joy:

"I congratulate you heartily, for I know there were many applicants. You owe it to the letters from your professors."

His mother bent her head, and in a low tone said: "I am very glad you have succeeded."

After dinner he went to the company's offices to obtain information about many matters, and asked the name of the surgeon of the *Picardie,* that was to sail the next day, in order that he might inquire about the details of his new life, and the special conditions that he would have to meet.

As Dr. Pirette was on board, he went to his room, a little steamer cabin, and was received by a young man with a light beard, who looked like his brother. They had a long conversation.

In the sonorous depths of the huge ship, a confused, ceaseless disturbance was going on in which the letting down of merchandise into the hold was blended with the sound of steps, with voices, with the movement of the derricks hoisting in the cargo, with the whistles of the boatswains, with the clang of chains dragging along the decks or wound on the capstan, with the hoarse puffing of the engine, which set up a slight vibration in the whole mass of the great vessel.

But when Pierre had quitted his colleague and found himself in the street, a new melancholy fell on him, and enveloped him, like those fogs that sweep across the sea, coming from the ends of the earth, and bearing in their impalpable density something mysterious and impure, like a pestilential breath from distant and unhealthy shores.

Never, in the hours of his greatest suffering, had he found himself plunged into such a quagmire of misery. The last tie had been broken; he no longer cared for anything. In tearing from his heart the roots of all his affections, he had not until now felt that distress as of a lost dog which suddenly seized him.

It was no longer a moral and torturing pang; it was the wild despair of a shelterless beast, the material anguish of a vagabond creature who no longer has a roof, and whom rain, wind, storm, all the brute forces of the world are about to attack. As he set his foot on the steamer and entered the little cabin tossing on the waves, the very flesh of the man, who had always slept in a quiet, motionless bed, revolted against the insecurity of all his future days. Hitherto, he had felt himself protected by solid walls set in earth, and by the certainty of always sleeping in the same place, beneath a roof that resisted the winds. Now, everything that can endure in the warmth of a solid house would be a danger and a perpetual suffering.

No ground beneath his feet; only the sea that heaves, and roars, and engulfs. No space around him, in which to walk, run, lose his way; only a few feet of plank to walk on like a criminal in the midst of other prisoners. No trees, gardens, streets, houses; nothing but water and sky. And then he would feel, unceasingly, the movement of the ship beneath his feet. In stormy weather he would have to lean against the partitions, or cling to the doors, or hang on to the edge of his narrow berth, to avoid falling. In calm weather he would hear the whirring noise of the screw, and feel the ship flying along, bearing him with it in its regular, exasperating flight.

He found himself condemned to this life of a wandering convict, solely because his mother had yielded to a moment's weakness.

He walked straight before him, overcome, for the moment, by the despairing melancholy of those who are going to expatriate themselves.

He no longer felt in his heart his haughty contempt or disdainful hate of unknown passers-by, but a sad longing to speak to them, to tell them that he was going to leave France, and to be listened to and consoled. In his bosom there was a need, like that of the shamefaced mendicant who holds out his hand —a timid yet strong need of feeling that some one was sorry for his departure.

He thought of Marowsko. The old Pole was the only one who loved him well enough to feel a true, deep emotion, and the doctor resolved to call on him at once.

When he entered the shop, the druggist, who was pounding some powders in the bottom of a marble mortar, gave a slight start and quitted his work.

"We never see you now," he said.

The young man explained that he had numerous affairs to look after, without betraying the reason, and took his seat, asking:

"Well, how is business?"

Business was not prosperous. Competition was

terrible, sick folks scarce and poor in that working-man's quarter. There was no sale except for cheap medicines, and the doctors did not prescribe those rare and complex remedies that give a profit of five hundred per cent. The old fellow concluded:

"If it lasts three months longer like this, I must shut up shop. If I had n you to depend on, my dear doctor, I would have turned bootblack before this."

Pierre felt his heart contract, and he decided to strike the blow abruptly, as it had to be done.

"Oh, on me? I can no longer be of any assistance to you. I leave Havre at the beginning of next month."

Marowsko took off his glasses, so great was his emotion, and cried:

"You—you! What's that you say?"

"I say I am going away, my poor friend."

The old man was stunned; he felt his last hope crumble; and he took a sudden dislike to this man, whom he had followed, and loved, and in whom he had had such confidence, and who deserted him in this way.

He stammered out:

"You are not going to betray me in your turn, are you?"

Pierre felt himself so moved that he longed to embrace him.

"I am not betraying you. I could not find a good place to establish a practice here, and I am going as a doctor on a transatlantic steamer."

"Oh, Monsieur Pierre, you promised faithfully to help me along in life!"

"What would you have? I must live myself; I have not a sou!"

Marowsko repeated:

"It is wrong, it is wrong—what you are going to do. Nothing now for me but to die of hunger. At my age, it is all over. It is wrong. You abandon a poor old man who came here to be near you. It is wrong."

Pierre wished to explain, give his reasons, and prove that he could not act otherwise. The Pole would not listen, in his indignation at such desertion, and ended by saying, with an allusion, beyond question, to certain political events:

"You Frenchmen never keep your word!"

Then Pierre rose, annoyed in turn, and, taking a higher tone, said:

"You are unjust, Monsieur Marowsko. It required powerful motives to make me adopt the decision I have made, and you ought to understand that. Good-day. I hope that next time I shall find you more reasonable."

He left the shop.

"Well," he thought, "no one will regret me sincerely."

He thought over carefully all the people he knew or had known; and, in the midst of all the faces that flitted across his memory, there stood out the face of the girl in the beer shop, who had caused him to suspect his mother.

He hesitated, for he nursed an instinctive grudge against her; then, by a sudden change of thought, "She was right, after all," he decided, and set out to find the street where she lived.

The beer shop was, as it happened, full of people

and full of smoke. The customers—shopkeepers and workingmen, for it was a holiday—were shouting, laughing, calling for beer; and the landlord himself was serving them, running from table to table, carrying off the empty glasses, and bringing them back foaming.

When Pierre found a place, not far from the desk, he waited, hoping that the girl would see and recognize him.

She, however, passed and repassed in front of him, without a glance, trotting about with a little coquettish swing of her skirts.

At last he knocked on the table with a coin. She came up.

"What do you wish, sir?"

She did not look at him; her mind was lost in calculating the glasses that she had served.

"Is that the way to say 'Good-day' to one's friends?" he said.

She turned her eyes on him, and said hurriedly:

"Oh, it is you! You look well. But I have no time to-day. Do you want beer?"

"Yes, a 'bock.'"

When she brought it, he resumed:

"I came to say good-by; I am going away."

She replied with indifference:

"Oh, pshaw! Where are you going?"

"To America."

"They say it's a fine country."

Not a word more. He must indeed have been foolish to speak to her on such a day. There were too many people in the place.

Pierre walked toward the sea. When he reached the pier, he saw the *Pearl* coming in, with his father and Captain Beausire on board. The sailor, Papagris, was rowing, and the two others, sitting in the stern, smoked their pipes with an air of perfect happiness. As he saw them pass, he thought: "Blessed are the simple in spirit."

He seated himself on one of the benches of the breakwater, to try and benumb himself into an animal-like somnolence.

When he returned home in the evening, his mother, without daring to raise her eyes to him, said:

"You will need to get a great many things before you start, and I am rather perplexed. I ordered your body linen, and have seen the tailor about your clothes; but is there nothing else you need, things I do not know about, perhaps?"

He opened his lips to say "No, nothing," but he reflected that he must, at least, accept enough to dress himself decently, and replied, in a very calm tone:

"I do not know yet myself. I will ask at the office."

He obtained there a list of indispensable articles. His mother, on receiving it from his hands, looked at him, for the first time in a long while, and her eyes had the humble, soft, sad, appealing expression of a poor dog that has been whipped and is begging pardon.

On the first of October, the *Lorraine,* sailing from Saint Nazaire, entered the port of Havre, to sail on the seventh of the same month for her destination of New York. Pierre Roland had to take possession of the little floating cabin in which henceforth his life would be imprisoned.

The following day as he was going out he met his mother on the stairs; she was waiting for him, and said in an almost unintelligible voice:

"Do you not want me to help you in arranging your room on the boat?"

"No, thanks; everything is done."

"I want so much to see your cabin," she murmured.

"It is not worth the trouble. It is very ugly and very small."

He went on, leaving her stunned, leaning against the wall, with her face deathly pale.

Now, Roland, who had visited the *Lorraine* that very same day, talked during dinner of nothing but that magnificent ship, and was much astonished that his wife had no desire to see it, since their son was to sail in it.

Pierre was scarcely at home at all for the next few days. He was nervous, irritable, harsh, and his brutal remarks seemed to hit every one. But on the evening before his departure he suddenly appeared very much changed and softened. As he was embracing his parents before going to sleep on board for the first time, he said:

"You will come and say 'Good-by' to me to-morrow, at the ship?"

Roland cried:

"Yes, yes, by Jove! Won't we, Louise?"

"Certainly," she said, in a low voice.

Pierre continued:

"We leave at eleven, sharp. You must be down there at half-past nine, at the latest."

"Hello!" cried the father; "here's an idea. When we leave you, we will run as fast as we can and go aboard the *Pearl,* and wait for you outside the harbor, and get another sight of you. Shall we do that, Louise?"

"Yes, certainly."

Roland went on:

"In this way you will not lose sight of us in the crowd that covers the pier when the transatlantic liners sail. One can never find one's friends in the throng. Does that suit you?"

"Oh, yes. Let us arrange it so."

An hour later Pierre was stretched on his little sailor's bed, long and narrow as a coffin. He lay a long time with his eyes open, thinking of all that had passed during the last two months in his life, and, above all, in his soul. Through having suffered and made others suffer, his aggressive and vengeful grief had worn itself out, like a foaming wave. He had scarcely the courage to be angry with any one, for any cause whatever; he let his indignation drift, like his life. He felt so weary of struggling, weary of smiting, weary of hating, weary of everything, that he could bear it no longer, and he sought to numb his heart into forgetfulness, as when one falls asleep. He heard, vaguely, around him the strange sounds of the ship—slight sounds, scarcely perceptible in that calm night in the harbor—and in the wound in his heart hitherto so agonizing he felt only a painful tingling as of a scar that was healing.

He slept profoundly till he was awakened by the movements of the sailors. It was daylight, and the tidal train with the passengers from Paris arrived at the quay.

Then he wandered about the ship, among the busy, restless crowd of people looking for their cabins, calling to each other, questioning and answering one another, in all the bewilderment of the beginning of a voyage. After a salute to the captain, and a shake of the hand to his comrade the purser, he entered the cabin, where some Englishmen were already dozing in the corners. The large room, with its walls of white marble with gold borders, appeared still larger as it was reflected with its long tables flanked by two unlimited lines of revolving chairs covered with crimson velvet. This, then, was the vast floating cosmopolitan hall, where the rich people of every continent had to dine in common. Its opulent luxury was that of large hotels, theatres, public places—a luxury that was commonplace and self-asserting, which satisfied the eyes of millionaires. The doctor was about to enter the second cabin, when he remembered that on the previous evening a great horde of emigrants had embarked; so he went to the lower deck. When he entered there, he was struck by a nauseating stench of poor dirty humanity; the odor of human flesh, more sickening than that of the hair or wool of beasts. There, in a sort of low, dark tunnel, like the galleries in mines, he saw hundreds of men, women and children stretched on planks, tier above tier, or grovelling in heaps on the floor. He could not distinguish faces, but he dimly saw this filthy crowd in rags, this crowd of wretched men conquered by life, exhausted, crushed down—starting with an emaciated wife and half-starved children, for an unknown country, where they hoped not to die of hunger, perhaps.

As he thought of the past toil, the wasted toil, the barren efforts, the bitter strife renewed each

day in vain, the energy spent by these beggars who
were going to begin again, they did not know where,
this existence of horrible wretchedness, the doctor
felt a desire to cry out to them, "Dump yourselves
into the sea, with your women and your little ones!"
and his heart was so wrung by pity that he walked
away, unable to bear the sight.

His father, his mother, his brother, and Madame
Rosémilly were already waiting for him in his
cabin.

"So soon?" he said.

"Yes," replied Madame Roland, with a trembling
voice; "we wished to have time to see you a little."

He looked at her. She was in black as if in
mourning, and he suddenly perceived that her hair,
that was merely gray the month before, had now
become quite white.

He could with difficulty seat the four visitors in
his little cabin, and he himself got up on his bunk.
Through the open door they saw a crowd as numerous as that in the streets on a holiday; for all the
friends of the passengers, and an army of mere
sightseers, had invaded the huge liner. They walked
along the corridors, through the saloons, everywhere, and some heads were poked into the room,
while voices outside muttered, "That's the doctor's
room."

Then Pierre closed the door; but when he found
himself shut up with his friends he longed to open
it again, for the movement on the ship concealed
their constraint and their silence.

At length Madame Rosémilly determined to speak.

"Very little air comes through these small windows."

"It is a port hole," said Pierre.

He pointed out the thickness of the glass that rendered it capable of resisting the most violent shocks, and then he explained at length the method of closing it. Roland next asked:

"Do you keep your medicines here?"

The doctor opened a locker, and showed them a row of phials that bore white labels with Latin names.

He took one down and enumerated the properties of its contents; then a second, then a third, and delivered a lecture on therapeutics which seemed to be listened to with great attention.

Roland shook his head, repeating:

"Is it not interesting?"

A gentle knock at the door was heard.

"Come in," cried Pierre.

And Captain Beausire appeared.

He said, as he held out his hand:

"I am late in coming, because I did not want to disturb the family leavetaking."

He, too, had to sit on the bunk. Then the silence recommenced.

Suddenly, however, Captain Beausire pricked up his ears. Some order had reached him through the partition, and he remarked:

"It is time for us to go if we want to get on board the *Pearl* and see you again as you come out, and say 'Good-by' in the open sea."

Roland made a great point of doing this, doubtless with a view to impress the passengers on the *Lorraine,* and rose hurriedly.

"Come, good-by, my boy."

He kissed Pierre's whiskers, and then opened the door.

Madame Roland did not stir, and remained with downcast eyes and very pale face.

Her husband touched her on the arm.

"Come, let us be off. We have not a moment to lose."

She stood up, took a step toward her son, and held out to him, one after the other, two cheeks as white as wax, which he kissed without saying a word. Then he shook Madame Rosémilly's hand and his brother's, asking him:

"When is the wedding to be?"

"I do not yet know precisely. We will make it fit in with one of your voyages."

Finally they all left the room, and went up to the deck, which was encumbered with the public and porters and sailors.

The steam was roaring in the enormous belly of the ship, which seemed to tremble with impatience.

"Good-by," said Roland, hurriedly.

"Good-by," replied Pierre, standing at the top of one of the little wooden gangways leading from the *Lorraine* to the quay.

He again shook all their hands, and his family departed.

"Quick, quick, into the carriage!" cried old Roland.

A cab was waiting for them, and took them to the outer harbor, where Papagris had the *Pearl* all ready to put off.

There was not a breath of air; it was one of those calm, dry days of autumn, when the smooth sea seems cold and hard as steel.

PIERRE AND JEAN

Jean seized an oar, the sailor flung the other into the rowlocks, and they began to row. On the breakwaters, the piers, even on the granite breastworks, there was an innumerable crowd, jostling and noisy, waiting for the *Lorraine* to pass by.

The *Pearl* rowed out between these two billows of humanity, and was soon outside the dock.

Captain Beausire, seated between the two ladies, held the tiller, and said:

"You will see that we shall be directly in her course, down there."

The two rowers pulled with all their might to get out as far as possible. All at once Roland exclaimed:

"Here she is! I see her rigging and her two smokestacks. She is coming out of the basin."

"Pull, boys," repeated Beausire.

Madame Roland took her handkerchief from her pocket and held it to her eyes.

Roland was standing up and clinging to the mast.

"Now she is swinging into the outer harbor. She does not stir. She is in motion again. She has to take a tug. She is off! Hurrah! She is between the jetties. Don't you hear the people cheering her? It is the *Neptune* that is towing her—I see her bows just now. There she is—there she is! *Mon Dieu*, what a ship! Just look at her!"

Madame Rosémilly and Beausire turned round; the two men ceased to row; Madame Roland alone was motionless.

The huge vessel, towed by a powerful tugboat, which looked like a caterpillar before her, came slowly and royally out of the harbor. The good folk of Havre, massed on the piers, the beach and

167

at their windows, suddenly carried away with patriotic zeal, shouted, *"Vive la Lorraine!"* cheering and applauding her stately departure—this child of a great maritime city that gave to the sea her fairest daughter.

But as soon as she had cleared the narrow passage between the two granite walls, and at length found herself free, she cast off her tug, and started alone, like some huge monster racing across the water.

"Here she comes! Here she comes!" Roland kept crying. "She is coming straight toward us."

Beausire, radiant with delight, repeated:

"Did not I tell you so? Eh? Don't I know their course?"

Jean, in a low voice, whispered to his mother:

"Mamma, look—she is coming."

Madame Roland uncovered her eyes, that were blinded with her tears.

On came the *Lorraine,* at full speed after clearing the harbor, in the clear, calm, fine weather. Beausire, with his glass leveled, cried:

"Attention! Monsieur Pierre is at the stern, all alone, well in sight. Attention!"

The *Lorraine,* high as a mountain, swift as a train, passed the *Pearl* almost within touching distance. Madame Roland, distracted and heartbroken, stretched out her arms toward the ship, and saw her son, her son Pierre, with his gold-laced cap, fling to her with both hands his farewell kisses.

But he went away in the distance, gradually vanishing and disappearing, until he was an imperceptible speck on the gigantic vessel. She tried to distinguish him still, and could not recognize him.

Jean took her hand.

"You saw him?" he said.

"Yes, I saw him. How good he is!"

They headed their boat toward the town.

"By Jove, she goes fast!" M. Roland declared with enthusiastic conviction.

The steamer, indeed, diminished moment by moment, as if it had melted away into the ocean. Madame Roland saw it plunge into the horizon toward an unknown country at the other end of the world. On that ship which nothing could stop, on that ship which soon she would no longer see, was her son, her poor boy. And it seemed to her that half of her heart went with him; it seemed to her, also, as if her life was ended; it seemed to her that never more would she behold her child.

"Why are you crying?" asked her husband. "He will be back in less than a month."

She sobbed:

"I do not know. I cry because I am not well."

When they returned to land, Beausire left them at once to go and breakfast with a friend. Jean went on in front with Madame Rosémilly, and Roland said to his wife:

"He has a good figure, all the same, our Jean."

"Yes," replied the mother.

And, as she was too troubled in mind to think of what she was saying, she added:

"I am very glad he is going to marry Madame Rosémilly."

M. Roland was stupefied.

"Oh, pshaw! What? He is going to marry Madame Rosémilly?"

"Yes. We counted on asking your opinion this very day."

"Well, well! Is it long since this affair has been on hand?"

"No; only a few days. Jean wished to be sure of being accepted by her before consulting you."

Roland rubbed his hands.

"Excellent, excellent. Nothing could be better. I approve of it decidedly."

As they were about quitting the quay and taking the Boulevard François I, his wife turned once more to cast a last look at the open sea; but she saw nothing but a little gray trail of smoke, so distant, so slight, that it had the appearance of a wreath of mist.

THE END

FATHER AND SON

THE dogs fastened to the apple trees in the grounds in front of the house were giving tongue at the sight of the game bags carried by the gamekeepers and small boys. It was half farm and half manor house, one of those quasi seignorial country residences, now occupied by large farmers. In the spacious dining-room-kitchen, Hautot Senior and Hautot Junior, M. Bermont, the tax collector, and M. Mondaru, the notary, were eating a mouthful and drinking a glass before going out shooting, for it was the first day of the season.

Hautot Senior, proud of all his possessions, talked boastfully of the game which his guests were going to find on his lands. He was a big Norman, one of those powerful, ruddy men, with large bones, who lift wagon loads of apples on their shoulders. Half peasant, half gentleman, rich, respected, influential, autocratic, he obliged his son César to go through the third form at college so that he might be an educated man, and there he had brought his studies to an end, for fear of his becoming a fine gentleman and paying no attention to the land.

César Hautot, almost as tall as his father, but thinner, was a good son, docile, content with everything, full of admiration, respect, and deference for the wishes and opinions of Hautot Senior.

M. Bermont, the tax collector, a stout little man, who showed on his red cheeks a thin network of violet veins resembling the tributaries and the winding courses of rivers on maps, asked:

"And hares—are there any hares?"

Hautot Senior answered:

"As many as you wish, especially in the Puysatier land."

"How shall we set out?" asked the notary, an epicure of a notary, pale and corpulent, with a brand-new hunting costume, belted in, that he had bought at Rouen.

"Well, that way, through the bottoms. We will drive the partridges into the plain, and we can get them there."

And Hautot Senior rose up. They all followed his example, took their guns out of the corners, examined the locks, stamped their feet in order to adjust their boots, which were rather hard, not having become flexible from wear. Then they went out; and the dogs, standing on their hind legs at the ends of their leashes, gave tongue while beating the air with their paws.

They set out toward the bottoms referred to. These consisted of a little valley, or, rather, a long, undulating stretch of poor land, which had on that account remained uncultivated, furrowed with ditches and covered with ferns, an excellent preserve for game.

The sportsmen took up their positions at some distance form each other, Hautot Senior at the right, Hautot Junior at the left, and the two guests in the middle. The gamekeeper, and the men carrying the game bags, followed. It was the solemn moment when the first shot is awaited, when the heart beats a little, while the nervous finger keeps feeling the trigger.

Suddenly a shot went off. Hautot Senior had fired. They all stopped, and saw a partridge separate from a covey which had risen, and fall down into a deep ditch under a thick growth of brush. The sportsman, becoming excited, rushed forward with rapid strides, thrusting aside the briars which stood in his path, and disappeared in his turn into the thicket, in quest of his game.

Almost at the same instant, a second shot was heard.

"Ha! ha! the rascal!" exclaimed M. Bermont, "he must have started a hare down there."

They all waited, with their eyes riveted on the mass of brush which their gaze failed to penetrate.

The notary, making a speaking trumpet of his hands, shouted:

"Have you got them?"

Hautot Senior made no response.

Then César, turning toward the gamekeeper, said:

"Just go and assist him, Joseph. We must keep walking in line. We'll wait."

And Joseph, an old stump of a man, lean and knotty, all of whose joints formed protuberances, set off at an easy pace down into the ditch, searching every opening through which a passage could be effected with the cautiousness of a fox. Then, suddenly, he cried:

"Oh! come! come! an accident has occurred."

FATHER AND SON

They all hurried forward, plunging through the briars.

The elder Hautot had fallen on his side, in a faint, with both hands pressed to his abdomen, from which blood trickled through his shooting jacket, torn by a bullet. Letting go of his gun, in order to pick up the dead partridge, he had let the firearm fall, and the second discharge, going off with the shock, had torn open his entrails. They drew him out of the trench, removed his clothes, and saw a frightful wound, through which the intestines protruded. Then, after having ligatured him the best way they could, they brought him back to his own house, and awaited the doctor, who had been sent for, as well as the priest.

When the doctor arrived he gravely shook his head, and, turning toward young Hautot, who was sobbing on a chair, he said:

"My poor boy, this does not look favorable."

But, when the wound was dressed, the wounded man moved his fingers, opened his mouth, then his eyes, cast around him troubled, haggard glances, then appeared to be trying to recall, to understand, and he murmured:

"Ah! good God! this has finished me!"

The doctor held his hand.

"Why, no; why, no; some days of rest merely—it will be nothing."

Hautot returned:

"It has finished me! My abdomen is gashed! I know it well."

Then, all of a sudden:

"I want to talk to my son, if I have time."

4

FATHER AND SON

Hautot Junior, in spite of himself, shed tears, and kept repeating like a little boy:

"Papa, papa, poor papa!"

But the father, in a firm tone, said:

"Come! stop crying—this is no time for it. I have something to say to you. Sit down there, quite close to me. It will not take long, and I shall be more calm. As for the rest of you, kindly leave us alone for a minute."

They all went out, leaving the father and son together.

As soon as they were alone:

"Listen, son!" he said, "you are twenty-four; one can talk to you. And then there is not such mystery about these matters as we attach to them. You know, do you not, that your mother has been dead seven years, and that I am not more than forty-five years myself, seeing that I was married at nineteen. Is not that true?"

The son faltered:

"Yes, it is true."

"So then your mother is dead seven years, and I have remained a widower. Well! a man like me cannot remain without a wife at thirty-seven, isn't that true?"

The son replied:

"Yes, it is true."

The father, out of breath, very pale, and his face contracted with suffering, went on:

"God! how I suffer! Well, you understand. Man is not made to live alone, but I did not want to take a successor to your mother, since I promised her not to do so. Therefore—you understand?"

"Yes, father."

5

"Well, I kept a young girl at Rouen, number eighteen, Rue de l'Éperlan, on the third floor, the second door—I am telling you all this, don't forget —a young girl, who has been very nice to me, loving, devoted, a true woman, eh? You understand, my lad?"

"Yes, father."

"So then, if I am carried off, I owe something to her, something substantial, that will place her beyond the reach of want. You understand?"

"Yes, father."

"I tell you that she is a good girl, and, but for you, and the remembrance of your mother, and also because we three lived together in this house, I would have brought her here, and then married her. Listen—listen, my boy—I might have made a will— I haven't done so. I did not wish to do so—for it is not necessary to write down things—things of this sort—it is too damaging to the legitimate children—and then it makes confusion—it ruins every one! Look you, lawyers, there's no need of them— never consult one. If I am rich, it is because I never employed one in all my life. You understand, my son?"

"Yes, father."

"Listen again—listen attentively! So then, I have made no will—I did not desire to do so—and then I knew you; you have a good heart, you are not covetous, not stingy, and I said to myself that when my end approached I would tell you all about it, and that I would beg of you not to forget the girl. And then, listen again! When I am gone, go and see her at once—and make such arrangements that she may not blame my memory. You have plenty of means. You can spare it—I leave you enough. Listen! You won't find her at home every day in the week. She works at Madame Moreau's in the Rue Beauvoisine. Go there on a Thursday. That is the day she expects me. It has been my day for the past six years. Poor little girl! she will weep! I say all this to you, because I know you so well, my son. One does not tell these things in public, either to the notary or to the priest. They happen—every one knows that—but they are not talked about, save in case of necessity. Then there must be no outsider in the secret, nobody except the family, because the family consists of one person alone. You understand?"

"Yes, father."

"Do you promise?"

"Yes, father."

"Do you swear it?"

"Yes, father."

"I beg of you, I implore of you, son, do not forget. I insist on this."

"No, father."

"You will go yourself. I want you to make sure of everything."

"Yes, father."

"And then, you will see—you will see what she will explain to you. As for me, I can say no more to you. You have sworn to do it."

"Yes, father."

"That's good, my son. Embrace me. Farewell. I am going to die, I'm sure. Tell them they may come in."

Young Hautot embraced his father, groaning as he did so; then, always docile, he opened the door, and the priest appeared in a white surplice, carrying the holy oils.

But the dying man had closed his eyes and refused to open them again; he refused to answer, and even to show by a sign that he understood.

He had talked enough, this man; he could speak no longer. Besides, he now felt his heart at ease and wanted to die in peace. What need had he to make a confession to the deputy of God, since he had just confessed to his son, who constituted his family?

He received the last rites, was purified, and received absolution, surrounded by his friends and his servants on their bended knees, without any movement of his face indicating that he still lived.

He expired about midnight, after four hours of spasms, which showed that he must have suffered dreadfully.

PART II

HE was buried on Tuesday, the shooting season having opened on Sunday. On returning home after the funeral César Hautot spent the rest of the day weeping. He scarcely slept that night, and felt so sad on awaking that he asked himself how he could go on living.

However, he kept thinking that, in order to obey his father's dying wish, he must go to Rouen the following day, and see this girl Caroline Donet, who lived at eighteen Rue d'Éperlan, the third story, second door. He had muttered to himself this name and address a countless number of times, just as a child repeats a prayer, so that he might not forget them, and he ended by repeating them continually, without thinking, so impressed were they on his mind.

Accordingly, on the following day, about eight o'clock, he ordered Graindorge to be harnessed to the tilbury, and set forth, at the long, swinging pace of the heavy Norman horse, along the high road from Ainville to Rouen. He wore his black frock coat, his tall silk hat, and his trousers strapped under his shoes, and, being in mourning, did not put on his blue dust coat.

He entered Rouen just as it was striking ten o'clock, put up, as he had always done, at the Hotel des Bons-Enfants, in the Rue des Trois-Mares, and submitted to the embraces of the landlord and his wife and their five children, for they had heard the melancholy news; after that, he had to tell them all the particulars of the accident, which caused him to shed tears; to repel all the proffered attentions which they sought to thrust upon him merely because he was wealthy; and to decline even the luncheon they wanted him to partake of, thus wounding their sensibilities.

Then, having wiped the dust off his hat, brushed his coat, and removed the mud stains from his boots, he set forth in search of the Rue de l'Éperlan, without venturing to make inquiries from any one, for fear of being recognized and of arousing suspicion.

At length, unable to find the place, he saw a priest passing by, and, trusting to the professional discretion of the clergy, he questioned the ecclesiastic.

9

He had only a hundred steps farther to go; it was the second street to the right.

Then he hesitated. Up to that moment he had obeyed, like a mere animal, the expressed wish of the deceased. Now he felt quite agitated, confused, humiliated, at the idea of finding himself—the son —in the presence of this woman who had been his father's sweetheart. All the morality we possess, which lies buried at the bottom of our emotions through centuries of hereditary instruction, all that he had been taught since he had learned his catechism about creatures of evil life, the instinctive contempt which every man entertains toward them, even though he may marry one of them, all the narrow honesty of the peasant in his character, was stirred up within him, and held him back, making him grow red with shame.

But he said to himself:

"I promised the father. I must not break my promise."

So he pushed open the partly opened door of number eighteen, saw a gloomy-looking staircase, ascended three flights, perceived a door, then a second door, saw a bell rope, and pulled it. The ringing, which resounded in the apartment, sent a shiver through his frame. The door was opened, and he found himself face to face with a well-dressed young lady, a brunette with rosy cheeks, who gazed at him with eyes of astonishment.

He did not know what to say to her, and she, who suspected nothing, and who was waiting for the father, did not invite him to come in. They stood looking thus at one another for nearly half a minute, at the end of which she said in a questioning tone:

"Do you want anything, monsieur?"

He falteringly replied:

"I am M. Hautot's son."

She gave a start, turned pale, and stammered out as if she had known him for a long time:

"Monsieur César?"

"Yes."

"And what then?"

"I have come with a message to you from my father."

She exclaimed:

"Oh, my God!" and then drew back so that he might enter. He shut the door and followed her into the apartment. Then he perceived a little boy of four or five years playing with a cat, seated on the floor in front of a stove, from which rose an odor of food being kept hot.

"Take a seat," she said.

He sat down.

"Well?" she questioned.

He no longer ventured to speak, keeping his eyes fixed on the table which stood in the centre of the room, with three covers laid on it, one of which was for a child, and a bottle of claret that had been opened, and one of white wine that had not been uncorked. He glanced at the chair with its back turned to the fire. That was his father's chair! They were expecting him. That was his bread which he saw at his place, for the crust had been removed on account of Hautot's bad teeth. Then, raising his eyes, he noticed on the wall his father's portrait, the large photograph taken at Paris the year of the exhibition, the same as that which hung above the bed in the sleeping apartment at Ainville.

The young woman again asked:

"Well, Monsieur César?"

He kept staring at her. Her face was livid with anxiety, and she waited, her hands trembling with fear.

Then he took courage.

"Well, mam'zelle, papa died on Sunday last just after he had opened the shooting season."

She was so overwhelmed that she did not move. After a silence of a few seconds, she faltered in an almost inaudible tone:

"Oh, it is not possible!"

Then, on a sudden, tears came into her eyes, and, covering her face with her hands, she burst out sobbing.

At that point the little boy turned round, and, seeing his mother weeping, began to roar. Then, realizing that this sudden trouble was brought about by the stranger, he rushed at César, caught hold of his trousers with one hand and with the other hit him with all his strength on the thigh. And César remained bewildered, deeply affected; with this woman mourning for his father on the one hand, and the little boy defending his mother on the other. He felt their emotion taking possession of him, and his eyes were beginning to fill with tears; so, to recover his self-command, he began to talk:

"Yes," he said, "the accident occurred on Sunday, at eight o'clock——"

And he told all the facts as if she were listening to him, without forgetting a single detail, mentioning the most trivial matters with the minuteness of a countryman. And the child still kept attacking him, kicking his ankles.

When he came to what his father had said about her, she took her hands from her face and said:

"Pardon me! I was not following you; I would like to know—— Would you mind beginning over again?"

He repeated everything in the same words, with pauses and reflections of his own from time to time. She listened eagerly now, perceiving, with a woman's keen sensibility, all the sudden changes of fortune which his narrative implied, and trembling with horror, every now and then exclaiming:

"Oh, my God!"

The little fellow, believing that she had calmed down, ceased beating César, in order to take his mother's hand, and he listened, too, as if he understood.

When the narrative was finished, young Hautot continued:

"Now, we will settle matters together, in accordance with his wishes. I am well off, he has left me plenty of means. I don't want you to have anything to complain about——"

But she quickly interrupted him.

"Oh! Monsieur César, Monsieur César, not to-day. I am cut to the heart—another time—another day. No, not to-day. If I accept, listen—it is not for myself—no, no, no, I swear to you, it is for the child. Besides, this sum will be placed to his account."

Thereupon, César, horrified, guessed the truth, and stammered:

13

"So then—it is his—the child?"

"Why, yes," she said.

And Hautot Junior gazed at his brother with a confused emotion, intense and painful.

After a long silence, for she had begun to weep afresh, César, quite embarrassed, went on:

"Well, then, Mam'zelle Donet, I am going. When would you wish to talk this over with me?"

She exclaimed:

"Oh! no, don't go! don't go! Don't leave me all alone with Émile. I would die of grief. I have no longer any one, any one but my child. Oh! what wretchedness, what wretchedness, Monsieur César! Come, sit down again. Tell me something more. Tell me what he did at home all the week."

And César resumed his seat, accustomed to obey.

She drew over another chair for herself in front of the stove, where the dishes had all this time been heating, took Émile upon her knees, and asked César a thousand questions about his father—questions of an intimate nature, which made him feel, without reasoning on the subject, that she had loved Hautot with all the strength of her weak woman's heart.

And, by the natural sequence of his ideas—which were rather limited in number—he recurred once more to the accident, and set about telling the story over again with all the same details.

When he said:

"He had a hole in his stomach that you could put your two fists into," she gave a sort of shriek, and her eyes again filled with tears.

Then, seized by the contagion of her grief, César began to weep, too, and as tears always soften the fibres of the heart, he bent over Émile, whose forehead was close to his own mouth, and kissed him.

The mother, recovering her breath, murmured:

"Poor child, he is an orphan now!"

"And so am I," said César.

And they were silent.

But suddenly the practical instinct of the housewife, accustomed to think of everything, revived in the young woman's breast.

"You have perhaps had nothing to eat all the morning, Monsieur César."

"No, mam'zelle."

"Oh! you must be hungry. You will eat a morsel."

"Thank you," he said, "I am not hungry; I have had too much sorrow."

She replied:

"In spite of sorrow, we must live. You will not refuse to let me get something for you! And then you will remain a little longer. When you are gone, I don't know what will become of me."

He yielded after some further resistance, and, sitting down with his back to the fire, facing her, he ate a plateful of tripe, which had been drying up in the gravy, and drank a glass of red wine. But he would not allow her to uncork the bottle of white wine. He several times wiped the mouth of the little boy, who had smeared all his chin with gravy.

As he rose to take his leave, he asked:

"When would you like me to come back to talk about this matter, Mam'zelle Donet?"

"If it is all the same to you, say next Thursday, Monsieur César. In that way I shall not waste my time, as I always have my Thursdays free."

"That will suit me—next Thursday."

"You will come to luncheon, won't you?"

"Oh! As to that I can't promise."

"The reason I suggested it is, that people can chat better when they are eating. One has more time, too."

"Well, be it so. About twelve o'clock, then."

And he took his departure, after he had again kissed little Émile, and pressed Mademoiselle Donet's hand.

PART III

THE week appeared long to César Hautot. He had never before lived alone, and the isolation seemed to him unendurable. Till now, he had lived at his father's side, just like his shadow, followed him into the fields, superintended the execution of his orders, and if they were separated for a short time they again met at dinner. They spent the evenings smoking their pipes together, sitting opposite each other, chatting about horses, cows, or sheep; and the grip of their hands when they rose in the morning was a manifestation of deep family affection.

Now César was alone. He went mechanically about his autumn duties on the farm, expecting any moment to see his father's tall, energetic outline rising up at the end of a level field. To kill time, he visited his neighbors, told about the accident to all who had not heard of it, and sometimes repeated it to the others. Then, having exhausted his occupations and his reflections, he would sit down at the side of the road, asking himself whether this kind of life was going to last forever.

He frequently thought of Mademoiselle Donet. He liked her. He considered her thoroughly respectable, a gentle, good young woman, as his father had said. Yes, undoubtedly she was a good girl. He resolved to act handsomely toward her, and to give her two thousand francs a year, settling the capital on the child. He even experienced a certain pleasure in thinking that he was going to see her on the following Thursday and arrange this matter with her. And then the thought of this brother, this little chap of five, who was his father's son, worried him, annoyed him a little, and, at the same time, pleased him. He had, as it were, a family in this youngster, sprung from a clandestine alliance, who would never bear the name of Hautot—a family which he might take or leave, just as he pleased, but which reminded him of his father.

And so, when he saw himself on the road to Rouen on Thursday morning, borne along by Graindorge with his measured trot, he felt his heart lighter, more at peace than it had been since his bereavement.

On entering Mademoiselle Donet's apartment, he saw the table laid as on the previous Thursday, with the sole difference that the crust had not been removed from the bread. He pressed the young woman's hand, kissed Émile on both cheeks, and sat down, more or less as if he were in his own house, although his heart was full. Mademoiselle Donet seemed to him a little thinner and paler. She must have grieved sorely. She now wore an air of constraint in his presence, as if she understood what she had not felt the week before under the first blow of her misfortune, and she exhibited an excessive deference toward him, a mournful humility, and made touching efforts to please him, as if to repay by her attentions the kindness he had manifested toward her. They were a long time at luncheon, talking over the business which had brought him there. She did not want so much money. It was too much. She earned enough to live on herself, but she only wished that Émile might find a few sous awaiting him when he grew up. César was firm, however, and even added a gift of a thousand francs for herself, for the expenses of mourning.

When he had taken his coffee, she asked:

"Do you smoke?"

"Yes—I have my pipe."

He felt in his pocket. Good heavens! He had forgotten it! He was becoming quite distressed about it when she offered him a pipe of his father's that had been put away in a closet. He took it up in his hand, recognized it, smelled it, spoke of its quality in a tone of emotion, filled it with tobacco, and lighted it. Then, he set Émile astride his knee, and gave him a ride, while she removed the table-cloth, and piled the soiled dishes under the sideboard, intending to wash them as soon as he was gone.

About three o'clock he rose regretfully, quite annoyed at the thought of having to go.

"Well! Mademoiselle Donet," he said, "I wish you good evening, and am delighted to have found you like this."

She remained standing before him, blushing, much

affected, and gazed at him while she thought of the father.

"Shall we not see one another again?" she said. He replied simply:

"Why, yes, mademoiselle, if it gives you pleasure."

"Certainly, Monsieur César. Will next Thursday suit you?"

"Yes, Mademoiselle Donet."

"You will come to luncheon, of course?"

"Well—if you are so kind as to invite me, I can't refuse."

"It is understood, then, Monsieur César—next Thursday, at twelve, the same as to-day."

"Thursday at twelve, Mademoiselle Donet!"

Vol. 1—14

THE MASK

THERE was a masquerade ball at the Elysée-Montmartre that evening. It was the *Mi-Carême,* and the crowds were pouring into the brightly lighted passage which leads to the dance hall, like water flowing through the open lock of a canal. The loud call of the orchestra, bursting like a storm of sound, shook the rafters, swelled through the whole neighborhood and awoke, in the streets and in the depths of the houses, an irresistible desire to jump, to get warm, to have fun, which slumbers within each human animal.

The patrons came from every quarter of Paris; there were people of all classes who love noisy pleasures, a little low and tinged with debauch. There were clerks and girls—girls of every description, some wearing common cotton, some the finest batiste; rich girls, old and covered with diamonds, and poor girls of sixteen, full of the desire to revel, to belong to men, to spend money. Elegant black evening suits, in search of fresh or faded but appetizing novelty, wandering through the excited crowds, looking, searching, while the masqueraders seemed moved above all by the desire for amusement. Already the far-famed quadrilles had attracted around them a curious crowd. The moving hedge which encircled the four dancers swayed in and out like a snake, sometimes nearer and sometimes farther away, according to the motions of the performers. The two women, whose lower limbs seemed to be attached to their bodies by rubber springs, were making wonderful and surprising motions with their legs. Their partners hopped and skipped about, waving their arms about. One could imagine their panting breath beneath their masks.

One of them, who had taken his place in the most famous quadrille, as substitute for an absent celebrity, the handsome *"Songe-au-Gosse,"* was trying to keep up with the tireless *"Arête-de-Veau"* and was making strange fancy steps which aroused the joy and sarcasm of the audience.

He was thin, dressed like a dandy, with a pretty varnished mask on his face. It had a curly blond mustache and a wavy wig. He looked like a wax figure from the Musée Grévin, like a strange and fantastic caricature of the charming young man of fashion plates, and he danced with visible effort, clumsily, with a comical impetuosity. He appeared rusty beside the others when he tried to imitate their gambols: he seemed overcome by rheumatism, as heavy as a great Dane playing with greyhounds. Mocking bravos encouraged him. And he, carried away with enthusiasm, jigged about with such frenzy that suddenly, carried away by a wild spurt, he pitched head foremost into the living wall formed by the audience, which opened up before him to allow him to pass, then closed around the inanimate body of the dancer, stretched out on his face.

Some men picked him up and carried him away, calling for a doctor. A gentleman stepped forward, young and elegant, in well-fitting evening clothes, with large pearl studs. "I am a professor of the

Faculty of Medicine," he said in a modest voice. He was allowed to pass, and he entered a small room full of little cardboard boxes, where the still lifeless dancer had been stretched out on some chairs. The doctor at first wished to take off the mask, and he noticed that it was attached in a complicated manner, with a perfect network of small metal wires which cleverly bound it to his wig and covered the whole head. Even the neck was imprisoned in a false skin which continued the chin and was painted the color of flesh, being attached to the collar of the shirt.

All this had to be cut with strong scissors. When the physician had slit open this surprising arrangement, from the shoulder to the temple, he opened this armor and found the face of an old man, worn out, thin and wrinkled. The surprise among those who had brought in this seemingly young dancer was so great that no one laughed, no one said a word.

All were watching this sad face as he lay on the straw chairs, his eyes closed, his face covered with white hair, some long, falling from the forehead over the face, others short, growing around the face and the chin, and, beside this poor head, that pretty little, neat, varnished, smiling mask.

The man regained consciousness after being inanimate for a long time, but he still seemed to be so weak and sick that the physician feared some dangerous complication. He asked: "Where do you live?"

The old dancer seemed to be making an effort to remember, and then he mentioned the name of the street, which no one knew. He was asked for more definite information about the neighborhood. He answered with a great slowness, indecision and difficulty, which revealed his upset state of mind. The physician continued:

"I will take you home myself."

Curiosity had overcome him to find out who this strange dancer, this phenomenal jumper might be. Soon the two rolled away in a cab to the other side of Montmartre.

They stopped before a high building of poor appearance. They went up a winding staircase. The doctor held to the banister, which was so grimy that the hand stuck to it, and he supported the dizzy old man, whose forces were beginning to return. They stopped at the fourth floor.

The door at which they had knocked was opened by an old woman, neat looking, with a white night-cap enclosing a thin face with sharp features, one of those good, rough faces of a hard-working and faithful woman. She cried out:

"For goodness sake! What's the matter?"

He told her the whole affair in a few words. She became reassured and even calmed the physician himself by telling him that the same thing had happened many times. She said: "He must be put to bed, monsieur, that is all. Let him sleep and to-morrow he will be all right."

The doctor continued: "But he can hardly speak."

"Oh! that's just a little drink, nothing more; he has eaten no dinner, in order to be nimble, and then he took a few absinthes in order to work himself up to the proper pitch. You see, drink gives strength to his legs, but it stops his thoughts and words. He is too old to dance as he does. Really, his lack of common sense is enough to drive one mad!"

The doctor, surprised, insisted:

"But why does he dance like that at his age?"

She shrugged her shoulders and turned red from the anger which was slowly rising within her and she cried out:

"Ah! yes, why? So that the people will think him young under his mask; so that the women will still take him for a young dandy and whisper nasty things into his ears; so that he can rub up against all their dirty skins, with their perfumes and powders and cosmetics. Ah! it s a fine business! What a life I have had for the last forty years! But we must first get him to bed, so that he may have no ill effects. Would you mind helping me? When he is like that I can't do anything with him alone."

The old man was sitting on his bed, with a tipsy look, his long white hair falling over his face. His companion looked at him with tender yet indignant eyes. She continued:

"Just see the fine head he has for his age, and yet he has to go and disguise himself in order to make people think that he is young. It's a perfect shame! Really, he has a fine head, monsieur! Wait, I'll show it to you before putting him to bed."

She went to a table on which stood the washbasin, a pitcher of water, soap and a comb and brush. She took the brush, returned to the bed and pushed back the drunkard's tangled hair. In a few seconds she made him look like a model fit for a great painter, with his long white locks flowing on his neck. Then she stepped back in order to observe him, saying: "There! Isn't he fine for his age?"

"Very," agreed the doctor, who was beginning to be highly amused.

She added: "And if you had known him when he

was twenty-five! But we must get him to bed, otherwise the drink will make him sick. Do you mind drawing off that sleeve? Higher—like that—that's right. Now the trousers. Wait, I will take his shoes off—that's right. Now, hold him upright while I open the bed. There—let us put him in. If you think that he is going to disturb himself when it is time for me to get in you are mistaken. I have to find a little corner any place I can. That doesn't bother him! Bah! You old pleasure seeker!"

As soon as he felt himself stretched out in his sheets the old man closed his eyes, opened them, closed them again, and over his whole face appeared an energetic resolve to sleep. The doctor examined him with an ever-increasing interest and asked: "Does he go to all the fancy balls and try to be a young man?"

"To all of them, monsieur, and he comes back to me in the morning in a deplorable condition. You see, it's regret that leads him on and that makes him put a pasteboard face over his own. Yes, the regret of no longer being what he was and of no longer making any conquests!"

He was sleeping now and beginning to snore. She looked at him with a pitying expression and continued: "Oh! how many conquests that man has made! More than one could believe, monsieur, more than the finest gentlemen of the world, than all the tenors and all the generals."

"Really? What did he do?"

"Oh! it will surprise you at first, as you did not know him in his palmy days. When I met him it was also at a ball, for he has always frequented them. As soon as I saw him I was caught—caught

like a fish on a hook. Ah! how pretty he was, monsieur, with his curly raven locks and black eyes as
large as saucers! Indeed, he was good looking! He
took me away that evening and I never have left him
since, never, not even for a day, no matter what he
did to me! Oh! he has often made it hard for me!"

The doctor asked: "Are you married?"

She answered simply: "Yes, monsieur, otherwise
he would have dropped me as he did the others. I
have been his wife and his servant, everything,
everything that he wished. How he has made me
cry—tears which I did not show him; for he would
tell all his adventures to me—to me, monsieur—without understanding how it hurt me to listen."

"But what was his business?"

"That's so. I forgot to tell you. He was the
foreman at Martel's—a foreman such as they never
had had—an artist who averaged ten francs an
hour."

"Martel?—who is Martel?"

"The hairdresser, monsieur, the great hairdresser
of the Opera, who had all the actresses for customers. Yes, sir, all the smartest actresses had their
hair dressed by Ambrose, and they would give him
tips that made a fortune for him. Ah! monsieur, all
the women are alike, yes, all of them. When a man
pleases their fancy they offer themselves to him. It
is so easy—and it hurt me so to hear about it. For
he would tell me everything—he simply could not
hold his tongue—it was impossible. Those things
please the men so much! They seem to get even
more enjoyment out of telling than doing.

"When I would see him coming in the evening, a
little pale, with a pleased look and a bright eye, I

would say to myself: 'One more. I am sure that he has caught one more.' Then I felt a wild desire to question him, and then, again, not to know, to stop his talking if he should begin. And we would look at each other.

"I knew that he would not keep still, that he would come to the point. I could feel that from his manner, which seemed to laugh and say: 'I had a fine adventure to-day, Madeleine.' I would pretend to notice nothing, to guess nothing; I would set the table, bring on the soup and sit down opposite him.

"At those times, monsieur, it was as if my friendship for him had been crushed in my body as with a stone. It hurt. But he did not understand; he did not know; he felt a need to tell all those things to some one, to boast, to show how much he was loved, and I was the only one he had to whom he could talk—the only one. And I would have to listen and drink it in, like poison.

"He would begin to take his soup and then he would say: 'One more, Madeleine.'

"And I would think: 'Here it comes! Goodness! what a man! Why did I ever meet him?'

"Then he would begin: 'One more! And a beauty, too.' And it would be some little one from the Vaudeville or else from the Variétés, and some of the big ones, too, some of the most famous. He would tell me their names, how their apartments were furnished, everything, everything, monsieur. Heartbreaking details. And he would go over them and tell his story over again from beginning to end, so pleased with himself that I would pretend to laugh so that he would not get angry with me.

"Everything may not have been true! He liked

to glorify himself and was quite capable of inventing such things! They may perhaps also have been true! On those evenings he would pretend to be tired and wish to go to bed after supper. We would take supper at eleven, monsieur, for he could never get back from work earlier.

"When he had finished telling about his adventure he would walk round the room and smoke cigarettes, and he was so handsome, with his mustache and curly hair, that I would think: 'It's true, just the same, what he is telling. Since I myself am crazy about that man, why should not others be the same?' Then I would feel like crying, shrieking, running away and jumping out of the window while I was clearing the table and he was smoking. He would yawn in order to show how tired he was, and he would say two or three times before going to bed: 'Ah! how well I shall sleep this evening!'

"I bear him no ill will, because he did not know how he was hurting me. No, he could not know! He loved to boast about the women just as a peacock loves to show his feathers. He got to the point where he thought that all of them looked at him and desired him.

"It was hard when he grew old. Oh, monsieur, when I saw his first white hair I felt a terrible shock and then a great joy—a wicked joy—but so great, so great! I said to myself: 'It's the end—it's the end.' It seemed as if I were about to be released from prison. At last I could have him to myself, all to myself, when the others would no longer want him.

"It was one morning in bed. He was still sleeping and I leaned over him to wake him up with a kiss, when I noticed in his curls, over his temple, a little thread which shone like silver. What a surprise! I should not have thought it possible! At first I thought of tearing it out so that he would not see it, but as I looked carefully I noticed another farther up. White hair! He was going to have white hair! My heart began to thump and perspiration stood out all over me, but away down at the bottom I was happy.

"It was mean to feel thus, but I did my housework with a light heart that morning, without waking him up, and, as soon as he opened his eyes of his own accord, I said to him: 'Do you know what I discovered while you were asleep?'

" 'No.'

" 'I found white hairs.'

"He started up as if I had tickled him and said angrily: 'It's not true!'

" 'Yes, it is. There are four of them over your left temple.'

"He jumped out of bed and ran over to the mirror. He could not find them. Then I showed him the first one, the lowest, the little curly one, and I said: 'It's no wonder, after the life that you have been leading. In two years all will be over for you.'

"Well, monsieur, I had spoken true; two years later one could not recognize him. How quickly a man changes! He was still handsome, but he had lost his freshness, and the women no longer ran after him. Ah! what a life I led at that time! How he treated me! Nothing suited him. He left his trade to go into the hat business, in which he ate up all his money. Then he unsuccessfully tried to be an actor, and finally he began to frequent public balls. Fortunately, he had had common sense enough to save a little something on which we now live. It is sufficient, but it is not enormous. And to think that at one time he had almost a fortune!

"Now you see what he does. This habit holds him like a frenzy. He has to be young; he has to dance with women who smell of perfume and cosmetics. You poor old darling!"

She was looking at her old snoring husband fondly, ready to cry. Then, gently tiptoeing up to him, she kissed his hair. The physician had risen and was getting ready to leave, finding nothing to say to this strange couple. Just as he was leaving she asked:

"Would you mind giving me your address? If he should grow worse, I could go and get you."

THE PENGUINS' ROCK

THIS is the season for penguins.

From April to the end of May, before the Parisian visitors arrive, one sees, all at once, on the little beach at Étretat several old gentlemen, booted and belted in shooting costume. They spend four or five days at the Hotel Hauville, disappear, and return again three weeks later. Then, after a fresh sojourn, they go away altogether.

One sees them again the following spring.

These are the last penguin hunters, what remain of the old set. There were about twenty enthusiasts thirty or forty years ago; now there are only a few of the enthusiastic sportsmen.

The penguin is a very rare bird of passage, with peculiar habits. It lives the greater part of the year in the latitude of Newfoundland and the islands of St. Pierre and Miquelon. But in the breeding season a flight of emigrants crosses the ocean and comes every year to the same spot to lay their eggs, to the Penguins' Rock near Étretat. They are found nowhere else, only there. They have always come there, have always been chased away, but return again, and will always return. As soon as the young birds are grown they all fly away, and disappear for a year.

Why do they not go elsewhere? Why not choose some other spot on the long white, unending cliff

1

that extends from the Pas-de-Calais to Havre? What force, what invincible instinct, what custom of centuries impels these birds to come back to this place? What first migration, what tempest, possibly, once cast their ancestors on this rock? And why do the children, the grandchildren, all the descendants of the first parents always return here?

There are not many of them, a hundred at most, as if one single family, maintaining the tradition, made this annual pilgrimage.

And each spring, as soon as the little wandering tribe has taken up its abode on the rock, the same sportsmen also reappear in the village. One knew them formerly when they were young; now they are old, but constant to the regular appointment which they have kept for thirty or forty years. They would not miss it for anything in the world.

It was an April evening in one of the later years. Three of the old sportsmen had arrived; one was missing—M. d'Arnelles.

He had written to no one, given no account of himself. But he was not dead, like so many of the rest; they would have heard of it. At length, tired of waiting for him, the other three sat down to table. Dinner was almost over when a carriage drove into the yard of the hotel, and the late comer presently entered the dining room.

He sat down, in a good humor, rubbing his hands, and ate with zest. When one of his comrades remarked with surprise at his being in a frock-coat, he replied quietly:

"Yes, I had no time to change my clothes."

2

THE PENGUINS' ROCK

They retired on leaving the table, for they had to set out before daybreak in order to take the birds unawares.

There is nothing so pretty as this sport, this early morning expedition.

At three o'clock in the morning the sailors awoke the sportsmen by throwing sand against the windows. They were ready in a few minutes and went down to the beach. Although it was still dark, the stars had paled a little. The sea ground the shingle on the beach. There was such a fresh breeze that it made one shiver slightly in spite of one's heavy clothing.

Presently two boats were pushed down the beach, by the sailors, with a sound as of tearing cloth, and were floated on the nearest waves. The brown sail was hoisted, swelled a little, fluttered, hesitated and swelling out again as round as a paunch, carried the boats towards the large arched entrance that could be faintly distinguished in the darkness.

The sky became clearer, the shadows seemed to melt away. The coast still seemed veiled, the great white coast, perpendicular as a wall.

They passed through the Manne-Porte, an enormous arch beneath which a ship could sail; they doubled the promontory of La Courtine, passed the little valley of Antifer and the cape of the same name; and suddenly caught sight of a beach on which some hundreds of seagulls were perched.

That was the Penguins' Rock. It was just a little protuberance of the cliff, and on the narrow ledges of rock the birds' heads might be seen watching the boats.

They remained there, motionless, not venturing

3

to fly off as yet. Some of them perched on the edges, seated upright, looked almost like bottles, for their little legs are so short that when they walk they glide along as if they were on rollers. When they start to fly they cannot make a spring and let themselves fall like stones almost down to the very men who are watching them.

They know their limitation and the danger to which it subjects them, and cannot make up their minds to fly away.

But the boatmen begin to shout, beating the sides of the boat with the wooden boat pins, and the birds, in affright, fly one by one into space until they reach the level of the waves. Then, moving their wings rapidly, they scud, scud along until they reach the open sea, if a shower of lead does not knock them into the water.

For an hour the firing is kept up, obliging them to give up, one after another. Sometimes the mother birds will not leave their nests, and are riddled with shot, causing drops of blood to spurt out on the white cliff, and the animal dies without having deserted her eggs.

The first day M. d'Arnelles fired at the birds with his habitual zeal; but when the party returned toward ten o'clock, beneath a brilliant sun, which cast great triangles of light on the white cliffs along the coast he appeared a little worried, and absent-minded, contrary to his accustomed manner.

As soon as they got on shore a kind of servant dressed in black came up to him and said something in a low tone. He seemed to reflect, hesitate, and then replied:

"No, to-morrow."

The following day they set out again. This time M. d'Arnelles frequently missed his aim, although the birds were close by. His friends teased him, asked him if he were in love, if some secret sorrow was troubling his mind and heart. At length he confessed.

"Yes, indeed, I have to leave soon, and that annoys me."

"What, you must leave? And why?"

"Oh, I have some business that calls me back. I cannot stay any longer."

They then talked of other matters.

As soon as breakfast was over the valet in black appeared. M. d'Arnelles ordered his carriage, and the man was leaving the room when the three sportsmen interfered, insisting, begging, and praying their friend to stay. One of them at last said:

"Come now, this cannot be a matter of such importance, for you have already waited two days."

M. d'Arnelles, altogether perplexed, began to think, evidently baffled, divided between pleasure and duty, unhappy and disturbed.

After reflecting for some time he stammered:

"The fact is—the fact is—I am not alone here. I have my son-in-law."

There were exclamations and shouts of "Your son-in-law! Where is he?"

He suddenly appeared confused and his face grew red.

"What! do you not know? Why—why—he is in the coach house. He is dead."

They were all silent in amazement.

M. d'Arnelles continued, more and more disturbed:

"I had the misfortune to lose him; and as I was taking the body to my house, in Briseville, I came round this way so as not to miss our appointment. But you can see that I cannot wait any longer."

Then one of the sportsmen, bolder than the rest, said:

"Well, but—since he is dead—it seems to me—that he can wait a day longer."

The others chimed in:

"That cannot be denied."

M. d'Arnelles appeared to be relieved of a great weight, but a little uneasy, nevertheless, he asked:

"But, frankly—do you think——"

The three others, as one man, replied:

"Parbleu! my dear boy, two days more or less can make no difference in his present condition."

And, perfectly calmly, the father-in-law turned to the undertaker's assistant, and said:

"Well, then, my friend, it will be the day after to-morrow."

A FAMILY

I WAS to see my old friend, Simon Radevin, of whom I had lost sight for fifteen years. At one time he was my most intimate friend, the friend who knows one's thoughts, with whom one passes long, quiet, happy evenings, to whom one tells one's secret love affairs, and who seems to draw out those rare, ingenious, delicate thoughts born of that sympathy that gives a sense of repose.

For years we had scarcely been separated; we had lived, travelled, thought and dreamed together; had liked the same things, had admired the same books, understood the same authors, trembled with the same sensations, and very often laughed at the same individuals, whom we understood completely by merely exchanging a glance.

Then he married. He married, quite suddenly, a little girl from the provinces, who had come to Paris in search of a husband. How in the world could that little thin, insipidly fair girl, with her weak hands, her light, vacant eyes, and her clear, silly voice, who was exactly like a hundred thousand marriageable dolls, have picked up that intelligent, clever young fellow? Can any one understand these things? No doubt he had hoped for happiness, simple, quiet and long-enduring happiness, in the arms of a good, tender and faithful woman; he had seen all that in the transparent looks of that schoolgirl with light hair.

He had not dreamed of the fact that an active, living and vibrating man grows weary of everything as soon as he understands the stupid reality, unless, indeed, he becomes so brutalized that he understands nothing whatever.

What would he be like when I met him again? Still lively, witty, light-hearted and enthusiastic, or in a state of mental torpor induced by provincial life? A man may change greatly in the course of fifteen years!

The train stopped at a small station, and as I got out of the carriage, a stout, a very stout man with red cheeks and a big stomach rushed up to me with open arms, exclaiming: "George!" I embraced him, but I had not recognized him, and then I said, in astonishment: "By Jove! You have not grown thin!" And he replied with a laugh: "What did you expect? Good living, a good table and good nights! Eating and sleeping, that is my existence!"

I looked at him closely, trying to discover in that broad face the features I held so dear. His eyes alone had not changed, but I no longer saw the same expression in them, and I said to myself: "If the expression be the reflection of the mind, the thoughts in that head are not what they used to be formerly; those thoughts which I knew so well."

Yet his eyes were bright, full of happiness and friendship, but they had not that clear, intelligent expression which shows as much as words the brightness of the intellect. Suddenly he said: "Here are my two eldest children." A girl of four-

teen, who was almost a woman, and a boy of thirteen, in the dress of a boy from a *lycée,* came forward in a hesitating and awkward manner, and I
said in a low voice: "Are they yours?" "Of course
they are," he replied, laughing. "How many have
you?" "Five! There are three more at home."

He said this in a proud, self-satisfied, almost triumphant manner, and I felt profound pity, mingled
with a feeling of vague contempt, for this vain-
glorious and simple reproducer of his species.

I got into a carriage which he drove himself, and
we set off through the town, a dull, sleepy, gloomy
town where nothing was moving in the streets except a few dogs and two or three maidservants.
Here and there a shopkeeper, standing at his door,
took off his hat, and Simon returned his salute and
told me the man's name; no doubt to show me that
he knew all the inhabitants personally, and the
thought struck me that he was thinking of becoming
a candidate for the Chamber of Deputies, that dream
of all those who bury themselves in the provinces.

We were soon out of the town, and the carriage
turned into a garden that was an imitation of a park,
and stopped in front of a turreted house, which
tried to look like a château.

"That is my den," said Simon, so that I might
compliment him on it. "It is charming," I replied.

A lady appeared on the steps, dressed for company, and with company phrases all ready prepared.
She was no longer the light-haired, insipid girl I
had seen in church fifteen years previously, but a
stout lady in curls and flounces, one of those ladies
of uncertain age, without intellect, without any of
those things that go to make a woman. In short,

she was a mother, a stout, commonplace mother, a human breeding machine which procreates without any other preoccupation but her children and her cook-book.

She welcomed me, and I went into the hall, where three children, ranged according to their height, seemed set out for review, like firemen before a mayor, and I said: "Ah! ah! so there are the others?" Simon, radiant with pleasure, introduced them: "Jean, Sophie and Gontran."

The door of the drawing-room was open. I went in, and in the depths of an easy-chair, I saw something trembling, a man, an old, paralyzed man. Madame Radevin came forward and said: "This is my grandfather, monsieur; he is eighty-seven." And then she shouted into the shaking old man's ears: "This is a friend of Simon's, papa." The old gentleman tried to say "good-day" to me, and he muttered: "Oua, oua, oua," and waved his hand, and I took a seat saying: "You are very kind, monsieur."

Simon had just come in, and he said with a laugh: "So! You have made grandpapa's acquaintance. He is a treasure, that old man; he is the delight of the children. But he is so greedy that he almost kills himself at every meal; you have no idea what he would eat if he were allowed to do as he pleased. But you will see, you will see. He looks at all the sweets as if they were so many girls. You never saw anything so funny; you will see presently."

I was then shown to my room, to change my dress for dinner, and hearing a great clatter behind me on the stairs, I turned round and saw that all the children were following me behind their father; to do me honor, no doubt.

My windows looked out across a dreary, interminable plain, an ocean of grass, of wheat and of oats, without a clump of trees or any rising ground, a striking and melancholy picture of the life which they must be leading in that house.

A bell rang; it was for dinner, and I went downstairs. Madame Radevin took my arm in a ceremonious manner, and we passed into the dining-room. A footman wheeled in the old man in his armchair. He gave a greedy and curious look at the dessert, as he turned his shaking head with difficulty from one dish to the other.

Simon rubbed his hands: "You will be amused," he said; and all the children, understanding that I was going to be indulged with the sight of their greedy grandfather, began to laugh, while their mother merely smiled and shrugged her shoulders, and Simon, making a speaking trumpet of his hands, shouted at the old man: "This evening there is sweet creamed rice!" The wrinkled face of the grandfather brightened, and he trembled more violently, from head to foot, showing that he had understood and was very pleased. The dinner began.

"Just look!" Simon whispered. The old man did not like the soup, and refused to eat it; but he was obliged to do it for the good of his health, and the footman forced the spoon into his mouth, while the old man blew so energetically, so as not to swallow the soup, that it was scattered like a spray all over the table and over his neighbors. The children writhed with laughter at the spectacle, while their father, who was also amused, said: "Is not the old man comical?"

During the whole meal they were taken up solely with him. He devoured the dishes on the table with his eyes, and tried to seize them and pull them over to him with his trembling hands. They put them almost within his reach, to see his useless efforts, his trembling clutches at them, the piteous appeal of his whole nature, of his eyes, of his mouth and of his nose as he smelt them, and he slobbered on his table napkin with eagerness, while uttering inarticulate grunts. And the whole family was highly amused at this horrible and grotesque scene.

Then they put a tiny morsel on his plate, and he ate with feverish gluttony, in order to get something more as soon as possible, and when the sweetened rice was brought in, he nearly had a fit, and groaned with greediness, and Gontran called out to him: "You have eaten too much already; you can have no more." And they pretended not to give him any. Then he began to cry; he cried and trembled more violently than ever, while all the children laughed. At last, however, they gave him his helping, a very small piece; and as he ate the first mouthful, he made a comical noise in his throat, and a movement with his neck as ducks do when they swallow too large a morsel, and when he had swallowed it, he began to stamp his feet, so as to get more.

I was seized with pity for this saddening and ridiculous Tantalus, and interposed on his behalf: "Come, give him a little more rice!" But Simon replied: "Oh! no, my dear fellow, if he were to eat too much, it would harm him, at his age."

A FAMILY

I held my tongue, and thought over those words. Oh, ethics! Oh, logic! Oh, wisdom! At his age! So they deprived him of his only remaining pleasure out of regard for his health! His health! What would he do with it, inert and trembling wreck that he was? They were taking care of his life, so they said. His life? How many days? Ten, twenty, fifty, or a hundred? Why? For his own sake? Or to preserve for some time longer the spectacle of his impotent greediness in the family.

There was nothing left for him to do in this life, nothing whatever. He had one single wish left, one sole pleasure; why not grant him that last solace until he died?

After we had played cards for a long time, I went up to my room and to bed; I was low-spirited and sad, sad, sad! and I sat at my window. Not a sound could be heard outside but the beautiful warbling of a bird in a tree, somewhere in the distance. No doubt the bird was singing in a low voice during the night, to lull his mate, who was asleep on her eggs.

And I thought of my poor friend's five children, and pictured him to myself, snoring by the side of his ugly wife.

SUICIDES

To Georges Legrand

HARDLY a day goes by without our reading a news item like the following in some newspaper:

> "On Wednesday night the people living in No. 40 Rue de ——, were awakened by two successive shots. The explosions seemed to come from the apartment occupied by M. X——. The door was broken in and the man was found bathed in his blood, still holding in one hand the revolver with which he had taken his life.
> "M. X—— was fifty-seven years of age, enjoying a comfortable income, and had everything necessary to make him happy. No cause can be found for his action."

What terrible grief, what unknown suffering, hidden despair, secret wounds drive these presumably happy persons to suicide? We search, we imagine tragedies of love, we suspect financial troubles, and, as we never find anything definite, we apply to these deaths the word "mystery."

A letter found on the desk of one of these "suicides without cause," and written during his last night, beside his loaded revolver, has come into our hands. We deem it rather interesting. It reveals none of those great catastrophes which we always expect to find behind these acts of despair; but it shows us the slow succession of the little vexations of life, the disintegration of a lonely existence,

whose dreams have disappeared; it gives the reason
for these tragic ends, which only nervous and high-
strung people can understand.

Here it is:

"It is midnight. When I have finished this letter I shall kill myself. Why? I shall attempt to
give the reasons, not for those who may read these
lines, but for myself, to kindle my waning courage,
to impress upon myself the fatal necessity of this act
which can, at best, be only deferred.

"I was brought up by simple-minded parents who
were unquestioning believers. And I believed as
they did.

"My dream lasted a long time. The last veil has
just been torn from my eyes.

"During the last few years a strange change has
been taking place within me. All the events of Life,
which formerly had to me the glow of a beautiful
sunset, are now fading away. The true meaning of
things has appeared to me in its brutal reality; and
the true reason for love has bred in me disgust even
for this poetic sentiment: 'We are the eternal toys
of foolish and charming illusions, which are always
being renewed.'

"On growing older, I had become partly recon-
ciled to the awful mystery of life, to the uselessness
of effort; when the emptiness of everything appeared to me in a new light, this evening, after
dinner.

"Formerly, I was happy! Everything pleased
me: the passing women, the appearance of the
streets, the place where I lived; and I even took an
interest in the cut of my clothes. But the repetition

of the same sights has had the result of filling my
heart with weariness and disgust, just as one would
feel were one to go every night to the same theatre.

"For the last thirty years I have been rising at
the same hour; and, at the same restaurant, for
thirty years, I have been eating at the same hours
the same dishes brought me by different waiters.

"I have tried travel. The loneliness which one
feels in strange places terrified me. I felt so alone,
so small on the earth that I quickly started on my
homeward journey.

"But here the unchanging expression of my furniture, which has stood for thirty years in the same
place, the smell of my apartments (for, with time,
each dwelling takes on a particular odor) each
night, these and other things disgust me and make
me sick of living thus.

"Everything repeats itself endlessly. The way
in which I put my key in the lock, the place where
I always find my matches, the first object which
meets my eye when I enter the room, make me feel
like jumping out of the window and putting an end
to those monotonous events from which we can
never escape.

"Each day, when I shave, I feel an inordinate
desire to cut my throat; and my face, which I see in
the little mirror, always the same, with soap on my
cheeks, has several times made me weak from sadness.

"Now I even hate to be with people whom I used
to meet with pleasure; I know them so well, I can
tell just what they are going to say and what I am
going to answer. Each brain is like a circus, where
the same horse keeps circling around eternally. We

must circle round always, around the same ideas, the same joys, the same pleasures, the same habits, the same beliefs, the same sensations of disgust.

"The fog was terrible this evening. It enfolded the boulevard, where the street lights were dimmed and looked like smoking candles. A heavier weight than usual oppressed me. Perhaps my digestion was bad.

"For good digestion is everything in life. It gives the inspiration to the artist, amorous desires to young people, clear ideas to thinkers, the joy of life to everybody, and it also allows one to eat heartily (which is one of the greatest pleasures). A sick stomach induces scepticism, unbelief, nightmares and the desire for death. I have often noticed this fact. Perhaps I would not kill myself, if my digestion had been good this evening.

"When I sat down in the arm-chair where I have been sitting every day for thirty years, I glanced around me, and just then I was seized by such a terrible distress that I thought I must go mad.

"I tried to think of what I could do to run away from myself. Every occupation struck me as being worse even than inaction. Then I bethought me of putting my papers in order.

"For a long time I have been thinking of clearing out my drawers; for, for the last thirty years, I have been throwing my letters and bills pell-mell into the same desk, and this confusion has often caused me considerable trouble. But I feel such moral and physical laziness at the sole idea of putting anything in order that I have never had the courage to begin this tedious business.

"I therefore opened my desk, intending to

choose among my old papers and destroy the majority of them.

"At first I was bewildered by this array of documents, yellowed by age, then I chose one.

"Oh! if you cherish life, never disturb the burial place of old letters!

"And if, perchance, you should, take the contents by the handful, close your eyes that you may not read a word, so that you may not recognize some forgotten handwriting which may plunge you suddenly into a sea of memories; carry these papers to the fire; and when they are in ashes, crush them to an invisible powder, or otherwise you are lost—just as I have been lost for an hour.

"The first letters which I read did not interest me greatly. They were recent, and came from living men whom I still meet quite often, and whose presence does not move me to any great extent. But all at once one envelope made me start. My name was traced on it in a large, bold handwriting; and suddenly tears came to my eyes. That letter was from my dearest friend, the companion of my youth, the confidant of my hopes; and he appeared before me so clearly, with his pleasant smile and his hand outstretched, that a cold shiver ran down my back. Yes, yes, the dead come back, for I saw him! Our memory is a more perfect world than the universe: it gives back life to those who no longer exist.

"With trembling hand and dimmed eyes I reread everything that he told me, and in my poor sobbing heart I felt a wound so painful that I began to groan as a man whose bones are slowly being crushed.

"Then I travelled over my whole life, just as one

travels along a river. I recognized people, so long forgotten that I no longer knew their names. Their faces alone lived in me. In my mother's letters I saw again the old servants, the shape of our house and the little insignificant odds and ends which cling to our minds.

"Yes, I suddenly saw again all my mother's old gowns, the different styles which she adopted and the several ways in which she dressed her hair. She haunted me especially in a silk dress, trimmed with old lace; and I remembered something she said one day when she was wearing this dress. She said: 'Robert, my child, if you do not stand up straight you will be round-shouldered all your life.'

"Then, opening another drawer, I found myself face to face with memories of tender passions: a dancing-pump, a torn handkerchief, even a garter, locks of hair and dried flowers. Then the sweet romances of my life, whose living heroines are now white-haired, plunged me into the deep melancholy of things. Oh, the young brows where blond locks curl, the caress of the hands, the glance which speaks, the hearts which beat, that smile which promises the lips, those lips which promise the embrace! And the first kiss—that endless kiss which makes you close your eyes, which drowns all thought in the immeasurable joy of approaching possession!

"Taking these old pledges of former love in both my hands, I covered them with furious caresses, and in my soul, torn by these memories, I saw them each again at the hour of surrender; and I suffered a torture more cruel than all the tortures invented in all the fables about hell.

"One last letter remained. It was written by me

and dictated fifty years ago by my writing teacher. Here it is:

"'My Dear Little Mamma:

"'I am seven years old to-day. It is the age of reason. I take advantage of it to thank you for having brought me into this world.

"'Your little son, who loves you,
"'Robert.'

"It is all over. I had gone back to the beginning, and suddenly I turned my glance on what remained to me of life. I saw hideous and lonely old age, and approaching infirmities, and everything over and gone. And nobody near me!

"My revolver is here, on the table. I am loading it. . . . Never reread your old letters!"

And that is how many men come to kill themselves; and we search in vain to discover some great sorrow in their lives.

DISCOVERY

THE steamer was crowded with people and the crossing promised to be good. I was going from Havre to Trouville.

The ropes were thrown off, the whistle blew for the last time, the whole boat started to tremble, and the great wheels began to revolve, slowly at first, and then with ever-increasing rapidity.

We were gliding along the pier, black with people. Those on board were waving their handkerchiefs, as though they were leaving for America, and their friends on shore were answering in the same manner.

The big July sun was shining down on the red parasols, the light dresses, the joyous faces and on the ocean, barely stirred by a ripple. When we were out of the harbor, the little vessel swung round the big curve and pointed her nose toward the distant shore which was barely visible through the early morning mist. On our left was the broad estuary of the Seine, her muddy water, which never mingles with that of the ocean, making large yellow streaks clearly outlined against the immense sheet of the pure green sea.

As soon as I am on a boat I feel the need of walking to and fro, like a sailor on watch. Why? I do not know. Therefore I began to thread my way along the deck through the crowd of travellers. Suddenly I heard my name called. I turned around. I beheld one of my old friends, Henri Sidoine, whom I had not seen for ten years.

We shook hands and continued our walk together, talking of one thing or another. Suddenly Sidoine, who had been observing the crowd of passengers, cried out angrily:

"It's disgusting, the boat is full of English people!"

It was indeed full of them. The men were standing about, looking over the ocean with an all-important air, as though to say: "We are the English, the lords of the sea! Here we are!"

The young girls, formless, with shoes which reminded one of the naval constructions of their fatherland, wrapped in multi-colored shawls, were smiling vacantly at the magnificent scenery. Their small heads, planted at the top of their long bodies, wore English hats of the strangest build.

And the old maids, thinner yet, opening their characteristic jaws to the wind, seemed to threaten one with their long, yellow teeth. On passing them, one could notice the smell of rubber and of tooth wash.

Sidoine repeated, with growing anger:

"Disgusting! Can we never stop their coming to France?"

I asked, smiling:

"What have you got against them? As far as I am concerned, they don't worry me."

He snapped out:

"Of course they don't worry you! But *I* married one of them."

I stopped and laughed at him.

"Go ahead and tell me about it. Does she make you very unhappy?"

2

He shrugged his shoulders.

"No, not exactly."

"Then she—is not true to you?"

"Unfortunately, she is. That would be cause for a divorce, and I could get rid of her."

"Then I'm afraid I don't understand!"

"You don't understand? I'm not surprised. Well, she simply learned how to speak French—that's all! Listen.

"I didn't have the least desire of getting married when I went to spend the summer at Étretat two years ago. There is nothing more dangerous than watering-places. You have no idea how it suits young girls. Paris is the place for women and the country for young girls.

"Donkey rides, surf-bathing, breakfast on the grass, all these things are traps set for the marriageable man. And, really, there is nothing prettier than a child about eighteen, running through a field or picking flowers along the road.

"I made the acquaintance of an English family who were stopping at the same hotel where I was. The father looked like those men you see over there, and the mother was like all other Englishwomen.

"They had two sons, the kind of boys who play rough games with balls, bats or rackets from morning till night; then came two daughters, the elder a dry, shrivelled-up Englishwoman, the younger a dream of beauty, a heavenly blonde. When those chits make up their minds to be pretty, they are divine. This one had blue eyes, the kind of blue which seems to contain all the poetry, all the dreams, all the hopes and happiness of the world!

"What an infinity of dreams is caused by two such

3

eyes! How well they answer the dim, eternal question of our heart!

"It must not be forgotten either that we Frenchmen adore foreign women. As soon as we meet a Russian, an Italian, a Swede, a Spaniard, or an Englishwoman with a pretty face, we immediately fall in love with her. We enthuse over everything which comes from outside—clothes, hats, gloves, guns and—women. But what a blunder!

"I believe that that which pleases us in foreign women is their accent. As soon as a woman speaks our language badly we think she is charming, if she uses the wrong word she is exquisite and if she jabbers in an entirely unintelligible jargon, she becomes irresistible.

"My little English girl, Kate, spoke a language to be marvelled at. At the beginning I could understand nothing, she invented so many new words; then I fell absolutely in love with this queer, amusing dialect. All maimed, strange, ridiculous terms became delightful in her mouth. Every evening, on the terrace of the Casino, we had long conversations which resembled spoken enigmas.

"I married her! I loved her wildly, as one can only love in a dream. For true lovers only love a dream which has taken the form of a woman.

"Well, my dear fellow, the most foolish thing I ever did was to give my wife a French teacher. As long as she slaughtered the dictionary and tortured the grammar I adored her. Our conversations were simple. They revealed to me her surprising gracefulness and matchless elegance; they showed her to me as a wonderful speaking jewel, a living doll made to be kissed, knowing, after a fashion, how to express what she loved. She reminded me of the pretty little toys which say 'papa' and 'mamma' when you pull a string.

"Now she talks—badly—very badly. She makes as many mistakes as ever—but I can understand her.

"I have opened my doll to look inside—and I have seen. And how I have to talk to her!

"Ah! you don't know, as I do, the opinions, the ideas, the theories of a well-educated young English girl, whom I can blame in nothing, and who repeats to me from morning till night sentences from a French reader prepared in England for the use of young ladies' schools.

"You have seen those cotillon favors, those pretty gilt papers, which enclose candies with an abominable taste. I have one of them. I tore it open. I wished to eat what was inside and it disgusted me so that I feel nauseated at seeing her compatriots.

"I have married a parrot to whom some old English governess might have taught French. Do you understand?"

* * * * * * * *

The harbor of Trouville was now showing its wooden piers covered with people.

I said:

"Where is your wife?"

He answered:

"I took her back to Étretat."

"And you, where are you going?"

"I? Oh, I am going to rest up here at Trouville."

Then, after a pause, he added:

"You have no idea what a fool a woman can be at times!"

5

THE ACCURSED BREAD

DADDY TAÏLLE had three daughters: Anna, the eldest, who was scarcely ever mentioned in the family; Rose, the second girl, who was eighteen, and Clara, the youngest, who was a girl of fifteen.

Old Taïlle was a widower and a foreman in M. Lebrument's button manufactory. He was a very upright man, very well thought of, abstemious; in fact, a sort of model workman. He lived at Havre, in the Rue d'Angoulême.

When Anna ran away from home the old man flew into a fearful rage. He threatened to kill the head clerk in a large draper's establishment in that town, whom he suspected. After a time, when he was told by various people that she was very steady and investing money in government securities, that she was no gadabout, but was a great friend of Monsieur Dubois, who was a judge of the Tribunal of Commerce, the father was appeased.

He even showed some anxiety as to how she was getting on, and asked some of her old friends who had been to see her, and when told that she had her own furniture, and that her mantelpiece was covered with vases and the walls with pictures, that there were clocks and carpets everywhere, he gave a broad contented smile. He had been working for thirty years to get together a wretched five or six thousand francs. This girl was evidently no fool.

One fine morning the son of Touchard, the cooper, at the other end of the street, came and asked him for the hand of Rose, the second girl. The old man's heart began to beat, for the Touchards were rich and in a good position. He was decidedly lucky with his girls.

The marriage was agreed upon, and it was settled that it should be a grand affair, and the wedding dinner was to be held at Sainte-Adresse, at Mother Jusa's restaurant. It would cost a lot certainly, but never mind, it did not matter just for once in a way.

But one morning, just as the old man was going home to luncheon with his two daughters, the door opened suddenly, and Anna appeared. She was well dressed and looked undeniably pretty and nice. She threw her arms round her father's neck before he could say a word, then fell into her sisters' arms with many tears and then asked for a plate, so that she might share the family soup. Taille was moved to tears in his turn and said several times:

"That is right, dear, that is right."

Then she told them about herself. She did not wish Rose's wedding to take place at Sainte-Adresse —certainly not. It should take place at her house and would cost her father nothing. She had settled everything and arranged everything, so it was "no good to say any more about it—there!"

"Very well, my dear! very well!" the old man said; "we will leave it so." But then he felt some doubt. Would the Touchards consent? But Rose, the bride-elect, was surprised and asked: "Why

should they object, I should like to know? Just
leave that to me; I will talk to Philip about it."

She mentioned it to her lover the very same day,
and he declared it would suit him exactly. Father
and Mother Touchard were naturally delighted at
the idea of a good dinner which would cost them
nothing and said:

"You may be quite sure that everything will be in
first-rate style."

They asked to be allowed to bring a friend, Madame Florence, the cook on the first floor, and Anna
agreed to everything.

The wedding was fixed for the last Tuesday of the
month.

II

After the civil formalities and the religious ceremony the wedding party went to Anna's house.
Among those whom the Tailles had brought was a
cousin of a certain age, a Monsieur Sauvetanin, a
man given to philosophical reflections, serious, and
always very self-possessed, and Madame Lamondois,
an old aunt.

Monsieur Sautevanin had been told off to give
Anna his arm, as they were looked upon as the two
most important persons in the company.

As soon as they had arrived at the door of Anna's
house she let go her companion's arm, and ran on
ahead, saying: "I will show you the way," and ran
upstairs while the invited guests followed more
slowly; and, when they got upstairs, she stood on one
side to let them pass, and they rolled their eyes and
turned their heads in all directions to admire this
mysterious and luxurious dwelling.

THE ACCURSED BREAD

The table was laid in the drawing-room, as the dining-room had been thought too small. Extra knives, forks and spoons had been hired from a neighboring restaurant, and decanters stood full of wine under the rays of the sun which shone in through the window.

The ladies went into the bedroom to take off their shawls and bonnets, and Father Touchard, who was standing at the door, made funny and suggestive signs to the men, with many a wink and nod. Daddy Taille, who thought a great deal of himself, looked with fatherly pride at his child's well-furnished rooms and went from one to the other, holding his hat in his hand, making a mental inventory of everything, and walking like a verger in a church.

Anna went backward and forward, ran about giving orders and hurrying on the wedding feast. Soon she appeared at the door of the dining-room and cried: "Come here, all of you, for a moment," and as the twelve guests entered the room they saw twelve glasses of Madeira on a small table.

Rose and her husband had their arms round each other's waists and were kissing each other in every corner. Monsieur Sauvetanin never took his eyes off Anna.

They sat down, and the wedding breakfast began, the relations sitting at one end of the table and the young people at the other. Madame Touchard, the mother, presided on the right and the bride on the left. Anna looked after everybody, saw that the glasses were kept filled and the plates well supplied. The guests evidently felt a certain respectful embarrassment at the sight of all the sumptuousness of the rooms and at the lavish manner in which they were

4

treated. They all ate heartily of the good things provided, but there were no jokes such as are prevalent at weddings of that sort; it was all too grand, and it made them feel uncomfortable. Old Madame Touchard, who was fond of a bit of fun, tried to enliven matters a little, and at the beginning of the dessert she exclaimed: "I say, Philip, do sing us something." The neighbors in their street considered that he had the finest voice in all Havre.

The bridegroom got up, smiled, and, turning to his sister-in-law, from politeness and gallantry, tried to think of something suitable for the occasion, something serious and correct, to harmonize with the seriousness of the repast.

Anna had a satisfied look on her face, and leaned back in her chair to listen, and all assumed looks of attention, though prepared to smile should smiles be called for.

The singer announced "The Accursed Bread," and, extending his right arm, which made his coat ruck up into his neck, he began.

It was decidedly long, three verses of eight lines each, with the last line and the last but one repeated twice.

All went well for the first two verses; they were the usual commonplaces about bread gained by honest labor and by dishonesty. The aunt and the bride wept outright. The cook, who was present, at the end of the first verse looked at a roll which she held in her hand, with streaming eyes, as if it applied to her, while all applauded vigorously. At the end of the second verse the two servants, who were standing with their backs to the wall, joined loudly in the chorus, and the aunt and the bride wept outright.

Daddy Taille blew his nose with the noise of a trombone, and old Touchard brandished a whole loaf half over the table, and the cook shed silent tears on the crust which she was still holding.

Amid the general emotion Monsieur Sauvetanin said:

"That is the right sort of song; very different from the nasty, risky things one generally hears at weddings."

Anna, who was visibly affected, kissed her hand to her sister and pointed to her husband with an affectionate nod, as if to congratulate her.

Intoxicated by his success, the young man continued, and unfortunately the last verse contained words about the "bread of dishonor" gained by young girls who had been led astray. No one took up the refrain about this bread, supposed to be eaten with tears, except old Touchard and the two servants. Anna had grown deadly pale and cast down her eyes, while the bridegroom looked from one to the other without understanding the reason for this sudden coldness, and the cook hastily dropped the crust as if it were poisoned.

Monsieur Sauvetanin said solemnly, in order to save the situation: "That last couplet is not at all necessary"; and Daddy Taille, who had got red up to his ears, looked round the table fiercely.

Then Anna, her eyes swimming in tears, told the servants in the faltering voice of a woman trying to stifle her sobs, to bring the champagne.

All the guests were suddenly seized with exuberant joy, and all their faces became radiant again. And when old Touchard, who had seen, felt and understood nothing of what was going on, and pointing to the guests so as to emphazise his words, sang the last words of the refrain:

"Children, I warn you all to eat not of that bread,"
the whole company, when they saw the champagne bottles, with their necks covered with gold foil, appear, burst out singing, as if electrified by the sight:

"Children, I warn you all to eat not of that bread."

BESIDE SCHOPENHAUER'S CORPSE

HE was slowly dying, as consumptives die. I saw him each day, about two o'clock, sitting beneath the hotel windows on a bench in the promenade, looking out on the calm sea. He remained for some time without moving, in the heat of the sun, gazing mournfully at the Mediterranean. Every now and then, he cast a glance at the lofty mountains with beclouded summits that shut in Mentone; then, with a very slow movement, he would cross his long legs, so thin that they seemed like two bones, around which fluttered the cloth of his trousers, and he would open a book, always the same book. And then he did not stir any more, but read on, read on with his eye and his mind; all his wasting body seemed to read, all his soul plunged, lost, disappeared, in this book, up to the hour when the cool air made him cough a little. Then, he got up and re-entered the hotel.

He was a tall German, with fair beard, who breakfasted and dined in his own room, and spoke to nobody.

A vague curiosity attracted me to him. One day, I sat down by his side, having taken up a book, too, to keep up appearances, a volume of Musset's poems.

And I began to look through "Rolla."

Suddenly, my neighbor said to me, in good French:

"Do you know German, monsieur?"

"Not at all, monsieur."

"I am sorry for that. Since chance has thrown us side by side, I could have lent you, I could have shown you, an inestimable thing—this book which I hold in my hand."

"What is it, pray?"

"It is a copy of my master, Schopenhauer, annotated with his own hand. All the margins, as you may see, are covered with his handwriting."

I took the book from him reverently, and I gazed at these forms incomprehensible to me, but which revealed the immortal thoughts of the greatest shatterer of dreams who had ever dwelt on earth.

And Musset's verses arose in my memory:

"Hast thou found out, Voltaire, that it is bliss to die,
And does thy hideous smile over thy bleached bones
     fly?"

And involuntarily I compared the childish sarcasm, the religious sarcasm of Voltaire with the irresistible irony of the German philosopher whose influence is henceforth ineffaceable.

Let us protest and let us be angry, let us be indignant, or let us be enthusiastic, Schopenhauer has marked humanity with the seal of his disdain and of his disenchantment.

A disabused pleasure-seeker, he overthrew beliefs, hopes, poetic ideals and chimeras, destroyed the aspirations, ravaged the confidence of souls, killed love, dragged down the chivalrous worship of women, crushed the illusions of hearts, and accomplished the most gigantic task ever attempted by scepticism. He spared nothing with his mocking spirit, and exhausted everything. And even to-day those who execrate him seem to carry in their own souls particles of his thought.

"So, then, you were intimately acquainted with Schopenhauer?" I said to the German.

He smiled sadly.

"Up to the time of his death, monsieur."

And he spoke to me about the philosopher and told me about the almost supernatural impression which this strange being made on all who came near him.

He gave me an account of the interview of the old iconoclast with a French politician, a doctrinaire Republican, who wanted to get a glimpse of this man, and found him in a noisy tavern, seated in the midst of his disciples, dry, wrinkled, laughing with an unforgettable laugh, attacking and tearing to pieces ideas and beliefs with a single word, as a dog tears with one bite of his teeth the tissues with which he plays.

He repeated for me the comment of this Frenchman as he went away, astonished and terrified: "I thought I had spent an hour with the devil."

Then he added:

"He had, indeed, monsieur, a frightful smile, which terrified us even after his death. I can tell you an anecdote about it that is not generally known, if it would interest you."

And he began, in a languid voice, interrupted by frequent fits of coughing.

"Schopenhauer had just died, and it was arranged that we should watch, in turn, two by two, till morning.

"He was lying in a large apartment, very simple, vast and gloomy. Two wax candles were burning on the stand by the bedside.

"It was midnight when I went on watch, together with one of our comrades. The two friends whom we replaced had left the apartment, and we came and sat down at the foot of the bed.

"The face was not changed. It was laughing. That pucker which we knew so well lingered still around the corners of the lips, and it seemed to us that he was about to open his eyes, to move and to speak. His thought, or rather his thoughts, enveloped us. We felt ourselves more than ever in the atmosphere of his genius, absorbed, possessed by him. His domination seemed to be even more sovereign now that he was dead. A feeling of mystery was blended with the power of this incomparable spirit.

"The bodies of these men disappear, but they themselves remain; and in the night which follows the cessation of their heart's pulsation I assure you, monsieur, they are terrifying.

"And in hushed tones we talked aout him, recalling to mind certain sayings, certain formulas of his, those startling maxims which are like jets of flame flung, in a few words, into the darkness of the Unknown Life.

" 'It seems to me that he is going to speak,' said my comrade. And we stared with uneasiness bordering on fear at the motionless face, with its eternal laugh. Gradually, we began to feel ill at ease, oppressed, on the point of fainting. I faltered:

" 'I don't know what is the matter with me, but, I assure you I am not well.'

"And at that moment we noticed that there was an unpleasant odor from the corpse.

"Then, my comrade suggested that we should go into the adjoining room, and leave the door open; and I assented to his proposal.

"I took one of the wax candles which burned on the stand, and I left the second behind. Then we went and sat down at the other end of the adjoining apartment, in such a position that we could see the bed and the corpse, clearly revealed by the light.

"But he still held possession of us. One would have said that his immaterial essence, liberated, free, all-powerful and dominating, was flitting around us. And sometimes, too, the dreadful odor of the decomposed body came toward us and penetrated us, sickening and indefinable.

"Suddenly a shiver passed through our bones: a sound, a slight sound, came from the death-chamber. Immediately we fixed our glances on him, and we saw, yes, monsieur, we saw distinctly, both of us, something white pass across the bed, fall on the carpet, and vanish under an armchair.

"We were on our feet before we had time to think of anything, distracted by stupefying terror, ready to run away. Then we stared at each other. We were horribly pale. Our hearts throbbed fiercely enough to have raised the clothing on our chests. I was the first to speak:

" 'Did you see?'

" 'Yes, I saw.'

" 'Can it be that he is not dead?'

" 'Why, when the body is putrefying?'

" 'What are we to do?'

"My companion said in a hesitating tone:

" 'We must go and look.'

"I took our wax candle and entered first, glancing into all the dark corners in the large apartment. Nothing was moving now, and I approached the bed. But I stood transfixed with stupor and fright: Schopenhauer was no longer laughing! He was grinning in a horrible fashion, with his lips pressed together and deep hollows in his cheeks. I stammered out:

" 'He is not dead!'

"But the terrible odor ascended to my nose and stifled me. And I no longer moved, but kept staring fixedly at him, terrified as if in the presence of an apparition.

"Then my companion, having seized the other wax candle, bent forward. Next, he touched my arm without uttering a word. I followed his glance, and saw on the ground, under the armchair by the side of the bed, standing out white on the dark carpet, and open as if to bite, Schopenhauer's set of artificial teeth.

"The work of decomposition, loosening the jaws, had made it jump out of the mouth.

"I was really frightened that day, monsieur."

And as the sun was sinking toward the glittering sea, the consumptive German rose from his seat, gave me a parting bow, and retired into the hotel.

THE UMBRELLA

MME. OREILLE was a very economical woman; she knew the value of a centime, and possessed a whole storehouse of strict principles with regard to the multiplication of money, so that her cook found the greatest difficulty in making what the servants call their market-penny, and her husband was hardly allowed any pocket money at all They were, however, very comfortably off, and had no children; but it really pained Mme. Oreille to see any money spent; it was like tearing at her heartstrings when she had to take any of those nice crown-pieces out of her pocket; and whenever she had to spend anything, no matter how necessary it might be, she slept badly the next night.

Oreille was continually saying to his wife:

"You really might be more liberal, as we have no children, and never spend our income."

"You don't know what may happen," she used to reply. "It is better to have too much than too little."

She was a little woman of about forty, very active, rather hasty, wrinkled, very neat and tidy, and with a very short temper.

Her husband frequently complained of all the privations she made him endure; some of them were

I

particularly painful to him, as they touched his vanity.

He was one of the head clerks in the War Office, and only stayed on there in obedience to his wife's wish, to increase their income which they did not nearly spend.

For two years he had always come to the office with the same old patched umbrella, to the great amusement of his fellow clerks. At last he got tired of their jokes, and insisted upon his wife buying him a new one. She bought one for eight francs and a half, one of those cheap articles which large houses sell as an advertisement. When the men in the office saw the article, which was being sold in Paris by the thousand, they began their jokes again, and Oreille had a dreadful time of it. They even made a song about it, which he heard from morning till night all over the immense building.

Oreille was very angry, and peremptorily told his wife to get him a new one, a good silk one, for twenty francs, and to bring him the bill, so that he might see that it was all right.

She bought him one for eighteen francs, and said, getting red with anger as she gave it to her husband:

"This will last you for five years at least."

Oreille felt quite triumphant, and received a small ovation at the office with his new acquisition.

When he went home in the evening his wife said to him, looking at the umbrella uneasily:

"You should not leave it fastened up with the elastic; it will very likely cut the silk. You must take care of it, for I shall not buy you a new one in a hurry."

THE UMBRELLA

She took it, unfastened it, and remained dumfounded with astonishment and rage; in the middle of the silk there was a hole as big as a sixpenny-piece; it had been made with the end of a cigar.

"What is that?" she screamed.

Her husband replied quietly, without looking at it:

"What is it? What do you mean?"

She was choking with rage, and could hardly get out a word.

"You—you—have—burned—your umbrella! Why —you must be—mad! Do you wish to ruin us outright?"

He turned round, and felt that he was growing pale.

"What are you talking about?"

"I say that you have burned your umbrella. Just look here."

And rushing at him, as if she were going to beat him, she violently thrust the little circular burned hole under his nose.

He was so utterly struck dumb at the sight of it that he could only stammer out:

"What—what is it? How should I know? I have done nothing, I will swear. I don't know what is the matter with the umbrella."

"You have been playing tricks with it at the office; you have been playing the fool and opening it, to show it off!" she screamed.

"I only opened it once, to let them see what a nice one it was, that is all, I swear."

But she shook with rage, and got up one of those conjugal scenes which make a peaceable man dread

3

the domestic hearth more than a battlefield where bullets are raining.

She mended it with a piece of silk cut out of the old umbrella, which was of a different color, and the next day Oreille went off very humbly with the mended article in his hand. He put it into a cupboard, and thought no more of it than of some unpleasant recollection.

But he had scarcely got home that evening when his wife took the umbrella from him, opened it, and nearly had a fit when she saw what had befallen it, for the disaster was irreparable. It was covered with small holes, which evidently proceeded from burns, just as if some one had emptied the ashes from a lighted pipe on to it. It was done for utterly, irreparably.

She looked at it without a word, in too great a passion to be able to say anything. He, also, when he saw the damage, remained almost dumfounded, in a state of frightened consternation.

They looked at each other, then he looked at the floor; and the next moment she threw the useless article at his head, screaming out in a transport of the most violent rage, for she had recovered her voice by that time:

"Oh! you brute! you brute! You did it on purpose, but I will pay you out for it. You shall not have another."

And then the scene began again, and after the storm had raged for an hour, he at last was able to explain himself. He declared that he could not understand it at all, and that it could only proceed from malice or from vengeance.

THE UMBRELLA

A ring at the bell saved him; it was a friend whom they were expecting to dinner.

Mme. Oreille submitted the case to him. As for buying a new umbrella, that was out of the question; her husband should not have another.

The friend very sensibly said that in that case his clothes would be spoiled, and they were certainly worth more than the umbrella. But the little woman, who was still in a rage, replied:

"Very well, then, when it rains he may have the kitchen umbrella, for I will not give him a new silk one."

Oreille utterly rebelled at such an idea.

"All right," he said; "then I shall resign my post. I am not going to the office with the kitchen umbrella."

The friend interposed.

"Have this one re-covered; it will not cost much."

But Mme. Oreille, being in the temper that she was, said:

"It will cost at least eight francs to re-cover it. Eight and eighteen are twenty-six. Just fancy, twenty-six francs for an umbrella! It is utter madness!"

The friend, who was only a poor man of the middle classes, had an inspiration:

"Make your fire assurance pay for it. The companies pay for all articles that are burned, as long as the damage has been done in your own house."

On hearing this advice the little woman calmed down immediately, and then, after a moment's reflection, she said to her husband:

"To-morrow, before going to your office, you

will go to the Maternelle Assurance Company, show them the state your umbrella is in, and make them pay for the damage."

M. Oreille fairly jumped, he was so startled at the proposal.

"I would not do it for my life! It is eighteen francs lost, that is all. It will not ruin us."

The next morning he took a walking-stick when he went out, and, luckily, it was a fine day.

Left at home alone, Mme. Oreille could not get over the loss of her eighteen francs by any means. She had put the umbrella on the dining-room table, and she looked at it without being able to come to any determination.

Every moment she thought of the assurance company, but she did not dare to encounter the quizzical looks of the gentlemen who might receive her, for she was very timid before people, and blushed at a mere nothing, and was embarrassed when she had to speak to strangers.

But the regret at the loss of the eighteen francs pained her as if she had been wounded. She tried not to think of it any more, and yet every moment the recollection of the loss struck her painfully. What was she to do, however? Time went on, and she could not decide; but suddenly, like all cowards, on making a resolve, she became determined.

"I will go, and we will see what will happen."

But first of all she was obliged to prepare the umbrella so that the disaster might be complete, and the reason of it quite evident. She took a match from the mantelpiece, and between the ribs she burned a hole as big as the palm of her hand; then she delicately rolled it up, fastened it with the elastic band, put on her bonnet and shawl, and went quickly toward the Rue de Rivoli, where the assurance office was.

But the nearer she got, the slower she walked. What was she going to say, and what reply would she get?

She looked at the numbers of the houses; there were still twenty-eight. That was all right, so she had time to consider, and she walked slower and slower. Suddenly she saw a door on which was a large brass plate with "La Maternelle Fire Assurance Office" engraved on it. Already! She waited a moment, for she felt nervous and almost ashamed; then she walked past, came back, walked past again, and came back again.

At last she said to herself:

"I must go in, however, so I may as well do it sooner as later."

She could not help noticing, however, how her heart beat as she entered.

She went into an enormous room with grated doors all round it, and above them little openings at which a man's head appeared, and as a gentleman carrying a number of papers passed her, she stopped him and said timidly:

"I beg your pardon, monsieur, but can you tell me where I must apply for payment for anything that has been accidentally burned?"

He replied in a sonorous voice:

"The first door on the left; that is the department you want."

This frightened her still more, and she felt inclined to run away, to put in no claim, to sacrifice her eighteen francs. But the idea of that sum re-

vived her courage, and she went upstairs, out of
breath, stopping at almost every other step.

She knocked at a door which she saw on the first
landing, and a clear voice said, in answer:

"Come in!"

She obeyed mechanically, and found herself in a
large room where three solemn gentlemen, all with
a decoration in their buttonholes, were standing
talking.

One of them asked her: "What do you want, madame?"

She could hardly get out her words, but stammered: "I have come—I have come on account of
an accident, something——"

He very politely pointed out a seat to her.

"If you will kindly sit down I will attend to you
in a moment."

And, returning to the other two, he went on with
the conversation.

"The company, gentlemen, does not consider
that it is under any obligation to you for more than
four hundred thousand francs, and we can pay no
attention to your claim to the further sum of a hundred thousand, which you wish to make us pay. Besides that, the surveyor's valuation——"

One of the others interrupted him:

"That is quite enough, monsieur; the law courts
will decide between us, and we have nothing further
to do than to take our leave." And they went out
after mutual ceremonious bows.

Oh! if she could only have gone away with them,
how gladly she would have done it; she would have
run away and given up everything. But it was too
late, for the gentleman came back, and said, bowing:

THE UMBRELLA

"What can I do for you, madame?"

She could scarcely speak, but at last she managed to say:

"I have come—for this."

The manager looked at the object which she held out to him in mute astonishment.

With trembling fingers she tried to undo the elastic, and succeeding, after several attempts, she hastily opened the damaged remains of the umbrella.

"It looks to me to be in a very bad state of health," he said compassionately.

"It cost me twenty francs," she said, with some hesitation.

He seemed astonished. "Really! As much as that?"

"Yes, it was a capital article, and I wanted you to see the condition it is in."

"Yes, yes, I see; very well. But I really do not understand what it can have to do with me."

She began to feel uncomfortable; perhaps this company did not pay for such small articles, and she said:

"But—it is burned."

He could not deny it.

"I see that very well," he replied.

She remained open-mouthed, not knowing what to say next; then, suddenly recollecting that she had left out the main thing, she said hastily:

"I am Mme. Oreille; we are assured in La Maternelle, and I have come to claim the value of this damage."

"I only want you to have it re-covered," she added quickly, fearing a positive refusal.

9

The manager was rather embarrassed, and said:

"But, really, madame, we do not sell umbrellas; we cannot undertake such kinds of repairs."

The little woman felt her courage reviving; she was not going to give up without a struggle; she was not even afraid any more, and said:

"I only want you to pay me the cost of repairing it; I can quite well get it done myself."

The gentleman seemed rather confused.

"Really, madame, it is such a very small matter! We are never asked to give compensation for such trivial losses. You must allow that we cannot make good pocket-handkerchiefs, gloves, brooms, slippers, all the small articles which are every day exposed to the chances of being burned."

She got red in the face, and felt inclined to fly into a rage.

"But, monsieur, last December one of our chimneys caught fire, and caused at least five hundred francs' damage; M. Oreille made no claim on the company, and so it is only just that it should pay for my umbrella now."

The manager, guessing that she was telling a lie, said, with a smile:

"You must acknowledge, madame, that it is very surprising that M. Oreille should have asked no compensation for damages amounting to five hundred francs, and should now claim five or six francs for mending an umbrella."

She was not the least put out, and replied:

"I beg your pardon, monsieur, the five hundred francs affected M. Oreille's pocket, whereas this damage, amounting to eighteen francs, concerns

Mme. Oreille's pocket only, which is a totally different matter."

As he saw that he had no chance of getting rid of her, and that he would only be wasting his time, he said resignedly:

"Will you kindly tell me how the damage was done?"

She felt that she had won the victory, and said:

"This is how it happened, monsieur: In our hall there is a bronze stick and umbrella stand, and the other day, when I came in, I put my umbrella into it. I must tell you that just above there is a shelf for the candlesticks and matches. I put out my hand, took three or four matches, and struck one, but it missed fire, so I struck another, which ignited, but went out immediately, and a third did the same."

The manager interrupted her to make a joke.

"I suppose they were government matches, then?"

She did not understand him, and went on:

"Very likely. At any rate, the fourth caught fire, and I lit my candle, and went into my room to go to bed; but in a quarter of an hour I fancied that I smelt something burning, and I have always been terribly afraid of fire. If ever we have an accident it will not be my fault, I assure you. I am terribly nervous since our chimney was on fire, as I told you; so I got up, and hunted about everywhere, sniffing like a dog after game, and at last I noticed that my umbrella was burning. Most likely a match had fallen between the folds and burned it. You can see how it has damaged it."

The manager had taken his cue, and asked her:

"What do you estimate the damage at?"

She did not know what to say, as she was not certain what value to put on it, but at last she replied:

"Perhaps you had better get it done yourself. I will leave it to you."

He, however, naturally refused.

"No, madame, I cannot do that. Tell me the amount of your claim, that is all I want to know."

"Well, I think that—— Look here, monsieur, I do not want to make any money out of you, so I will tell you what we will do. I will take my umbrella to the maker, who will re-cover it in good, durable silk, and I will bring the bill to you. Will that suit you, monsieur?"

"Perfectly, madame; we will settle it so. Here is a note for the cashier, who will repay you whatever it costs you."

He gave Mme. Oreille a slip of paper, who took it, got up and went out, thanking him, for she was in a hurry to escape lest he should change his mind.

She went briskly through the streets, looking out for a really good umbrella maker, and when she found a shop which appeared to be a first-class one, she went in, and said, confidently:

"I want this umbrella re-covered in silk, good silk. Use the very best and strongest you have; I don't mind what it costs."

BELHOMME'S BEAST

THE coach for Havre was ready to leave
Criquetot, and all the passengers were waiting for their names to be called out, in the
courtyard of the Commercial Hotel kept by Monsieur Malandain, Jr.

It was a yellow wagon, mounted on wheels which
had once been yellow, but were now almost gray
through the accumulation of mud. The front
wheels were very small, the back ones, high and
fragile, carried the large body of the vehicle,
which was swollen like the belly of an animal.
Three white horses, with enormous heads and great
round knees, were the first things one noticed. They
were harnessed ready to draw this coach, which had
something of the appearance of a monster in its
massive structure. The horses seemed already
asleep in front of the strange vehicle.

The driver, Césaire Horlaville, a little man with
a big paunch, supple nevertheless, through his constant habit of climbing over the wheels to the top
of the wagon, his face all aglow from exposure to
the brisk air of the plains, to rain and storms, and
also from the use of brandy, his eyes twitching from
the effect of constant contact with wind and hail,
appeared in the doorway of the hotel, wiping his
mouth on the back of his hand. Large round bas-
kets, full of frightened poultry, were standing in

1

front of the peasant women. Césaire Horlaville took them one after the other and packed them on the top of his coach; then, more gently, he loaded on those containing eggs; finally he tossed up from below several little bags of grain, small packages wrapped in handkerchiefs, pieces of cloth, or paper. Then he opened the back door, and drawing a list from his pocket he called:

"Monsieur le curé de Gorgeville."

The priest advanced. He was a large, powerful, robust man with a red face and a genial expression. He hitched up his cassock to lift his foot, just as the women hold up their skirts, and climbed into the coach.

"The schoolmaster of Rollebosc-les-Grinets."

The man hastened forward, tall, timid, wearing a long frock coat which fell to his knees, and he in turn disappeared through the open door.

"Maître Poiret, two seats."

Poiret approached, a tall, round-shouldered man, bent by the plow, emaciated through abstinence, bony, with a skin dried by a sparing use of water. His wife followed him, small and thin, like a tired animal, carrying a large green umbrella in her hands.

"Maître Rabot, two seats."

Rabot hesitated, being of an undecided nature. He asked:

"You mean me?"

The driver was going to answer with a jest, when Rabot dived head first towards the door, pushed forward by a vigorous shove from his wife, a tall, square woman with a large, round stomach like a barrel, and hands as large as hams.

2

Rabot slipped into the wagon like a rat entering a hole.

"Maître Caniveau."

A large peasant, heavier than an ox, made the springs bend, and was in turn engulfed in the interior of the yellow chest.

"Maître Belhomme."

Belhomme, tall and thin, came forward, his neck bent, his head hanging, a handkerchief held to his ear as if he were suffering from a terrible toothache.

All these people wore the blue blouse over quaint and antique coats of a black or greenish cloth, Sunday clothes which they would only uncover in the streets of Havre. Their heads were covered by silk caps at high as towers, the emblem of supreme elegance in the small villages of Normandy.

Césaire Horlaville closed the door, climbed up on his box and snapped his whip.

The three horses awoke and, tossing their heads, shook their bells.

The driver then yelling "Get up!" as loud as he could, whipped up his horses. They shook themselves, and, with an effort, started off at a slow, halting gait. And behind them came the coach, rattling its shaky windows and iron springs, making a terrible clatter of hardware and glass, while the passengers were tossed hither and thither like so many rubber balls.

At first all kept silent out of respect for the priest, that they might not shock him. Being of a loquacious and genial disposition, he started the conversation.

"Well, Maître Caniveau," said he, "how are you getting along?"

The enormous farmer who, on account of his size, girth and stomach, felt a bond of sympathy for the representative of the Church, answered with a smile:

"Pretty well, Monsieur le curé, pretty well. And how are you?"

"Oh! I'm always well and healthy."

"And you, Maître Poiret?" asked the abbé.

"Oh! I'd be all right only the colzas ain't a-goin' to give much this year, and times are so hard that they are the only things worth while raisin'."

"Well, what can you expect? Times are hard."

"Huh! I should say they were hard," sounded the rather virile voice of Rabot's big consort.

As she was from a neighboring village, the priest only knew her by name.

"Is that you, Blondel?" he said.

"Yes, I'm the one that married Rabot."

Rabot, slender, timid, and self-satisfied, bowed smilingly, bending his head forward as though to say: "Yes, I'm the Rabot whom Blondel married."

Suddenly Maître Belhomme, still holding his handkerchief to his ear, began groaning in a pitiful fashion. He was going "Oh—oh—oh!" and stamping his foot in order to show his terrible suffering.

"You must have an awful toothache," said the priest.

The peasant stopped moaning for a minute and answered:

"No, Monsieur le curé, it is not the teeth. It's my ear—away down at the bottom of my ear."

"Well, what have you got in your ear? A lump of wax?"

"I don't know whether it's wax; but I know that it is a bug, a big bug, that crawled in while I was asleep in the haystack."

'A bug! Are you sure?"

"Am I sure? As sure as I am of heaven, Monsieur le curé! I can feel it gnawing at the bottom of my ear! It's eating my head for sure! It's eating my head! Oh—oh—oh!" And he began to stamp his foot again.

Great interest had been aroused among the spectators. Each one gave his bit of advice. Poiret claimed that it was a spider, the teacher thought it might be a caterpillar. He had already seen such a thing once, at Campemuret, in Orne, where he had been for six years. In this case the caterpillar had gone through the head and out at the nose. But the man remained deaf in that ear ever after, the drum having been pierced.

"It's more likely to be a worm," said the priest.

Maître Belhomme, his head resting against the door, for he had been the last one to enter, was still moaning.

"Oh—oh—oh! I think it must be an ant, a big ant—there it is biting again. Oh, Monsieur le curé, how it hurts! how it hurts!"

"Have you seen the doctor?" asked Caniveau.

"I should say not!"

"Why?"

The fear of the doctor seemed to cure Belhomme. He straightened up without, however, dropping his handkerchief.

"What! You have money for them, for those

5

loafers? He would have come once, twice, three
times, four times, five times! That means two five-
franc pieces, two five-franc pieces, for sure. And
what would he have done, the loafer, tell me, what
would he have done? Can you tell me?"

Caniveau was laughing.

"No, I don't know. Where are you going?"

"I am going to Havre, to see Chambrelan."

"Who is Chambrelan?"

"The healer, of course."

"What healer?"

"The healer who cured my father."

"Your father?"

"Yes, the healer who cured my father years ago."

"What was the matter with your father?"

"A draught caught him in the back, so that he
couldn't move hand or foot."

"Well, what did your friend Chambrelan do to
him?"

"He kneaded his back with both hands as though
he were making bread! And he was all right in a
couple of hours!"

Belhomme thought that Chambrelan must also
have used some charm, but he did not dare say so
before the priest. Caniveau replied, laughing:

"Are you sure it isn't a rabbit that you have in
your ear? He might have taken that hole for his
home. Wait, I'll make him run away."

Whereupon Caniveau, making a megaphone of
his hands, began to mimic the barking of hounds.
He snapped, howled, growled, barked. And everybody in the carriage began to roar, even the schoolmaster, who, as a rule, never even smiled.

However, as Belhomme seemed angry at their

making fun of him, the priest changed the conversation and turning to Rabot's big wife, said:

"You have a large family, haven't you?"

"Oh, yes, Monsieur le curé—and it's a pretty hard matter to bring them up!"

Rabot agreed, nodding his head as though to say: "Oh, yes, it's a hard thing to bring up!"

"How many children?"

She replied authoritatively in a strong, clear voice:

"Sixteen children, Monsieur le curé, fifteen of them by my husband!"

And Rabot smiled broadly, nodding his head. He was responsible for fifteen, he alone, Rabot! His wife said so! Therefore there could be no doubt about it. And he was proud!

And whose was the sixteenth? She didn't tell. It was doubtless the first. Perhaps everybody knew, for no one was surprised. Even Caniveau kept mum.

But Belhomme began to moan again:

"Oh—oh—oh! It's scratching about in the bottom of my ear! Oh, dear, oh, dear!"

The coach just then stopped at the Café Polyte. The priest said:

"If someone were to pour a little water into your ear, it might perhaps drive it out. Do you want to try?"

"Sure! I am willing."

And everybody got out in order to witness the operation. The priest asked for a bowl, a napkin and a glass of water, then he told the teacher to hold the patient's head over on one side, and, as

7

soon as the liquid should have entered the ear, to turn his head over suddenly on the other side.

But Caniveau, who was already peering into Belhomme's ear to see if he couldn't discover the beast, shouted:

"Gosh! What a mess! You'll have to clear that out, old man. Your rabbit could never get through that; his feet would stick."

The priest in turn examined the passage and saw that it was too narrow and too congested for him to attempt to expel the animal. It was the teacher who cleared out this passage by means of a match and a bit of cloth. Then, in the midst of the general excitement, the priest poured into the passage half a glass of water, which trickled over the face through the hair and down the neck of the patient. Then the schoolmaster quickly twisted the head round over the bowl, as though he were trying to unscrew it. A couple of drops dripped into the white bowl. All the passengers rushed forward. No insect had come out.

However, Belhomme exclaimed: "I don't feel anything any more." The priest triumphantly exclaimed: "Certainly it has been drowned." Everybody was happy and got back into the coach.

But hardly had they started when Belhomme began to cry out again. The bug had aroused itself and had become furious. He even declared that it had now entered his head and was eating his brain. He was howling with such contortions that Poirat's wife, thinking him possessed by the devil, began to cry and to cross herself. Then, the pain abating a little, the sick man began to tell how it was running round in his ear. With his finger he imitated the

8

movements of the body, seeming to see it, to follow it with his eyes: "There is goes up again! Oh— oh—oh—what torture!"

Caniveau was getting impatient. "It's the water that is making the bug angry. It is probably more accustomed to wine."

Everybody laughed, and he continued: "When we get to the Café Bourbeux, give it some brandy, and it won't bother you any more, I wager."

But Belhomme could contain himself no longer; he began howling as though his soul were being torn from his body. The priest was obliged to hold his head for him. They asked Césaire Horlaville to stop at the nearest house. It was a farmhouse at the side of the road. Belhomme was carried into it and laid on the kitchen table in order to repeat the operation. Caniveau advised mixing brandy and water in order to benumb and perhaps kill the insect. But the priest preferred vinegar.

They poured the liquid in drop by drop this time, that it might penetrate down to the bottom, and they left it several minutes in the organ that the beast had chosen for its home.

A bowl had once more been brought; Belhomme was turned over bodily by the priest and Caniveau, while the schoolmaster was tapping on the healthy ear in order to empty the other.

Césaire Horlaville himself, whip in hand, had come in to observe the proceedings.

Suddenly, at the bottom of the bowl appeared a little brown spot, no bigger than a tiny seed. However, it was moving. It was a flea! First there were cries of astonishment and then shouts of laughter. A flea! Well, that was a good joke, a mighty good one! Caniveau was slapping his thigh, Césaire Horlaville snapped his whip, the priest laughed like a braying donkey, the teacher cackled as though he were sneezing, and the two women were giving little screams of joy, like the clucking of hens.

Belhomme had seated himself on the table and had taken the bowl between his knees; he was observing, with serious attention and a vengeful anger in his eye, the conquered insect which was twisting round in the water. He grunted, "You rotten little beast!" and he spat on it.

The driver, wild with joy, kept repeating: "A flea, a flea, ah! there you are, damned little flea, damned little flea, damned little flea!" Then having calmed down a little, he cried: "Well, back to the coach! We've lost enough time."

THE DOWRY

THE marriage of Maitre Simon Lebrument with Mademoiselle Jeanne Cordier was a surprise to no one. Maitre Lebrument had bought out the practice of Maitre Papillon; naturally, he had to have money to pay for it; and Mademoiselle Jeanne Cordier had three hundred thousand francs clear in currency, and in bonds payable to bearer.

Maitre Lebrument was a handsome man. He was stylish, although in a provincial way; but, nevertheless, he was stylish—a rare thing at Boutigny-le-Rebours.

Mademoiselle Cordier was graceful and fresh-looking, although a trifle awkward; nevertheless, she was a handsome girl, and one to be desired.

The marriage ceremony turned all Boutigny topsy-turvy. Everybody admired the young couple, who quickly returned home to domestic felicity, having decided simply to take a short trip to Paris, after a few days of retirement.

This tête-à-tête was delightful, Maitre Lebrument having shown just the proper amount of delicacy. He had taken as his motto: "Everything comes to him who waits." He knew how to be at the same time patient and energetic. His success was rapid and complete.

After four days, Madame Lebrument adored her

husband. She could not get along without him.
She would sit on his knees, and taking him by the
ears she would say: "Open your mouth and shut
your eyes." He would open his mouth wide and
partly close his eyes, and he would try to nip her
fingers as she slipped some dainty between his teeth.
Then she would give him a kiss, sweet and long,
which would make chills run up and down his spine.
And then, in his turn, he would not have enough
caresses to please his wife from morning to night
and from night to morning.

When the first week was over, he said to his
young companion:

"If you wish, we will leave for Paris next Tuesday. We will be like two lovers, we will go to
the restaurants, the theatres, the concert halls,
everywhere, everywhere!"

She was ready to dance for joy.

"Oh! yes, yes. Let us go as soon as possible."

He continued:

"And then, as we must forget nothing, ask your
father to have your dowry ready; I shall pay Maitre
Papillon on this trip."

She answered:

"All right! I will tell him to-morrow morning."

And he took her in his arms once more, to renew
those sweet games of love which she had so enjoyed
for the past week.

The following Tuesday, father-in-law and
mother-in-law went to the station with their daughter and their son-in-law who were leaving for the
capital.

The father-in-law said:

THE DOWRY

"I tell you it is very imprudent to carry so much money about in a pocketbook." And the young lawyer smiled.

"Don't worry; I am accustomed to such things. You understand that, in my profession, I sometimes have as much as a million about me. In this manner, at least, we avoid a great amount of red tape and delay. You needn't worry."

The conductor was crying:

"All aboard for Paris!"

They scrambled into a car, where two old ladies were already seated.

Lebrument whispered into his wife's ear:

"What a bother! I won't be able to smoke."

She answered in a low voice:

"It annoys me too, but not on account of your cigar."

The whistle blew and the train started. The trip lasted about an hour, during which time they did not say very much to each other, as the two old ladies did not go to sleep.

As soon as they were in front of the Saint-Lazare Station, Maitre Lebrument said to his wife:

"Dearie, let us first go over to the Boulevard and get something to eat; then we can quietly return and get our trunk and bring it to the hotel."

She immediately assented.

"Oh! yes. Let's eat at the restaurant. Is it far?"

He answered:

"Yes, it's quite a distance, but we will take the omnibus."

She was surprised:

"Why don't we take a cab?"

He began to scold her smilingly:

3

THE DOWRY

"Is that the way you save money? A cab for a five minutes' ride at six cents a minute! You would deprive yourself of nothing."

"That's so," she said, a little embarrassed.

A big omnibus was passing by, drawn by three big horses, which were trotting along. Lebrument called out:

"Conductor! Conductor!"

The heavy carriage stopped. And the young lawyer, pushing his wife, said to her quickly:

"Go inside; I'm going up on top, so that I may smoke at least one cigarette before lunch."

She had no time to answer. The conductor, who had seized her by the arm to help her up the step, pushed her inside, and she fell into a seat, bewildered, looking through the back window at the feet of her husband as he climbed up to the top of the vehicle.

And she sat there motionless, between a fat man who smelled of cheap tobacco and an old woman who smelled of garlic.

All the other passengers were lined up in silence —a grocer's boy, a young girl, a soldier, a gentleman with gold-rimmed spectacles and a big silk hat, two ladies with a self-satisfied and crabbed look, which seemed to say: "We are riding in this thing, but we don't *have* to," two sisters of charity and an undertaker. They looked like a collection of caricatures.

The jolting of the wagon made them wag their heads and the shaking of the wheels seemed to stupefy them—they all looked as though they were asleep.

The young woman remained motionless.

4

"Why didn't he come inside with me?" she was saying to herself. An unaccountable sadness seemed to be hanging over her. He really need not have acted so.

The sisters motioned to the conductor to stop, and they got off one after the other, leaving in their wake the pungent smell of camphor. The bus started up and soon stopped again. And in got a cook, red-faced and out of breath. She sat down and placed her basket of provisions on her knees. A strong odor of dish-water filled the vehicle.

"It's further than I imagined," thought Jeanne. The undertaker went out, and was replaced by a coachman who seemed to bring the atmosphere of the stable with him. The young girl had as a successor a messenger, the odor of whose feet showed that he was continually walking.

The lawyer's wife began to feel ill at ease, nauseated, ready to cry without knowing why.

Other persons left and others entered. The stage went on through interminable streets, stopping at stations and starting again.

"How far it is!" thought Jeanne. "I hope he hasn't gone to sleep! He has been so tired the last few days."

Little by little all the passengers left. She was left alone, all alone. The conductor cried:

"Vaugirard!"

Seeing that she did not move, he repeated:

"Vaugirard!"

She looked at him, understanding that he was speaking to her, as there was no one else there. For the third time the man said:

"Vaugirard!"

Then she asked:

"Where are we?"

He answered gruffly:

"We're at Vaugirard, of course! I have been yelling it for the last half hour!"

"Is it far from the Boulevard?" she said.

"Which boulevard?"

"The Boulevard des Italiens."

"We passed that a long time ago!"

"Would you mind telling my husband?"

"Your husband! Where is he?"

"On the top of the bus."

"On the top! There hasn't been anybody there for a long time."

She started, terrified.

"What? That's impossible! He got on with me. Look well! He must be there."

The conductor was becoming uncivil:

"Come on, little one, you've talked enough! You can find ten men for every one that you lose. Now run along. You'll find another one somewhere."

Tears were coming to her eyes. She insisted:

"But, monsieur, you are mistaken; I assure you that you must be mistaken. He had a big portfolio under his arm."

The man began to laugh:

"A big portfolio! Oh, yes! He got off at the Madeleine. He got rid of you, all right! Ha! ha! ha!"

The stage had stopped. She got out and, in spite of herself, she looked up instinctively to the roof of the bus. It was absolutely deserted.

Then she began to cry, and, without thinking that

anybody was listening or watching her, she said out loud:

"What is going to become of me?"

An inspector approached:

"What's the matter?"

The conductor answered, in a bantering tone of voice:

"It's a lady who got left by her husband during the trip."

The other continued:

"Oh! that's nothing. You go about your business."

Then he turned on his heels and walked away.

She began to walk straight ahead, too bewildered, too crazed even to understand what had happened to her. Where was she to go? What could she do? What could have happened to him? How could he have made such a mistake? How could he have been so forgetful?

She had two francs in her pocket. To whom could she go? Suddenly she remembered her cousin Barral, one of the assistants in the offices of the Ministry of the Navy.

She had just enough to pay for a cab. She drove to his house. He met her just as he was leaving for his office. He was carrying a large portfolio under his arm, just like Lebrument.

She jumped out of the carriage.

"Henry!" she cried.

He stopped, astonished:

"Jeanne! Here—all alone! What are you doing? Where have you come from?"

Her eyes full of tears, she stammered:

"My husband has just got lost!"

7

THE DOWRY

"Lost! Where?"

"On an omnibus."

"On an omnibus?"

Weeping, she told him her whole adventure.

He listened, thought, and then asked:

"Was his mind clear this morning?"

"Yes."

"Good. Did he have much money with him?"

"Yes, he was carrying my dowry."

"Your dowry! The whole of it?"

"The whole of it—in order to pay for the practice which he bought."

"Well, my dear cousin, by this time your husband must be well on his way to Belgium."

She could not understand. She kept repeating:

"My husband—you say——"

"I say that he has disappeared with your—your capital—that's all!"

She stood there, a prey to conflicting emotions, sobbing.

"Then he is—he is—he is a villain!"

And, faint from excitement, she leaned her head on her cousin's shoulder and wept.

As people were stopping to look at them, he pushed her gently into the vestibule of his house, and, supporting her with his arm around her waist, he led her up the stairs, and as his astonished servant opened the door, he ordered:

"Sophie, run to the restaurant and get a luncheon for two. I am not going to the office to-day."

OLD JUDAS

THIS entire stretch of country was amazing;
it was characterized by a grandeur that was
almost religious, and yet it had an air of
sinister desolation.

A great, wild lake, filled with stagnant, black
water, in which thousands of reeds were waving to
and fro, lay in the midst of a vast circle of naked
hills, where nothing grew but broom, or here and
there an oak curiously twisted by the wind.

Just one house stood on the banks of that dark
lake, a small, low house inhabited by Uncle Joseph,
an old boatman, who lived on what he could make
by his fishing. Once a week he carried the fish he
caught into the surrounding villages, returning with
the few provisions that he needed for his sustenance.

I went to see this old hermit, who offered to take
me with him to his nets, and I accepted.

His boat was old, worm-eaten and clumsy, and
the skinny old man rowed with a gentle and monotonous stroke that was soothing to the soul, already
oppressed by the sadness of the land round about.

It seemed to me as if I were transported to
olden times, in the midst of that ancient country, in
that primitive boat, which was propelled by a man
of another age.

He took up his nets and threw the fish into the
bottom of the boat, as the fishermen of the Bible

might have done. Then he took me down to the end of the lake, where I suddenly perceived a ruin on the other side of the bank, a dilapidated hut, with an enormous red cross on the wall that looked as if it might have been traced with blood, as it gleamed in the last rays of the setting sun.

"What is that?" I asked.

"That is where Judas died," the man replied, crossing himself.

I was not surprised, being almost prepared for this strange answer. Still I asked:

"Judas? What Judas?"

"The Wandering Jew, monsieur," he added.

I asked him to tell me this legend.

But it was better than a legend, being a true story, and quite a recent one, since Uncle Joseph had known the man.

This hut had formerly been occupied by a large woman, a kind of beggar, who lived on public charity.

Uncle Joseph did not remember from whom she had this hut. One evening an old man with a white beard, who seemed to be at least two hundred years old, and who could hardly drag himself along, asked alms of this forlorn woman, as he passed her dwelling.

"Sit down, father," she replied; "everything here belongs to all the world, since it comes from all the world."

He sat down on a stone before the door. He shared the woman's bread, her bed of leaves, and her house.

He did not leave her again, for he had come to the end of his travels.

"It was Our Lady the Virgin who permitted this, monsieur," Joseph added, "it being a woman who had opened her door to a Judas, for this old vagabond was the Wandering Jew. It was not known at first in the country, but the people suspected it very soon, because he was always walking; it had become a sort of second nature to him."

And suspicion had been aroused by still another thing. This woman, who kept that stranger with her, was thought to be a Jewess, for no one had ever seen her at church. For ten miles around no one ever called her anything else but the Jewess.

When the little country children saw her come to beg they cried out:

"Mamma, mamma, here is the Jewess!"

The old man and she began to go out together into the neighboring districts, holding out their hands at all the doors, stammering supplications into the ears of all the passers. They could be seen at all hours of the day, on by-paths, in the villages, or again eating bread, sitting in the noon heat under the shadow of some solitary tree.

And the country people began to call the beggar Old Judas.

One day he brought home in his sack two little live pigs, which a farmer had given him after he had cured the farmer of some sickness.

Soon he stopped begging, and devoted himself entirely to his pigs. He took them out to feed by the lake, or under isolated oaks, or in the near-by valleys. The woman, however, went about all day begging, but she always came back to him in the evening.

He also did not go to church, and no one ever

3

had seen him cross himself before the wayside crucifixes. All this gave rise to much gossip.

One night his companion was attacked by a fever and began to tremble like a leaf in the wind. He went to the nearest town to get some medicine, and then he shut himself up with her, and was not seen for six days.

The priest, having heard that the "Jewess" was about to die, came to offer the consolation of his religion and administer the last sacrament. Was she a Jewess? He did not know. But in any case, he wished to try to save her soul.

Hardly had he knocked at the door when old Judas appeared on the threshold, breathing hard, his eyes aflame, his long beard agitated, like rippling water, and he hurled blasphemies in an unknown language, extending his skinny arms in order to prevent the priest from entering.

The priest attempted to speak, offered his purse and his aid, but the old man kept on abusing him, making gestures with his hands as if throwing stones at him.

Then the priest retired, followed by the curses of the beggar.

The companion of old Judas died the following day. He buried her himself, in front of his door. They were people of so little account that no one took any interest in them.

Then they saw the man take his pigs out again to the lake and up the hillsides. And he also began begging again to get food. But the people gave him hardly anything, as there was so much gossip about him. Every one knew, moreover, how he had treated the priest.

4

OLD JUDAS

Then he disappeared. That was during Holy Week, but no one paid any attention to him.

But on Easter Sunday the boys and girls who had gone walking out to the lake heard a great noise in the hut. The door was locked; but the boys broke it in, and the two pigs ran out, jumping like goats. No one ever saw them again.

The whole crowd went in; they saw some old rags on the floor, the beggar's hat, some bones, clots of dried blood and bits of flesh in the hollows of the skull.

His pigs had devoured him.

"This happened on Good Friday, monsieur." Joseph concluded his story, "three hours after noon."

"How do you know that?" I asked him.

"There is no doubt about that," he replied.

I did not attempt to make him understand that it could easily happen that the famished animals had eaten their master, after he had died suddenly in his hut.

As for the cross on the wall, it had appeared one morning, and no one knew what hand traced it in that strange color.

Since then no one doubted any longer that the Wandering Jew had died on this spot.

I myself believed it for one hour.

THE LITTLE CASK

HE was a tall man of forty or thereabout, this Jules Chicot, the innkeeper of Épreville, with a red face and a round stomach, and said by those who knew him to be a smart business man. He stopped his buggy in front of Mother Magloire's farmhouse, and, hitching the horse to the gatepost, went in at the gate.

Chicot owned some land adjoining that of the old woman, which he had been coveting for a long while, and had tried in vain to buy a score of times, but she had always obstinately refused to part with it.

"I was born here, and here I mean to die," was all she said.

He found her peeling potatoes outside the farmhouse door. She was a woman of about seventy-two, very thin, shriveled and wrinkled, almost dried up in fact and much bent, but as active and untiring as a girl. Chicot patted her on the back in a friendly fashion and then sat down by her on a stool.

"Well, mother, you are always pretty well and hearty, I am glad to see."

"Nothing to complain of, considering, thank you. And how are you, Monsieur Chicot?"

"Oh, pretty well, thank you, except a few rheumatic pains occasionally; otherwise I have nothing to complain of."

"So much the better."

1

THE LITTLE CASK

And she said no more, while Chicot watched her going on with her work. Her crooked, knotted fingers, hard as a lobster's claws, seized the tubers, which were lying in a pail, as if they had been a pair of pincers, and she peeled them rapidly, cutting off long strips of skin with an old knife which she held in the other hand, throwing the potatoes into the water as they were done. Three daring fowls jumped one after the other into her lap, seized a bit of peel and then ran away as fast as their legs would carry them with it in their beak.

Chicot seemed embarrassed, anxious, with something on the tip of his tongue which he could not say. At last he said hurriedly:

"Listen, Mother Magloire——"

"Well, what is it?"

"You are quite sure that you do not want to sell your land?"

"Certainly not; you may make up your mind to that. What I have said I have said, so don't refer to it again."

"Very well; only I think I know of an arrangement that might suit us both very well."

"What is it?"

"Just this. You shall sell it to me and keep it all the same. You don't understand? Very well, then follow me in what I am going to say."

The old woman left off peeling her potatoes and looked at the innkeeper attentively from under her heavy eyebrows, and he went on:

"Let me explain myself. Every month I will give you a hundred and fifty francs. You understand me, I suppose? Every month I will come and bring you thirty crowns,* and it will not make the slightest

2

difference in your life—not the very slightest. You will have your own home just as you have now, need not trouble yourself about me, and will owe me nothing; all you will have to do will be to take my money. Will that arrangement suit you?"

He looked at her good-humoredly, one might almost have said benevolently, and the old woman returned his looks distrustfully, as if she suspected a trap, and said:

"It seems all right as far as I am concerned, but it will not give you the farm."

"Never mind about that," he said; "you may remain here as long as it pleases God Almighty to let you live; it will be your home. Only you will sign a deed before a lawyer making it over to me after your death. You have no children, only nephews and nieces for whom you don't care a straw. Will that suit you? You will keep everything during your life, and I will give you the thirty crowns a month. It is pure gain as far as you are concerned."

The old woman was surprised, rather uneasy, but, nevertheless, very much tempted to agree, and answered:

"I don't say that I will not agree to it, but I must think about it. Come back in a week, and we will talk it over again, and I will then give you my definite answer."

And Chicot went off as happy as a king who had conquered an empire.

Mother Magloire was thoughtful, and did not sleep at all that night; in fact, for four days she was in a fever of hesitation. She suspected that there was something underneath the offer which was not to her advantage; but then the thought of thirty crowns a month, of all those coins clinking in her apron, falling to her, as it were, from the skies, without her doing anything for it, aroused her covetousness.

She went to the notary and told him about it. He advised her to accept Chicot's offer, but said she ought to ask for an annuity of fifty instead of thirty, as her farm was worth sixty thousand francs at the lowest calculation.

"If you live for fifteen years longer," he said, "even then he will only have paid forty-five thousand francs for it."

The old woman trembled with joy at this prospect of getting fifty crowns a month, but she was still suspicious, fearing some trick, and she remained a long time with the lawyer asking questions without being able to make up her mind to go. At last she gave him instructions to draw up the deed and returned home with her head in a whirl, just as if she had drunk four jugs of new cider.

When Chicot came again to receive her answer she declared, after a lot of persuading, that she could not make up her mind to agree to his proposal, though she was all the time trembling lest he should not consent to give the fifty crowns, but at last, when he grew urgent, she told him what she expected for her farm.

He looked surprised and disappointed and refused.

Then, in order to convince him, she began to talk about the probable duration of her life.

"I am certainly not likely to live more than five or six years longer. I am nearly seventy-three, and far from strong, even considering my age. The other evening I thought I was going to die, and could hardly manage to crawl into bed."

But Chicot was not going to be taken in.

"Come, come, old lady, you are as strong as the church tower, and will live till you are a hundred at least; you will no doubt see me put under ground first."

The whole day was spent in discussing the money, and as the old woman would not give in, the inn-keeper consented to give the fifty crowns, and she insisted upon having ten crowns over and above to strike the bargain.

Three years passed and the old dame did not seem to have grown a day older. Chicot was in despair, and it seemed to him as if he had been paying that annuity for fifty years, that he had been taken in, done, ruined. From time to time he went to see the old lady, just as one goes in July to see when the harvest is likely to begin. She always met him with a cunning look, and one might have supposed that she was congratulating herself on the trick she had played him. Seeing how well and hearty she seemed, he very soon got into his buggy again, growling to himself:

"Will you never die, you old hag?"

He did not know what to do, and he felt inclined to strangle her when he saw her. He hated her with a ferocious, cunning hatred, the hatred of a peasant who has been robbed, and began to cast about for some means of getting rid of her.

One day he came to see her again, rubbing his hands as he did the first time he proposed the bargain, and, after having chatted for a few minutes, he said:

THE LITTLE CASK

"Why do you never come and have a bit of dinner at my place when you are in Épreville? The people are talking about it, and saying we are not on friendly terms, and that pains me. You know it will cost you nothing if you come, for I don't look at the price of a dinner. Come whenever you feel inclined; I shall be very glad to see you."

Old Mother Magloire did not need to be asked twice, and the next day but one, as she had to go to the town in any case, it being market day, she let her man drive her to Chicot's place, where the buggy was put in the barn while she went into the house to get her dinner.

The innkeeper was delighted and treated her like a lady, giving her roast fowl, black pudding, leg of mutton and bacon and cabbage. But she ate next to nothing. She had always been a small eater, and had generally lived on a little soup and a crust of bread and butter.

Chicot was disappointed and pressed her to eat more, but she refused, and she would drink little, and declined coffee, so he asked her:

"But surely you will take a little drop of brandy or liqueur?"

"Well, as to that, I don't know that I will refuse." Whereupon he shouted out:

"Rosalie, bring the superfine brandy—*the special* —you know."

The servant appeared, carrying a long bottle ornamented with a paper vine-leaf, and he filled two liqueur glasses.

"Just try that; you will find it first rate."

The good woman drank it slowly in sips, so as to

make the pleasure last all the longer, and when she
had finished her glass, she said:

"Yes, that is first rate!"

Almost before she had said it Chicot had poured
her out another glassful. She wished to refuse, but
it was too late, and she drank it very slowly, as she
had done the first, and he asked her to have a third.
She objected, but he persisted.

"It is as mild as milk, you know; I can drink ten
or a dozen glasses without any ill effects; it goes
down like sugar and does not go to the head; one
would think that it evaporated on the tongue. It is
the most wholesome thing you can drink."

She took it, for she really enjoyed it, but she left
half the glass.

Then Chicot, in an excess of generosity, said:

"Look here, as it is so much to your taste, I will
give you a small keg of it, just to show that you and
I are still excellent friends." So she took one away
with her, feeling slightly overcome by the effects of
what she had drunk.

The next day the innkeeper drove into her yard
and took a little iron-hooped keg out of his gig. He
insisted on her tasting the contents, to make sure it
was the same delicious article, and, when they had
each of them drunk three more glasses, he said as
he was going away:

"Well, you know when it is all gone there is more
left; don't be modest, for I shall not mind. The
sooner it is finished the better pleased I shall be."

Four days later he came again. The old woman
was outside her door cutting up the bread for her
soup.

He went up to her and put his face close to hers,

so• that he might smell her breath; and when he smelt the alcohol he felt pleased.

"I suppose you will give me a glass of the special?" he said. And they had three glasses each.

Soon, however, it began to be whispered abroad that Mother Magloire was in the habit of getting drunk all by herself. She was picked up in her kitchen, then in her yard, then in the roads in the neighborhood, and she was often brought home like a log.

The innkeeper did not go near her any more, and, when people spoke to him about her, he used to say, putting on a distressed look:

"It is a great pity that she should have taken to drink at her age, but when people get old there is no remedy. It will be the death of her in the long run."

And it certainly was the death of her. She died the next winter. About Christmas time she fell down, unconscious, in the snow, and was found dead the next morning.

And when Chicot came in for the farm, he said:

"It was very stupid of her; if she had not taken to drink she would probably have lived ten years longer."

BOITELLE

FATHER BOITELLE (Antoine) made a specialty of undertaking dirty jobs all through the countryside. Whenever there was a ditch or a cesspool to be cleaned out, a dunghill removed, a sewer cleansed, or any dirt hole whatever, he was always employed to do it.

He would come with the instruments of his trade, his sabots covered with dirt, and set to work, complaining incessantly about his occupation. When people asked him then why he did this loathsome work, he would reply resignedly:

"Faith, 'tis for my children, whom I must support. This brings me in more than anything else."

He had, indeed, fourteen children. If any one asked him what had become of them, he would say with an air of indifference:

"There are only eight of them left in the house. One is out at service and five are married."

When the questioner wanted to know whether they were well married, he replied vivaciously:

"I did not oppose them. I opposed them in nothing. They married just as they pleased. We shouldn't go against people's likings, it turns out badly. I am a night scavenger because my parents went against my likings. But for that I would have become a workman like the others."

1

BOITELLE

Here is the way his parents had thwarted him in his likings:

He was at the time a soldier stationed at Havre, not more stupid than another, or sharper either, a rather simple fellow, however. When he was not on duty, his greatest pleasure was to walk along the quay, where the bird dealers congregate. Sometimes alone, sometimes with a soldier from his own part of the country, he would slowly saunter along by cages containing parrots with green backs and yellow heads from the banks of the Amazon, or parrots with gray backs and red heads from Senegal, or enormous macaws, which look like birds reared in hot-houses, with their flower-like feathers, their plumes and their tufts. Parrots of every size, who seem painted with minute care by the miniaturist, God Almighty, and the little birds, all the smaller birds hopped about, yellow, blue and variegated, mingling their cries with the noise of the quay, and adding to the din caused by unloading the vessels, as well as by passengers and vehicles, a violent clamor, loud, shrill and deafening, as if from some distant forest of monsters.

Boitelle would pause, with wondering eyes, wide-open mouth, laughing and enraptured, showing his teeth to the captive cockatoos, who kept nodding their white or yellow topknots toward the glaring red of his breeches and the copper buckle of his belt. When he found a bird that could talk he put questions to it, and if it happened at the time to be disposed to reply and to hold a conversation with him he would carry away enough amusement to last him till evening. He also found heaps of amusement in looking at the monkeys, and could conceive no

2

greater luxury for a rich man than to own these animals as one owns cats and dogs. This kind of taste for the exotic he had in his blood, as people have a taste for the chase, or for medicine, or for the priesthood. He could not help returning to the quay every time the gates of the barracks opened, drawn toward it by an irresistible longing.

On one occasion, having stopped almost in ecstasy before an enormous macaw, which was swelling out its plumes, bending forward and bridling up again as if making the court curtseys of parrot-land, he saw the door of a little café adjoining the bird dealer's shop open, and a young negress appeared, wearing on her head a red silk handkerchief. She was sweeping into the street the corks and sand of the establishment.

Boitelle's attention was soon divided between the bird and the woman, and he really could not tell which of these two beings he contemplated with the greater astonishment and delight.

The negress, having swept the rubbish into the street, raised her eyes, and, in her turn, was dazzled by the soldier's uniform. There she stood facing him with her broom in her hands as if she were bringing him a rifle, while the macaw continued bowing. But at the end of a few seconds the soldier began to feel embarrassed at this attention, and he walked away quietly so as not to look as if he were beating a retreat.

But he came back. Almost every day he passed before the Café des Colonies, and often he could distinguish through the window the figure of the little black-skinned maid serving "bocks" or glasses of brandy to the sailors of the port. Frequently, too, she would come out to the door on seeing him; soon, without even having exchanged a word, they smiled at one another like acquaintances; and Boitelle felt his heart touched when he suddenly saw, glittering between the dark lips of the girl, a shining row of white teeth. At length, one day he ventured to enter, and was quite surprised to find that she could speak French like every one else. The bottle of lemonade, of which she was good enough to accept a glassful, remained in the soldier's recollection memorably delicious, and it became a custom with him to come and absorb in this little tavern on the quay all the agreeable drinks which he could afford.

For him it was a treat, a happiness, on which his thoughts dwelt constantly, to watch the black hand of the little maid pouring something into his glass while her teeth laughed more than her eyes. At the end of two months they became fast friends, and Boitelle, after his first astonishment at discovering that this negress had as good principles as honest French girls, that she exhibited a regard for economy, industry, religion and good conduct, loved her more on that account, and was so charmed with her that he wanted to marry her.

He told her his intentions, which made her dance with joy. She had also a little money, left her by a female oyster dealer, who had picked her up when she had been left on the quay at Havre by an American captain. This captain had found her, when she was only about six years old, lying on bales of cotton in the hold of his ship, some hours after his departure from New York. On his arrival in Havre he abandoned to the care of this compassionate oyster dealer the little black creature, who had been hidden on board his vessel, he knew not why or by whom.

The oyster woman having died, the young negress became a servant at the Colonial Tavern.

Antoine Boitelle added: "This will be all right if my parents don't oppose it. I will never go against them, you understand, never! I'm going to say a word or two to them the first time I go back to the country."

On the following week, in fact, having obtained twenty-four hours' leave, he went to see his family, who cultivated a little farm at Tourteville, near Yvetot.

He waited till the meal was finished, the hour when the coffee baptized with brandy makes people more open-hearted, before informing his parents that he had found a girl who satisfied his tastes, all his tastes, so completely that there could not exist any other in all the world so perfectly suited to him.

The old people, on hearing this, immediately assumed a cautious manner and wanted explanations. He had concealed nothing from them except the color of her skin.

She was a servant, without much means, but strong, thrifty, clean, well-conducted and sensible. All these things were better than money would be in the hands of a bad housewife. Moreover, she had a few sous, left her by a woman who had reared her, a good number of sous, almost a little dowry, fifteen hundred francs in the savings bank. The old people, persuaded by his talk, and relying also on their own judgment, were gradually weakening, when he came to the delicate point. Laughing in rather a constrained fashion, he said:

"There's only one thing you may not like. She is not a white slip."

They did not understand, and he had to explain at some length and very cautiously, to avoid shocking them, that she belonged to the dusky race of which they had only seen samples in pictures at Épinal. Then they became restless, perplexed, alarmed, as if he had proposed a union with the devil.

The mother said: "Black? How much of her is black? Is the whole of her?"

He replied: "Certainly. Everywhere, just as you are white everywhere."

The father interposed: "Black? Is it as black as the pot?"

The son answered: "Perhaps a little less than that. She is black, but not disgustingly black. The curé's cassock is black, but it is not uglier than a surplice, which is white."

The father said: "Are there more black people besides her in her country?"

And the son, with an air of conviction, exclaimed: "Certainly!"

But the old man shook his head.

"That must be unpleasant."

And the son:

"It isn't more disagreeable than anything else when you get accustomed to it."

The mother asked:

"It doesn't soil the underwear more than other skins, this black skin?"

"Not more than your own, as it is her proper color."

Then, after many other questions, it was agreed

that the parents should see this girl before coming to any decision, and that the young fellow, whose term of military service would be over in a month, should bring her to the house in order that they might examine her and decide by talking the matter over whether or not she was too dark to enter the Boitelle family.

Antoine accordingly announced that on Sunday, the 22d of May, the day of his discharge, he would start for Tourteville with his sweetheart.

She had put on, for this journey to the house of her lover's parents, her most beautiful and most gaudy clothes, in which yellow, red and blue were the prevailing colors, so that she looked as if she were adorned for a national festival.

At the terminus, as they were leaving Havre, people stared at her, and Boitelle was proud of giving his arm to a person who commanded so much attention. Then, in the third-class carriage, in which she took a seat by his side, she aroused so much astonishment among the country folks that the people in the adjoining compartments stood up on their benches to look at her over the wooden partition which divides the compartments. A child, at sight of her, began to cry with terror, another concealed his face in his mother's apron. Everything went off well, however, up to their arrival at their destination. But when the train slackened its rate of motion as they drew near Yvetot, Antoine felt ill at ease, as he would have done at a review when he did not know his drill practice. Then, as he leaned his head out, he recognized in the distance his father, holding the bridle of the horse harnessed to a carryall, and his mother, who had come forward to the grating, behind which stood those who were expecting friends.

He alighted first, gave his hand to his sweetheart, and holding himself erect, as if he were escorting a general, he went to meet his family.

The mother, on seeing this black lady in variegated costume in her son's company, remained so stupefied that she could not open her mouth; and the father found it hard to hold the horse, which the engine or the negress caused to rear continuously. But Antoine, suddenly filled with unmixed joy at seeing once more the old people, rushed forward with open arms, embraced his mother, embraced his father, in spite of the nag's fright, and then turning toward his companion, at whom the passengers on the platform stopped to stare with amazement, he proceeded to explain:

"Here she is! I told you that, at first sight, she is not attractive; but as soon as you know her, I can assure you there's not a better sort in the whole world. Say good-morning to her so that she may not feel badly."

Thereupon Mère Boitelle, almost frightened out of her wits, made a sort of curtsy, while the father took off his cap, murmuring:

"I wish you good luck!"

Then, without further delay, they climbed into the carryall, the two women at the back, on seats which made them jump up and down as the vehicle went jolting along the road, and the two men in front on the front seat.

Nobody spoke. Antoine, ill at ease, whistled a barrack-room air; his father whipped the nag; and his mother, from where she sat in the corner, kept casting sly glances at the negress, whose forehead and cheekbones shone in the sunlight like well-polished shoes.

Wishing to break the ice, Antoine turned round.

"Well," said he, "we don't seem inclined to talk."

"We must have time," replied the old woman.

He went on:

"Come! Tell us the little story about that hen of yours that laid eight eggs."

It was a funny anecdote of long standing in the family. But, as his mother still remained silent, paralyzed by her emotion, he undertook himself to tell the story, laughing as he did so at the memorable incident. The father, who knew it by heart, brightened at the opening words of the narrative; his wife soon followed his example; and the negress herself, when he reached the drollest part of it, suddenly gave vent to a laugh, such a loud, rolling torrent of laughter that the horse, becoming excited, broke into a gallop for a while.

This served to cement their acquaintance. They all began to chat.

They had scarcely reached the house and had all alighted, when Antoine conducted his sweetheart to a room, so that she might take off her dress, to avoid staining it, as she was going to prepare a nice dish, intended to win the old people's affections through their stomachs. He drew his parents outside the house, and, with beating heart, asked:

"Well, what do you say now?"

The father said nothing. The mother, less timid, exclaimed:

9

"She is too black. No, indeed, this is too much for me. It turns my blood."

"You will get used to it," said Antoine.

"Perhaps so, but not at first."

They went into the house, where the good woman was somewhat affected at the spectacle of the negress engaged in cooking. She at once proceeded to assist her, with petticoats tucked up, active in spite of her age.

The meal was an excellent one, very long, very enjoyable. When they were taking a turn after dinner, Antoine took his father aside.

"Well, dad, what do you say about it?"

The peasant took care never to compromise himself.

"I have no opinion about it. Ask your mother."

So Antoine went back to his mother, and, detaining her behind the rest, said:

"Well, mother, what do you think of her?"

"My poor lad, she is really too black. If she were only a little less black, I would not go against you, but this is too much. One would think it was Satan!"

He did not press her, knowing how obstinate the old woman had always been, but he felt a tempest of disappointment sweeping over his heart. He was turning over in his mind what he ought to do, what plan he could devise, surprised, moreover, that she had not conquered them already as she had captivated himself. And they, all four, walked along through the wheat fields, having gradually relapsed into silence. Whenever they passed a fence they saw a countryman sitting on the stile, and a group of brats climbed up to stare at them, and every one rushed out into the road to see the "black" whom young Boitelle had brought home with him. At a distance they noticed people scampering across the fields just as when the drum beats to draw public attention to some living phenomenon. Père and Mère Boitelle, alarmed at this curiosity, which was exhibited everywhere through the country at their approach, quickened their pace, walking side by side, and leaving their son far behind. His dark companion asked what his parents thought of her.

He hesitatingly replied that they had not yet made up their minds.

But on the village green people rushed out of all the houses in a flutter of excitement; and, at the sight of the gathering crowd, old Boitelle took to his heels, and regained his abode, while Antoine, swelling with rage, his sweetheart on his arm, advanced majestically under the staring eyes, which opened wide in amazement.

He understood that it was at an end, and there was no hope for him, that he could not marry his negress. She also understood it; and as they drew near the farmhouse they both began to weep. As soon as they had got back to the house, she once more took off her dress to aid the mother in the household duties, and followed her everywhere, to the dairy, to the stable, to the hen house, taking on herself the hardest part of the work, repeating always: "Let me do it, Madame Boitelle," so that, when night came on, the old woman, touched but inexorable, said to her son: "She is a good girl, all the same. It's a pity she is so black; but indeed she is too black. I could not get used to it. She must go back again. She is too, too black!"

And young Boitelle said to his sweetheart:

"She will not consent. She thinks you are too black. You must go back again. I will go with you to the train. No matter—don't fret. I am going to talk to them after you have started."

He then took her to the railway station, still cheering her with hope, and, when he had kissed her, he put her into the train, which he watched as it passed out of sight, his eyes swollen with tears.

In vain did he appeal to the old people. They would never give their consent.

And when he had told this story, which was known all over the country, Antoine Boitelle would always add:

"From that time forward I have had no heart for anything—for anything at all. No trade suited me any longer, and so I became what I am—a night scavenger."

People would say to him:

"Yet you got married."

"Yes, and I can't say that my wife didn't please me, seeing that I have fourteen children; but she is not the other one, oh, no—certainly not! The other one, mark you, my negress, she had only to give me one glance, and I felt as if I were in Heaven."

A WIDOW

THIS story was told during the hunting season
at the Château Baneville. The autumn had
been rainy and sad. The red leaves, instead
of rustling under the feet, were rotting under the
heavy downfalls.

The forest was as damp as it could be. From it
came an odor of must, of rain, of soaked grass and
wet earth; and the sportsmen, their backs hunched
under the downpour, mournful dogs, with tails between their legs and hairs sticking to their sides, and
the young women, with their clothes drenched, returned every evening, tired in body and in mind.

After dinner, in the large drawing-room, everybody played lotto, without enjoyment, while the wind
whistled madly around the house. Then they tried
telling stories like those they read in books, but no
one was able to invent anything amusing. The
hunters told tales of wonderful shots and of the
butchery of rabbits; and the women racked their
brains for ideas without revealing the imagination
of Scheherezade. They were about to give up this
diversion when a young woman, who was idly caressing the hand of an old maiden aunt, noticed a little
ring made of blond hair, which she had often seen
without paying any attention to it.

She fingered it gently and asked, "Auntie, what

is this ring? It looks as if it were made from the hair of a child."

The old lady blushed, grew pale, then answered in a trembling voice: "It is sad, so sad that I never wish to speak of it. All the unhappiness of my life comes from that. I was very young then, and the memory has remained so painful that I weep every time I think of it."

Immediately everybody wished to know the story, but the old lady refused to tell it. Finally, after they had coaxed her for a long time, she yielded. Here is the story:

"You have often heard me speak of the Santèze family, now extinct. I knew the last three male members of this family. They all died in the same manner; this hair belongs to the last one. He was thirteen when he killed himself for me. That seems strange to you, doesn't it?

"Oh! it was a strange family—mad, if you will, but a charming madness, the madness of love. From father to son, all had violent passions which filled their whole being, which impelled them to do wild things, drove them to frantic enthusiasm, even to crime. This was born in them, just as burning devotion is in certain souls. Trappers have not the same nature as minions of the drawing-room. There was a saying: 'As passionate as a Santèze.' This could be noticed by looking at them. They all had wavy hair, falling over their brows, curly beards and large eyes whose glance pierced and moved one, though one could not say why.

"The grandfather of the owner of this hair, of whom it is the last souvenir, after many adventures, duels and elopements, at about sixty-five fell madly in love with his farmer's daughter. I knew them both. She was blond, pale, distinguished-looking, with a slow manner of talking, a quiet voice and a look so gentle that one might have taken her for a Madonna. The old nobleman took her to his home and was soon so captivated with her that he could not live without her for a minute. His daughter and daughter-in-law, who lived in the château, found this perfectly natural, love was such a tradition in the family. Nothing in regard to a passion surprised them, and if one spoke before them of parted lovers, even of vengeance after treachery, both said in the same sad tone: 'Oh, how he must have suffered to come to that point!' That was all. They grew sad over tragedies of love, but never indignant, even when they were criminal.

"Now, one day a young man named Monsieur de Gradelle, who had been invited for the shooting, eloped with the young girl.

"Monsieur de Santèze remained calm as if nothing had happened, but one morning he was found hanging in the kennels, among his dogs.

"His son died in the same manner in a hotel in Paris during a journey which he made there in 1841, after being deceived by a singer from the opera.

"He left a twelve-year-old child and a widow, my mother's sister. She came to my father's house with the boy, while we were living at Bertillon. I was then seventeen.

"You have no idea how wonderful and precocious this Santèze child was. One might have thought that all the tenderness and exaltation of the whole race had been stored up in this last one. He was always dreaming and walking about alone in a great alley

3

of elms leading from the château to the forest. I watched from my window this sentimental boy, who walked with thoughtful steps, his hands behind his back, his head bent, and at times stopping to raise his eyes as if he could see and understand things that were not comprehensible at his age.

"Often, after dinner on clear evenings, he would say to me: 'Let us go outside and dream, cousin.' And we would go outside together in the park. He would stop quickly before a clearing where the white vapor of the moon lights the woods, and he would press my hand, saying: 'Look! look! but you don't understand me; I feel it. If you understood me, we should be happy. One must love to know!' I would laugh and then kiss this child, who loved me madly.

"Often, after dinner, he would sit on my mother's knees. 'Come, auntie,' he would say, 'tell me some love-stories.' And my mother, as a joke, would tell him all the old legends of the family, all the passionate adventures of his forefathers, for thousands of them were current, some true and some false. It was their reputation for love and gallantry which was the ruin of every one of these men; they gloried in it and then thought that they had to live up to the renown of their house.

"The little fellow became exalted by these tender or terrible stories, and at times he would clap his hands, crying: 'I, too, I, too, know how to love, better than all of them!'

"Then he began to court me in a timid and tender manner, at which every one laughed, it was so amusing. Every morning I had some flowers picked by him, and every evening before going to his room he would kiss my hand and murmur: 'I love you!'

4

A WIDOW

"I was guilty, very guilty, and I grieved continually about it, and I have been doing penance all my life; I have remained an old maid—or, rather, I have lived as a widowed *fiancée*, his widow.

"I was amused at this childish tenderness, and I even encouraged him. I was coquettish, as charming as with a man, alternately caressing and severe. I maddened this child. It was a game for me and a joyous diversion for his mother and mine. He was twelve! think of it! Who would have taken this atom's passion seriously? I kissed him as often as he wished; I even wrote him little notes, which were read by our respective mothers; and he answered me by passionate letters, which I have kept. Judging himself as a man, he thought that our loving intimacy was secret. We had forgotten that he was a Santèze.

"This lasted for about a year. One evening in the park he fell at my feet and, as he madly kissed the hem of my dress, he kept repeating: 'I love you! I love you! I love you! If ever you deceive me, if ever you leave me for another, I'll do as my father did.' And he added in a hoarse voice, which gave me a shiver: 'You know what he did!'

"I stood there astonished. He arose, and standing on the tips of his toes in order to reach my ear, for I was taller than he, he pronounced my first name: 'Genevieve!' in such a gentle, sweet, tender tone that I trembled all over. I stammered: 'Let us return! let us return!' He said no more and followed me; but as we were going up the steps of the porch, he stopped me, saying: 'You know, if ever you leave me, I'll kill myself.'

"This time I understood that I had gone too far,

5

and I became quite reserved. One day, as he was reproaching me for this, I answered: 'You are now too old for jesting and too young for serious love. I'll wait.'

"I thought that this would end the matter. In the autumn he was sent to a boarding-school. When he returned the following summer I was engaged to be married. He understood immediately, and for a week he became so pensive that I was quite anxious.

"On the morning of the ninth day I saw a little paper under my door as I got up. I seized it, opened it and read: 'You have deserted me and you know what I said. It is death to which you have condemned me. As I do not wish to be found by another than you, come to the park just where I told you last year that I loved you and look in the air.'

"I thought that I should go mad. I dressed as quickly as I could and ran wildly to the place that he had mentioned. His little cap was on the ground in the mud. It had been raining all night. I raised my eyes and saw something swinging among the leaves, for the wind was blowing a gale.

"I don't know what I did after that. I must have screamed at first, then fainted and fallen, and finally have run to the château. The next thing that I remember I was in bed, with my mother sitting beside me.

"I thought that I had dreamed all this in a frightful nightmare. I stammered: 'And what of him, what of him, Gontran?' There was no answer. It was true!

"I did not dare see him again, but I asked for a lock of his blond hair. Here—here it is!"

And the old maid stretched out her trembling

hand in a despairing gesture. Then she blew her nose several times, wiped her eyes and continued: "I broke off my marriage—without saying why. And I—I always have remained the—the widow of this thirteen-year-old boy." Then her head fell on her breast and she wept for a long time.

As the guests were retiring for the night a large man, whose quiet she had disturbed, whispered in his neighbor's ear: "Isn't it unfortunate to be so sentimental?"

THE EFFEMINATES

HOW often we hear people say, "He is charming, that man, but he is a girl, a regular girl." They are alluding to the effeminates, the bane of our land.

For we are all girl-like men in France—that is, fickle, fanciful, innocently treacherous, without consistency in our convictions or our will, violent and weak as women are.

But the most irritating of girl-men is assuredly the Parisian and the boulevardier, in whom the appearance of intelligence is more marked and who combines in himself all the attractions and all the faults of those charming creatures in an exaggerated degree in virtue of his masculine temperament.

Our Chamber of Deputies is full of girl-men. They form the greater number of the amiable opportunists whom one might call "The Charmers." These are they who control by soft words and deceitful promises, who know how to shake hands in such a manner as to win hearts, how to say "My dear friend" in a certain tactful way to people he knows the least, to change his mind without suspecting it, to be carried away by each new idea, to be sincere in their weathercock convictions, to let themselves be deceived as they deceive others, to forget the next morning what he affirmed the day before.

The newspapers are full of these effeminate men. That is probably where one finds the most, but it is also where they are most needed. The *Journal des Débats* and the *Gazette de France* are exceptions.

Assuredly, every good journalist must be somewhat effeminate—that is, at the command of the public, supple in following unconsciously the shades of public opinion, wavering and varying, sceptical and credulous, wicked and devout, a braggart and a true man, enthusiastic and ironical, and always convinced while believing in nothing.

Foreigners, our anti-types, as Mme. Abel called them, the stubborn English and the heavy Germans, regard us with a certain amazement mingled with contempt, and will continue to so regard us till the end of time. They consider us frivolous. It is not that, it is that we are girls. And that is why people love us in spite of our faults, why they come back to us despite the evil spoken of us; these are lovers' quarrels! . . .

The effeminate man, as one meets him in this world, is so charming that he captivates you after five minutes' chat. His smile seems made for you; one cannot believe that his voice does not assume specially tender intonations on their account. When he leaves you it seems as if one had known him for twenty years. One is quite ready to lend him money if he asks for it. He has enchanted you, like a woman.

If he commits any breach of manners towards you, you cannot bear any malice, he is so pleasant when you next meet him. If he asks your pardon

2

you long to ask pardon of him. Does he tell lies? You cannot believe it. Does he put you off indefinitely with promises that he does not keep? One lays as much store by his promises as though he had moved heaven and earth to render them a service.

When he admires anything he goes into such raptures that he convinces you. He once adored Victor Hugo, whom he now treats as a back number. He would have fought for Zola, whom he has abandoned for Barbey and d'Aurevilly. And when he admires, he permits no limitation, he would slap your face for a word. But when he becomes scornful, his contempt is unbounded and allows of no protest.

In fact, he understands nothing.

Listen to two girls talking.

"Then you are angry with Julia?" "I slapped her face." "What had she done?" "She told Pauline that I had no money thirteen months out of twelve, and Pauline told Gontran—you understand." "You were living together in the Rue Clanzel?" "We lived together four years in the Rue Bréda; we quarrelled about a pair of stockings that she said I had worn—it wasn't true—silk stockings that she had bought at Mother Martin's. Then I gave her a pounding and she left me at once. I met her six months ago and she asked me to come and live with her, as she has rented a flat that is twice too large."

One goes on one's way and hears no more. But on the following Sunday as one is on the way to Saint Germain two young women get into the same railway carriage. One recognizes one of them at once; it is Julia's enemy. The other is—Julia!

And there are endearments, caresses, plans. "Say, Julia—listen, Julia," etc.

The girl-man has his friendships of this kind. For three months he cannot bear to leave his old Jack, his dear Jack. There is no one but Jack in the world. He is the only one who has any intelligence, any sense, any talent. He alone amounts to anything in Paris. One meets them everywhere together, they dine together, walk about in company, and every evening walk home with each other back and forth without being able to part with one another.

Three months later, if Jack is mentioned:

"There is a drinker, a sorry fellow, a scoundrel for you. I know him well, you may be sure. And he is not even honest, and ill-bred," etc., etc.

Three months later, and they are living together.

But one morning one hears that they have fought a duel, then embraced each other, amid tears, on the duelling ground.

Just now they are the dearest friends in the world, furious with each other half the year, abusing and loving each other by turns, squeezing each other's hands till they almost crush the bones, and ready to run each other through the body for a misunderstanding.

For the relations of these effeminate men are uncertain. Their temper is by fits and starts, their delight unexpected, their affection turn-about-face, their enthusiasm subject to eclipse. One day they love you, the next day they will hardly look at you, for they have in fact a girl's nature, a girl's charm, a girl's temperament, and all their sentiments are like the affections of girls.

THE EFFEMINATES

They treat their friends as women treat their pet dogs.

It is the dear little Toutou whom they hug, feed with sugar, allow to sleep on the pillow, but whom they would be just as likely to throw out of a window in a moment of impatience, whom they turn round like a sling, holding it by the tail, squeeze in their arms till they almost strangle it, and plunge, without any reason, in a pail of cold water.

Then, what a strange thing it is when one of these beings falls in love with a real girl! He beats her, she scratches him, they execrate each other, cannot bear the sight of each other and yet cannot part, linked together by no one knows what mysterious psychic bonds. She deceives him, he knows it, sobs and forgives her. He despises and adores her without seeing that she would be justified in despising him. They are both atrociously unhappy and yet cannot separate. They cast invectives, reproaches and abominable accusations at each other from morning till night, and when they have reached the climax and are vibrating with rage and hatred, they fall into each other's arms and kiss each other ardently.

The girl-man is brave and a coward at the same time. He has, more than another, the exalted sentiment of honor, but is lacking in the sense of simple honesty, and, circumstances favoring him, would defalcate and commit infamies which do not trouble his conscience, for he obeys without questioning the oscillations of his ideas, which are always impulsive.

To him it seems permissible and almost right to cheat a haberdasher. He considers it honorable

5

not to pay his debts, unless they are gambling debts
—that is, somewhat shady. He dupes people whenever the laws of society admit of his doing so.
When he is short of money he borrows in all ways,
not always being scrupulous as to tricking the
lenders, but he would, with sincere indignation, run
his sword through anyone who should suspect him
of only lacking in politeness.

OLD AMABLE

PART I

THE humid, gray sky seemed to weigh down on
the vast brown plain. The odor of autumn,
the sad odor of bare, moist lands, of fallen
leaves, of dead grass made the stagnant evening air
more thick and heavy. The peasants were still at
work, scattered through the fields, waiting for the
stroke of the Angelus to call them back to the farm-
houses, whose thatched roofs were visible here and
there through the branches of the leafless trees which
protected the apple-gardens against the wind.

At the side of the road, on a heap of clothes, a
very small boy seated with his legs apart was playing
with a potato, which he now and then let fall on his
dress, whilst five women were bending down plant-
ing slips of colza in the adjoining plain. With a
slow, continuous movement, all along the mounds of
earth which the plough had just turned up, they
drove in sharp wooden stakes and in the hole thus
formed placed the plant, already a little withered,
which sank on one side; then they patted down the
earth and went on with their work.

A man who was passing, with a whip in his hand,
and wearing wooden shoes, stopped near the child,
took it up and kissed it. Then one of the women
rose up and came across to him. She was a big, red-

I

haired girl, with large hips, waist and shoulders, a tall Norman woman, with yellow hair in which there was a blood-red tint.

She said in a resolute voice:

"Why, here you are, Césaire—well?"

The man, a thin young fellow with a melancholy air, murmured:

"Well, nothing at all—always the same thing."

"He won't have it?"

"He won't have it."

"What are you going to do?"

"What do you say I ought to do?"

"Go see the curé."

"I will."

"Go at once!"

"I will."

And they stared at each other. He held the child in his arms all the time. He kissed it once more and then put it down again on the woman's clothes.

In the distance, between two farm-houses, could be seen a plough drawn by a horse and driven by a man. They moved on very gently, the horse, the plough and the laborer, in the dim evening twilight.

The woman went on:

"What did your father say?"

"He said he would not have it."

"Why wouldn't he have it?"

The young man pointed toward the child whom he had just put back on the ground, then with a glance he drew her attention to the man drawing the plough yonder there.

And he said emphatically:

"Because 'tis his—this child of yours."

2

The girl shrugged her shoulders and in an angry tone said:

"Faith, every one knows it well—that it is Victor's. And what about it after all? I made a slip. Am I the only woman that did? My mother also made a slip before me, and then yours did the same before she married your dad! Who is it that hasn't made a slip in the country? I made a slip with Victor because he took advantage of me while I was asleep in the barn, it's true, and afterward it happened between us when I wasn't asleep. I certainly would have married him if he weren't a servant man. Am I a worse woman for that?"

The man said simply:

"As for me, I like you just as you are, with or without the child. It's only my father that opposes me. All the same, I'll see about settling the business."

She answered:

"Go to the curé at once."

"I'm going to him."

And he set forth with his heavy peasant's tread, while the girl, with her hands on her hips, turned round to plant her colza.

In fact, the man who thus went off, Césaire Houlbrèque, the son of deaf old Amable Houlbrèque, wanted to marry, in spite of his father, Céleste Lévesque, who had a child by Victor Lecoq, a mere laborer on her parents' farm, who had been turned out of doors for this act.

The hierarchy of caste, however, does not exist in the country, and if the laborer is thrifty, he becomes, by taking a farm in his turn, the equal of his former master.

3

So Césaire Houlbrèque went off, his whip under his arm, brooding over his own thoughts and lifting up one after the other his heavy wooden shoes daubed with clay. Certainly he desired to marry Céleste Lévesque. He wanted her with her child because she was the wife he wanted. He could not say why, but he knew it, he was sure of it. He had only to look at her to be convinced of it, to feel quite queer, quite stirred up, simply stupid with happiness. He even found a pleasure in kissing the little boy, Victor's little boy, because he belonged to her.

And he gazed, without hate, at the distant outline of the man who was driving his plough along the horizon.

But old Amable did not want this marriage. He opposed it with the obstinacy of a deaf man, with a violent obstinacy.

Césaire in vain shouted in his ear, in that ear which still heard a few sounds:

"I'll take good care of you, daddy. I tell you she's a good girl and strong, too, and also thrifty."

The old man repeated:

"As long as I live I won't see her your wife."

And nothing could get the better of him, nothing could make him waver. One hope only was left to Césaire. Old Amable was afraid of the curé through the apprehension of death which he felt drawing nigh. he had not much fear of God, nor of the Devil, nor of Hell, nor of Purgatory, of which he had no conception, but he dreaded the priest, who represented to him burial, as one might fear the doctors through horror of diseases. For the last eight days Céleste, who knew this weakness of the old man, had been urging Césaire to go and find the

4

curé, but Césaire always hesitated, because he had
not much liking for the black robe, which represented to him hands always stretched out for collec-
tions or for blessed bread.

However, he had made up his mind, and he proceeded toward the presbytery, thinking in what manner he would speak about his case.

The Abbé Raffin, a lively little priest, thin and
never shaved, was awaiting his dinner-hour while
warming his feet at his kitchen fire.

As soon as he saw the peasant entering he asked,
merely turning his head:

"Well, Césaire, what do you want?"

"I'd like to have a talk with you, M. le Curé."

The man remained standing, intimidated, holding
his cap in one hand and his whip in the other.

"Well, talk."

Césaire looked at the housekeeper, an old woman
who dragged her feet while putting on the cover for
her master's dinner at the corner of the table in front
of the window.

He stammered:

" 'Tis—'tis a sort of confession."

Thereupon the Abbé Raffin carefully surveyed his
peasant. He saw his confused countenance, his air
of constraint, his wandering eyes, and he gave orders to the housekeeper in these words:

"Marie, go away for five minutes to your room,
while I talk to Césaire."

The servant cast on the man an angry glance and
went away grumbling.

The clergyman went on:

"Come, now, tell your story."

The young fellow still hesitated, looked down at

his wooden shoes, moved about his cap, then, all of a sudden, he made up his mind:

"Here it is: I want to marry Céleste Lévesque."

"Well, my boy, what's there to prevent you?"

"The father won't have it."

"Your father?"

"Yes, my father."

"What does your father say?"

"He says she has a child."

"She's not the first to whom that happened, since our Mother Eve."

"A child by Victor Lecoq, Anthime Loisel's servant man."

"Ha! ha! So he won't have it?"

"He won't have it."

"What! not at all?"

"No, no more than an ass that won't budge an inch, saving your presence."

"What do you say to him yourself in order to make him decide?"

"I say to him that she's a good girl, and strong, too, and thrifty also."

"And this does not make him agree to it. So you want me to speak to him?"

"Exactly. You speak to him."

"And what am I to tell your father?"

"Why, what you tell people in your sermons to make them give you sous."

In the peasant's mind every effort of religion consisted in loosening the purse strings, in emptying the pockets of men in order to fill the heavenly coffer. It was a kind of huge commercial establishment, of which the curés were the clerks, sly, crafty clerks, sharp as any one must be who does business for the good God at the expense of the country people.

He knew full well that the priests rendered services, great services to the poorest, to the sick and dying, that they assisted, consoled, counselled, sustained, but all this by means of money, in exchange for white pieces, for beautiful glittering coins, with which they paid for sacraments and masses, advice and protection, pardon of sins and indulgences, purgatory and paradise according to the yearly income and the generosity of the sinner.

The Abbé Raffin, who knew his man and who never lost his temper, burst out laughing.

"Well, yes, I'll tell your father my little story; but you, my lad, you'll come to church."

Houlbrèque extended his hand in order to give a solemn assurance:

"On the word of a poor man, if you do this for me, I promise that I will."

"Come, that's all right. When do you wish me to go and find your father?"

"Why, the sooner the better—to-night, if you can."

"In half an hour, then, after supper."

"In half an hour."

"That's understood. So long, my lad."

"Good-by till we meet again, Monsieur le Curé; many thanks."

"Not at all, my lad."

And Césaire Houlbrèque returned home, his heart relieved of a great weight.

He held on lease a little farm, quite small, for they were not rich, his father and he. Alone with a female servant, a little girl of fifteen, who made the soup, looked after the fowls, milked the cows and

7

churned the butter, they lived frugally, though Césaire was a good cultivator. But they did not possess either sufficient lands or sufficient cattle to earn more than the indispensable.

The old man no longer worked. Sad, like all deaf people, crippled with pains, bent double, twisted, he went through the fields leaning on his stick, watching the animals and the men with a hard, distrustful eye. Sometimes he sat down on the side of the road and remained there without moving for hours, vaguely pondering over the things that had engrossed his whole life, the price of eggs and corn, the sun and the rain which spoil the crops or make them grow. And, worn out with rheumatism, his old limbs still drank in the humidity of the soul, as they had drunk in for the past sixty years, the moisture of the walls of his low house thatched with damp straw.

He came back at the close of the day, took his place at the end of the table in the kitchen and when the earthen bowl containing the soup had been placed before him he placed round it his crooked fingers, which seemed to have kept the round form of the bowl and, winter and summer, he warmed his hands, before commencing to eat, so as to lose nothing, not even a particle of the heat that came from the fire, which costs a great deal, neither one drop of soup into which fat and salt have to be put, nor one morsel of bread, which comes from the wheat.

Then he climbed up a ladder into a loft, where he had his straw-bed, while his son slept below stairs at the end of a kind of niche near the chimneypiece and the servant shut herself up in a kind of cellar, a black hole which was formerly used to store the potatoes.

8

OLD AMABLE

Césaire and his father scarcely ever talked to each other. From time to time only, when there was a question of selling a crop or buying a calf, the young man would ask his father's advice, and, making a speaking-trumpet of his two hands, he would bawl out his views into his ear, and old Amable either approved of them or opposed them in a slow, hollow voice that came from the depths of his stomach.

So one evening Césaire, approaching him as if about to discuss the purchase of a horse or a heifer, communicated to him at the top of his voice his intention to marry Céleste Lévesque.

Then the father got angry. Why? On the score of morality? No, certainly. The virtue of a girl is of slight importance in the country. But his avarice, his deep, fierce instinct for saving, revolted at the idea that his son should bring up a child which he had not begotten himself. He had thought suddenly, in one second, of the soup the little fellow would swallow before becoming useful on the farm. He had calculated all the pounds of bread, all the pints of cider that this brat would consume up to his fourteenth year, and a mad anger broke loose from him against Césaire, who had not bestowed a thought on all this.

He replied in an unusually strong voice:

"Have you lost your senses?"

Thereupon Césaire began to enumerate his reasons, to speak about Céleste's good qualities, to prove that she would be worth a thousand times what the child would cost. But the old man doubted these advantages, while he could have no doubts as to the child's existence; and he replied with em-

9

phatic repetition, without giving any further explanation:

"I will not have it! I will not have it! As long as I live, this won't be done!"

And at this point they had remained for the last three months, without one or the other giving in, resuming at least once a week the same discussion, with the same arguments, the same words, the same gestures and the same fruitlessness.

It was then that Céleste had advised Césaire to go and ask for the curé's assistance.

On arriving home the peasant found his father already seated at table, for he came late through his visit to the presbytery.

They dined in silence, face to face, ate a little bread and butter after the soup and drank a glass of cider. Then they remained motionless in their chairs, with scarcely a glimmer of light, the little servant girl having carried off the candle in order to wash the spoons, wipe the glasses and cut the crusts of bread to be ready for next morning's breakfast.

There was a knock at the door, which was immediately opened, and the priest appeared. The old man raised toward him an anxious eye full of suspicion, and, foreseeing danger, he was getting ready to climb up his ladder when the Abbé Raffin laid his hand on his shoulder and shouted close to his temple:

"I want to have a talk with you, Father Amable."

Césaire had disappeared, taking advantage of the door being open. He did not want to listen, for he was afraid and did not want his hopes to crumble slowly with each obstinate refusal of his father. He preferred to learn the truth at once, good or bad, later on; and he went out into the night. It was a moonless, starless night, one of those misty nights when the air seems thick with humidity. A vague odor of apples floated through the farmyard, for it was the season when the earliest applies were gathered, the "early ripe," as they are called in the cider country. As Césaire passed along by the cattlesheds the warm smell of living beasts asleep on manure was exhaled through the narrow windows, and he heard the stamping of the horses, who were standing at the end of the stable, and the sound of their jaws tearing and munching the hay on the racks.

He went straight ahead, thinking about Céleste. In this simple nature, whose ideas were scarcely more than images generated directly by objects, thoughts of love only formulated themselves by calling up before the mind the picture of a big red-haired girl standing in a hollow road and laughing, with her hands on her hips.

It was thus he saw her on the day when he first took a fancy for her. He had, however, known her from infancy, but never had he been so struck by her as on that morning. They had stopped to talk for a few minutes and then he went away, and as he walked along he kept repeating:

"Faith, she's a fine girl, all the same. 'Tis a pity she made a slip with Victor."

Till evening he kept thinking of her and also on the following morning.

When he saw her again he felt something tickling the end of his throat, as if a cock's feather had been driven through his mouth into his chest, and since then, every time he found himself near her, he was astonished at this nervous tickling which always commenced again.

In three months he made up his mind to marry her, so much did she please him. He could not have said whence came this power over him, but he explained it in these words:

"I am possessed by her," as if the desire for this girl within him were as dominating as one of the powers of hell. He scarcely bothered himself about her transgression. It was a pity, but, after all, it did her no harm, and he bore no grudge against Victor Lecoq.

But if the curé should not succeeed, what was he to do? He did not dare to think of it, the anxiety was such a torture to him.

He reached the presbytery and seated himself near the little gateway to wait for the priest's return.

He was there perhaps half an hour when he heard steps on the road, and although the night was very dark, he presently distinguished the still darker shadow of the cassock.

He rose up, his legs giving way under him, not even venturing to speak, not daring to ask a question.

The clergyman perceived him and said gaily:

"Well, my lad, it's all right."

Césaire stammered:

"All right, 'tisn't possible."

"Yes, my lad, but not without trouble. What an old ass your father is!"

The peasant repeated:

" 'Tisn't possible!"

"Why, yes. Come and look me up to-morrow at

midday in order to settle about the publication of the banns."

The young man seized the curé's hand. He pressed it, shook it, bruised it as he stammered:

"True—true—true, Monsieur le Curé, on the word of an honest man, you'll see me to-morrow—at your sermon."

PART II

The wedding took place in the middle of December. It was simple, the bridal pair not being rich. Césaire, attired in new clothes, was ready since eight o'clock in the morning to go and fetch his betrothed and bring her to the mayor's office, but it was too early. He seated himself before the kitchen table and waited for the members of the family and the friends who were to accompany him.

For the last eight days it had been snowing, and the brown earth, the earth already fertilized by the autumn sowing, had become a dead white, sleeping under a great sheet of ice.

It was cold in the thatched houses adorned with white caps, and the round apples in the trees of the enclosures seemed to be flowering, covered with white as they had been in the pleasant month of their blossoming.

This day the big clouds to the north, the big great snow clouds, had disappeared and the blue sky showed itself above the white earth on which the rising sun cast silvery reflections.

Césaire looked straight before him through the window, thinking of nothing, quite happy.

The door opened, two women entered, peasant women in their Sunday clothes, the aunt and the cousin of the bridegroom; then three men, his cousins; then a woman who was a neighbor. They sat down on chairs and remained, motionless and silent, the women on one side of the kitchen, the men on the other, suddenly seized with timidity, with that embarrassed sadness which takes possession of people assembled for a ceremony. One of the cousins soon asked:

"Is it not the hour?"

Césaire replied:

"I am much afraid it is."

"Come on! Let us start," said another.

Those rose up. Then Césaire, whom a feeling of uneasiness had taken possession of, climbed up the ladder of the loft to see whether his father was ready. The old man, always as a rule an early riser, had not yet made his appearance. His son found him on his bed of straw, wrapped up in his blanket, with his eyes open and a malicious gleam in them.

He bawled into his ear: "Come, daddy, get up. It's time for the wedding."

The deaf man murmured in a doleful tone:

"I can't get up. I have a sort of chill over me that freezes my back. I can't stir."

The young man, dumbfounded, stared at him, guessing that this was a dodge.

"Come, daddy; you must make an effort."

"I can't do it."

"Look here! I'll help you."

And he stooped toward the old man, pulled off his blanket, caught him by the arm and lifted him up. But old Amable began to whine:

14

OLD AMABLE

"Ooh! ooh! ooh! What suffering! Ooh! I can't. My back is stiffened up. The cold wind must have rushed in through this cursed roof."

"Well, you'll get no dinner, as I'm having a spread at Polyte's inn. This will teach you what comes of acting mulishly."

And he hurried down the ladder and started out, accompanied by his relatives and guests.

The men had turned up the bottoms of their trousers so as not to get them wet in the snow. The women held up their petticoats and showed their lean ankles with gray woollen stockings and their bony shanks resembling broomsticks. And they all moved forward with a swinging gait, one behind the other, without uttering a word, moving cautiously, for fear of losing the road which was hidden beneath the flat, uniform, uninterrupted stretch of snow.

As they approached the farmhouses they saw one or two persons waiting to join them, and the procession went on without stopping and wound its way forward, following the invisible outlines of the road, so that it resembled a living chaplet of black beads undulating through the white countryside.

In front of the bride's door a large group was stamping up and down the open space awaiting the bridegroom. When he appeared they gave him a loud greeting, and presently Céleste came forth from her room, clad in a blue dress, her shoulders covered with a small red shawl and her head adorned with orange flowers.

But every one asked Césaire:

"Where's your father?"

He replied with embarrassment:

"He couldn't move on account of the pains."

And the farmers tossed their heads with a sly, incredulous air.

They directed their steps toward the mayor's office. Behind the pair about to be wedded a peasant woman carried Victor's child, as if it were going to be baptized; and the men, in pairs now, with arms linked, walked through the snow with the movements of a sloop at sea.

After having been united by the mayor in the little municipal house the pair were made one by the curé, in his turn, in the modest house of God. He blessed their union by promising them fruitfulness, then he preached to them on the matrimonial virtues, the simple and healthful virtues of the country, work, concord and fidelity, while the child, who was cold, began to fret behind the bride.

As soon as the couple reappeared on the threshold of the church shots were discharged from the ditch of the cemetery. Only the barrels of the guns could be seen whence came forth rapid jets of smoke; then a head could be seen gazing at the procession. It was Victor Lecoq celebrating the marriage of his old sweetheart, wishing her happiness and sending her his good wishes with explosions of powder. He had employed some friends of his, five or six laboring men, for these salvos of musketry. It was considered a nice attention.

The repast was given in Polyte Cacheprune's inn. Twenty covers were laid in the great hall where people dined on market days, and the big leg of mutton turning before the spit, the fowls browned under their own gravy, the chitterlings sputtering over the bright, clear fire filled the house with a thick odor of live coal sprinkled with fat—the powerful, heavy odor of rustic fare.

They sat down to table at midday and the soup was poured at once into the plates. All faces had already brightened up; mouths opened to utter loud jokes and eyes were laughing with knowing winks. They were going to amuse themselves and no mistake.

The door opened, and old Amable appeared. He seemed in a bad humor and his face wore a scowl as he dragged himself forward on his sticks, whining at every step to indicate his suffering. As soon as they saw him they stopped talking, but suddenly his neighbor, Daddy Malivoire, a big joker, who knew all the little tricks and ways of people, began to yell, just as Césaire used to do, by making a speaking-trumpet of his hands.

"Hallo, my cute old boy, you have a good nose on you to be able to smell Polyte's cookery from your own house!"

A roar of laughter burst forth from the throats of those present. Malivoire, excited by his success, went on:

"There's nothing for the rheumatics like a chitterling poultice! It keeps your belly warm, along with a glass of three-six!"

The men uttered shouts, banged the table with their fists, laughed, bending on one side and raising up their bodies again as if they were working a pump. The women clucked like hens, while the servants wriggled, standing against the walls. Old Amable was the only one that did not laugh, and, without making any reply, waited till they made room for him.

17

They found a place for him in the middle of the table, facing his daughter-in-law, and, as soon as he was seated, he began to eat. It was his son who was paying, after all; it was right he should take his share. With each ladleful of soup that went into his stomach, with each mouthful of bread or meat crushed between his gums, with each glass of cider or wine that flowed through his gullet he thought he was regaining something of his own property, getting back a little of his money which all those gluttons were devouring, saving in fact a portion of his own means. And he ate in silence with the obstinacy of a miser who hides his coppers, with the same gloomy persistence with which he formerly performed his daily labors.

But all of a sudden he noticed at the end of the table Céleste's child on a woman's lap, and his eye remained fixed on the little boy. He went on eating, with his glance riveted on the youngster, into whose mouth the woman who minded him every now and then put a little morsel which he nibbled at. And the old man suffered more from the few mouthfuls sucked by this little chap than from all that the others swallowed.

The meal lasted till evening. Then every one went back home.

Césaire raised up old Amable.

"Come, daddy, we must go home," said he.

And he put the old man's two sticks in his hands.

Céleste took her child in her arms, and they went on slowly through the pale night whitened by the snow. The deaf old man, three-fourths tipsy, and even more malicious under the influence of drink, refused to go forward. Several times he even sat down with the object of making his daughter-in-law catch cold, and he kept whining, without uttering a word, giving vent to a sort of continuous groaning as if he were in pain.

When they reached home he at once climbed up to his loft, while Césaire made a bed for the child near the deep niche where he was going to lie down with his wife. But as the newly wedded pair could not sleep immediately, they heard the old man for a long time moving about on his bed of straw, and he even talked aloud several times, whether it was that he was dreaming or that he let his thoughts escape through his mouth, in spite of himself, not being able to keep them back, under the obsession of a fixed idea.

When he came down his ladder next morning he saw his daughter-in-law looking after the house-keeping.

She cried out to him:

"Come, daddy, hurry on! Here's some good soup."

And she placed at the end of the table the round black earthen bowl filled with steaming liquid. He sat down without giving any answer, seized the hot bowl, warmed his hands with it in his customary fashion, and, as it was very cold, even pressed it against his breast to try to make a little of the living heat of the boiling liquid enter into him, into his old body stiffened by so many winters.

Then he took his sticks and went out into the fields, covered with ice, till it was time for dinner, for he had seen Céleste's youngster still asleep in a big soap-box.

He did not take his place in the household. He

lived in the thatched house, as in bygone days, but he seemed not to belong to it any longer, to be no longer interested in anything, to look upon those people, his son, the wife and the child as strangers whom he did not know, to whom he never spoke.

The winter glided by. It was long and severe.

Then the early spring made the seeds sprout forth again, and the peasants once more, like laborious ants, passed their days in the fields, toiling from morning till night, under the wind and under the rain, along the furrows of brown earth which brought forth the bread of men.

The year promised well for the newly married pair. The crops grew thick and strong. There were no late frosts, and the apples bursting into bloom scattered on the grass their rosy white snow which promised a hail of fruit for the autumn.

Césaire toiled hard, rose early and left off work late, in order to save the expense of a hired man.

His wife said to him sometimes:

"You'll make yourself ill in the long run."

He replied:

"Certainly not. I'm a good judge."

Nevertheless one evening he came home so fatigued that he had to get to bed without supper. He rose up next morning at the usual hour, but he could not eat, in spite of his fast on the previous night, and he had to come back to the house in the middle of the afternoon in order to go to bed again. In the course of the night he began to cough; he turned round on his straw couch, feverish, with his forehead burning, his tongue dry and his throat parched by a burning thirst.

However, at daybreak he went toward his grounds,

but next morning the doctor had to be sent for and pronounced him very ill with inflammation of the lungs.

And he no longer left the dark recess in which he slept. He could be heard coughing, gasping and tossing about in this hole. In order to see him, to give his medicine and to apply cupping-glasses they had to bring a candle to the entrance. Then one could see his narrow head with his long matted beard underneath a thick lacework of spiders' webs, which hung and floated when stirred by the air. And the hands of the sick man seemed dead under the dingy sheets.

Céleste watched him with restless activity, made him take physic, applied blisters to him, went back and forth in the house, while old Amable remained at the edge of his loft, watching at a distance the gloomy cavern where his son lay dying. He did not come near him, through hatred of the wife, sulking like an ill-tempered dog.

Six more days passed, then one morning, as Céleste, who now slept on the ground on two loose bundles of straw, was going to see whether her man was better, she no longer heard his rapid breathing from the interior of his recess. Terror stricken, she asked:

"Well, Césaire, what sort of a night had you?"

He did not answer. She put out her hand to touch him, and the flesh on his face felt cold as ice. She uttered a great cry, the long cry of a woman overpowered with fright. He was dead.

At this cry the deaf old man appeared at the top of his ladder, and when he saw Céleste rushing to call for help, he quickly descended, placed his hand on his son's face, and suddenly realizing what had happened, went to shut the door from the inside, to prevent the wife from re-entering and resuming possession of the dwelling, since his son was no longer living.

Then he sat down on a chair by the dead man's side.

Some of the neighbors arrived, called out and knocked. He did not hear them. One of them broke the glass of the window and jumped into the room. Others followed. The door was opened again and Céleste reappeared, all in tears, with swollen face and bloodshot eyes. Then old Amable, vanquished, without uttering a word, climbed back to his loft.

The funeral took place next morning. Then, after the ceremony, the father-in-law and the daughter-in-law found themselves alone in the farmhouse with the child.

It was the usual dinner hour. She lighted the fire, made some soup and placed the plates on the table, while the old man sat on the chair waiting without appearing to look at her. When the meal was ready she bawled in his ear:

"Come, daddy, you must eat." He rose up, took his seat at the end of the table, emptied his soup bowl, masticated his bread and butter, drank his two glasses of cider and then took himself off.

It was one of those warm days, one of those enjoyable days when life ferments, pulsates, blooms all over the surface of the soil.

Old Amable pursued a little path across the fields. He looked at the young wheat and the young oats, thinking that his son was now under the earth, his poor boy! He walked along wearily, dragging his legs after him in a limping fashion. And, as he was all alone in the plain, all alone under the blue sky, in the midst of the growing crops, all alone with the larks which he saw hovering above his head, without hearing their light song, he began to weep as he proceeded on his way.

Then he sat down beside a pond and remained there till evening, gazing at the little birds that came there to drink. Then, as the night was falling, he returned to the house, supped without saying a word and climbed up to his loft. And his life went on as in the past. Nothing was changed, except that his son Césaire slept in the cemetery.

What could he, an old man, do? He could work no longer; he was now good for nothing except to swallow the soup prepared by his daughter-in-law. And he ate it in silence, morning and evening, watching with an eye of rage the little boy also taking soup, right opposite him, at the other side of the table. Then he would go out, prowl about the fields after the fashion of a vagabond, hiding behind the barns where he would sleep for an hour or two as if he were afraid of being seen and then come back at the approach of night.

But Céleste's mind began to be occupied by graver anxieties. The farm needed a man to look after it and cultivate it. Somebody should be there always to go through the fields, not a mere hired laborer, but a regular farmer, a master who understood the business and would take an interest in the farm. A lone woman could not manage the farming, watch the price of corn and direct the sale and purchase of cattle. Then ideas came into her head, simple practical ideas, which she had turned over in her head at night. She could not marry again before the end of the year, and it was necessary at once to take care of pressing interests, immediate interests.

Only one man could help her out of her difficulties, Victor Lecoq, the father of her child. He was strong and understood farming; with a little money in his pocket he would make an excellent cultivator. She was aware of his skill, having known him while he was working on her parents' farm.

So one morning, seeing him passing along the road with a cart of manure, she went out to meet him. When he perceived her, he drew up his horses and she said to him as if she had met him the night before:

"Good-morrow, Victor—are you quite well, the same as ever?"

He replied:

"I'm quite well, the same as ever—and how are you?"

"Oh, I'd be all right, only that I'm alone in the house, which bothers me on account of the farm."

Then they remained chatting for a long time, leaning against the wheel of the heavy cart. The man every now and then lifted up his cap to scratch his forehead and began thinking, while she, with flushed cheeks, went on talking warmly, told him about her views, her plans, her projects for the future. At last he said in a low tone:

"Yes, it can be done."

She opened her hand like a countryman clinching a bargain and asked:

"Is it agreed?"

He pressed her outstretched hand.

"'Tis agreed."

OLD AMABLE

"It's settled, then, for next Sunday?"
"It's settled for next Sunday."
"Well, good-morning, Victor."
"Good-morning, Madame Houlbrèque."

PART III

This particular Sunday was the day of the village festival, the annual festival in honor of the patron saint, which in Normandy is called the assembly.

For the last eight days quaint-looking vehicles in which live the families of strolling fair exhibitors, lottery managers, keepers of shooting galleries and other forms of amusement or exhibitors of curiosities whom the peasants call "wonder-makers" could be seen coming along the roads drawn slowly by gray or sorrel horses.

The dirty wagons with their floating curtains, accompanied by a melancholy-looking dog, who trotted, with his head down, between the wheels, drew up one after the other on the green in front of the town hall. Then a tent was erected in front of each ambulant abode, and inside this tent could be seen, through the holes in the canvas, glittering things which excited the envy or the curiosity of the village youngsters.

As soon as the morning of the fête arrived all the booths were opened, displaying their splendors of glass or porcelain, and the peasants on their way to mass looked with genuine satisfaction at these modest shops which they saw again, nevertheless, each succeeding year.

OLD AMABLE

Early in the afternoon there was a crowd on the green. From every neighboring village the farmers arrived, shaken along with their wives and children in the two-wheeled open chars à bancs, which rattled along, swaying like cradles. They unharnessed at their friends' houses and the farmyards were filled with strange-looking traps, gray, high, lean, crooked, like long-clawed creatures from the depths of the sea. And each family, with the youngsters in front and the grown-up ones behind, came to the assembly with tranquil steps, smiling countenances and open hands, big hands, red and bony, accustomed to work and apparently tired of their temporary rest.

A clown was blowing a trumpet. The barrel-organ accompanying the carrousel sent through the air its shrill jerky notes. The lottery-wheel made a whirring sound like that of cloth tearing, and every moment the crack of the rifle could be heard. And the slow-moving throng passed on quietly in front of the booths resembling paste in a fluid condition, with the motions of a flock of sheep and the awkwardness of heavy animals who had escaped by chance.

The girls, holding one another's arms in groups of six or eight, were singing; the youths followed them, making jokes, with their caps over their ears and their blouses stiffened with starch, swollen out like blue balloons.

The whole countryside was there—masters, laboring men and women servants.

Old Amable himself, wearing his old-fashioned green frock coat, had wished to see the assembly, for he never failed to attend on such an occasion.

OLD AMABLE

He looked at the lotteries, stopped in front of the shooting galleries to criticize the shots and interested himself specially in a very simple game which consisted in throwing a big wooden ball into the open mouth of a mannikin carved and painted on a board.

Suddenly he felt a tap on his shoulder. It was Daddy Malivoire, who exclaimed:

"Ha, daddy! Come and have a glass of brandy."

And they sat down at the table of an open-air restaurant.

They drank one glass of brandy, then two, then three, and old Amable once more began wandering through the assembly. His thoughts became slightly confused, he smiled without knowing why, he smiled in front of the lotteries, in front of the wooden horses and especially in front of the killing game. He remained there a long time, filled with delight, when he saw a holiday-maker knocking down the gendarme or the curé, two authorities whom he instinctively distrusted. Then he went back to the inn and drank a glass of cider to cool himself. It was late, night came on. A neighbor came to warn him:

"You'll get back home late for the stew, daddy."

Then he set out on his way to the farmhouse. A soft shadow, the warm shadow of a spring night, was slowly descending on the earth.

When he reached the front door he thought he saw through the window which was lighted up two persons in the house. He stopped, much surprised, then he went in, and he saw Victor Lecoq seated at the table, with a plate filled with potatoes before

him, taking his supper in the very same place where
his son had sat.

And he turned round suddenly as if he wanted to
go away. The night was very dark now. Céleste
started up and shouted at him:

"Come quick, daddy! Here's some good stew to
finish off the assembly with."

He complied through inertia and sat down, watching in turn the man, the woman and the child. Then
he began to eat quietly as on ordinary days.

Victor Lecoq seemed quite at home, talked from
time to time to Céleste, took up the child in his lap
and kissed him. And Céleste again served him with
food, poured out drink for him and appeared happy
while speaking to him. Old Amable's eyes followed
them attentively, though he could not hear what
they were saying.

When he had finished supper (and he had scarcely
eaten anything, there was such a weight at his
heart) he rose up, and instead of ascending to his
loft as he did every night he opened the gate of the
yard and went out into the open air.

When he had gone, Céleste, a little uneasy, asked:
"What is he going to do?"

Victor replied in an indifferent tone:

"Don't bother yourself. He'll come back when
he's tired."

Then she saw after the house, washed the plates
and wiped the table, while the man quietly took off
his clothes. Then he slipped into the dark and hollow bed in which she had slept with Césaire.

The yard gate opened and old Amable again appeared. As soon as he entered the house he looked
round on every side with the air of an old dog on

28

the scent. He was in search of Victor Lecoq. As he did not see him, he took the candle off the table and approached the dark niche in which his son had died. In the interior of it he perceived the man lying under the bed clothes and already asleep. Then the deaf man noiselessly turned round, put back the candle and went out into the yard.

Céleste had finished her work. She put her son into his bed, arranged everything and waited for her father-in-law's return before lying down herself.

She remained sitting on a chair, without moving her hands, and with her eyes fixed on vacancy.

As he did not come back, she murmured in a tone of impatience and annoyance:

"This good-for-nothing old man will make us burn four sous' worth of candles."

Victor answered from under the bed clothes:

"It's over an hour since he went out. We ought to see whether he fell asleep on the bench outside the door."

"I'll go and see," she said.

She rose up, took the light and went out, shading the light with her hand in order to see through the darkness.

She saw nothing in front of the door, nothing on the bench, nothing on the dung heap, where the old man used sometimes to sit in hot weather.

But, just as she was on the point of going in again, she chanced to raise her eyes toward the big apple tree, which sheltered the entrance to the farmyard, and suddenly she saw two feet—two feet at the height of her face belonging to a man who was hanging.

She uttered terrible cries:

"Victor! Victor! Victor!"

He ran out in his shirt. She could not utter another word, and turning aside her head so as not to see, she pointed toward the tree with her outstretched arm.

Not understanding what she meant, he took the candle in order to find out, and in the midst of the foliage lit up from below he saw old Amable hanging high up with a stable-halter round his neck.

A ladder was leaning against the trunk of the apple tree.

Victor ran to fetch a bill-hook, climbed up the tree and cut the halter. But the old man was already cold and his tongue protruded horribly with a frightful grimace.

THE CHRISTENING

"WELL, doctor, a little brandy?"

"With pleasure."

The old ship's surgeon, holding out his glass, watched it as it slowly filled with the golden liquid. Then, holding it in front of his eyes, he let the light from the lamp stream through it, smelled it, tasted a few drops and smacked his lips with relish. Then he said:

"Ah! the charming poison! Or rather the seductive murderer, the delightful destroyer of peoples!

"You people do not know it the way I do. You may have read that admirable book entitled *L'Assommoir,* but you have not, as I have, seen alcohol exterminate a whole tribe of savages, a little kingdom of negroes—alcohol calmly unloaded by the barrel by red-bearded English seamen.

"Right near here, in a little village in Brittany near Pont-l'Abbé, I once witnessed a strange and terrible tragedy caused by alcohol. I was sepnding my vacation in a little country house left me by my father. You know this flat coast where the wind whistles day and night, where one sees, standing or prone, these giant rocks which in the olden times were regarded as guardians, and which still retain something majestic and imposing about them. I always expect to see them come to life and start to walk across the country with the slow and ponderous tread of giants, or to unfold enormous granite wings and fly toward the paradise of the Druids.

"Everywhere is the sea, always ready on the slightest provocation to rise in its anger and shake its foamy mane at those bold enough to brave its wrath.

"And the men who travel on this terrible sea, which, with one motion of its green back, can overturn and swallow up their frail barks—they go out in the little boats, day and night, hardy, weary and drunk. They are often drunk. They have a saying which says: 'When the bottle is full you see the reef, but when it is empty you see it no more.'

"Go into one of their huts; you will never find the father there. If you ask the woman what has become of her husband, she will stretch her arms out over the dark ocean which rumbles and roars along the coast. He remained there one night, when he had had too much to drink; so did her oldest son. She has four more big, strong, fair-haired boys. Soon it will be their time.

"As I said, I was living in a little house near Pont-l'Abbé. I was there alone with my servant, an old sailor, and with a native family which took care of the grounds in my absence. It consisted of three persons, two sisters and a man, who had married one of them, and who attended to the garden.

"A short time before Christmas my gardener's wife presented him with a boy. The husband asked me to stand as god-father. I could hardly deny the request, and so he borrowed ten francs from me for the cost of the christening, as he said.

"The second day of January was chosen as the date of the ceremony. For a week the earth had been covered by an enormous white carpet of snow, which made this flat, low country seem vast and limitless. The ocean appeared to be black in contrast with this white plain; one could see it rolling, raging and tossing its waves as though wishing to annihilate its pale neighbor, which appeared to be dead, it was so calm, quiet and cold.

"At nine o'clock the father, Kerandec, came to my door with his sister-in-law, the big Kermagan, and the nurse, who carried the infant wrapped up in a blanket. We started for the church. The weather was so cold that it seemed to dry up the skin and crack it open. I was thinking of the poor little creature who was being carried on ahead of us, and I said to myself that this Breton race must surely be of iron, if their children were able, as soon as they were born, to stand such an outing.

"We came to the church, but the door was closed; the priest was late.

"Then the nurse sat down on one of the steps and began to undress the child. At first I thought there must have been some slight accident, but I saw that they were leaving the poor little fellow naked, completely naked, in the icy air. Furious at such imprudence, I protested:

"'Why, you are crazy! You will kill the child!'

"The woman answered quietly: 'Oh, no, sir; he must wait naked before the Lord.'

"The father and the aunt looked on undisturbed. It was the custom. If it were not adhered to misfortune was sure to attend the little one.

"I scolded, threatened and pleaded. I used force to try to cover the frail creature. All was in vain. The nurse ran away from me through the snow, and the body of the little one turned purple. I was about to leave these brutes when I saw the priest coming across the country, followed by the sexton and a young boy. I ran towards him and gave vent to my indignation. He showed no surprise nor did he quicken his pace in the least. He answered:

" 'What can you expect, sir? It's the custom. They all do it, and it's of no use trying to stop them.'

" 'But at least hurry up!' I cried.

"He answered: 'But I can't go any faster.'

"He entered the vestry, while we remained outside on the church steps. I was suffering. But what about the poor little creature who was howling from the effects of the biting cold!

"At last the door opened. He went into the church. But the poor child had to remain naked throughout the ceremony. It was interminable. The priest stammered over the Latin words and mispronounced them horribly. He walked slowly and with a ponderous tread. His white surplice chilled my heart. It seemed as though, in the name of a pitiless and barbarous god, he had wrapped himself in another kind of snow in order to torture this little piece of humanity that suffered so from the cold.

"Finally the christening was finished according to the rites and I saw the nurse once more take the frozen, moaning child and wrap it up in the blanket.

"The priest said to me: 'Do you wish to sign the register?'

"Turning to my gardener, I said: "Hurry up and get home quickly so that you can warm that child.' I gave him some advice so as to ward off, if not too late, a bad attack of pneumonia. He promised to

4

follow my instructions and left with his sister-in-law and the nurse. I followed the priest into the vestry, and when I had signed he demanded five francs for expenses.

"As I had already given the father ten francs, I refused to pay twice. The priest threatened to destroy the paper and to annul the ceremony. I, in turn, threatened him with the district attorney. The dispute was long, and I finally paid five francs.

"As soon as I reached home I went down to Kerandec's to find out whether everything was all right. Neither father, nor sister-in-law, nor nurse had yet returned. The mother, who had remained alone, was in bed, shivering with cold and starving, for she had had nothing to eat since the day before.

"'Where the deuce can they have gone?' I asked. She answered without surprise or anger, 'They're going to drink something to celebrate.' It was the custom. Then I thought of my ten francs which were to pay the church and would doubtless pay for the alcohol.

"I sent some broth to the mother and ordered a good fire to be built in the room. I was uneasy and furious and promised myself to drive out these brutes, wondering with terror what was going to happen to the poor infant.

"It was already six, and they had not yet returned. I told my servant to wait for them and I went to bed. I soon fell asleep and slept like a top. At daybreak I was awakened by my servant, who was bringing me my hot water.

"As soon as my eyes were open I asked: 'How about Kerandec?'

"The man hesitated and then stammered: 'Oh!

he came back, all right, after midnight, and so drunk that he couldn't walk, and so were Kermagan and the nurse. I guess they must have slept in a ditch, for the little one died and they never even noticed it.'

"I jumped up out of bed, crying:

"'What! The child is dead?'

"'Yes, sir. They brought it back to Mother Kerandec. When she saw it she began to cry, and now they are making her drink to console her.'

"'What's that? They are making her drink!'

"'Yes, sir. I only found it out this morning. As Kerandec had no more brandy or money, he took some wood alcohol, with monsieur gave him for the lamp, and all four of them are now drinking that. The mother is feeling pretty sick now.'

"I had hastily put on some clothes, and seizing a stick, with the intention of applying it to the backs of these human beasts, I hastened towards the gardener's house.

"The mother was raving drunk beside the blue body of her dead baby. Kerandec, the nurse, and the Kermagan woman were snoring on the floor. I had to take care of the mother, who died towards noon."

The old doctor was silent. He took up the brandy-bottle and poured out another glass. He held it up to the lamp, and the light streaming through it imparted to the liquid the amber color of molten topaz. With one gulp he swallowed the treacherous drink.

THE FARMER'S WIFE

SAID the Baron René du Treilles to me:
"Will you come and open the hunting season with me at my farm at Marinville? I shall be delighted if you will, my dear boy. In the first place, I am all alone. It is rather a difficult ground to get at, and the place I live in is so primitive that I can invite only my most intimate friends."

I accepted his invitation, and on Saturday we set off on the train going to Normandy. We alighted at a station called Almivare, and Baron René, pointing to a carryall drawn by a timid horse and driven by a big countryman with white hair, said:

"Here is our equipage, my dear boy."

The driver extended his hand to his landlord, and the baron pressed it warmly, asking:

"Well, Maître Lebrument, how are you?"

"Always the same, M'sieu le Baron."

We jumped into this swinging hencoop perched on two enormous wheels, and the young horse, after a violent swerve, started into a gallop, pitching us into the air like balls. Every fall backward on the wooden bench gave me the most dreadful pain.

The peasant kept repeating in his calm, monotonous voice:

"There, there! All right all right, Moutard, all right!"

But Moutard scarcely heard, and kept capering along like a goat.

Our two dogs behind us, in the empty part of the hencoop, were standing up and sniffing the air of the plains, where they scented game.

The baron gazed with a sad eye into the distance at the vast Norman landscape, undulating and melancholy, like an immense English park, where the farmyards, surrounded by two or four rows of trees and full of dwarfed apple trees which hid the houses, gave a vista as far as the eye could see of forest trees, copses and shrubbery such as landscape gardeners look for in laying out the boundaries of princely estates.

And René du Treilles suddenly exclaimed:

"I love this soil; I have my very roots in it."

He was a pure Norman, tall and strong, with a slight paunch, and of the old race of adventurers who went to found kingdoms on the shores of every ocean. He was about fifty years of age, ten years less perhaps than the farmer who was driving us.

The latter was a lean peasant, all skin and bone, one of those men who live a hundred years.

After two hours' travelling over stony roads, across that green and monotonous plain, the vehicle entered one of those orchard farmyards and drew up before an old structure falling into decay, where an old maid-servant stood waiting beside a young fellow, who took charge of the horse.

We entered the farmhouse. The smoky kitchen was high and spacious. The copper utensils and the crockery shone in the reflection of the hearth. A cat lay asleep on a chair, a dog under the table. One perceived an odor of milk, apples, smoke, that

2

indescribable smell peculiar to old farmhouses, the odor of the earth, of the walls, of furniture, the odor of spilled stale soup, of former wash-days and of former inhabitants, the smell of animals and of human beings combined, of things and of persons, the odor of time, and of things that have passed away.

I went out to have a look at the farmyard. It was very large, full of apple trees, dwarfed and crooked, and laden with fruit which fell on the grass around them. In this farmyard the Norman smell of apples was as strong as that of the bloom of orange trees on the shores of the south of France.

Four rows of beeches surrounded this inclosure. They were so tall that they seemed to touch the clouds at this hour of nightfall, and their summits, through which the night winds passed, swayed and sang a mournful, interminable song.

I reëntered the house.

The baron was warming his feet at the fire, and was listening to the farmer's talk about country matters. He talked about marriages, births and deaths, then about the fall in the price of grain and the latest news about cattle. The "Veularde" (as he called a cow that had been bought at the fair of Veules) had calved in the middle of June. The cider had not been first-class last year. Apricots were almost disappearing from the country.

Then we had dinner. It was a good rustic meal, simple and abundant, long and tranquil. And while we were dining I noticed the special kind of friendly familiarity which had struck me from the start between the baron and the peasant.

Outside, the beeches continued sighing in the night wind, and our two dogs, shut up in a shed,

3

were whining and howling in an uncanny fashion. The fire was dying out in the big fireplace. The maid-servant had gone to bed. Maître Lebrument said in his turn:

"If you don't mind, M'sieu le Baron, I'm going to bed. I am not used to staying up late."

The baron extended his hand toward him and said: "Go, my friend," in so cordial a tone that I said, as soon as the man had disappeared:

"He is devoted to you, this farmer?"

"Better than that, my dear fellow! It is a drama, an old drama, simple and very sad, that attaches him to me. Here is the story:

"You know that my father was colonel in a cavalry regiment. His orderly was this young fellow, now an old man, the son of a farmer. When my father retired from the army he took this former soldier, then about forty, as his servant. I was at that time about thirty. We were living in our old château of Valrenne, near Caudebec-en-Caux.

"At this period my mother's chambermaid was one of the prettiest girls you could see, fair-haired, slender and sprightly in manner, a genuine soubrette of the old type that no longer exists. To-day these creatures spring up into hussies before their time. Paris, with the aid of the railways, attracts them, calls them, takes hold of them, as soon as they are budding into womanhood, these little sluts who in old times remained simple maid-servants. Every man passing by, as recruiting sergeants did formerly, looking for recruits, with conscripts, entices and ruins them—these foolish lassies—and we have now only the scum of the female sex for servant maids, all that is dull, nasty, common and ill-formed, too ugly even for gallantry.

"Well, this girl was charming, and I often gave her a kiss in dark corners; nothing more, I swear to you! She was virtuous, besides; and I had some respect for my mother's house, which is more than can be said of the blackguards of the present day.

"Now, it happened that my man-servant, the ex-soldier, the old farmer you have just seen, fell madly in love with this girl, perfectly daft. The first thing we noticed was that he forgot everything, he paid no attention to anything.

"My father said incessantly:

"'See here, Jean, what's the matter with you? Are you ill?'

"He replied:

"'No, no, M'sieu le Baron. There's nothing the matter with me.'

"He grew thin; he broke glasses and let plates fall when waiting on the table. We thought he must have been attacked by some nervous affection, and sent for the doctor, who thought he could detect symptoms of spinal disease. Then my father, full of anxiety about his faithful man-servant, decided to place him in a private hospital. When the poor fellow heard of my father's intentions he made a clean breast of it.

"'M'sieu le Baron——'

"'Well, my boy?'

"'You see, the thing I want is not physic.'

"'Ha! what is it, then?'

"'It's marriage!'

"My father turned round and stared at him in astonishment.

" 'What's that you say, eh?'

" 'It's marriage.'

" 'Marriage! So, then, you jackass, you're in love.'

" 'That's how it is, M'sieu le Baron.'

"And my father began to laugh so immoderately that my mother called out through the wall of the next room:

" 'What in the world is the matter with you, Gontran?'

"He replied:

" 'Come here, Catherine.'

"And when she came in he told her, with tears in his eyes from sheer laughter, that his idiot of a servant-man was lovesick.

"But my mother, instead of laughing, was deeply affected.

" 'Who is it that you have fallen in love with, my poor fellow?' she asked.

"He answered without hesitation:

" 'With Louise, Madame le Baronne.'

"My mother said with the utmost gravity: 'We must try to arrange this matter the best way we can.'

"So Louise was sent for and questioned by my mother; and she said in reply that she knew all about Jean's liking for her, that in fact Jean had spoken to her about it several times, but that she did not want him. She refused to say why.

"And two months elapsed during which my father and mother never ceased to urge this girl to marry Jean. As she declared she was not in love with any other man, she could not give any serious reason for her refusal. My father at last overcame her resistance by means of a big present of money, and started the pair of them on a farm—this very farm. I did not see them for three years, and then I learned that Louise had died of consumption. But my father and mother died, too, in their turn, and it was two years more before I found myself face to face with Jean.

"At last one autumn day about the end of October the idea came into my head to go hunting on this part of my estate, which my father had told me was full of game.

"So one evening, one wet evening, I arrived at this house. I was shocked to find my father's old servant with perfectly white hair, though he was not more than forty-five or forty-six years of age. I made him dine with me, at the very table where we are now sitting. It was raining hard. We could hear the rain battering at the roof, the walls, and the windows, flowing in a perfect deluge into the farmyard; and my dog was howling in the shed where the other dogs are howling to-night.

"All of a sudden, when the servant-maid had gone to bed, the man said in a timid voice:

" 'M'sieu le Baron.'

" 'What is it, my dear Jean?'

" 'I have something to tell you.'

" 'Tell it, my dear Jean.'

" 'You remember Louise, my wife.'

" 'Certainly, I remember her.'

" 'Well, she left me a message for you.'

" 'What was it?'

" 'A—a—well, it was what you might call a confession.'

" 'Ha—and what was it about?'

" 'It was—it was—I'd rather, all the same, tell you
nothing about it—but I must—I must. Well, it's
this—it wasn't consumption she died of at all. It
was grief—well, that's the long and short of it. As
soon as she came to live here after we were married,
she grew thin; she changed so that you wouldn't
know her, M'sieu le Baron. She was just as I was
before I married her, but it was just the opposite, just
the opposite.

" 'I sent for the doctor. He said it was her liver
that was affected—he said it was what he called a
"hepatic" complaint—I don't know these big words,
M'sieu le Baron. Then I bought medicine for her,
heaps on heaps of bottles that cost about three hundred francs. But she'd take none of them; she
wouldn't have them; she said: "It's no use, my poor
Jean; it wouldn't do me any good." I saw well that
she had some hidden trouble; and then I found her
one time crying, and I didn't know what to do, no, I
didn't know what to do. I bought her caps, and
dresses, and hair oil, and earrings. Nothing did her
any good. And I saw that she was going to die.
And so one night at the end of November, one
snowy night, after she had been in bed the whole
day, she told me to send for the curé. So I went for
him. As soon as he came——

" ' "Jean," she said, "I am going to make a confession to you. I owe it to you, Jean. I have never
been false to you, never! never, before or after you
married me. M'sieu le Curé is there, and can tell
you so; he knows my soul. Well, listen, Jean. If
I am dying, it is because I was not able to console
myself for leaving the château, because I was too
fond of the young Baron Monsieur René, too fond

of him, mind you, Jean, there was no harm in it! This is the thing that's killing me. When I could see him no more I felt that I should die. If I could only have seen him, I might have lived, only seen him, nothing more. I wish you'd tell him some day, by and by, when I am no longer here. You will tell him, swear you will, Jean—swear it—in the presence of M'sieu le Curé! It will console me to know that he will know it one day, that this was the cause of my death! Swear it!"

" 'Well, I gave her my promise, M'sieu le Baron, and on the faith of an honest man I have kept my word.'

"And then he ceased speaking, his eyes filling with tears.

"Good God! my dear boy, you can't form any idea of the emotion that filled me when I heard this poor devil, whose wife I had killed without suspecting it, telling me this story on that wet night in this very kitchen.

"I exclaimed: 'Ah! my poor Jean! my poor Jean!'

"He murmured: 'Well, that's all, M'sieu le Baron. I could not help it, one way or the other—and now it's all over!'

"I caught his hand across the table, and I began to weep.

"He asked, 'Will you come and see her grave?' I nodded assent, for I couldn't speak. He rose, lighted a lantern, and we walked through the blinding rain by the light of the lantern.

"He opened a gate, and I saw some crosses of black wood.

"Suddenly he stopped before a marble slab and

said: 'There it is,' and he flashed the lantern close to it so that I could read the inscription:

"'To LOUISE HORTENSE MARINET,
"'Wife of Jean-François Lebrument, Farmer,
"'SHE WAS A FAITHFUL WIFE. GOD REST HER SOUL.'

"We fell on our knees in the damp grass, he and I, with the lantern between us, and I saw the rain beating on the white marble slab. And I thought of the heart of her sleeping there in her grave. Ah! poor heart! poor heart!

"Since then I come here every year. And I don't know why, but I feel as if I were guilty of some crime in the presence of this man who always looks as if he forgave me."

THE DEVIL

THE peasant and the doctor stood on opposite sides of the bed, beside the old, dying woman. She was calm and resigned and her mind quite clear as she looked at them and listened to their conversation. She was going to die, and she did not rebel at it, for her time was come, as she was ninety-two.

The July sun streamed in at the window and the open door and cast its hot flames on the uneven brown clay floor, which had been stamped down by four generations of clodhoppers. The smell of the fields came in also, driven by the sharp wind and parched by the noontide heat. The grasshoppers chirped themselves hoarse, and filled the country with their shrill noise, which was like that of the wooden toys which are sold to children at fair time.

The doctor raised his voice and said: "Honoré, you cannot leave your mother in this state; she may die at any moment." And the peasant, in great distress, replied: "But I must get in my wheat, for it has been lying on the ground a long time, and the weather is just right for it; what do you say about it, mother?" And the dying old woman, still tormented by her Norman avariciousness, replied yes with her eyes and her forehead, and thus urged her son to get in his wheat, and to leave her to die alone.

But the doctor got angry, and, stamping his foot, he said: "You are no better than a brute, do you hear, and I will not allow you to do it, do you understand? And if you must get in your wheat today, go and fetch Rapet's wife and make her look after your mother; I will have it, do you understand me? And if you do not obey me, I will let you die like a dog, when you are ill in your turn; do you hear?"

The peasant, a tall, thin fellow with slow movements, who was tormented by indecision, by his fear of the doctor and his fierce love of saving, hesitated, calculated, and stammered out: "How much does La Rapet charge for attending sick people?" "How should I know?" the doctor cried. "That depends upon how long she is needed. Settle it with her, by Heaven! But I want her to be here within an hour, do you hear?"

So the man decided. "I will go for her," he replied; "don't get angry, doctor." And the latter left, calling out as he went: "Be careful, be very careful, you know, for I do not joke when I am angry!" As soon as they were alone the peasant turned to his mother and said in a resigned voice: "I will go and fetch La Rapet, as the man will have it. Don't worry till I get back."

And he went out in his turn.

La Rapet, who was an old washerwoman, watched the dead and the dying of the neighborhood, and then, as soon as she had sewn her customers into that linen cloth from which they would emerge no more, she went and took up her iron to smooth out the linen of the living. Wrinkled like a last year's apple, spiteful, envious, avaricious with a phenomenal avarice, bent double, as if she had been broken in half across the loins by the constant motion of passing the iron over the linen, one might have said that she had a kind of abnormal and cynical love of a death struggle. She never spoke of anything but of the people she had seen die, of the various kinds of deaths at which she had been present, and she related with the greatest minuteness details which were always similar, just as a sportsman recounts his luck.

When Honoré Bontemps entered her cottage, he found her preparing the starch for the collars of the women villagers, and he said: "Good-evening; I hope you are pretty well, Mother Rapet?"

She turned her head round to look at him, and said: "As usual, as usual, and you?" "Oh! as for me, I am as well as I could wish, but my mother is not well." "Your mother?" "Yes, my mother!" "What is the matter with her?" "She is going to turn up her toes, that's what's the matter with her!"

The old woman took her hands out of the water and asked with sudden sympathy: "Is she as bad as all that?" "The doctor says she will not last till morning." "Then she certainly is very bad!" Honoré hesitated, for he wanted to make a few preparatory remarks before coming to his proposition; but as he could hit upon nothing, he made up his mind suddenly.

"How much will you ask to stay with her till the end? You know that I am not rich, and I cannot even afford to keep a servant girl. It is just that which has brought my poor mother to this state—too much worry and fatigue! She did the

3

work of ten, in spite of her ninety-two years. You don't find any made of that stuff nowadays!"

La Rapet answered gravely: "There are two prices: Forty sous by day and three francs by night for the rich, and twenty sous by day and forty by night for the others. You shall pay me the twenty and forty." But the peasant reflected, for he knew his mother well. He knew how tenacious of life, how vigorous and unyielding she was, and she might last another week, in spite of the doctor's opinion; and so he said resolutely: "No, I would rather you would fix a price for the whole time until the end. I will take my chance, one way or the other. The doctor says she will die very soon. If that happens, so much the better for you, and so much the worse for her, but if she holds out till to-morrow or longer, so much the better for her and so much the worse for you!"

The nurse looked at the man in astonishment, for she had never treated a death as a speculation, and she hesitated, tempted by the idea of the possible gain, but she suspected that he wanted to play her a trick. "I can say nothing until I have seen your mother," she replied.

"Then come with me and see her."

She washed her hands, and went with him immediately.

They did not speak on the road; she walked with short, hasty steps, while he strode on with his long legs, as if he were crossing a brook at every step.

The cows lying down in the fields, overcome by the heat, raised their heads heavily and lowed feebly at the two passersby, as if to ask them for some green grass.

THE DEVIL

When they got near the house, Honoré Bontemps murmured: "Suppose it is all over?" And
his unconscious wish that it might be so showed
itself in the sound of his voice.

But the old woman was not dead. She was lying
on her back, on her wretched bed, her hands covered
with a purple cotton counterpane, horribly thin,
knotty hands, like the claws of strange animals,
like crabs, half closed by rheumatism, fatigue and
the work of nearly a century which she had accomplished.

La Rapet went up to the bed and looked at the
dying woman, felt her pulse, tapped her on the
chest, listened to her breathing, and asked her questions, so as to hear her speak; and then, having
looked at her for some time, she went out of the
room, followed by Honoré. Her decided opinion
was that the old woman would not last till night. He
asked: "Well?" And the sick-nurse replied: "Well,
she may last two days, perhaps three. You will
have to give me six francs, everything included."

"Six francs! six francs!" he shouted. "Are you
out of your mind? I tell you she cannot last more
than five or six hours!" And they disputed angrily
for some time, but as the nurse said she must go
home, as the time was going by, and as his wheat
would not come to the farmyard of its own accord,
he finally agreed to her terms.

"Very well, then, that is settled; six francs, including everything, until the corpse is taken out."

And he went away, with long strides, to his
wheat which was lying on the ground under the
hot sun which ripens the grain, while the sick-nurse
went in again to the house.

THE DEVIL

She had brought some work with her, for she worked without ceasing by the side of the dead and dying, sometimes for herself, sometimes for the family which employed her as seamstress and paid her rather more in that capacity. Suddenly she asked: "Have you received the last sacraments, Mother Bontemps?"

The old peasant woman shook her head, and La Rapet, who was very devout, got up quickly: "Good heavens, is it possible? I will go and fetch the curé"; and she rushed off to the parsonage so quickly that the urchins in the street thought some accident had happened, when they saw her running.

The priest came immediately in his surplice, preceded by a choir boy who rang a bell to announce the passage of the Host through the parched and quiet country. Some men who were working at a distance took off their large hats and remained motionless until the white vestment had disappeared behind some farm buildings; the women who were making up the sheaves stood up to make the sign of the cross; the frightened black hens ran away along the ditch until they reached a well-known hole, through which they suddenly disappeared, while a foal which was tied in a meadow took fright at the sight of the surplice and began to gallop round and round, kicking out every now and then. The acolyte, in his red cassock, walked quickly, and the priest, with his head inclined toward one shoulder and his square biretta on his head, followed him, muttering some prayers; while last of all came La Rapet, bent almost double as if she wished to prostrate herself, as she walked with folded hands as they do in church.

6

Honoré saw them pass in the distance, and he asked: "Where is our priest going?" His man, who was more intelligent, replied: "He is taking the sacrament to your mother, of course!"

The peasant was not surprised, and said: "That may be," and went on with his work.

Mother Bontemps confessed, received absolution and communion, and the priest took his departure, leaving the two women alone in the suffocating room, while La Rapet began to look at the dying woman, and to ask herself whether it could last much longer.

The day was on the wane, and gusts of cooler air began to blow, causing a view of Epinal, which was fastened to the wall by two pins, to flap up and down; the scanty window curtains, which had formerly been white, but were now yellow and covered with fly-specks, looked as if they were going to fly off, as if they were struggling to get away, like the old woman's soul.

Lying motionless, with her eyes open, she seemed to await with indifference that death which was so near and which yet delayed its coming. Her short breathing whistled in her constricted throat. It would stop altogether soon, and there would be one woman less in the world; no one would regret her.

At nightfall Honoré returned, and when he went up to the bed and saw that his mother was still alive, he asked: "How is she?" just as he had done formerly when she had been ailing, and then he sent La Rapet away, saying to her: "To-morrow morning at five o'clock, without fail." And she replied: "To-morrow, at five o'clock."

She came at daybreak, and found Honoré eating

his soup, which he had made himself before going to work, and the sick-nurse asked him: "Well, is your mother dead?" "She is rather better, on the contrary," he replied, with a sly look out of the corner of his eyes. And he went out.

La Rapet, seized with anxiety, went up to the dying woman, who remained in the same state, lethargic and impassive, with her eyes open and her hands clutching the counterpane. The nurse perceived that this might go on thus for two days, four days, eight days, and her avaricious mind was seized with fear, while she was furious at the sly fellow who had tricked her, and at the woman who would not die.

Nevertheless, she began to work, and waited, looking intently at the wrinkled face of Mother Bontemps. When Honoré returned to breakfast he seemed quite satisfied and even in a bantering humor. He was decidedly getting in his wheat under very favorable circumstances.

La Rapet was becoming exasperated; every minute now seemed to her so much time and money stolen from her. She felt a mad inclination to take this old woman, this headstrong old fool, this obstinate old wretch, and to stop that short, rapid breath, which was robbing her of her time and money, by squeezing her throat a little. But then she reflected on the danger of doing so, and other thoughts came into her head; so she went up to the bed and said: "Have you ever seen the Devil?" Mother Bontemps murmured: "No."

Then the sick-nurse began to talk and to tell her tales which were likely to terrify the weak mind of the dying woman. Some minutes before one dies

the Devil appears, she said, to all who are in the
death throes. He has a broom in his hand, a saucepan on his head, and he utters loud cries. When
anybody sees him, all is over, and that person has
only a few moments longer to live. She then enumerated all those to whom the Devil had appeared
that year: Joséphine Loisel, Eulalie Ratier, Sophie
Padaknau, Séraphine Grospied.

Mother Bontemps, who had at last become disturbed in mind, moved about, wrung her hands, and
tried to turn her head to look toward the end of the
room. Suddenly La Rapet disappeared at the foot
of the bed. She took a sheet out of the cupboard
and wrapped herself up in it; she put the iron
saucepan on her head, so that its three short bent
feet rose up like horns, and she took a broom in
her right hand and a tin pail in her left, which she
thew up suddenly, so that it might fall to the
ground noisily.

When it came down, it certainly made a terrible
noise. Then, climbing upon a chair, the nurse lifted
up the curtain which hung at the bottom of the bed,
and showed herself, gesticulating and uttering shrill
cries into the iron saucepan which covered her face,
while she menaced the old peasant woman, who was
nearly dead, with her broom.

Terrified, with an insane expression on her face,
the dying woman made a superhuman effort to get
up and escape; she even got her shoulders and chest
out of bed; then she fell back with a deep sigh. All
was over, and La Rapet calmly put everything back
into its place; the broom into the corner by the
cupboard, the sheet inside it, the saucepan on the
hearth, the pail on the floor, and the chair against

the wall. Then, with professional movements, she closed the dead woman's large eyes, put a plate on the bed and poured some holy water into it, placing in it the twig of boxwood that had been nailed to the chest of drawers, and kneeling down, she fervently repeated the prayers for the dead, which she knew by heart, as a matter of business.

And when Honoré returned in the evening he found her praying, and he calculated immediately that she had made twenty sous out of him, for she had only spent three days and one night there, which made five francs altogether, instead of the six which he owed her.